MW00772911

DON'T BLAME

THE

GUITARIST

By

KATHLEEN MAYES

This book is fiction. All characters, names, places, and events are either a product of the author's imagination or are used fictitiously. Any resemblance to actual persons, living or dead, events, or locales is entirely coincidental.

ISBN:

E-Book: 978-1-963764-02-4

Paperback: 978-1-963764-33-8

Hardcover: 978-1-963764-03-1

This book is dedicated to my husband, Joseph Mayes, the most supportive person I've ever known ...

even if he couldn't stop himself from asking, over and over, "When will it be done?"

Chapter 1

New Jersey
Spring 2013
Friday, May 10

Suzanna closed her set with a swinging Brazilian samba to match the room's upbeat vibe. Keep the customers happy. Keep those tips rolling in. The crowd at the Haddonfield Bistro was full of life, chatting and drinking with a weekend gusto. Her classical guitar rang out bright and fast with notes bouncing off the restaurant's tile and woodwork. The spirited conversations merged with her music.

Typical Friday.

She stretched her arm under her music stand and shut off the amp. Two men at a nearby table were debating the liberal values of Haddonfield's new mayor. She abruptly tuned it out. During her earliest background music jobs, she'd been guilty of eavesdropping, especially when it included juicy gossip. But now, after two years of working all manner of gigs, including three nights a week here at the Haddonfield Bistro, she was content to mind her own business.

As she fastened the guitar to its rack, her hair fell across her face. The warmth and humidity of New Jersey's early spring had transformed her cropped, brunette bob into unruly curls. Pushing a strand back into place, she spied a pudgy man approaching. His cheap cologne reached her first.

He tossed a dollar in her tip jar. "Your music is lovely, so relaxing!"

What did he expect her to do with one dollar? But then, a dollar might be a lot to this guy and dollars add up.

"Your fingers practically dance over those strings." He took one of her business cards and read it through Coke-bottle glasses. "Suzanna Archer."

She eyed him with slight suspicion and tried to assess whether he actually liked her music or was just hitting on her. He might be one of those creepy guys who go gaga over female performers. That would be unusual at this restaurant, where she didn't even play on a stage.

Suzanna glanced down at her traditional performance clothes—black blouse and black slacks. Even though they fit snugly to her petite frame, they were decidedly unsexy. She rubbed her arms against a vulnerable shiver. Displaying her natural good looks while not attracting unwanted attention was a trick she hadn't quite mastered. Still, she kept to her rule: never be unsociable to an audience member. Swallowing her unease, she plastered on a professional smile and said, "I was named for a song, but—"

"Like 'Oh! Susanna'?" Behind the glasses, his eyes lit up.

Uh-oh. She shook her head and hoped a rendition of the Stephen Foster song wasn't coming up, but …

"Oh! Susanna, oh, don't you cry for me. I come from Alabama with a geetar on my knee," he sang in a nasal tenor voice.

It took all her effort not to roll her eyes. Instead, she faked a laugh along with him, then slipped away to the long, antique bar. How many times had she been serenaded with that song? A million? And everyone who replaced banjo with guitar thought they'd cracked their own original joke. Here, in small-town Haddonfield, New Jersey, it was a rare occasion when someone guessed her actual namesake. She sighed, put the encounter behind her, and hopped up on a barstool.

Swiveling from side to side, Suzanna scanned the faces of the cheerful couples and families packed into the dark, wood-and-leather booths. That well-dressed gentleman in the corner looked like a prime tipping candidate. She hoped so, anyway. Tips made up the core of her income; hourly wages were just icing. Even after four stellar years at the Philadelphia Conservatory, she didn't have the credentials to do any other music job. No orchestra jobs for classical guitarists. Solo concerts took gobs of money, and college positions required a master's degree. If she wanted to make a living playing music, background was it. For now.

Inhaling deeply, Suzanna took in the scrumptious aroma of burgers and fries. Her mouth watered just smelling the fatty scent permeating every inch of the place. All the local restaurant critics claimed the Haddonfield Bistro served the best pub grub in New Jersey. She agreed.

A dark-gray shadow rippled across her arms. She gazed out the window for the source. A black sedan the size of a stretch limo cruised by the front of the restaurant. Odd to see such a bulky car on the historic streets of Haddonfield. It was gonna take finesse to park that monster around here. She strained her neck to get a better look, but it was gone.

Suzanna swiveled to face the bar. The Haddonfield Bistro's trade name, *HB*, was etched into the bar rail. She ran her fingers over the carving's distinctive, sloping letters.

Vinny's back was to her, but she caught his eye in the mirrored back wall. "Busy night," she said.

He pulled a wineglass down from the hanging racks and skimmed it across the top of the bar in one smooth motion. "Yo, Suzanna, the place is rockin'."

Vinny's slicked-back, black hair, strong chin, and accent reminded her of a younger, more handsome Sylvester Stallone, thoroughly South Philly Italian.

He poured out a chardonnay and handed the glass off to a waitress. Then, propping his elbows on the bar, he beamed at her. "How's Baby holding up?"

Suzanna smiled at the thought of her creaky, old, 1974 Maverick, aka "Baby." The only car she ever owned.

Vinny's dark eyes were practically laughing. "I can still hook you up with my buddy to get you a better ride."

One corner of her mouth twisted up. "But I haven't got all my use out of him yet."

"That's one ugly—"

A woman at the other end of the bar held up two fingers, and Vinny slid across the floor as if his feet were roller skates.

It was true; her car was no great beauty. Rusty holes dotted the faded, midnight-blue paint job like copper constellations, and wires aggressively poked through the back seat's shredded cloth covering. No hubcaps, no power brakes or steering, no electric windows, no electronic anything—Baby was humble, but he was hers. The HB was only a few blocks from her apartment, but she couldn't manage to drag all her gig paraphernalia on foot. She needed Baby.

While Vinny made his way back to Suzanna's end of the bar, he gathered a bouquet of emptied wine glasses in each bear-paw hand.

"Saw Baby parked in your favorite spot." He sloshed the glasses in soapy water.

"Yep, got lucky." For Suzanna, that tiny stretch of macadam outside the HB's side door held a little magic. Not that she was superstitious or anything, but every time she parked there, she had an excellent tip night.

She spotted Emily breezing across the room in her crisp, all-black uniform, arms loaded with dirty dishes. The Haddonfield Bistro's blue HB logo, stitched on her collar and pocket apron, looked refined next to the rose tattoo on her forearm. Her miniskirt showed off her long and shapely legs, a quality that Suzanna, being on the short side, secretly envied.

Emily coaxed the dishes into the bus cart at the end of the bar. She straightened her apron, tightened her ponytail, and plopped down beside Suzanna. "That guy you were talking to … the chubby one with the goggles. Was he bothering you?"

"Sort of."

"I saw him lurking around while you were playing."

"Just a fanboy."

"More like a fucktard."

HB's owner, Harry, strolled by. "Watch your language, Em. This is a family restaurant." Harry, being ex-military, ran a tight ship.

Emily grimaced and sighed dramatically in his direction. He fixed his gaze on her with a frown but then winked. She grinned back and said, "You look very *Denzel* tonight."

Flagged down by a customer, Emily grabbed the coffeepot. She marched over to the table with a huge smile, her strawberry-blonde ponytail bopping up and down. On her way back, she bumped shoulders with the busboy and splashed half of the pot of coffee on the floor.

"The legend lives on." Suzanna chuckled at Emily's well-known butterfingers. "How you manage to keep from spilling all over your customers is beyond me."

Suzanna inched slowly by the puddle of coffee on her way to the HB's side door. She'd left her clamp-on, electronic tuner out in her car. Early in her background music career, she learned that a tuner measuring vibrations, rather than pitch, was a must in a noisy restaurant.

As she pushed the door open, the sun's last rays threw Baby's profile into relief. Her car's sporty, sloped back tried hard to make the boxy chassis look sexy, but Baby just wasn't a Mustang, more like a wannabe. Didn't matter to her.

Suzanna could see her tuner sitting on Baby's dash. All she had to do was cross the doublewide sidewalk.

A sudden silver-white flash pierced her eyes. Intense heat enveloped her as a loud boom shook the ground. Somewhere, glass shattered. Every inch of her body trembled.

Like the smack of a surging ocean wave, a thump on her chest whisked her backward into the HB. Her head clipped a barstool as she rammed into Emily. The two ended up sprawled on the floor, hearts pounding.

The side entrance no longer had a door, only a bare, dangling hinge. Eyes burning, Suzanna peered out through a veil of smoke at a flaming hunk of metal ablaze in her favorite parking spot. A flaming hunk that used to be Baby.

Chapter 2

Suzanna lay flat on her back atop the chill tile floor where the explosion had dumped her. Through a black-gray haze, she squinted up at the HB's pressed-copper ceiling and tried to pull together her splintered thoughts. She was sure of only one thing. When she walked over to the now nonexistent side door, that stupid coffee spill had slowed her pace. Just enough. She would be dead right now if Emily wasn't such a klutz.

A confusion of tramping feet and shouting whirled around her, muffled by a low, constant rumbling in her ears. Her lungs burned from the fumes of melting plastic. She wiggled her fingers and pulled her legs up to her chin. No injuries, only a throbbing bump on the back of her head.

Suzanna craned her neck toward her performance area with a growing sense of alarm. That spot, positioned between the HB's front door and a bank of oversized windows, was where she played background music for the restaurant's customers. It was also home to all her gear. Holding her breath, she stared across the room and checked on her amp, music stand, and precious classical guitar. Miraculous. All untouched.

With fragile relief, Suzanna jacked herself up enough to sit cross-legged and let her head droop into her shaking hands.

Far-off sirens blared and swelled as they closed in. Harry charged out of his back office. He took one look at the thick smoke pouring through the HB's blown-out doorway, snatched up a fire extinguisher, and started spraying.

As Suzanna kneaded the bump on her head, an older man, pressing a napkin to his mouth, shoved past, almost knocking her flat again. Bracing herself, she slid back on her elbows. Her fingertips skimmed over something solid and crackly. She jerked her arm back and squeezed her eyes shut. Was that a bug? She opened one eye to a squint. It was only a scorched paperback. It must have hurtled in from the sidewalk, just like she did. She wiped her watery eyes and examined the cover. Although it was singed various shades of brown, she could still read the title, *The Jersey Devil: Phantom of the Pines*. "What the—"

Vinny thrust his beefy hands under Suzanna's arms and whooshed her up on a barstool. "Is your head okay?" he asked, out of breath.

She could see his lips moving, but her ears were totally out of service. Still clutching the paperback, she gave him a weak nod. Over his shoulder, she saw Emily spread-eagled on the floor.

"Oh my God, Emmy?" Suzanna frantically pointed at her friend.

Vinny spun around and knelt by Emily. "You all right?"

"What do you think? We just got blasted!" Emily's eyes flitted back and forth along the length of the HB. "I'm not hurt, but what the hell *was* that?"

Vinny gripped Em's elbow and helped her up. "Let's find out. Come on, Harry's up front."

Suzanna watched them plunge into the crowd but decided to stay put. From her barstool, she stretched her neck to look out through the jagged hole that had once been the side door. A firefighter was hosing down Baby's remains. The torrents of water blew the sharp scent of burning tires into the restaurant and turned her stomach. She held her nose.

Three police officers barged through the gaping doorway and brushed past her. Harry left his post, guiding families out the front door, and rushed to join them, his burly frame cutting a swath through the crowd.

Suzanna's teeth began to chatter even though she wasn't cold. She tried to slow her heart rate and dial down the adrenaline coursing through her veins. A light tap on her shoulder nearly made her fall off her barstool.

The tapper, a police officer, grasped her elbow, stopping her fall. "Suzanna Archer?"

She cupped her hand to her ear and tilted her head.

The officer shouted, "Suzanna Archer?"

She nodded and shouted back, "What happened? Is anybody hurt? Is it my fault?"

"Only minor injuries. You're the main victim." He pointed at her head. "I'm Officer Cline. That waitress over there is very worried about you." He tipped his head in Emily's direction.

"Was it a terrorist attack or something, Officer ...?" She couldn't remember his name to save her life and had a vague feeling she was being impolite.

"Just call me Jason. We don't know much yet. The detective and CSI guy are working the scene outside. They'll talk to you when they're done inspecting your vehicle."

She whimpered to no one in particular, "Baby, my Baby ..."

Jason clutched her wrists. "What baby? My God, was there a baby in that car?"

"Oh, no. Baby's my car's name. Or *was* his name."

He released her arms and let out a heavy sigh.

"Sorry," she said.

"That's one for the books." Gently, he slanted her head forward and examined the growing lump in the back. "It looks superficial to me, but there's an EMT in the ambulance out front. Should I get him?"

Even though her head *did* ache, Suzanna just wanted everyone to leave her alone. She needed time to puzzle out this nightmare. Why in the world did Baby go up in flames? A gas leak? Some sort of spontaneous combustion? "No. Thanks ... really."

Jason nodded. "I can't force you, but see a doctor if it doesn't feel better soon. Call out if you need me." He turned and took charge of the room. With an authoritative voice, he said, "All right, everybody, relax. There's a car fire on the side street, but limited damage. We're evacuating to play it safe."

Emily scanned the empty room. Only two stragglers lingered. Everyone else was already out on the sidewalk, gathered around the burnished town clock. She let out a short snort of laughter. "Yeah, come on, everybody. Both of you, out here."

Sometimes Suzanna admired Em's ability to make light of almost any problem. But other times, like right now, they just added to Suzanna's stress.

Jason ignored the wisecrack, drew back his shoulders, and led the last customers out.

Emily hurried over to Suzanna and gave her a quick hug. "Do you think this had anything to do with one of your fans? Like that goggles guy?"

"My ears are rumbling. Speak up."

Em cupped her hand around Suzanna's ear and shouted, "Could Goggles Guy be responsible?"

"God, Em, I hope not."

"Well, earlier, I wanted to knock his teeth out. He called me bubbly!"

"You *are* kind of bubbly." Suzanna attempted a snicker but ended up just sniffling.

"Whatever. How ya feeling?"

"My head hurts, but it's minor. That's what Jason said anyway."

"Is that his name? Jason, huh."

Emily hooked her elbow on the bar, and despite all the mayhem, she coolly leaned over and exclaimed in Suzanna's ear, "Did you see the muscles on him? Gotta *love* a man in uniform!"

A half hour later, Emily and her team of waitresses had swept up all the debris, toweled off the booths, and wiped layers of soot from the pendant lamps hovering above each table. Harry flipped on the ceiling fans and ushered customers back in through the front door. Handing out free pints, Vinny cajoled and thanked everyone for staying.

Suzanna tried to chip in, but Em ordered her to sit in a booth and gave her an ice pack. Harry kept hounding her to go to the ER, but that was the last place she wanted to go … waiting for hours in a packed, stuffy room, all the insurance forms, and then only to be sent home with what, a couple of Tylenol and a prescription to take it easy?

As she slumped in her booth, ice pack glued to her head, the rumble in her ears softened. Now, everything just sounded a bit muted. It was like she'd been enclosed in a bubble after taking too much cold medicine.

Jason sat down across from her.

"Where's this detective?" Suzanna asked.

"They're almost done out there. Detective O'Brien will be with you soon. Sit tight."

She nodded. She was in no shape to go anywhere, anyway. Her hands were shaking like she had stage fright, and she wasn't even sure how she would get home.

Jason stood up and patted her hand. "After that, I'll drive you home."

He must have read her mind. Her lips tried to curl into a smile, but only one side worked.

Harry had called Vinny's cousin to install a replacement door. Already, he was doing the final touchups with several piercing hammer strikes. Suzanna hugged herself against the sound; each whack jolted her jittery stomach.

Harry barreled through the new doorway, stepped back, and inspected the job with an air of proud ownership. Suzanna caught sight of him, glasses teetering on his sweating, bald head, giving Vinny's cousin an approving pat on the back. He appeared to be handling the whole exploding car thing reasonably well. She couldn't help but feel responsible for the demolished door. As he turned, she averted her eyes, but he'd spied her and her ice pack. With broad strides, he crossed the room to her booth. "Stow your things and go home."

"I'm so sorry about the door. Did anything else get wrecked?"

"Don't give that another thought. Just go home. I'll take you."

"But I still have to talk to the detective."

"No one's interviewed you yet?" His lips puckered with concern. Under his breath, he said, "Bravo, Sierra!"

"Really, Harry. I can wait." She mustered a lopsided smile.

Harry shook his head in resignation and tramped back to his office.

Leaving the ice pack behind, Suzanna went to her performance area to put her guitar away. While bending over her guitar case, she thought she heard a deep voice saying her name. She twisted to gaze up at a lanky, middle-aged man in a neatly pressed suit and tie. An enormous, horseshoe-style mustache covered the lower portion of his face. She'd never seen anything like it. White and gray tinged the edges of the thick, brown whiskers. The ends of the horseshoe extended an inch below his bottom lip with a slight upward curl.

The man blathered on, but from her muted bubble, she could barely understand. She straightened up and took in the man's full height. Just to look him in the face, she had to roll her sore head back as far as it would go.

He wore sky-blue latex gloves that reflected annoying speckles while he soundlessly tapped on his notepad. To Suzanna, the tapping looked like exasperation. Exasperation with her. Panic gripped her chest, and her comprehension dwindled. She just stared at him—and that mustache. Finally, he thrust his business card at her.

She sat down and willed her eyes to focus on the tiny print. "Detective O'Brien."

He pulled up a chair and aimed for her ear. "Suzanna Archer, right? It's your vehicle that's been damaged?"

She frowned and raised her hand. "That's me."

"The crime scene investigator just finished bagging and tagging all the evidence. It has to go to the county's lab for processing, but I hope to get results by morning."

She nodded. "Why did my car—"

"First, tell me exactly what happened to you in just a sentence or two."

"I was pushing the door open. There was a flash and an explosion. It whooshed me inside the building."

"I want to assure you that you're safe now."

"I didn't think I wasn't. What's going on?" Her panic threatened to soar.

"Hold on. Any physical injuries besides your head?"

"No."

"Is this your only workplace?"

"I play at another restaurant, too. And do private gigs, like parties and weddings."

"So, except for the restaurants, you never know where you'll be working from week to week?"

"Yeah. I mean, it's not much of a living right now, but when I go back to school for my music master's, I'll be able to get a college teaching position."

Detective O'Brien's face was turning a vivid shade of red. Was he agitated with her again? Her fluky gig work must make his job tough.

"I get free meals, too," Suzanna said. "It's the best perk of playing background music at a restaurant. At least on the days I gig, I eat well." Why did she feel like she had to explain herself to this guy?

"Indeed." The detective kept his eyes on his notes. "My preliminary suspicion is that your vehicle had a bomb attached somewhere under the front end."

Unsure she'd heard him right, she asked, "Bomb?"

"Yes, bomb." The detective looked into her eyes for the first time. "Any knowledge of that?"

"Are you kidding?" She said it so loud her ears popped, making her bubble shrink by half.

Detective O'Brien's next words stuck a thumbtack into the last of her bubble. "I'm hoping County can help us determine who planted it."

Suzanna gasped. "Someone did this on purpose?"

The detective held up his blue-gloved hand like it was a crossing guard's stop sign. "Relax. This is day one of the investigation. We don't know anything for certain yet." He dropped his hand and shrugged. "Could have been totally random, or someone mistook your car for another. Hard to imagine that mistake, though. An old Maverick is pretty distinctive. Very few left on the road."

Fighting a wave of nausea, she asked, "But why?"

"That's what I'm here to find out."

Something about his tone sent her back to her childhood, remembering the way Mighty Mouse would say, "Here I come to save the day."

"Our crime scene guy thinks another vehicle was involved. He found a front bumper at the end of the block."

"Huh." Suzanna saw a black flash out of the corner of her eye and spun around. Nothing there. Was she seeing things now? She looked back, and the detective was staring at her.

"Can you think of anyone who might want to harm you?" he asked. His eyes snapped back to his notes.

She sat straight up. This can't be happening. The detective's businesslike manner and lack of eye contact strained her nerves. He should take a class in customer relations, for sure.

"Listen, I'm only a guitarist." She spread her arms. "I mean, sometimes I make mistakes when I'm playing, but that's no reason—"

"So, no ideas then?"

"Not one."

O'Brien frowned and stroked one side of his mustache. "Have any substance abuse problems?"

She shook her head.

"Any criminal associates?"

"Of course not!" Suzanna glared at him, but his eyes stayed pinned to his notes.

The detective pulled a clear, plastic evidence bag from his pocket. "Can you identify this item we found in the wreckage?" He handed her the bag, which held a warped, laminated car registration card. Its brownish-yellow edges had melted and were sticking to the inside of the bag. She turned it over in her hand. It looked cold and abandoned. Stroking it with her thumb like it was an old friend, she spoke to the card rather than the detective. "It was in my glove compartment."

O'Brien nodded and gently tugged it out of her reluctant hand.

That's when Suzanna remembered the paperback. "I've got something, too." She held up *The Jersey Devil: Phantom of the Pines.* "I found it on the floor where I landed." Ashes floated from the book's pages as she handed it to him, stirring up a whiff of charcoal.

"Does this belong to you?" he asked.

"No. It flew inside the door with me. Maybe it was on the street beside my car?"

"Do you know anyone who might have put this book *inside* your car?"

She shook her head as she clapped ashes off her palms.

O'Brien turned it over and read the back cover. "No author credited. Unusual. I'm putting it in evidence." He took out another plastic bag and dropped the paperback inside.

Three loud, staccato chimes boomed out, setting Suzanna's heart pounding. It sounded like someone was striking a gong right next to her head. She slapped her hands over her tortured ears.

O'Brien snatched his cell from his pocket and held it up. "Just my phone."

"Oh, man, that scared me!" She closed her eyes and pressed her hand to her chest. Being a musician was never supposed to be scary or dangerous. Suzanna reviewed the reasons she'd gone into the music field. Getting blown up wasn't one of them.

When she opened her eyes, she saw Harry leaning against the frame of his office door, watching them. She wasn't surprised when he marched across the room and said, "That's enough, Detective. Talk to her more tomorrow."

O'Brien nodded and looked at Suzanna. "In that case, I need you to come to the station in the morning."

Her eyes grew wide, and an involuntary tear rolled down her cheek.

Harry whispered, "Detective, someplace less stark where she'd feel calm."

O'Brien shrugged. Facing Suzanna, he snapped, "Starbucks down the street. Tomorrow. Eleven o'clock. Can you be there?"

"Are you buying?" she asked, trying a feeble attempt to lighten things up the way Emily did.

He wrinkled his nose. "If you prefer the police station …"

Her cheeks blushed pink. Emily's jokes never fell flat like that. "Geez, I was only kidding. See you at Starbucks."

The detective linked eyes with her. "This is no time to be kidding around, Suzanna. We don't know what we're dealing with."

He broke eye contact and focused on his shiny, polished shoes. "The patrol car across the street will drive you home, and another will be stationed outside your apartment overnight."

The detective rose, and Suzanna reflexively shrank back from his imposing height. She kept a careful watch as he hurried away with the evidence bags.

Harry gave her shoulder a squeeze. "Go use my office phone and call your insurance company. Then, go home."

"Thanks, Harry," she said, noting that her boss could give the detective some pointers in empathy.

The slog to the back office felt like wading through molasses. How could someone be after her? Must be some mistake. Thankfully, there would be overnight police protection. And although she didn't always like having Chris, her roommate, around, she was glad she wouldn't be alone tonight. Just wait till she got home and told him the whole story.

Suzanna hunkered down in Harry's king-size leather chair and called her insurance company. The assigned agent politely listened as she did her best to describe the situation.

"After we inspect it," the agent said, "we'll determine if the car can be repaired or if it's totaled."

Even in her confused state, Suzanna couldn't help but snicker. "Oh, it's totaled all right. There's not much left to inspect."

"In any case, you can pick up a rental car at your local Enterprise and use it until we work out the details."

She hadn't even considered how she would get anywhere without Baby. A rental car. What an unexpected consolation prize.

Chapter 3

Across the river in Philadelphia, Arty was pulling his tattered robe around his waist and shuffling to the kitchen. Just an hour before, he'd nailed the Haddonfield job—fast, clean, and unseen. He was a pro and proud of it. Now, it was 'Miller Time.' He grabbed a beer from the fridge and settled down at his rickety kitchen table.

In his heart, Arty was still twenty-five, young and strong, with a swagger. But if he was going, to be honest, his thinning, gray hair, slight paunch, and stooped shoulders smacked of his seventy-four years of age. Not that long ago, his hair was a lady-killing, wavy, sable brown. But just yesterday, he noticed that white was even creeping into his thick eyebrows.

He didn't want anyone to get him wrong now. He was in great shape for seventy-four. Thanks to the brawny build he inherited from his pop, he could still bench-press two hundred pounds. And every one of his original teeth gleamed in his mouth. All the same, there was no denying he had matured. Retirement was calling.

But instead of taking his ease, Arty had to drum up more work—and quick. The Haddonfield job was a good start. A couple more jobs like that, and he'd be set.

His current need for employment was out-and-out embarrassing. Last month, he'd been on track to retire, but then, in one wild, Atlantic City weekend, he gambled away most of his nest egg. Before that, he'd always kept himself in check, never betting the whole ball of wax. But that weekend in AC, winning looked like a sure thing.

All the signs were there. The slot machines jangled and pinged a joyful chorus, the clinking roulette wheels set the beat, and the buxom dealer at his table gave him that "you-can-fuck-me-if-you're-lucky" smile. Arty peeked at his hand—a straight flush, jack high. The best hand he'd ever been dealt. Chances were about one in sixty thousand. The hand of a lifetime. Only a royal flush could beat it, and even after drawing and discarding, the odds of that happening to another player at his table were astronomical. In his jacket pocket, he rubbed his lucky Harrah's poker chip between his thumb and index finger.

The big slots winner siren blared out behind him, and a thousand different colored lights flashed—his favorite fanfare in the world. That was the last sign he needed. Arty went all in.

Beside him, a chump wearing a damfool bolo tie smiled and laid down the royal flush. Arty almost choked. He'd been beaten like a red-haired stepchild. In a daze, he left the table.

The stairs leading out of the casino soared steeper than usual as he shuffled up and out to the boardwalk. He went all the way to the end of the jetty and chucked his *lucky* chip in the ocean.

He'd really screwed the pooch this time.

Shaking his head, he tried to erase the memory of the entire cock-up. Arty shoved his chair back and pushed himself up with one hand clamped to his aching knee. The bones scraped against each other in the place where cartilage used to be. Every damn day, it seemed like some new ailment cropped up. Getting old was no fucking joke. He paced the floor with a vague limp.

The kitchen still held the sweet smell of peppers and eggs from breakfast, making him peckish. As he turned to the counter for some sandwich fixings, a sudden shaft of light from the setting sun streamed through the window. The glowing warmth surrounded him, and his mind slipped away to tropical climes. What he really wanted to do— really, *really* longed to do—was retire down in Florida.

Arty pulled his chair in line with the sun's last rays and flopped into it. Letting his eyelids droop shut, he stretched his legs out as though lounging in a beach chair and folded his arms behind his head. With high-fidelity memories of ocean waves crashing in his ears, he conjured up a bikini-clad waitress bringing him a festive cocktail with a teensy umbrella jutting over the rim. Later, he might play a little bocce ball.

The sun dipped below the horizon, shading his face. He frowned and sat up, remembering that his savings had taken a hike, forcing his dreams out of reach.

Arty gave his kitchen a once-over, examining the only remaining asset to his name—the house he'd inherited from his pop. The old Cape Cod wasn't much to look at. It stood on a meager lot in a substandard Philly suburb. Yesterday, coming up the walk, he stomped on a chunk of withered stucco the size of a fist and flattened it to a pancake. As he scraped it off his sole, he glanced up at the house. Most of the exterior was cracking and peeling. He whistled through his teeth. When did that happen?

The exterior was one thing, but the entire house needed a boatload of repairs. He couldn't afford a handyman, and no way was he doing the work himself. Ever since he lost everything, a mighty small social security check was his only income, and it barely paid the gas bill. Time to make some big money. No penny-ante, little, shit jobs.

Arty sat up straight, pencil in hand and took a crack at making a list of his repeat clients. He struggled for a few minutes, writing down only two names. Dammit, he couldn't remember anything anymore! He snorted and drummed his fingers on the table.

Racking his brain, he tried to dig up the name of the stupid guy who'd hired him six months ago. It was right on the tip of his tongue. He could almost picture it. Did it start with a G? Son of a bitch! Arty hurled the pencil across the room. It smacked the wall, angled off a shred of ripped wallpaper, and rolled over the linoleum. He was about to throw the pad of paper, too, when the phone rang. As he reached for it, it went silent.

A mistaken call? Maybe it was the same client who had hired him for the Haddonfield job. The guy had called out of the blue that morning in the midst of Arty's breakfast. He'd been a soft talker with a shaky voice. Annoying as hell. Arty had kept his cool, though, until he got a handle on the potential client. He always did. He had to. The caller could have been virtually anyone looking for his help. He'd done work for mobsters, TV stars, and everyone in between. Didn't bother him. As long as they could pay, he handled things.

Arty had warned his potential client that he was pissing up a rope if the job wasn't major. That's when the guy said the magic words—he wanted someone *neutralized*. Arty liked that his profession included a range of tasks. Sometimes, his work required cleanup, sometimes breaking and entering, and sometimes, like this morning's job, rubbing out a target. A pleasant variety.

He'd charged the new client a bundle, and the guy didn't even blink. All the detailed pictures and documents had been printed out on Arty's fax machine. He loved the sound of the muffled distortion and squeal when that machine fired up.

Now, his stomach was growling like a foghorn. He stopped thinking about the new client and remembered that he had a hankering for a sandwich. Arty stuffed pickles and bologna into slices of bread and ate standing over the sink. While taking a bite, he caught his hands shaking. Where the hell did that come from? Another damn part of growing old? During this morning's conversation with the new client, he had to increase the volume on the phone. And yesterday, it pissed him off royally when he had to turn up the TV. Did he need a hearing aid now? Imagine that … a fixer with a butt-ugly hearing aid.

Swallowing the last mouthful of sandwich, Arty sat back down at the table. A sudden pang of melancholy hit him in the gut, and he knew why. His target in Haddonfield had been female. Bumping off a member of the weaker sex always made him a bit gloomy, reminding him of his poor mum. Cancer had taken her before her time when he was only nine, the very year they moved into this Cape Cod from an abysmal tenement in West Philly. That's why, when he decided on a plan to take out today's target, he kept his mum in mind and settled on a method with no muss, no fuss, and no personal contact.

All the components had been in his special accessory drawer—power supply, initiator, tape, and explosives. Old parts, but all salvageable. After making a quick job of building the bomb, he'd thrown everything in his knapsack and driven over the bridge to New Jersey. Once he had made it to Haddonfield, the entire operation took only a few minutes.

A heavy thud shook the house. Arty jumped in his chair. It definitely came from the living room. He eased across the hall and peeked in. Nothing. Strange sounds and scents pestered him from time to time, and items moved around on their own, mostly wall hangings and food. He was sure a poltergeist haunted his house. Sometimes, he thought the ghost was his mum. He hoped it was his mum, anyway, and not one of his past targets. After years of coping with perplexing and eerie events in his own house, he'd developed a fascination with all things supernatural.

Arty shuffled back to the kitchen and carried his laptop from the counter to the table. He was ready to do some heavy research. Earlier that day, right before he left for Haddonfield, his long-haired, geeky neighbor from across the street had stopped by with a fascinating book. Their conversation had piqued his interest in the legend of the Jersey Devil. He thought through the neighbor's visit, trying to figure out why he'd been sucked in.

When the doorbell rang, he'd been wary out of habit and squinted through the peephole. Relieved to see only his bespectacled neighbor, he yanked the door open and was blasted with the earthy stench of pot smoke.

"Hey, man." Arty's neighbor pulled back an oily strand of hair and shoved his glasses up on his nose. "So I just read this really cool book, and like, I thought of you." Sunlight ricocheted off the book's shiny cover as he waved it around. The guy was about as excited as a stoner could get. "Like, I figure we're brothers in the study of the supernatural."

Under his breath, Arty said, "Dammit." Ever since they'd talked in his driveway about their mutual love of the *Ghost Hunters* TV show, this guy seemed to think they were asshole buddies.

"I got some new findings. Wanna hear?"

Arty's lips broke into a half smile. "Listen, son, I've been interested in the paranormal since the Dead Sea was still sick. I doubt you've got anything I don't know."

"But this phenom's local. Happened right over in South Jersey."

Arty's face went blank. What a nerd. The guy was fidgeting around so much, it looked like he had to take a leak. But he had to admit, it was kinda nice talking to another hardcore paranormal fan.

Shading his eyes from the glare of the cover, Arty snatched the paperback from his neighbor. He tilted the book until the flaming reds and oranges transformed into a recognizable shape—a cartoon of a creature whose body combined the torso of a snake-like dragon with the hideous features of the devil. Above the drawing, the title glowed in cherry-red, balloon-shaped letters, *The Jersey Devil: Phantom of the Pines*.

"Aw, come on." He shook his head. "I've heard of the Jersey Devil, a proven hoax."

"No, it's a real thing. Read the book, read the book." Spittle flew out of the geek's mouth and landed on Arty's shirt.

Arty pressed his lips together and let out a faint sigh. He'd tucked the book under his arm and mumbled thanks. He watched his neighbor meander back across the street with the spring's breeze swirling his long, stringy hair in five different directions.

Did the guy even have a job? Stopping by in the middle of the day on a weekday was odd. Maybe he was a dope dealer. He sure smelled like one.

There had only been time to page through *The Jersey Devil: Phantom of the Pines* and throw it in his knapsack before Arty left for Haddonfield. But the whole time he was planting the bomb, he couldn't get the Jersey Devil off his mind. His paranormal curiosity was surging.

Now, as he opened his laptop, he wanted to know everything there was to know about New Jersey's monster.

Chapter 4

After sending Suzanna home from the HB with Officer Cline, Detective O'Brien interviewed the head waitress, Emily. Talkative and amusing, she seemed to be Suzanna's closest friend. He jotted down *live wire* in his notes. Unfortunately, she only gave him one piece of crucial data—Suzanna had a new boyfriend. Emily didn't know his name. She just called him Cello Boy.

Next, O'Brien joined the owner, Harry, gazing out the window of the HB's replaced side door. The police force had cleared away the vehicle's remains and replaced it with cones and a rectangle of yellow hazard tape.

Noting the droop in Harry's broad shoulders, O'Brien understood. Today's havoc was enough to weigh anyone down. He held out his business card. Harry lifted it as though it was made of lead, then shoved it in his pocket.

"On the plus side," O'Brien said, "there were no major injuries and minimal damage to your establishment."

Harry nodded and gave O'Brien a tired smile. "That's quite a mustache you've got there, Detective. You look like—"

O'Brien cut him off with a weary bite in his voice. "I know, Yosemite Sam."

"Sorry, I was gonna say Wyatt Earp. Didn't mean …"

"No problem. Can you answer some questions?"

"Of course. Like a cup of joe?"

"No, I got a whiff of your coffee. Not for me."

Harry crossed his arms. "Well, we're not Dunkin' Donuts. You a connoisseur or something?"

"Of coffee? You bet. Now, tell me about your restaurant and Suzanna's role here."

Harry took a seat at the bar and motioned for O'Brien to join him. "I opened this place five years ago when I left the Marines, but it turned out different than I'd planned."

"How so?" O'Brien wrote down *Marine*. A Marine might have a working knowledge of explosives.

"I'd come to Haddonfield to open a gourmet restaurant. The town might be small, but it has always been upscale. You know, close to Philly and all the classy architecture. I was betting the ritzy trend would continue."

"Good bet. But your place looks more like a British pub, not a—"

Harry held up his hand. "My plan was to start with a pub grub menu and then, a little at a time, branch out to haute cuisine. But turns out, I make the best hamburger in the state of New Jersey."

O'Brien shot him a skeptical glance.

"I'm not exaggerating." Harry pointed at five small plaques hanging behind the bar. "I won the Best in New Jersey Award five times for my Bistro Burger."

A sudden craving for a hamburger washed over O'Brien, and he licked his lips.

Harry chuckled. "Bet you'd like one right now."

O'Brien forced a tightlipped smile. "But now your bistro doesn't jibe with Haddonfield's classy shops and restaurants."

"Ah, but I've learned that every town, no matter how well-heeled, needs a pub."

O'Brien nodded. He hesitated, taking time to form his next question. "I hate to be impolitic, but there aren't many African Americans in Haddonfield, much less shop owners. Had any trouble?"

"Nah, that's why I keep a tight rein on the place. I have to. I'm the example."

"Hmm …" That wasn't quite what O'Brien was getting at. "Could this have been a racially motivated attack and Suzanna's vehicle a random by-product?"

"Nothing like that." Harry shook his head vigorously. "Not here."

O'Brien pulled at the side of his mustache. "How did you meet Suzanna?"

"She showed up one day two years ago looking for a background job. The flyer she handed me was cute as all get out, and she offered one free night of music. The customers raved, and she's been playing here ever since."

"So she plays guitar while everyone eats?"

"Exactly. Why not come in sometime and have a burger? She works Thursday through Saturday."

Ignoring the question, O'Brien wrote down Suzanna's work schedule. "Two years. You must know her fairly well by now."

Harry sat back with a gentle smile. "I'm not *that* much older than her, but she makes me feel fatherly … like protective. Probably cause she's pint-size."

O'Brien met Harry's eyes. "Do you know anyone who might want to harm her?"

Harry's smile faded, and he slowly shook his head.

"Do you have a video surveillance system? Maybe it caught something before the car exploded."

"No, but I've already put in a call to have one installed." Harry nodded toward the front door. "But come to think of it, that jewelry store across the street has one."

O'Brien squinted through the front windows and noted the address of Haddonfield Jewelers.

"Have you seen anyone hanging around? Anyone who didn't seem kosher?"

A wrinkle ran along Harry's forehead. "Now that you mention it …"

O'Brien gazed at him eagerly. "Go on."

"I can't remember what day it was, but I saw a guy in a gray hoodie standing outside the window over there." Harry nodded his head toward Suzanna's performance area. "Right behind where she plays."

"What made you notice him?"

"Don't know. He was just staring at her, weird-like."

"What was he wearing besides the hoodie?"

"Who knows? But there was gold lettering on the front. I couldn't read it, though."

"Describe his face."

"Aw, man. Detective, I'm not gonna be much help." Harry dragged his palm across his bald head. "He had glasses, which I could see, but he had the hood up, and it hid the rest of his face."

Vinny leaned over the bar. "You two want anything?"

O'Brien shook his head and asked, "Did you see your boss's guy in a hoodie?"

"Nope." Vinny nodded toward Harry. "He told me, but I never seen him."

"Any ideas about why that car exploded?"

"Nope." A customer motioned, and Vinny slipped away.

O'Brien looked at Harry. "Anything else you can tell me?"

"No, but if I can help in any way …"

A familiar tickle ran along the bridge of O'Brien's nose. Things weren't falling into place neatly the way he liked. He'd have to do a lot of digging before this case started making any sense.

The salty scent of French fries floated under their noses as Emily stopped behind them, loaded down with a huge tray. "Hey, Detective O'Brien."

O'Brien twisted around to the waitress.

"Where does a mustache go for a drink?" She waited a beat. O'Brien turned back to the bar, knowing what was coming.

"A handle bar!" She continued past them, her laughter trailing away along with the smell of French fries.

Detective O'Brien stomped out of the HB and headed to his car. Mustache jokes. He got enough of those back at the station house. He'd shave the damn thing off if it would do any good, but those knuckleheads at the precinct would just ride him about something else.

When the captain had first introduced him to the boys in the Haddonfield squad room, the place erupted in snide comments. "Howdy, Pardner." "Hey, Super Mario, where's your brother?" "Stay away from the schoolmarm, you varmint." He couldn't understand it. In New York, his mustache was idiosyncratic. But here in Haddonfield, it was the funniest thing anyone had ever seen.

The evening air cooled his temper as O'Brien strolled down the wide sidewalks of the town's main road, King's Boulevard. Radiant moonlight mingled with the glow of ornamental, vintage lampposts showing off the tree-lined street. Blocks of Victorian row houses provided homes for artsy stores, coffeehouses, and trendy restaurants. He agreed with Harry—"ritzy" described Haddonfield's character to a T. Even better, "hippie chic."

The sidewalk crowd thinned as the town slowed for the night. The detective came to a pedestrian crossing and registered disbelief, as he always did, when the Haddonfield drivers stopped. He swore that in most Jersey towns, the drivers actually aimed for the foot traffic.

Almost two years had passed since O'Brien transferred from the NYPD into the Haddonfield Police Force. In that entire, interminable time, this car bomb case was the most interesting thing to cross his desk. The town's crimes generally consisted of nothing more than stolen bicycles, littering, and jaywalking.

When he'd first learned of Haddonfield's open, lead-detective position, he thought he'd found the perfect low-stress replacement for his New York job. But now, with two years under his belt, he secretly hoped this new case would jazz things up a bit.

Nearing his car, O'Brien rounded a corner into a dark alley. The symptoms the doc predicted had begun—his night vision was deteriorating fast. He misjudged the curb, and his toes slammed into cement. As he pitched forward, he smacked into the front of his car. Leaning on the hood for support, he ran his hands along the car's side rim until he found the door handle.

Only two years ago, on his fiftieth birthday, he'd received the bleak diagnosis. His expensive, New York ophthalmologist had held out little hope. No treatment existed for macular degeneration—no medication, no surgery, no cure.

He clambered into the driver's seat and flicked on the overhead light. Still, as he tried to put his notes away, he strained to see the latch on his briefcase. He took a blind jab at it, and papers spilled all over the floor mat.

The doc had explained in detail the gradual and gloomy process O'Brien faced. First, wavy lines would blur his sight. Then, he'd need increasingly more light, eventually losing his night vision completely. Finally, he would lose his central field of vision. In the end, only his peripheral vision would remain intact. In other words, he'd be legally blind. Not much of a birthday present, Doc. Not much use for a half-blind cop. But the thought of going out on disability made his skin crawl. They'd have to drag him out, kicking.

It was only a matter of time before his New York buddies blew the whistle on his problem, so he jumped ahead of the curve and transferred to Haddonfield. Here in "Podunk" New Jersey, where they talked slow and moved even slower, he'd make it to retirement without anyone being wiser.

O'Brien drove the two miles back to his apartment, squinting through the windshield. He hated driving at night, but this kind of case didn't stop when the sun went down.

His route home went by the local Chinese restaurant, the only cuisine New Jersey seemed to do right. After picking up some dinner, he got back in his car and lit a cigarette. He pondered it burning in his fingers. He was an idiot. The doc had given him a few ways to manage his macular degeneration and slow its progress—avoid stress, fatty foods, obesity, and smoking. The dietary changes he could deal with; he was already skinny as a pencil. And he'd dealt with the stress by moving. But quitting cigarettes … he'd been trying for two years.

The detective pulled over alongside one of the black, wrought iron trash cans dotting the roads of Haddonfield. Deciding to quit that minute, he tossed his pack. As he merged back into traffic, an SUV swerved away, almost sideswiping him. It just missed his bumper. He hadn't seen it at all. It was like it came out of nowhere. He clenched the wheel. This wasn't the first near miss he'd had at night. Clearly, he was fighting a losing battle with his eyes. He snickered at the irony. Clear for everyone to see but him.

With a tired hunger in his gut, he arrived at his apartment on the edge of town. His apartment complex consisted of a series of boxy, brick buildings with connecting yards and slender, cement walks. Each building held four one-bedroom apartments. In an effort to live up to Haddonfield's standard, the owners had attached Victorian gingerbread to the exterior gables. Like a tacky veneer, it just made the buildings look cheaper. But O'Brien didn't care how much the decor missed the mark. His apartment was cheap, clean, and one mile from work.

The detective carried his pork lo mein under his arm and reflexively reached into his pocket for a cigarette. Dammit. He forgot he quit.

Entering his apartment, he ran smack into a wall of stale smoke. He slammed the door and barely got his coat off before heading to the kitchen to raid his emergency cigarette stash. On his way, he stumbled over a ripped chunk of linoleum in front of the fridge—the same one he tripped over every time he walked through the kitchen. He cursed at himself for neglecting to fix it or at least calling the landlord.

His cigarette stash lived in the highest kitchen cabinet above the countertop that held his prized possession—an elaborate coffee machine, the only up-to-date appliance in the apartment. It ground beans, brewed coffee or espresso, steamed milk for cappuccino, and did it all on a timer. He ripped the cellophane off a fresh pack of smokes and lit up with a deep, satisfying drag.

His apartment was sparsely furnished, only the essentials. The walls were bare, no artwork or family photos. Cobwebs grew from unpacked boxes he'd strewn in the corner the first day he moved in. Only his closet was well-kept, fully stocked with pressed suits and starched shirts. Knowing he could pick up and leave at any moment was reassuring.

O'Brien opened the refrigerator and contemplated the three items in it: a bottle of ketchup with brown, congealed goop caked around the rim, a jar of mayonnaise that had probably gone bad, and a six-pack of Guinness. He pulled out a Guinness.

While he ate from the take-out containers, he mulled over the key points from his interviews.

Suzanna. Musician, petite, short, dark-brown hair. Possible target. Plays classical guitar at HB Thursday, Friday, Saturday nights. Get name of other restaurant. Miscellaneous other workplaces. Clueless about bomb. Offered no suspects. Investigate family and roommate.

Emily. Head waitress, tall, long, blonde hair. Tough girl trying to soften. Perfect fit for restaurant biz. Upbeat, live wire. Psychology student. Good friends with Suzanna. Offered possible suspect—new guy dating Suzanna, Cello Boy. Get name.

Harry. HB owner. Ex-marine. Only African American proprietor in Haddonfield? Racial issues? Witnessed suspicious guy in gray hoodie with yellow letters staring at Suzanna.

Vinny. Bartender, Tony Danza vibe. Didn't know anything. Couldn't corroborate hoodie guy. Mob connections?

Carrying his Guinness, O'Brien moved to the living room and sank down into his saggy, Naugahyde recliner, the only place to sit in the room. The silence in this apartment was unsettling. Only the ticking clock disturbed it. Through the thin walls in NY, he used to hear yelling, fighting, babies crying, TVs … Now, he couldn't decide which environment he liked less.

Not turning on the lights, he sat in the noiseless dark and brooded over his new case. If he was right about the explosion being caused by a planted car bomb, nothing made any sense. A car bomb was the strategy of a hit man. Why would an assassin turn up in this sleepy, New Jersey town?

Chapter 5

Suzanna slammed the apartment door with her hip, a technique developed over years of coming and going with her hands full. Her gig bag and amp were slung over one shoulder, and her guitar case was strapped to her back like a backpack. Thank heavens for the police ride home. For that matter, as long as she was being grateful, thank heavens she was still in one piece!

Her roommate's voice carried over from the next room. "There are musicians, and then … there are Musicians with a capital M," Chris said with a pompous drawl. "I'm the pure-of-heart kind of musician. What one would call an 'arteest.'"

A jumble of battered sneakers and jackets—not hers or Chris's—lay scattered by the entrance. Chris's friends. Suzanna let her gig bag fall to the ground with a thud. A medley of male voices rose from the living room. She was already a stressed-out mess. How was she going to deal with a houseful?

As she pulled her guitar off her back, a stiff neck reminded her how much heavier this guitar case was than her old one. The new case, the latest technology, looked like some futuristic, metallic casket and weighed a ton. The strain of carrying it didn't help her aching head any.

Pausing, she steadied herself before rounding the corner into the living room. There she found Chris lounging on the sofa, surrounded by a group of drunk, male, twentysomethings. He passed the guitar in his hands to one of his gang and focused on Suzanna.

"And here, we have a 'take-every-gig' guitarist," he said, losing the drawl. "She'll even play a wedding!"

Chris's friends all turned toward Suzanna. Their eyes fixed on her face.

"That work, including the dreaded wedding gig, paid your half of the rent last month. You still owe me."

She sized up Chris's gang. They were all skinny, dirty, and wasted. Then, she took in the room. The dregs of food from their fridge littered her secondhand, but polished, coffee table. Drained beer bottles were strewn across the old, hardwood floor. An empty bag of chips sat crumpled on the window seat—*her* vinegar and sea salt chips.

Suzanna wanted to scream, *My car just burned up, and you dorks ate my chips!* but thought better of sharing her problems with Chris's drunken horde.

Through steeled lips, she said, "You didn't tell me you invited guests tonight."

Chris gripped his beer bottle by the neck and swung it in lazy circles. All eyes turned back to him. "But we're having a wonderful celebration."

Suzanna sucked in a breath and held it. Two years ago, her brief romance with Chris had ended on the day they graduated from the Philadelphia Conservatory. But for the past six months, they'd been rooming together "platonically" out of necessity, and it wasn't going very well.

She picked up the empty bag of chips, the masking tape with her name still plastered on the front. Her chips were sacred. Chris knew that.

One of the guests said, "Those were delicious."

She lost it. "Okay, everybody out!"

Chris flinched and clutched his chest in fake surprise. Suzanna outstared him, and he dropped the act. He gave his friends a gloomy nod. Obediently, they put on jackets, packed up guitars, and shuffled out the door. Chris didn't bother seeing them out.

Impolite. When they were dating, that was the first rotten quality she'd seen in Chris. Stupidly, she'd ignored it, but then, she was in love. During those heady days, she had found his long, blond hair and movie-star face irresistible. Now? Not so much.

"You're home awfully early, Miss Sellout." Reproach tinged Chris's voice.

Her eyes welled up. He hadn't even noticed how upset she was. Suzanna flopped down on the sofa. "I have to talk to you. Something big happened at work—"

"You call that work?" Chris shook his head at her. "I call it white noise for a bunch of losers."

"Stop it! This is serious."

Chris scuffed over to the bay window, pulled back the curtain, and peeked out. In that brief moment, the streetlight glistened in his eyes, and she realized how bloodshot they were.

"So what hap— Hey!" The drape fell from his hand, and he swung toward her. "What's going on out there? A patrol car is sitting across the street."

Suzanna looked him square in the eye. "Baby exploded. If I'd been any closer, I wouldn't be here."

"What?" His nose and lips scrunched together like he'd just smelled a Deptford pig farm.

While she gave him a rundown of the blowup, he squeezed in beside her on the small sofa and wrapped his arm around her shoulders. This was the Chris she'd fallen in love with. He'd been so sweet and affectionate … in the beginning.

Chris patted her hand. "Sorry about Baby. But you've got to admit, that car *was* a hunk of junk."

"Right, but what am I—"

"I'll ask around about used cars for sale. Almost anything would be a step up. Insurance should cover it." He unsqueezed himself from the sofa and returned to looking out the window. "So, how long will that patrol car be parked over there?"

"How should I know?" A wave of pain rolled behind Suzanna's eyes. Chris was more worried about the cop outside than her crisis. "And I have a bump on my head."

She swallowed a sob, and suddenly, all the tears she'd fended off since the explosion poured out.

"Hey, hey." Chris squatted in front of her and put his hands on her knees. His breath smelled like he'd drunk an entire keg of Heineken. "Calm down."

"Do you think someone is out to get me?" She sniffled and wiped her nose.

"Course not."

"Well, why—"

"Wait. Before I forget. I can't transfer my rent money tomorrow. I'll have it in a couple days, along with last month's."

"Late again!" Suzanna shoved him away and he tumbled over. Selfish bastard! Couldn't take a moment from his own issues to think about her. This reminded her all too well of why she broke up with him. It hadn't taken long to realize he was just a gorgeous jerk. Turned out he was selfish in every way, including in the bedroom. How shallow she'd been. Drawn in by his handsome features and the fact he played classical guitar, too. Chalk it up to inexperience. After they'd split up, she never looked back. That is, until six months ago when he showed up at her door. She blew her nose and wiped her eyes.

From the floor, he said, "It's a higher calling to follow one's principles than gain riches."

"Come off it. You can have principles and make money, too."

He propped his back against the sofa and held up his bottle as though making a toast. "You'll see. No more background music for me." Chris's fine, blond hair flopped in his face; he swept it out of his eyes with a practiced flick of his head. "I'm targeting elite gigs and concerts where I'll perform for people who are truly listening."

Suzanna was in no mood for this conversation. What was he talking about, anyway? It was hard enough to make a living in music without limiting the gigs. The problem was that their musical goals were miles apart. She simply wanted to earn an independent income playing music. Chris wanted fame.

Kneading her stiff neck, she lamented the loss of her old roommate, Zelda, a violinist friend from the conservatory. "Wonder how Zelda's doing."

"What a great pal she was, leaving you in the lurch like that."

"I haven't heard from her since she shacked up with what's-his-name."

"Lucky that I turned up to take over the lease. Don't you think?"

She didn't answer. He was fishing for compliments. Just because Zelda left her holding the bag on a lease that wasn't up for another year and a half didn't make him a hero.

"Saved both our butts." Chris puffed out his chest.

Suzanna's scowl twitched with cynicism. She didn't know how Chris discovered Zelda had moved away, and his motives were still unclear. He'd come to her in an uproar, saying his folks had kicked him out and begged her to let him move in. Later, she found out it was all a lie. Fortunately, she'd made it plain that there would be no rekindling of the romance. Now, six months in, they were butting heads on everything from work ethics to musical phrasing, and he was being a real scumbag. She was ready to throw in the towel.

"At least when you moved in," she said, "I could stop borrowing money from my mom. God, I hate that."

Suzanna often dreamed of having the apartment to herself. It was old but had so much character. She'd have to look far and wide to find a place with its vintage charm for the bargain basement rent they paid. Only dreams. She could play background music until her fingers fell off and still not afford it on her own. Even if she could scrape by without a roommate, she'd never be able to save up for her main goal—a master's degree. And now, on top of everything, she had to buy a new car.

"Was any of your gear in Baby when he blew?" Chris asked.

Suzanna's stomach tightened. She pictured her tuner melted somewhere within Baby's smoldering remains and the charred Jersey Devil book flying into the HB.

"What do you know about the Jersey Devil?" she asked.

Chris shot her a puzzled look. "Where did that come from?"

"A paperback all about the Jersey Devil blasted into the HB with me. The police took it."

"Are we talking the Jersey hockey team?"

"No, the urban legend. You know, monster in the Pine Barrens."

"Isn't it supposed to be half devil, half something else? A horse, maybe?"

"Who knows? But where would you get a book about it?"

Chris shrugged and, without words, only inflection, said, "I don't know."

"I'll find out," Suzanna said with a determined nod that made her head hurt. "I want my own copy."

The sofa rocked as Chris pushed off. On his way to the kitchen, he picked his way over a mound of empty beer bottles. Suzanna regarded his striking face and flowing hair. Young and attractive—that could take you far in the classical music world just like any other. Chris's looks, she often thought, were the reason he'd booked *any* paying concerts. She wondered if he would still land concerts when he grew bald and wrinkled. For that matter, would she still get background gigs or a college position when her hair turned gray?

Chris took a seat at their small, butcher-block island. Suzanna followed him into the kitchen and opened the fridge. Her shoulders slumped. Empty. No pickles, no yogurt, no nothing.

"Did I see Piano Dan in your group of revelers?" she asked.

"Yep, he just got a job coding for Comcast and bought all the beer."

"Another one bites the dust." Suzanna had stopped counting how many conservatory friends had given up on their music dreams. One by one, they took non-musical day gigs to get by, then those jobs morphed into careers.

"You won't catch me taking a damn day job," Chris said, "not me."

Suzanna's eyes teared up again, but she held back the tears. He just couldn't think of anyone but himself.

"I blame the conservatory," Chris proclaimed. "Not one music-business course."

Suzanna gave him a mopey nod. She'd never forget how utterly unprepared she'd been to begin life as an independent musician. Having to learn marketing, publicity, management, and God knows what else on the job. But she'd done the work. As far as she knew, Chris had never even tried.

"I hate the business side," he said.

"Self-promotion is part of the gig."

"But it has nothing to do with music."

Suzanna's mind wandered as Chris driveled on. Where could she get her own Jersey Devil book? Amazon?

Piled high on the kitchen countertop sat a stack of sardine packages, Chris's favorite snack. She watched him unwrap a pack, slurp the sardines straight out of the tin, and wash them down with beer. The oily juice splattered all over the front of his ragged T-shirt.

Practically holding her nose against the fishy odor, she said, "Look, I know you're having financial … issues. But if you don't start coughing up rent on time, I'm phoning your parents and asking them for it."

He gave her a dismissive wave and tossed the empty tin.

Suzanna had never met Chris's elusive mom and dad and knew only two things about them—they were Evangelical preachers, and they had money. Enough money to mail Chris a check every month. If only those dollars didn't fly through his fingers like a flurry of sixteenth notes. "They might want to know how much you're drinking, too."

"You've been making that ridiculous threat for months now."

"Well, I can't front your rent forever."

"This is called blackmail." Chris emphasized each word with a swish of his beer bottle.

"So you've said." Suzanna laced her guitar to her back. "Or is it extortion? I had a debate about this with the HB crew just the other day."

He stuck his nose in the air. "That's quite a seedy bunch you're associating with."

Her face flushed pink. How did he always know exactly what to say to piss her off?

"Speaking of my parents," Chris said, "they called today, and get this, they're thinking about visiting. You could do your blackmail thing with them in person."

Too angry to comment, she held her tongue.

"And they want to come in two weeks. What do you think?"

Suzanna bundled up her gig bag with a bitter frown. "Let them come." Scraping down the hall, she carted all her gear to her bedroom and propped her guitar against her dresser. She softly latched the door, leaned her back against it, and shut her eyes. The relief of being alone enveloped her like a soothing, hot bath. She could still hear Chris spouting off about his parents; he hadn't even noticed she'd left. Typical.

She scanned her room, the high ceilings and hardwood floors, and her heart ached at the thought of losing the apartment. If she called it quits with Chris, she only had three choices: track down a new roommate (exhausting), move back with Mom (ouch), or find a smaller, cheaper place (if that was even possible.) In her opinion, they already had the best, cheap walk-up in South Jersey.

Occupying the entire second floor of a partitioned, Victorian row house, it had two small bedrooms, crown molding, and her favorite feature—floor-to-ceiling windows in every room. Outside, an unvarnished pine staircase led up from a gravel parking area to a tiny deck and private entrance. The whole house was holding up pretty well, considering it had been built in the 1800s. A few flaws gave away its age: hairline cracks in plaster walls, sloping floors, and windows so loose, they shook in their frames whenever a plane flew overhead. It was an old house in a town of old houses, but she loved it.

Suzanna collapsed on her bed. The mattress bobbed in time to Chris's passing footsteps as he lumbered down the hall to his room. Cradling her sore head in one arm, she dragged her laptop from her bedside table with the other.

At least she didn't have a knock-down, drag-out fight with Chris tonight. That would have been the perfect end to a horrible day. Fights with Chris seemed to happen when he drank, and lately, he'd been drinking all the time. Those fights always ended with him dishing out personal digs, especially about her appearance. Her haircut was tragic, her clothes were old, her nose was just too big. Okay, she could use a fresh wardrobe. But being so darn short meant she might as well thumb her nose at all the fashion trends. And speaking of noses, he couldn't lay off that most hurtful topic. She hadn't heard so many gigantic schnoz insults since grade school.

With her fingertips, Suzanna massaged her tired eyes. At least she knew her eyes were pretty—large and jade green with long, full lashes. They were her mother's eyes. She'd inherited all her mom's features, except one. Her nose was the only physical trait she knew for certain came from her father.

Suzanna snapped her laptop open and brought up the empty Google search screen. What did she want to learn about the Jersey Devil? Background? Maybe. But she was more interested in *Jersey Devil: Phantom of the Pines* and its provenance than its topic.

Scrolling through Amazon's offering of Jersey Devil books, she found several interesting selections, but not *her* book. Odd. Must be published by a small press or even self-published. Not listing the author didn't help.

She switched strategies, ending up on Wikipedia's Jersey Devil page. The long table of contents guaranteed a wealth of information. She promised herself that she would read it all another time. Instead, she scrolled to the bottom of the page and scoured the footnotes, hoping *Jersey Devil: Phantom of the Pines* would show up in the reference section. No luck.

The final footnote caught her eye though, a shop called the Devil's Lair, specializing in Jersey Devil lore, books, and gifts. The shop didn't have a website, only a street address. It sat right in the middle of the Pine Barrens in the town of Indian Mills, a forty-five-minute drive from Haddonfield. Monday was her next day off. It could be fun to go and explore. If any store sold her book, the Devil's Lair would be it. And they might know who else bought it.

Suzanna clicked on the *Images* link at the top of the screen. Dozens of pictures of the Jersey Devil popped up. No photographs, only disturbing drawings and etchings. To her surprise, a different, gruesome beast appeared in each illustration. Apparently, no one had a clue what the thing actually looked like. The creepiest Jersey Devils were pictured with evil-snarling snouts and fangs dripping with blood.

In the center of the screen, an old-fashioned engraving grabbed her attention. Attributed to the *Philadelphia Bulletin*, January 1909, it stood out from all the others. The simple, crosshatched pencil sketch depicted an incredibly goofy-looking creature. Giant-size with gangly, skinny bones, it had a horse-like face, sprawling bat wings, cloven hooves, and a spiky, forked tail. It stood on its back legs with tiny, bent front arms, like a kangaroo. This Jersey Devil appeared to be smiling. Suzanna didn't find it creepy, just peculiar.

Leave it to New Jersey to have a horsey-kangaroo monster! She chuckled for the first time since the explosion.

Chapter 6

Arty sat at his kitchen table as night came on. His laptop's dim glow played across his face, darkening the fleshy bags under his eyes. The remaining room lay in shadow.

Staring into the computer screen, his stubby fingers stiffly mashing the keys, he read page after page of Jersey Devil lore—the origin story, sighting locations and dates, names of experts in the field … everything. The legend reminded him of Bigfoot, and he knew Bigfoot was real. His cousin in Washington State had actual photographs.

A wisp of his mother's old, jasmine perfume flooded his senses and abruptly vanished. The scent provoked a twinge of nostalgia, and a memory from his youth sprang to mind—standing with his mum on the front steps of the Cape Cod, the one he still lived in, both of them waving. They must've been waving to his pop.

A dull thump came from the living room. He crept across the hall. A leather-bound book lay on the floor next to his pop's bookshelf, full of books Arty had never read. He crouched down, sure it hadn't been there earlier. As he picked it up, an old snapshot fluttered out. He held the photo up and peered into the past. They'd looked so happy. It was him, about eight or nine, with his mum, both waving, the exact moment he'd just been remembering. Turning it over, he saw his mum's scrawled handwriting … *Leaving for Florida 1948*. He got the cold shudders. Was his mum trying to tell him something?

Arty padded back to his kitchen table. Surveying its many repairs, some so-so, some lousy, he decided the table looked a lot like he felt—old. The yellowed snapshot reinforced the idea.

He turned back to his laptop and clicked on a hyperlink that took him to an inventory of authentic witness accounts of Jersey Devil sightings. After reading them, he kicked back and wagged his head. He had to hand it to the geek. This paranormal activity *was* legit. And to his surprise, the Jersey Devil made its most spectacular appearance in the very town he had just visited—Haddonfield.

A mysterious, faint-red box floated across the bottom of the web page. When he clicked on it, a grainy, black-and-white photo appeared of a gloomy, stone house sitting atop a craggy hill. Arty took in a sharp breath. Secluded and in a state of decay, the place looked seriously creepy. A heavy mist, shimmering like a giant spiderweb, encircled the thing.

Arty zoomed in on the image. What a dump! It was in worse shape than the Cape Cod. Dead branches flanked the crumbling stone walls while brambles snaked their way through the cracks. A weather-worn chimney covered more than half of the front. Any fireplace attached to that chimney would be sizable, likely the sole heat source. The entire house couldn't have more than two rooms.

The caption stated, *Location of the Jersey Devil's Birth*. He rubbed his thick arms against a creeping chill. The page listed directions from multiple locales. Tucked away in the Pine Barrens, the house stood near the shore town of Leeds, New Jersey. On the spot, he vowed to go there and check it out, maybe even take along his geeky neighbor. He jotted down the directions.

Clicking back to the magnified house, Arty stared at the screen until everything blurred. He could swear a long spike, like an animal's tail, was poking out from behind the house. He kneaded his eyes with his knuckles. Glaring back, he saw only the house—no animal, no tail.

With a slap, he closed his laptop. How could he ever have believed the Jersey Devil was a hoax? These new findings inspired him to take another look at his neighbor's book. He reached into his knapsack and groped through the clutter. *The Jersey Devil: Phantom of the Pines* was gone.

Arty pulled the knapsack up to his face. All his tools were there, but no book. He emptied everything onto the table. No book. Did he lose it?

He flopped down in his chair, baffled, and brooded. When the phone rang, he was so startled he knocked his knapsack to the floor. "Arty here."

"She's not dead!"

It took Arty a second to realize who it was. This morning, his client's voice sounded timid. Now, he sounded like a howling maniac.

Arty had to hold the phone away from his ear. "Really? How did—"

"Don't you know your job?"

"Okay, okay … dammit, man, switch to decaf! I'll take care of it."

"Do things right this time, or I'll find somebody to fix *you*."

Arty hung up, muttering, "Shithead." Was he losing it? He *had* done everything right but, somehow, still missed his target. Bad luck? He pictured his lucky chip tumbling end over end in the frothy waves.

Chapter 7

Saturday, May 11

Suzanna drove her brand-new, rented Civic hatchback down King's Boulevard toward her apartment. The compact car kept her snug and warm, safe from the early morning air holding the final chill of winter. For a moment, she forgot about last night's trauma.

She looked on with envy at the Haddonfieldites strolling along the cobblestone sidewalks, wordlessly proclaiming the weekend. Saturday was never a day of freedom for her, just another workday, or, rather, worknight. Weekends ranked as prime gig time. The stream of pedestrians acted like they were flat-out daring the coming storm to spoil their day off. Armed with umbrellas, they ignored the slate-gray sky, leaden with clouds, and went about their chores as though it were a sunny day. She drove by joggers and dog walkers, weaving their way around bundle-juggling shoppers, and watched hand-holding couples peruse artfully displayed breakfast menus hanging in café windows.

Above the shops, the second and third floors, with their candy-colored turrets and ornamental gingerbread, supplied affordable rental housing for people of modest income, like her. Three blocks beyond King's Boulevard, real estate prices soared above her pay grade. That part of town held historic, high-end mansions surrounded by massive grounds.

Haddonfield's location, right across the river from the city of Philadelphia, had proved ideal for Suzanna. She could get to Center City in less than fifteen minutes, where classical-guitar-gig opportunities increased tenfold. She played so many gigs, it sometimes felt like she was passing herself coming back as she drove over the bridge to Philly. But background music would never give her the financially independent life she craved. She had to get that master's.

As she passed the HB, she glimpsed a streak of yellow. Police tape. The image of a firefighter hosing down Baby flashed in her mind, and her heart rate skyrocketed. Last night's explosion kept poking its nose into her thoughts. At least the pain in her head had dwindled to a dull ache. Nothing aspirin couldn't fix.

Stopping at a crosswalk, Suzanna stamped both feet on the brake pedal. The Civic jerked to a standstill. The force and response of the brakes surprised her every time. Power brakes were something Baby never had.

The rental held other upgrades, too, playing in a whole different ballpark than Baby. Cherry red with that new-car smell, it boasted automatic windows, seat adjustments, and side mirrors. An impressive array of levers covered the steering wheel and armrest. Suzanna had yet to figure out what they did. And best of all, the Civic featured power steering along with those power brakes. She felt a pang of guilt, but maybe losing Baby wasn't so terrible after all.

Pausing on her deck, Suzanna looked over her shoulder, admiring the gleaming rental car she'd just parked in the gravel lot. Then, with a shudder, she scoured the area for any potential attackers.

Her mind was still focused on imaginary bombers as she turned the door key. A sour smell permeated the hallway. The sound of vomiting jarred her back to reality. "Chris?" When she left earlier that morning for Enterprise, he'd been sleeping.

Chris stumbled out of the bathroom and into the kitchen, wearing nothing but a ratty, old robe. "Had a few too many libations." He wiped his mouth on his sleeve, burped, and took a beer out of the fridge. His long, blond hair was matted to his face.

"You literally just puked from too much booze. Now you're at it again?"

"It does seem a bit plebeian," he said, slurring his words.

"It's ten in the morning."

"Morning? Already?" He turned his back on her and walked into the living room.

"This isn't normal," Suzanna said, following him. She didn't like to confront him, especially about drinking. His reactions could be explosive. Once, he hurled a full beer bottle across the room. But now, she didn't care how he reacted and just blurted out, "You're an alcoholic."

Chris ignored her. No response at all. Without even making eye contact, he sat down on the sofa and drank his beer.

Suzanna's fists clenched. His silence was worse than an overreaction. She cranked up her voice. "I've had it! If you don't get help, or at least start paying your rent on time, one of us has to go."

Out of habit, Chris flung his head back to toss his hair, but this time, the matted strands stuck flat to his forehead. "Go? I thought you were blackmailing me with my parents."

"I will, and soon, but you need to take a good, hard look at yourself."

"Suzanna, as usual, you're overreacting. Chill out, and we can deli … deliber … uh, talk about it."

"Not this time!"

She stomped out to the deck and slammed the door. Her appointment with Detective O'Brien wasn't for another hour, but after that dramatic exit, there was no way she was going back inside.

Between O'Brien's meeting and dealing with Chris, her daily routine was shot. Normally, she'd be practicing right now, but instead, she had to waste an hour. She could go shopping, visit friends, investigate the Jersey Devil … Her eyes lit up. She could go to the used bookstore up on

King's Boulevard, directly across the street from Starbucks. It was precisely the kind of shop that might sell *The Jersey Devil: Phantom of the Pines*.

Glancing down at the street, Suzanna did a double take. No police car. She clung to the deck railing and glared at the empty spot. Had it been there when she went for the rental? She couldn't remember. Trying to keep calm, she hurried down the steps, wondering where her protection had gone. She checked along both sides of the street, but no police car.

Peering up at the overcast sky that threatened rain any minute, Suzanna wrapped her arms around herself and started walking. An umbrella would be nice, but she wasn't going back. Her windbreaker would have to do. At least it had a hood.

Anyway, it was only a two-minute walk. A little water wouldn't hurt her, but she couldn't stop worrying about who or what could.

Chapter 8

After wasting that car bomb last night, Arty needed to whip up a new plan. No more screwups. The first order of business—find a good location to make the final attack on his target, a staging area, if you will. He drove to Haddonfield to check out her turf.

First, he scoped out her apartment, but it was too exposed. In fact, her entire block was too exposed. He struck it off his list.

Next, Arty attempted to explore the HB again. It could still be the best place to carry out the hit. While making his way down King's Boulevard, the sharp, fresh smell of ozone smacked him in the face. No question … any time now, it was gonna pour.

Tugging his collar up around his neck, he scowled at the creaking flower baskets swaying from swanky lampposts. Damn, fancy mucky-mucks. As he checked down the street for the HB, hoping to get there before the rain started, he was bowled over by a swinging placard embossed with shiny, gold print. The words pierced his eyes like a laser: *The Haddonfield Book Emporium—New and Gently Used Books*. He still had no idea how he lost his neighbor's Jersey Devil book, but this store might have a replacement.

Arty pulled on the emporium's inviting brass handle, but the door didn't budge. He tugged harder and then harder still. Finally, the door flew open with a bang and a high-pitched bell rattled. The clamor gave him a shock, a real whammy. He cursed through gritted teeth.

Overflowing, floor-to-ceiling bookshelves packed the place. Scattered among the mismatched shelves were beat-up, overstuffed chairs, wobbly end tables, and a collection of antique desks. Considering the snooty nature of the town, he thought the store looked surprisingly shabby. Maybe that's why there were so few customers milling about.

Arty stopped at a bulletin board and read the notices—*Nanny available*; *Book club meeting on Moby Dick*; *Wine tasting*; *Lost Persian cat*; *Historical society lecture about New Jersey's Revolutionary legislature fleeing from the British*. What a bunch of stuck-up Poindexters!

Pressing on, he wandered through the aisles, searching for the replacement book. Finally, he went to the front desk and asked the girl, who looked about eleven, if they had any books on the Jersey Devil.

"We sure do! On the second floor. I'll show you." The girl's smile was so saccharin it made his teeth hurt.

"No, I'll find it myself." Just his luck, it would be on the upper level. With some difficulty, he found a slender, wrought iron, spiral staircase against the back wall, almost hidden amid piles of paperbacks. Arty labored up the stairs, his lousy knee creaking on every step.

The second floor's single, large room was partitioned into columns of ceiling-high shelves crammed together even tighter than on the first floor. He scoured the rows of books and promptly zeroed in on *The Jersey Devil: Phantom of the Pines*. While he was at it, he snapped up two other books on the local monster.

Arty nosed around and came across a compact reading nook surrounded by the looming shelves. A table lamp cast just enough light on a roomy, overstuffed wing chair. He lowered himself into the cushy seat with a comfortable sigh and began to eyeball his new findings. It wasn't long before he was snoozing.

Chapter 9

Suzanna turned onto King's Boulevard and walked down its wide sidewalk toward the used bookstore. As she passed the Indian King Tavern, she ran a finger along the jagged, peeling paint of its navy-blue, clapboard storefront. The tavern was one of a handful of Revolutionary War–era structures interspersed between Haddonfield's shops and cafés. The community preserved its history with a vengeance, so most of the buildings from the 1700s had been transformed into well-maintained museums. She was thinking the Indian King looked a little worse for wear, when a group of painters hauling ladders, brushes, and scrapers swarmed by and got to work.

As she came up on her favorite pastry shop, The Upper Crust, a fleeting scent of buttery croissants drifted out. It reminded her she hadn't eaten anything that morning. She considered going in. She *should* eat something, but her nervous stomach disagreed.

Suzanna decided to give The Upper Crust a pass and waded through the mass of pedestrians toward the used bookstore. The ominous sky, paired with the jostling crowd, deepened her anxiety. The face of each passerby looked a little suspicious. Any one of them could have sabotaged Baby. Her unease mingled with her anger at Chris. Inside her sneakers, her toes stress-twitched.

A warning droplet grazed her forehead, and she jogged down the block, guided by the bookstore's swinging placard. Behind the glass of the emporium's spacious bay window, a fat tabby slept on the sill amid a display of tattered hardbacks. The books were haphazardly strewn about; the cat was contentment itself. Suzanna tugged on the brass doorknob extra hard, knowing the door would stick in the jamb. It always did. A small bell jingled as the door gave way. When she stepped inside, the scent of worn-out paper and vintage wood reminded her of childhood trips to the library with her mom.

Suzanna approached the girl behind the bookstore's counter, which, in this case, was the top of an antique, Queen Anne, fall-front desk. It held numerous tiny drawers, letter-size cubbyholes, and a miniature door hiding a secret compartment. While admiring the desk's cabinetwork, she asked, "Do you have any books on New Jersey or Jersey folklore?"

The girl flashed a broad smile. "We sure do." Waving for Suzanna to follow, she bounded out of her chair and rushed to the back of the store. Suzanna powerwalked to keep up and followed her to the top of the spiral staircase.

Leading the way through the cramped, second-floor aisles, the girl looked like an archeological adventurer searching for a mummy's tomb. Suzanna wanted to ask if there were any secret panels or hidden doors. After pointing out a low shelf, the girl spun around and disappeared down the stairs.

The room's primary light source was a wooden-framed skylight that covered most of the ceiling. In the past, Suzanna had been there only on sunny days when the massive skylight poured sunshine into every corner. But today's gray sky produced nothing but muted shadows. A few old floor lamps gave off the only gloomy reading light.

Suzanna dragged one of the lamps up to her shelf and browsed through the book spines. All the titles were related in some way to the state of New Jersey. The selection was surprisingly varied—*A History of Inventing in NJ*, *Jersey Shore Cookbook*, *Birds of NJ Field Guide* ... The books weren't in alphabetical order, or, for that matter, in any kind of order.

Toward the end of the shelf, her eyes were drawn to a book with a bright and colorful binding. Jumbo, glossy, orange letters spelled out *Weird New Jersey*. The book's weight surprised her as she pried it off the shelf and opened it on a small desk. Running her finger down the table of contents, Suzanna came across a whole chapter on the Jersey Devil. Twenty other chapters detailed a variety of eerie phenomena in the state. She leafed through the pages and became absorbed in a tale about a ghost choir haunting the remains of an abandoned mansion.

Startled by the sound of footsteps, she jerked her head out of the book. Apparently, she wasn't alone on the second floor. Stretching her neck, she tried to see where the noise had originated. The crammed bookshelves only allowed her to see a few feet in each direction. The dim lighting didn't help. She stood hushed, listening for any movement.

An enormous, winged shadow, inky black, flew across the skylight, momentarily throwing the room into utter darkness. Her jangling nerves, already on high alert, lit up. As if the shadow had been a prelude, a trumpet blast of thunder crashed. Suzanna flinched, and the heavy book fell to the floor with a smack. When she bent to retrieve it, her hands were trembling. What a dope. Scared of shadows and thunder.

Fat raindrops leisurely plopped onto the skylight. She pulled a wooden chair up to the desk and sat down, turning her attention back to *Weird New Jersey*'s ghoulish local monsters. As she flipped through the pages, the sky turned from gray to black. The rain quickened, filling the room with a piercing rat-a-tat. Suzanna cupped her hands over her ears and squinted through the dark at the worn book.

When it was almost time to head to Starbucks, she skipped to the chapter on the Jersey Devil. It began with a full-page picture of the monster with daggerlike fangs and grasping paws. As she read, the sky finally opened, and waves of water pounded onto the skylight with a deafening clatter.

Raspy panting floated out from the shelves behind her, cutting through the din. Suzanna sprang out of her chair.

The grating sound swelled into a snarl and ended with a sharp snort. Clutching *Weird New Jersey* in a sweaty grip, she stood on tiptoe, trying to see over the shelves.

Behind her, a crash rang out like a gunshot. She jumped about a foot in the air. Heart hammering in her ears, she dropped the book and flew down the spiral staircase. The emporium's sticky door was no match for her adrenaline-filled smack. The little bell jangled at full tilt.

Back on the sidewalk, Suzanna pushed through the throng and started running. She ran until it struck her that she didn't know where she was going. Soaking wet, she stopped and leaned against an antique shop storefront. Past the point of even trying to stay dry, she squeezed her eyes shut. She hadn't read much of *Weird New Jersey*, but it seemed to give her delusions of rasping, disembodied monsters. Or was she so jittery from last night's fiasco that any old noise freaked her out?

The buzz of the shopper's hubbub helped her shed the monster world and come back to real life. When she finally blinked her eyes open, the pouring rain had turned to a fine spray. Suzanna looked at all the umbrellas and raincoats self-consciously. Her hair and jacket were soaked. Slipping back into the stream of pedestrians, she headed to Starbucks. Now, ironically enough, she found being part of the crowd calming.

Chapter 10

When the downpour broke, Arty woke in the bookstore's comfy chair with a loud snort. He must have been snoring, but what a great nap! Time to beat feet. Still half asleep, he scooped up his trophies and shuffled toward the stairs.

Out of nowhere, pins 'n' needles throbbed through his leg. He staggered, and his books crashed on the wooden floor. The racket echoed off the walls and skylight like machine-gun fire. He stooped to pick them up, but his hands had gone numb. Dammit! Another malady? He shook his arms to get the feeling back.

A thud and the sound of running came from the next aisle. As the sensation in his hands returned, Arty gathered up his stack and stuck his head around the end of the shelves. A book lay flat on the floor. Its bright-orange title read, *Weird New Jersey*. He leafed through and checked the inside cover for the price. Only twenty-five cents. Who could pass up a bargain like that? He added it to his pile and trudged down the stairs.

Outside, under the eaves of the Haddonfield Book Emporium, Arty stood, waiting for the pounding rain to ease up. Despite the crappy weather, chatty weekenders surrounded him. He'd totally forgotten that it was Saturday, and Saturday meant all the snobby Haddonfieldites would be out on the town. Rainwater seeping into his shoes made matters worse, bringing on a chill that threatened to move up his spine. Arty flattened himself against the emporium's clapboard storefront and stamped his feet. Standing there, hanging on to a bagful of books, he wondered if his journey to Haddonfield would pay off. He didn't need a rainstorm; he needed a brainstorm for a new attack plan.

When the downpour finally slowed, he inched out from under the eaves, palm up. Only spitting.

About to get on his way, Arty pulled up short when the neighboring nail salon's door burst open, and out swarmed a mob of young girls. The din from their shrill voices sounded like skeletons tap-dancing on a tin roof. As the chatty teens surrounded him and jostled by, they twirled him in a full circle.

Tottering to a standstill, he gasped for air. "Christ on a raft!" He gave them his dirtiest stink eye. Muttering, he put the bag of books in his knapsack. When he turned around, an enormous, Black, bald jogger almost ran him over.

"Hey, dickweed, have a care!" The guy ignored him and jogged right by. Arty couldn't believe these people.

He headed toward the HB, but another swinging shop placard brought him up short. In bold typeface, it read *The Jersey Devil Brewery*. What was going on? The Jersey Devil was popping up everywhere! Maybe tomorrow he'd visit the birth site; the image of that stone house still played in his imagination. He shook his head and thought about the beer … a fresh craft ale straight from the tap. So inviting.

As Arty raised his foot to enter the brewery, a Chihuahua appeared and sniffed around his ankle. The dog's leash led back to a short, plump woman in sweatpants. She juggled a huge, polka-dot umbrella and two other leashes attached to two more frantically tugging little dogs. The Chihuahua shook its drenched body, flinging murky water all over Arty's khakis.

"No, Taco, leave the nice man alone!" The woman sounded like a cranky schoolteacher.

Arty eyed the three tiny dogs and groaned. "I hate little, yappy mutts." Teeth clenched, he jerked his leg out of sniffing range. The dog, Taco, glared up at him and yapped. Arty scowled down and yelled, "Put a sock in it!"

Shockingly, without warning, Taco bared his fangs and clamped them down on Arty's ankle. The razor-sharp choppers ripped right through his pants and sank into his flesh. He gulped and cried out, "Get this stinking monkey-humper away from me!" He swung his leg back and forth in ever-increasing arcs, trying to dislodge the snarling dog. But Taco doubled down and hung on tight.

A string of expletives came pouring out of Arty's mouth, ending with, "Fuck off, you little turd factory!" With that, Taco released his bite and trotted back to his owner.

The woman straightened her back, pushing out her well-endowed chest. "So sorry! Come along, Taco." She gave Arty a pompous look and strutted away with her nose in the air, the little dogs trailing behind.

Arty rubbed his shin and sized up the damage to his pants and leg. No blood and only a small rip. Surprising. Damnable fussbudgets and their yappy dogs. He decided against grabbing a beer. It was too early in the day anyhow, not that it ever stopped him before. Maybe he could use a good, strong cup of coffee instead. Deciding to treat himself, he crossed the street to Starbucks. After that unprovoked dog attack, he deserved it.

Chapter 11

At a table in Starbucks, facing its heavy, glass double doors, Suzanna tried unsuccessfully to pat and squeeze her hair dry with napkins. The rich aromas of mocha and cinnamon saturated the air, and she took a long whiff. Grinding, whirring, and chattering echoed off the giant windows looking out onto King's Boulevard. To her relief, all the noise masked the folksy, piped-in music. She just wasn't in the mood for singer-songwriters today.

She stretched her back and contemplated the cup of decaf in front of her. Decaf wasn't usually her thing, but why add caffeine to the situation? Taking a sip, she reconsidered last night's conversation with Detective O'Brien. She pulled his business card out of her pocket. Hopefully, he'll have details today proving that Baby's fire was nothing more than a mechanical problem, like an overheated engine or fuel leak. No bomb. But if a mystery car bomber was out there, and he was targeting her, should she really be walking around in public? Her stomach gurgled.

One by one, Suzanna surveyed the other Starbucks customers. With relief, instead of misreading every face as suspicious, she only saw normal, everyday townsfolk sipping coffee and nibbling muffins. None of these people could be a car bomber. She was particularly amused by a young man in the corner, sporting both a goatee and a mullet. He looked like a Renaissance gentleman haphazardly thrown into the 1980s.

Laughter attracted her attention. Three teenage girls on a leather couch were flipping through a magazine. At a high table beside them, an older man with a long, gray ponytail sipped a cappuccino as he read. He seemed lonely.

The man looked up from his book and grimaced at a couple across the room, preoccupied with a stroller parked next to their table. They were coaxing their baby to stop crying but making no headway. At the HB, Suzanna had to deal with noisy kids, too. So annoying. Sometimes she couldn't hear herself play because a brat was screaming at the top of their lungs. It's not that she didn't like children, but she was perfectly comfortable with her own biological clock running out.

Harry, in his jogging suit, strutted through the door. Chest held high and soaking wet, he looked every bit the Marine he once was. She recalled Emily's description of him—the three B's—bald, Black, and beautiful. She attempted a smile, but her lips only twitched.

"Suzanna! Glad I ran into you." He shook himself like a big puppy, sprinkling beads of rain on her arms. He gently put his damp but comforting hand on her shoulder. "How's the head?"

"My head is fine; my nerves are the problem. I'm really stressed out."

"You need some downtime." He squatted beside her and lowered his voice. "I want you to take tonight off. I think you're more upset about this car thing than you want to admit."

"Oh, I don't mind admitting it. Everything's making me jump."

He gave her hand a squeeze and walked to the counter. When he returned, he carried a tall cup with fluffy whipped cream piled high on top.

"Don't tell Vinny," he stage-whispered. "His coffee's great, but he doesn't make a Frappuccino." A glob of whipped cream slid down the side of his cup, and he licked it off.

Suzanna had to smile, and this time, her lips obeyed. One minute, Harry was jogging, and the next, sipping a calorie-ridden iced coffee.

"So, I won't see you back at the HB until Thursday. That gives you plenty of time to rest up, and if you need more, just say so."

Suzanna gave a quick, slight nod. Based on her current mental state, the last thing she wanted to do was play guitar for a room packed with strangers. But she couldn't help having mixed feelings. A night off meant a significant financial hit—musicians don't get paid sick days.

As Harry breezed out the glass door, he missed smacking into Detective O'Brien by a hair. Nimbly thrusting his drink high above his head, Harry didn't spill a drop.

"Hey there, Detective," Harry said. "Watch your step."

O'Brien shoved past, giving him an almost imperceptible nod. Suzanna watched the detective cross the room, his shiny dress shoes clicking on the tile floor. His full suit and tie looked out of place. She unsuccessfully tried to imagine him without the mustache.

The detective put in his order. He didn't even glance at Suzanna until he placed his cup of steaming, black coffee on her table. As he sat across from her, he pulled a small notepad and pencil from his suit coat pocket. In an official voice, he asked, "Any problems last night?"

"No pleasantries for you then?" she asked. "Not even a howdy, ma'am?"

O'Brien didn't respond, but she thought she heard a quiet snarl. Maybe she was getting better at this joking stuff. He blew on his coffee and waited, keeping his eyes on his notepad.

"No problems … but wait a second." Suzanna sat up and leaned forward. "Let me ask *you* a question. Exactly how long did that patrolman stay outside my place last night? Did he see anything?"

The detective's eyes widened. "A patrol car wasn't outside your apartment all night?"

"It wasn't there when I left to come here."

O'Brien shot up, knocking his chair over. He yanked his cell phone out. "Higgins! Why aren't you tracking Archer?" He turned away from Suzanna, as though she couldn't hear every word he yelled. Customers and baristas stopped talking and gawked.

Suzanna gleaned that the guy, Higgins, should've kept tabs on her apartment all night and all morning. Plus, he was supposed to follow her if she left. But instead, he abandoned her around 1 a.m. because he got tired. O'Brien was pissed. By the time he hung up, she was sure Higgins was in a heap of trouble. And did she hear that right? O'Brien had called him *smelly*. She scrunched her nose. Harsh.

The detective righted his chair and sank into it. Looking back down at his notes, he said, "Let me give you an update on the case."

"Sorry, I didn't mean to get anyone in hot water."

"Not your fault." Detective O'Brien dragged his thumb across his forehead, clearing beads of sweat that had formed during the phone call.

"The lab report is back from County. They determined that there was a motion-sensitive bomb planted under the front area of your vehicle, maybe in the wheel hub. The triggering mechanism was configured to go off when you opened the door. Based on the bumper we found, County thinks the bomb went off by mistake when another driver sideswiped your vehicle."

The detective leaned back and looked her in the eye. "Are you sure you can't think of someone who might be behind this?"

She glared at him. "No, why *would* anyone do this?"

"I was hoping you could tell me."

Chapter 12

The pungent smell of ground coffee beans filled Arty's lungs as he pressed through the heavy Starbucks door. With the eye of a professional fixer, he canvased the room. Midway to the counter, dumbstruck, he put on the brakes. There she sat, his target, Suzanna Archer, talking to a man in a suit looking very much like a cop. Arty rummaged through his jacket pocket for the photo from his client. He could hardly believe his eyes, but even sopping wet, she was a match.

Coffee in hand, he took a table close enough to eavesdrop and made the most of it.

Chapter 13

"In any case," O'Brien said, "we now believe you were the intended target."

"No!" Suzanna gasped and waited for some compassion to creep into the detective's voice. Maybe she was expecting too much; police must get jaded after a while.

He tapped his notes on the table and seemed to get lost in thought. "If someone wanted to harm you, they botched the job … possibly an amateur."

O'Brien wrote something down. Suzanna strained to read it but couldn't make it out.

"We'll know more when we get surveillance footage from Haddonfield Jewelers, hopefully Monday. In the meantime, if you think of anything … you still have my card?"

She held it up and waved it at him.

"Good. Now tell me more about yourself."

A surprisingly open-ended question. Suzanna chose to be succinct. "I grew up in Jersey, went to Cherry Hill High, and then the Philadelphia Conservatory." God, was her background that unremarkable?

The detective nodded and tapped his pencil on the table.

She guessed he wanted her to go on. "Now, I live with a roommate a couple blocks down the road."

"Tell me about her."

"*Him*. His name is Chris Boyd. He's a classical guitarist, too. We went to school together."

"And is this relationship," he asked suggestively, "close?"

"Oh, give me a break. We're 'just' friends," Suzanna said, making air quotes. She wasn't about to volunteer her past romances to the police.

"Do you think your roommate, or someone else close to you, could be the target instead of you?"

Suzanna flattened her back against the chair. Her mom? Emily? Neither of them could be in trouble. Chris? Who knew? But it was none of this detective's business. "No, absolutely not."

O'Brien shrugged. "Then tell me about your family."

"My mom lives in Cherry Hill. She's a campaign manager."

"And your dad?"

"No dad."

"No dad?"

"No dad."

"Wait a sec. Do you mean he passed away?"

"I don't know. It's possible," she said with irritation.

"Huh. Can you elaborate?"

Suzanna heaved a heavy sigh and began her time-worn explanation. "My mom was young. It was the end of the eighties, but she carried on like it was the sixties. She got her fill of drugs, sex, and rock and roll." Suzanna gazed up at the ceiling and folded her arms across her chest. "Let's just say Mom had a free spirit and enjoyed the European hostel scene." Looking down at the table, she spoke faster. "So, she spent a few years hitchhiking around Europe. By the time she realized she was pregnant, she was back in the States and had no idea who my father was."

She unfolded her arms and met the detective's eyes.

"Your mom sounds … interesting. I'll need to talk with her. Name?"

"You mean my mom's name?"

"No, the proper name of the King of Siam. Of course, your mom."

"Joan Archer."

The detective scribbled notes and took a sip of coffee. A disgusted scowl crossed his lips, and Suzanna thought he was going to spit it out. Instead, he choked it down and said, "That's revolting."

"What?" She gaped at him. "You don't like Starbucks?"

"You can't get good coffee any place around here. In New York, I could get it on any street corner. Here, I have to brew it myself."

"So, you're a coffee aficionado from New York."

O'Brien didn't skip a beat. "What about your friend Emily? I talked with her last night."

"Em and I are good friends, but we're sort of opposites. The only thing we have in common is the HB."

"Explain."

Suzanna thought for a moment. The relationship was hard to put into words. It had surprised her, along with everyone else, when she and Em became friends. The young waitress was all ballsy noise, while Suzanna was more like a light melody. Their backgrounds differed in so many ways, they'd never have even met if not for working together at the HB.

"Em comes from a big, blue-collar family with four younger brothers. She's the first in her family to go to college. And me, I'm an only child raised by an over-educated hippie." She shrugged a shoulder. "We're just ... different."

"Seems she has a little trouble getting the blue off her collar."

Suzanna slipped him a curious glance. Did he just make a joke? A disparaging joke at that. She couldn't get a read on this guy. Taking a swallow of decaf, she turned her thoughts back to Emily.

"Em's a little rough around the edges, but she's clever and hardworking." Suzanna surprised herself with how defensive the statement came out. "She's unpredictable, too. Half the time, she rattles on like a college professor, and the other half, she dishes dirt like a sailor."

O'Brien jotted in his notepad. "Emily told me you have a new boyfriend."

"What? How on earth did that come up?" She folded her arms and waited for an explanation.

"She said neither of you know him very well, and he seems suspicious."

Her eyes snapped wider. "Suspicious? How can she say that? And I wouldn't call him my boyfriend. We haven't even been on a date yet!"

"Emily called him Cello Boy. What's his name?"

"Adam Damon. He's a cellist in the Haddonfield Symphony. But I don't see how he could help."

O'Brien glanced up at her and held her eyes for a moment. "Any other friends or enemies I should know about?"

Throwing her hands up, she exclaimed, "As far as I know, I have no enemies. And now that we're talking about it, I don't seem to have many friends, either!"

The detective ignored her outburst. "Where will you be tonight and tomorrow?"

She settled back in her chair. "Tonight, well … Harry gave me the night off, so I guess I'll go to my mom's. When I called last night, she was pretty worried." Suzanna hadn't told her mom anything about a bomb, only that Baby burned up and she banged her head. She dreaded telling the whole story, knowing the grilling she'd get. Even so, her mom's house was the best place to go for comfort, and today, she needed comfort.

The detective peeked down at his notes and said, "Tell your mom"—he paused, skimming the page—"Joan Archer, right?"

"You mean the King of Siam?"

O'Brien cleared his throat. "Tell her I'll be stopping by soon. Where will you be tomorrow?"

"I play brunch at Ristorante Buena in Philly—"

"Ristorante Buena." His eyes lit up. "Good food. *Very* good food."

Ah, so he's a foodie. That explains the coffee. It was nice to see him perk up. "I play there every Sunday. You could come sometime and hear me."

"Sure," O'Brien said, his voice flattening.

Suzanna figured that meant "fat chance."

"Where after that?" he asked.

"A date with Adam." She squinted at the detective a little sheepishly. "Our first date."

"Where to?"

"Kimmel Center. Philly Orchestra, three o'clock matinee."

"Then what?"

"Back to HB, I guess."

O'Brien tapped his pencil on the table. "Any other concerns?"

"Can I have another look at that book I gave you?"

"It's in evidence."

"I tried to buy a copy online, but no one carried it. And the used bookstore doesn't have it, either."

"You'll have to come to the station to see it."

"But I found another shop that might sell it."

"A shop? Where?"

"In the middle of the Pine Barrens. I'm going there on Monday to see."

"Hang on. Don't even think about investigating anything on your own. If this shop is a credible lead, we'll look into it. What's its name?"

"The Devil's Lair. I'm only trying to find a connection."

In a scolding dad voice, O'Brien warned, "Leave it alone. Stay home."

Her eyes blazed. He was treating her like a child. Suzanna opened her mouth to protest, but instead of giving him a hard time, to her surprise, her eyes welled up.

His tone softened. "Listen, watch out for anyone looking dodgy and stay home."

"Okay." A sob caught in her throat. Everyone looked dodgy.

The detective's phone chimed. Suzanna flinched and almost knocked her coffee off the table. Would she ever get used to that ringtone?

O'Brien checked a text and then put his phone away. "A patrol car will be stationed outside your apartment all night, and another will tail you tomorrow during the day. I'll be in touch." He stuffed his pad and pencil in his suit coat. "You know you can call me anytime, right?" Not waiting for an answer, he stood, tossed his half-full cup in the trash, and walked out.

Chapter 14

Arty had listened intently and worked out his new strategy on a Starbucks napkin. He gave himself a five-star review. There was nothing like the buzz he got from finishing off a plan. He took a long pull on his double espresso and watched while the cop, and then his target, went out the door.

He relaxed with his coffee and read most of *The Jersey Devil: Phantom of the Pines*. It only reinforced his online searches. He'd give it to his neighbor when he got home, as though he had never lost the original. The nerd would be none the wiser.

A teenage girl with acne flitted up to his table. With nauseating cheerfulness, she asked, "Wanna go to a poetry reading tonight?" She plunked a colorful flyer in front of him.

Arty's mouth morphed into a sneer. "Do I look like somebody who'd go to a poetry reading? I'd rather eat glass."

"Chill out, mister!" She made a U-turn and stalked away.

That was it! He'd had enough. His mission for the day was accomplished. Now he wanted nothing more than to hotfoot it out of this hoity-toity little town with all these sniveling hippie-dippies. He drove back to Philly, irritated by the whole concept of Haddonfield. "The place should be called Assholeia or, better yet, Sphincterville."

Arty pulled out his wallet and paid the bridge toll. It aggravated him to no end that all five bridges connecting Pennsylvania to New Jersey bullied drivers into paying five bucks to cross. Shrewdly, they only required payment in one direction. Entering New Jersey cost zilch, but it took cash to get out. Now that he thought about it, though, it was worth every penny.

He parked his treasured Lincoln Continental in his driveway and crossed the street to his neighbor's house. He'd decided it was time to learn the geek's name. So, he opened the guy's mailbox and pulled out a handful of junk mail.

On his way to the front door, he read the name off a magazine label. No ... it can't be! Richard Wacker? He waited until he stopped laughing to ring the bell.

The geek peeked out the window and then unbolted the door. "Hey, man, what's up?"

Arty waved away the pot smoke. "Here's your mail, Mr. *Wacker*." He couldn't help cracking up again. "Did your parents hate you or something?"

"Oh man, it's like a family name." He blushed and shrugged it off.

"Okay, *Dick*, I've something for you."

"It's Rick ... and I heard all the jokes."

Arty stretched out his hand, holding *The Jersey Devil: Phantom of the Pines*.

"So what ya think? No hoax, right?"

"I gotta admit, you were dead on the money." Arty whipped out the other three volumes. "And I scored more research."

Rick's half-closed eyelids flew open.

Arty handed him *Weird New Jersey*. "You should check out the used bookstore in Haddonfield. These books were so cheap, they even fit in *my* budget."

"Cool."

"You start in on *Weird New Jersey*, and I'll tackle the other two. Then we'll swap."

Arty turned and sauntered home. Looking back, he saw Rick still standing in his doorway with pot smoke billowing around him, staring at *Weird New Jersey* with a Christmas-morning smile.

Chapter 15

Chris pulled his head out of the toilet and sat back on his haunches. He couldn't remember the last time a Saturday morning hangover included puking his guts out. It must have been yesterday's added recreational pharmaceuticals—the drugs he'd purchased with his rent money. He'd heard of throwing money down the toilet, but this … this felt like a high price to pay for a little oblivion. But right now, he needed oblivion.

Suzanna storming out and slamming the door hadn't helped his aching head any. A twinge in his arm made him check last night's results. The bruising was intense. The only other time he'd shot up, Micky, his dealer, did it for him. It had gone smooth as silk. Micky had given him all the paraphernalia required for another try—syringe, spoon, tourniquet—everything except instructions. If only he'd paid more attention. Last night, he tried to imitate Micky's fluid movements but had a terrible time sticking the needle in his own arm. Today, the inside of his elbow looked like a mashed strawberry. Up till now, he'd been crushing Oxy and snorting it. But once he'd felt the swift, powerful rush of shooting smack, he couldn't resist trying it again.

Chris snatched up a well-used bottle of drops from the sink and dabbed at his bloodshot eyes. Nothing to be done about the dark circles underneath, though, or the puffy eyelids. Coffee … that's what he needed. He splashed some water on his face, pulled on a T-shirt and jeans, and charged headlong for the kitchen.

Sitting down with a steaming mug, he popped a few aspirins and fretted over the next day's high-class gig, which would bring in a cool five hundred bucks. The prestigious Philadelphia Technology Council had hired him to play for their midday corporate retreat. The venue, Bala Country Club, ranked among Pennsylvania's most exclusive golf clubs. Even though it wouldn't be a fully staged concert, the cream of Philadelphia's society would be watching and listening only to him. Chris wouldn't be the background to anything.

This gig reminded him of the concerts he used to play in high school after he'd won the Curtis Young Performer Competition. The prize had been a year of performances scattered throughout the Tri-State area, mainly at schools and public events. Low-pressure gigs, and the audiences loved him. His parents nearly burst with pride. Back then, he'd felt like a prodigy. Back then, he thought he was going places.

All that came to a screeching halt when he got to the conservatory and discovered that every other student had won a similar competition. In performance class, he'd watched as most of the guitarists outdid him, especially Suzanna. His parents had expected him to keep up the star power, but he came up short. They lost faith in him. Now, with gin and painkillers on his side, he was on a mission to get that star power back. The one thing he knew for sure was that playing background music wouldn't get him there.

He seized his guitar from its case with determination. If only he could book a year of concerts now. Hanging his head, he plucked a sad, minor scale. He needed a drink. Chris flipped his hair back and sat up straight. "No," he said out loud. "Not today."

As he tossed off more scales, his hangover faded. The short program he'd prepared for the corporate gig was a no-brainer, but he played through it from beginning to end. After each piece, he basked in imaginary applause. By the time he put his guitar down, confidence warmed his chest as though he'd just kicked back a snifter of cognac.

That warmth was replaced by a familiar feeling the second he walked into the kitchen. A craving for a martini hit him. One drink wouldn't hurt anything, would it? Chris pulled down his gin and made himself a martini—olive and all. The ice clinked in the shaker, melting less quickly than his pledge to stay sober.

"Shaken, not stirred," Chris said to an invisible guest. Brandishing the strainer up and down, he poured his drink. The slender stem of the martini glass felt elegant between his fingers. He took a long swallow and licked his lips, swollen and cracked against his tongue, reminding him he was still hungover. No problem. As soon as he got one drink down, he'd return to form.

Three short raps on the door gave him a jolt. Chris inched the door ajar and peeked out. Emily stood on the deck, ducking under a giant umbrella. Drizzle stung his face as he pulled the door wide open. "Suzanna's out. Wanna come in and wait?"

"Sure, my shift doesn't start for a while. Where'd she go?"

"Not my turn to watch her."

Em flapped her umbrella as she stepped inside. "I was gonna give her a ride to work, but I see she got her rental. Pretty sweet."

"For real?" Chris stared down into the gravel lot at a shiny, red car. "Look at that!" How did she do it? A brand-new car. Just like that brand-new guitar case. Those high-tech cases cost a fortune. Every classical guitarist wanted one. Not a problem for Suzanna, though. Because of her exposure in a Ristorante Buena Facebook ad, all she had to do was give the guitar case a review, and the manufacturer gave her one for free. Infuriating!

As Emily sat down at the breakfast island, Chris stealthily slid his martini glass behind a cereal box. His face flushed when he spotted Em eyeing the bottle of gin on the counter. Crap. He'd forgotten the bottle. He mopped his sweaty brow with the kitchen cloth. Spotting a handy, long-sleeved shirt hanging on the back of a chair, he plucked it up by the collar and slapped it on over his T-shirt. Hoping the sleeve concealed his bruised arm, he flashed Emily a nervous grin. He pulled his glass out and took a sip, owning up to the martini. "Could I interest you in a libation? I have the makings for martinis."

Emily held up her bottle of Snapple. "A little early for me."

Chris returned the gin to its cabinet atop the fridge, the highest cabinet in the kitchen. "Suit yourself. The sun must be over the yardarm somewhere."

"I take it you're hiding that from Suzanna. There's no way she could reach up there."

"Not without a ladder," Chris said, and a staccato chuckle sputtered out. Em's accusation touched a nerve.

The door creaked, and Suzanna walked in dripping wet, peeled off her windbreaker, and hung it on the rack. A puddle formed on the floor beneath it. Chris hid his martini behind the cereal again and put on a smile.

Suzanna marched to the cabinet where she kept her precious chips. "Just checking."

Chris smirked as she opened it. He'd replaced the bag his friends had eaten. After her chip inspection, her eyes fell on an oversized brandy glass on the counter. "My tip jar. I thought I lost it last night!"

Letting his hair fall in his face, Chris bent over and retied his sneakers. "A cop dropped it off. Said you left it in his car."

"All I remember is the explosion." She picked up her tip jar and checked inside. "Where's my seed money?"

Usually, she kept a twenty in the glass all the time—because no one puts a tip in an empty jar. Her eyes narrowed, and she gave Chris a suspicious glance.

He tsked and shook his head. "Your jar is so déclassé, it's embarrassing. We're classical musicians, not common buskers."

"I make more in tips than regular pay." Suzanna scrunched up her face at him.

"Don't give me that lizard face. Tips are demeaning." Chris was dying for a sip of his martini but stuck it out. "Case in point: Last year, I played a small gig near the shore. A man came up to me and ripped a five-dollar bill in half. He handed one half to me and said, 'If I like your playing, I'll give you the other half.'"

Em nearly spit out her Snapple. "Like an exam? At least waitresses get a standard percentage."

Chris flipped his hair and turned to Emily. "That's just one of the many reasons I decided not to play background gigs anymore."

Suzanna held out her tip jar and threw her chin up. "I like to know if people enjoy my playing. Tips make it obvious."

Chris was devising a comeback when Suzanna's phone rang in her pocket. She answered, "Suzanna Archer. Classical Guitar." She put the phone on speaker with a knowing 'check this out' smirk toward Chris. "...

background music for a birthday party," said a friendly male voice.

"I only play classical guitar," Suzanna explained. "Are you sure that's the kind of guitar you want for your background music?"

The man's tone turned edgy. *"There are different kinds of guitars?"*

Chris had heard that question, and Suzanna's reply, far too many times.

Suzanna took a deep breath and rattled off, "Yep, classical guitars differ from the acoustic, steel-string guitars that singer-songwriters play and are nothing like the electric guitars rock bands use. They differ drastically in construction, string type, playing technique, sound—"

"I'm not certain classical music is what I want ..."

"Typical," Chris mumbled. He turned away from Suzanna and finished off his martini.

"No problem. Any style of music can be played on any kind of guitar. It just sounds different."

The man let out a sigh. *"I'll think about it and get back to you."*

"But wait, I can play blues, pop, samba, jazz ... all on a classical guitar."

Suzanna's voice grew tense as she tried to save the gig. Chris already knew she'd lost it. The click on the other end of the phone proved him right. He snorted and lumbered into the living room. "You should say solo guitar. Take the word *classical* off the table."

"But I want people to know what they're in for. Nothing worse than arriving at a gig and getting a request for Metallica."

"At least he didn't ask you to play Bruce."

"God, if I get one more Bruce request—"

A single knock thudded at the front door, and Chris sprang up to get it. This time, he knew who it was, and he wasn't happy about it. A young man in a tailored suit, slicked-back, black hair, and a crooked nose stood on the deck, brushing off his sleeves. Micky.

Chris summoned up a glowing smile. "Looks like the rain stopped."

"What tipped you off?" Micky snapped the words off like he took a bite out of them. Chris hurried his drug dealer down the hall to his room without a glance back at Suzanna and Em.

Chapter 16

Em thrust her hands on her hips. "What was all that about?"

Suzanna shrugged a shoulder. She had no idea what Chris was up to and was afraid to ask. Right now, she wanted to steer the subject in a totally different direction, and she wanted another set of eyes to do it. "Forget him. I've something to show you."

Em threw her Snapple bottle in the garbage. "Asshole. I can't believe you two were ever a couple."

Suzanna firmly gripped Em's sleeve and led her down the hall to her bedroom.

"Who was that guy, anyway?" Em cricked her arm at Chris's door. "He looked a little like Vinny."

Suzanna ignored the question; she didn't want to talk about Chris.

Em flopped on the bed. "How's your head?"

"All better." She didn't want to discuss her head bump or her jangling nerves, either.

Em pulled a crinkled piece of paper out from under her butt. Holding it up, she coughed out a laugh. Her voice climbed up to a squeak. "Look at the little guitar at the bottom."

Suzanna closed her door and sighed at the stationery. "My mom gave me a ream of that for my last birthday.

Everyone, even Mom, thinks I should get guitar gifts. One of my dresser drawers is jam-packed with them."

"Like mugs?"

"Yep, but other stuff like scarves, fridge magnets, key chains, posters—"

"Why don't you toss 'em?"

Suzanna shrugged. She picked up a T-shirt and hoodie from the floor. After giving the shirt a sniff, she threw them both beside her laundry basket, which was overflowing with clean clothes that needed folding. She heaped the clean clothes onto her dresser and tossed the dirty shirt and hoodie into the empty basket.

Emily shoved the paper aside. "So, what do you want to show me?"

Suzanna's eyes brightened. "I think I found a lead on my dad." Her heart beat faster as she slid an elongated, hardcover book out of her gig bag. There was only one problem. If her lead panned out, it would mean her mom had lied to her all her life.

Em wriggled backward on the bed until her butt touched the wall. "Can't say you're not stubborn. But I'd keep looking, too. That story of your mom's *is* a little hinky."

Suzanna hugged the slender, hardcover book to her chest. "Yeah, and stupid me, I believed every word right up till high school." She thought back to the night of her high school graduation party and the suspicious chat she'd had with her mother. That night, her mom drank one too many glasses of wine, and when it got late, she had pulled her daughter aside. With slurred words, she'd said she had a confession to make about her father. Suzanna gasped and waited, but her mom just staggered away. Ever since, her mom claims that Suzanna imagined the whole thing.

"Confession. That was the word she'd used that night."

Emily rolled her eyes. She had heard the story years ago. "Come on, she was drunk. I say all kinds of stupid things when I'm drunk."

"People tell secrets when they're drunk."

Em shook her head and patted the bed. "Whatcha find?"

Suzanna squeezed in. "I was digging around in Mom's basement for my old conservatory notebooks, and *look*." She plopped a leather-bound, high school yearbook in Em's lap.

Em ran her finger over the embossed numbers on the front cover. "The year is 1986. Is this your mom's?"

"Aha. Turns out Mom was in the same class as State Senator Bancroft. And check this out." Suzanna pointed at a youthful picture of Bancroft with a scrawled message beneath. In faded, blue ink, Bancroft had written: *To my Winter Lady. I'll never forget you. Don't have too much fun in Europe. Love, Don.*

As she read the note, Em's eyes widened. "Wow, do you think they had a thing?"

"I think so, 'cause …" Suzanna paged halfway through the book and put her finger on a photo. "They're both in this shot."

The bed rocked as Emily squeezed in closer. "They're holding hands!"

Suzanna pulled her laptop from the bedside table. "So I put together a timeline to work out if he could be my father."

"If he is, why didn't he say something?"

"Maybe it's some weird secret, or he disowned me, or who knows?"

Suzanna opened a spreadsheet, and Em leaned over her shoulder. Columns of years, ages, and events filled the screen. Suzanna's mom and Bancroft were shown as graduating in 1986, and Suzanna being born in 1989. "At first, I thought she got pregnant before she went to Europe, but that didn't pan out."

Suzanna scrolled down the column. "Now I'm thinking she could've slept with him after she got back. The timing's still off, but maybe her story about the whole hitchhiking around Europe thing is a load of crap."

"The senator," Em said. "Why would she lie about *him*?"

"You got me. But I'm confronting her tonight."

"After work?"

"Harry gave me the night off."

"Lucky you."

"Yeah, except for all the money I'm losing."

"When are you gonna get off your dead ass and go back to school?"

Suzanna looked away. "Soon. It's not as easy getting financial aid for a master's degree." Not much of an excuse. With a master's in classical guitar, she could get a college professorship. A dream job—salary, medical benefits, and tenure. Her current gigs could become a sideline.

Emily nudged her in the ribs. "Take out loans like me."

"I hate that whole idea."

"Then why not let your mom help this time?"

"I hate that even more."

Shrugging, Emily said, "Wanting to go it alone holds you back."

Suzanna nodded. Em was right. There was no future in playing background music. She had to go back to school. But she was procrastinating, and she wasn't entirely sure why.

"What's that?" Em pointed at an open web folder on the computer screen.

"I've been looking into the Jersey Devil, too." She filled the screen with one of the scary pictures of the monster and gave Em an account of her research. "I'm going to the Devil's Lair Monday. Wanna come with?"

"Can't. Work all day. You should ask your new squeeze."

"Hey, that's right." Suzanna sat up and faced her. "Where do you get off telling Detective O'Brien that Adam is suspicious?"

"Skip it. I'm just suspicious in general." Emily waved away Suzanna's complaint with a flick of her hand. "I may have a Jersey Devil resource for you, though. I'll get back to you."

"Resource? What kind—"

"Can we talk about Chris for a sec?" Em lowered her voice. "Why does he need privacy all of a sudden with what's-his-name?"

Suzanna frowned as she got off the bed. "Hard to say." She put the yearbook back in her gig bag and returned to folding laundry. "He's been so pretentious and mean lately. I can barely have a conversation with him."

"Why don't you just throw him out?"

Suzanna whirled around and snapped a towel in Em's direction. "You know I can't afford that."

"Yeah, but it's almost like you don't want to hurt his feelings."

"Maybe, for old times' sake?"

"Don't be stupid. He's got no problem hurting yours. I've heard him say on more than one occasion, 'You would be beautiful if it weren't for your—'"

Suzanna's hand automatically flew up to her nose. "Don't say it! I hear it enough from him." Turning back to her laundry, she wished Em didn't consider her such a pushover. "Could be I just don't want to move back with Mom."

"What? I'd give anything to have a mom like yours."

"Aw, come on, your family's right out of *The Waltons*."

"You don't have to live with them. If I had the money, I'd be out of there in a minute."

Suzanna chuckled. Em couldn't fool her; she knew how tight that family was.

Emily pushed off the bed. "This thing about Chris could be serious."

The rare, earnest tone in Em's voice made Suzanna uneasy. She threw a half-folded top on the dresser and met Em's eyes. "Last week, something weird happened. When I came home from work, Chris had a black eye and split lip."

"A fight?"

"He said he fell down the steps. I figure he was drunk and went into free fall."

"Sounds fishy. Is he still always late with his rent?"

Suzanna nodded. She didn't want to admit it out loud.

"Today," Em said, "I caught him sneaking a martini. Then he hid his bottle of gin. That's the behavior of an addict."

"I know he's an alcoholic. It's taking a toll on his playing."

"Jesus, Suzanna, that may be the least of his problems. Anything gone missing lately?"

"Like money?" She knew she'd lost a five-dollar bill about a month ago and was pretty sure Chris had taken it. And that's probably where her tip jar seed money went, too.

"Don't leave things lying around. Addiction changes people. I know. My brother went down that rabbit hole with the hard stuff." Emily shook her head. "I think he's gonna battle his habit the rest of his life, and who knows where Chris is heading."

Em hopped up from the bed. "I'm taking off. Gotta get to work."

Nodding, Suzanna walked her to the door.

Em put her index finger over her lips. "Shh. Don't let on I snitched about the gin, but keep your eye on him." As she went out the door, she said, "Let me know what happens with your mom."

Suzanna hurried back down the hallway to her room. She had to squeeze by Chris and the Vinny look-alike going in the opposite direction. The guy glanced at her, but she kept her head down and didn't get a full look at his face. Even so, she had a needling suspicion that she'd seen him before.

After the guy left, Chris shut the door with a hurried slam. He turned to her and flashed a big grin. "He's my new associate. I've just signed a couple of gig contracts."

"What, you got a manager?"

Chris's grin faded as he shook his head. "Event planner."

Suzanna patted him on the back. "Still great. Congrats." Encouraging. Working for an event planner was a respectable way to get gigs. Like general contractors, planners are employed to manage large events, and in turn, they hire everyone needed—caterer, music, venue, and wait staff. If Chris got on the good side of one of those guys, he could work every weekend.

"Does your planner have a specialty ... like weddings?"

"I'll never play a wedding." Chris pulled off his glasses and thoughtfully placed the temple tip in the corner of his mouth. "*My* planner deals in corporate affairs, actual performances." He flicked his hair back. "And covers all Jersey and PA."

"That's amazing. Where'd you find someone like that?"

On the way to his room, Chris said, "Don't remember."

Suzanna knew most of the local planners, but who was this guy? He must be big and from out of town. Philly, most likely. A planner wouldn't have come to the house unless he had work. Contracts to sign and gig details. It was just like Chris to keep it from her. Probably embarrassed that he needed help getting gigs. This might be the perfect thing to straighten him out.

She called down the hall, "How about the rent money?"

Chris looked back over his shoulder. "I'll have it in a couple days." He turned to her and with his finger, drew an 'X' across his chest. "Cross my heart."

Chapter 17

Joan Archer signed the last of a stack of fundraising letters on her desk with the squiggle that had become her signature. She made sure the squiggle didn't obscure her printed title—*Campaign Manager, Donald Bancroft for U.S. Representative of New Jersey*.

At this point in the election cycle, only a few dedicated employees worked on Saturdays. But when November 2016 drew near, campaign headquarters would turn into a beehive of activity on weekends as well as weekdays.

On this particular Saturday, even with the big Trenton rally coming up in two weeks, headquarters radiated an atmosphere of peace and quiet. Most offices were empty, half the lights were off, and everyone was dressed casually. Everyone except Joan. She wore her usual power suit and heels.

As she threw the sealed envelopes in her outgoing mail tray, yelling erupted from down the hall. Waiting a moment, she hoped things would calm down without her intervention. But then a thud penetrated through the soles of her shoes. Did that come from Don's office? She shoved back her chair and, with her heels snagging on the carpet, ran to the office of New Jersey State Senator Donald Bancroft.

Joan arrived just in time to see Bancroft punch his fist through his office wall. Her best intern, Anne, cowered against the wall at the senator's feet with her arm draped over her face. Bancroft pulled back his hand, drywall flaking off his knuckles, leaving a raggedy hole the size of a baseball above Anne's head.

Joan's hands flew to her hips. "What the hell is going on?"

"Devil's teeth!" Bancroft rubbed his punching hand and sat back at his desk as though nothing unusual had happened.

Joan rushed to Anne's side and helped the girl up. "Are you okay?"

Anne nodded and whispered, "I was only looking for a stapler." With a tear rolling down her cheek, she fled the room.

Joan turned to Don. "Explain."

"That girl was nosing around my desk."

"That's it?"

"I gave her a little push. I'm stressed about the rally."

"And what did the wall do?"

"You've no idea how much pressure I'm under."

"Come off it. You managed the pressure in all your other campaigns. If that intern—her name is Anne, by the way—blabs to the press, you and your favorability ratings will go down the drain."

"Sorry. I overreacted."

"Overreacted? Are you kidding? You pushed the panic button."

"Go talk to her. Calm her down. Just say I apologize." Bancroft dabbed at his knuckles where the skin had scraped off.

"Fine, but we're not done with this."

Joan left the senator's office to search for Anne. Had she hooked her wagon to the wrong star? Bancroft's running for U.S. Representative was quite a step up from his current state senator status. Managing his campaign should've been the crowning achievement of her career. So why didn't it feel that way?

She checked the ladies' room, but no Anne. The narrow, second-floor hallway of campaign headquarters contained ten offices. She opened each door and either asked for her or called her name. Finally, she found her sobbing in the lunchroom.

Joan stroked her hair until the tears stopped. "What happened in there? And don't sugarcoat it."

"Like I said, I needed a stapler. There wasn't one on his desk, so I went to open the top drawer. That's when Senator Bancroft came in."

"Well, you shouldn't go through other people's desk drawers, so you were in the wrong there. Go on."

"He shoved me away from his desk." Her eyes teared up again. "I slammed into the wall so hard, I thought I saw stars."

"Oh, God." Joan feigned calm but raged inside. "He asked me to tell you that he's very sorry."

Anne sniffled and wiped her nose with her hand.

Joan walked to the kitchenette counter and doubled back with the box of tissues, all the while trying to come up with some explanation or advice for the girl. She felt obligated to steer the interns in the right direction, but this was a rough one.

She sat down and handed the girl a tissue. "Anne, I'm so sorry, but politicians are passionate characters. The state senator is under a great deal of stress. Why don't you go home and relax? I'll talk to him, and we can work this all out."

"Okay. But Ms. Archer, I don't think I'm coming back."

Joan hugged her. "I understand. Don't make up your mind now. Call me on Monday, and we'll see."

Joan stomped into Bancroft's office and slammed the door behind her. She couldn't believe how calm he appeared, sitting at his desk reviewing printouts of polling data. He was down in the polls this week, but she doubted that stats were reason enough for his temper tantrum.

Looking up, he threw his pencil down. "What now?"

"Not like we need more to do, but after your little prank, we have an ethical issue, a professional issue, and possibly a legal issue on our hands."

"My bad. Let's clean it up and move on." He returned to his paperwork.

"Tell me why this happened and how you're going to make sure it doesn't happen again."

"Just suck it up and fix it. You're my campaign manager, not my confessor … or my wife. Last time I checked, you work for me."

That was a mean jab, considering their history. Shaking it off like a good campaign manager, she went into triage mode. "In essence, Anne just quit. You need to call her on Monday, apologize, and ask her to come back to work."

"Okay, remind me Monday morning."

Joan turned and was halfway out the door when Bancroft said, "Oh, and call maintenance to fix the hole in the wall."

She stormed down the hall to her office. The election for New Jersey's U.S. Representative was still over a year away. She'd have to manage Don a lot better if he was going to have any chance of beating his Republican rival, Craig Wallace. She slipped off her heels and massaged her feet.

Don's behavior had always been a bit erratic, even as a teenager. When Joan took the position three months ago, she'd been grateful they had a history. Anyone else might have looked at her checkered past and turned her away. But he knew her. In high school, they'd run against each other for student council president. She lost. A short-lived romance followed. It barely registered as a relationship, but they'd kept in touch—sort of. He knew all about her years after high school, traipsing around Europe. Still, he acknowledged that she'd paid her dues by returning to school, working hard in the field, and moving up the ranks of New Jersey politics.

Joan's promotion consultant, Samantha, darted into her office.

"What was all the noise? I'm half afraid to ask."

Joan gave her a blow-by-blow account. "Babysitting a man-child was not what I bargained for when I took this job," she said, rubbing her temples.

Samantha leaned in. "But this is physical abuse. What are you going to do?"

"I'll smooth things over."

"You're the woman!"

"I believe so strongly in his policies, I just hope he gets with the program." Joan put her shoes back on. "Keep a lid on this; I don't want it leaking. The only way this gets to the press is if I can't stop Anne from blabbing."

"You should be running instead of him."

"My past wouldn't hold up under scrutiny. Any opponent with half a brain would trounce me."

"People are more understanding these days. Who didn't have a wild youth?"

"But the illegitimate kid. Even now, it's unacceptable."

"Well, if you ever run, count me in."

"Thanks, Sam. Back to work."

Joan browsed through her email. Five new messages from the event planner for the Trenton rally. How many questions could this guy have? She methodically worked through each one.

The final message in her inbox was from Suzanna, saying she'd be coming over tonight. That was a relief. She could get the details on that car fire. Slumping back in her chair, Joan tried to subtotal her donor spreadsheet. Not a chance. Her concentration was shot.

She turned to her cluttered credenza and opened the day's paper. A photo of Baby's remains jumped off the bottom of the page. Her eyes popped as she speed-read the article discussing the attack. This wasn't how Suzanna had described things! Joan packed up her laptop and went home by way of the liquor store. Tonight—bottle of red.

Chapter 18

Suzanna parked in front of her mother's trendy, if not a bit time-worn, row house in Cherry Hill—the house she grew up in. Through the Civic's windshield, she admired the distant Philadelphia skyline ablaze in a scarlet sunset. The view could've been a postcard.

Her mom dashed out the front door in her customary leggings and leg warmers. A short, denim jacket bobbed around her shoulders. At home, Joan traded business suits and heels for clothes that echoed her youthful free spirit. With her long hair tied up in a flopping ponytail, she looked like she just teleported in from the 1980s.

In the mom category, Suzanna considered herself lucky. Looking back, she marveled at her mom's initiative and determination. She remembered endless evenings watching her study at the kitchen table and days of tagging along to intern jobs. Now, she proudly told anyone who'd listen that her mom was a "mover and shaker" in New Jersey politics. It would've been nice to have a dad while growing up, but her mom was really all she ever needed.

Joan opened the car door and nearly pulled Suzanna out. Wrapping her arms around her daughter, she squeezed tight, getting perilously close to cutting off her air supply. "I've been so worried. How's your head?"

"I'm fine, Mom. It's only a little bump." Suzanna forced out a thin laugh as she disentangled herself from her mom's embrace. "The thing that hurts most is losing Baby."

"Is that so?" Joan ran her hand across the roof of the Civic. "This is a tasty replacement, though. Insurance?"

Suzanna nodded and slid her laptop out of the car.

They linked arms and stepped through the stamp-size front yard to the house, the evening air still fresh from the afternoon's storm. The glistening grass squished underfoot with each step. In the doorway, Suzanna recognized the gloomy strains of Isaac Bellow's crooning coming from her mom's high-end stereo. No surprise there. Politics aside, her mom's true passions were poetry and melancholy music. Bellow was the king of both. So, as a devoted fan, naturally, Joan had given her only daughter the name of his best-known song.

"Mom, why don't you try listening to something else? There are lots of good singer-songwriters out there."

Joan grimaced. "No time. Each new Bellow album drains me. I can spend months lost in a single release."

"Guess I understand." Suzanna wrinkled her brow. "I once spent an entire month listening to nothing but Beethoven's Seventh Symphony."

"What about those Counting Crows albums you used to listen to night and day?"

"They're still my favorite indie band. I think their music gets to me the same way Bellow's gets to you."

They strolled past the stairs and down the hallway to the agreeably cluttered, country-style kitchen. As Suzanna squeezed through the Dutch door, she marveled at how such a big room could still feel cramped. It was the sound system that did it. A low buffet supported a multi-deck stereo extended across the only wall without appliances or cupboards. The premium system included a dual cassette deck, CD player, quality turntable, and three-foot-high speakers. Pine shelves packed with vinyl records and CDs surrounded the system. She was certain that in any other kitchen, that wall would be filled with pantry cabinets.

Suzanna placed her laptop on the long, pine kitchen table that dovetailed with the sound system. Dusk reflected off a row of casement windows lining the back wall. They sat across from each other in their customary seats—established over decades of meals, holidays, and heart-to-hearts. The table was a bit too big for the room, with seating for at least ten. Suzanna always thought it sad that the oversized table had never held a crowd. Most of the time, it was only her and her mom.

Joan snatched up an open bottle of merlot from the counter. She topped off her half-empty glass and put the bottle on the table.

Suzanna eyed the bottle and shook her head. "Oh boy, Isaac Bellow and red wine. Are you that upset about my car fire?" She reached around to the stereo controls and turned the volume down.

"Ye-es. Your car fire, or whatever it was. I read about it in the paper today and have done nothing but worry ever since. The article implied that it was an explosion and no accident."

Not wanting to worry her mom more, Suzanna kept it short and to the point. "The police think a bomb was planted in Baby on purpose. That someone could be targeting me." A nervous laugh accented her last words.

Joan's voice jumped up an octave. "The paper didn't say you were a target. Why didn't you tell me all this last night?" She clapped a hand over her open mouth and, through her fingers, asked, "Why would anyone want to hurt you?"

"I keep asking myself the same thing. Why does someone want me dead? Why me?"

"Dead?" Joan whispered.

Hearing the shock in her mother's voice, Suzanna tried to tone things down. "Well, not dead … injured." She saw what was coming. "Don't cross-examine me. I just told you everything I know, and the police don't know much, either."

Joan met Suzanna's eyes and frowned. "Who's the investigating officer?"

"Detective O'Brien."

"Are the police giving you protection?"

"Sure. A patrol car stayed outside my apartment last night, and I think he's following me around. Did you know all the Haddonfield police cars are SUVs now? What a waste of gas."

Joan's frown deepened. "Don't try to change the subject. I'll be speaking with your detective; you can count on that. Now let's go over this, one step at a time."

Suzanna slouched, retold the story, and answered every question her mom launched at her. More often than not, she could only answer, "I don't know," until finally, she squeezed her mom's hand and asked, "Enough about me. How's the campaign going?"

Joan exhaled with a huff. "Along with everything else, I had a little crisis at work today." She paused and swiftly added, "Nothing I couldn't handle."

"The senator is so lucky to have you. What happened?"

"New Jersey State Senator Donald Bancroft behaved like a lout, that's what."

Suzanna's eyes grew wider. She'd never heard her mom say a bad thing about Bancroft. Without thinking, words rushed out of her mouth. "You dated him in high school, right?"

"How did you know?"

"Your yearbook."

Joan's face flushed the same red as the merlot in her glass.

Suzanna flipped open her laptop. "I calculated a timeline. I think it works."

"Don't start with that tonight. He's not your father."

Suzanna's chin rose up in protest.

Joan took a swig of wine. "C'mon, I would've told you."

"I really thought he might be—"

Joan crossed her legs. "Nope, not your father." She crossed her arms, too, and looked away. "But today's crisis was all about him."

"What happened?"

Joan delivered a detailed version of the assault. At the end, she pulled her hair out of the ponytail, twirling the strands around her fingers. Suzanna squirmed in her chair. "Creepy. What does Bancroft say about it?"

Joan swirled the merlot in her glass with one hand and turned up the stereo with the other. "That's just it. He didn't even make an excuse. Just complained the girl nosed around his desk."

Suzanna's shoulders sagged, and her toes curled in her shoes. Finding the yearbook had seemed like the eureka moment she'd been waiting for, but now, she was sorry for ever considering Bancroft father material. She studied her mother's face. Joan had stunning green eyes with full lashes, flowing brown hair with a few strands of silver peeking through, and a small, perfect nose. In her prime, she must've been a knockout. Still was. Touching the tip of her own nose, she gloomily reflected on inheriting all those features except one.

"Let's see your timeline."

"Doesn't matter anymore." Suzanna snapped her laptop closed. "Did you ever work with Bancroft before?"

"Not until this campaign." A pinched smile flitted across her lips. "I always believed in him and what he could do for New Jersey, especially as his political star rose." Joan ran her fingers through her hair. "You're right, though. We briefly dated in high school. Very briefly."

"Why didn't you tell me?"

"Never thought it was relevant. Back then, Don was just getting interested in politics." Joan shook her head. "He wanted to be seen as a wholesome politician. That's when he came up with that stupid phrase, Devil's teeth, to use instead of profanity."

Joan sighed, and her eyes rolled up to the ceiling. "He's a Democrat, dammit! I *thought* a decent Democrat. It's like Clinton all over again."

"Sorry, Mom. I thought he was one of the good guys. He always gives me a great tip at the Ristorante … and the HB, too."

"I don't know if he's a bad guy or if he's a good guy doing bad things."

"You should quit his campaign and run for office yourself. Let them dig up your dirty laundry." Suzanna shrugged. "What's so awful about being a single mother, anyway? Just put it behind you. Other politicians do."

"Those *other* politicians are all men." Joan's shoulders sagged, and she gave her head a firm shake. "No. I won't risk it."

Suzanna got up and peered in the refrigerator, not sure what she was looking for. "So, my calculations were wrong about Bancroft." She came back to the table empty-handed. "But I've been thinking—"

"Uh-oh."

"Have you heard about these new genealogy DNA tests? If I got one, at least I could find out what country he's from—" The pained expression spreading across her mother's face stopped her.

"I get it, sweetheart. Anyone would want to know their father, but for you, it's impossible." Joan twisted in her chair and plucked a clean wineglass from the counter. "Have some wine, and I'll make dinner." She stood and put a pot of water on the stove. "Why not stay over in your old room tonight? Seems we both could use the company."

Suzanna yawned. "All right." Like so many times before, she gave up on discussing her unknown father. The sound of Bellow's unrelenting gravel baritone entwined with soprano harmonies nagged at her raw nerves. She reached over and turned down the melancholy strains. "I heard someone on the radio call Isaac Bellow 'the Barry White of folk.'" She chuckled. "He certainly doesn't shy away from sexual innuendo in his lyrics, and that bass voice …"

The boiling water sizzled as Joan stirred in penne pasta with a wooden spoon. "That's better than the critic who said his songs were 'music to commit suicide by.'"

"Now, that one, I get," Suzanna said. "His songs are filled with heartache and sorrow. Well-crafted lyrics, but I don't want to dwell on them."

"It's different for me." Joan stopped stirring and focused on the wall above the stove, her voice turning wistful. "His music gives me comfort. The poetry takes me deep, worth a little heartache."

"You should try Chopin." Suzanna gave her mom a mischievous grin. "Some of his music might be depressing enough for you."

"Funny, but except for your guitar playing, I prefer words with my music."

"Then listen to my Counting Crows. Catchy melodies. Interesting lyrics."

Joan turned to her daughter. "I've listened to plenty of singers." She accented each word with a shake of the spoon, paying no attention to the water dribbling off. "None of them measure up to Bellow."

Suzanna slumped back in her chair and crossed her arms.

Joan drew in a lungful of air. "Bellow writes about the world's suffering and connects it to the personal. Counting Crows just sing about their own little heartbreaks." Giving the spoon one last shake, she said, "The Crows' lead singer needs to stop whining, grow up, and get over that girl Maria he keeps singing about." She turned back to the stove.

Suzanna uncrossed her arms. Her mom was right. There certainly were a lot of references to someone named Maria in the Crows' songs.

The bottle of merlot looked tempting. Suzanna pulled it across the table and poured herself a glass. While enjoying the blend of fruity and spicy scents, a sudden whiff of something burning on the stove conjured the image of Baby ablaze. Again, she heard the rush of police and the stomping of fearful customers. She rubbed the bump on her head without thinking. When she saw her mom's concerned gaze, she dropped her hand and shrugged.

Joan turned to the counter, shaking her head. Slicing into an onion, she asked, "What's going on with Chris these days? Still drinking so much?"

"Yep. But I warned him again that if he didn't pay the rent on time, I'd call his parents about his finances and his drinking. He says I'm blackmailing him."

"Well, be careful. You don't want to fool around with the Boyds. They're very influential, especially with politicians they contribute to, like Don. They buy themselves a lot of pull."

"They certainly psych out Chris. Every time I threaten to call them, he acts like a scared, little kid."

While Joan got serious about the meal, Suzanna opened her laptop and browsed through her calendar for the coming week. The tangy aroma of her mom's bubbling red sauce made her hungry for the first time that day. Her eyes fell on tomorrow's date with Adam. Mom didn't even know Adam existed. "Before I'm too tired, I've got something else to tell you."

Joan whisked two brimming plates onto the table and sat down. She didn't say a word, but Suzanna saw her stiffen, bracing against some new calamity.

"I met someone. Someone I think I like a lot."

Joan's face lit up, and she spoke in a flurry. "Tell me. How'd you meet? What's his name? I want details!"

Suzanna held up her hands and laughed. "Hold on." Over the plates of pasta, she recounted her first meeting with Adam, how he was this sweet, attractive customer at the HB who'd been catching her eye for weeks. He first approached her when she'd been playing a cello transcription. He had asked about the transcription's key, and then they set off on a musical gabfest. She saved the best part for last.

"When he asked me my name, I said, 'Suzanna. I was named after a song, but not the one you think.'"

"Did he sing that stupid 'Oh! Susanna'?"

"No! He had asked if I was named for the Isaac Bellow song or the Randy Newman."

"Really? He knew the Bellow?" Joan's lips curled in surprise. "I didn't know Randy Newman wrote a song named 'Suzanna,' too."

"I know! Well, his song's actually just 'Suzanne.'"

"Close enough."

Suzanna leaned forward. "Now, I'm no Randy Newman expert, so I listened to it."

"What's it like?"

"Bluesy, funny, and a little strange." Suzanna bounced in her chair. "It's good."

"Seems like you and this guy have a lot in common."

Suzanna cleared the table and put the dirty plates in the sink. Turning back, she said, "And the other day, he asked me out."

Joan clapped her hands. "Great, for when?"

"Tomorrow, Philly Orchestra matinee."

"I'm not sure you should be going out right now, not if you're some kind of target."

"The cops seem to think it's okay, and they'll be watching me."

"Just keep your eyes open. I'll want to hear all about the date. Come over Monday and spill your guts. What's the orchestra playing?"

"Beethoven's Seventh. He got the tickets because I told him it was my favorite."

"Don't sleep with him on the first date."

"Ma-um." Putting on her most serious adult voice, she said, "Don't worry."

After washing the dishes, Suzanna padded up the carpeted stairs to her old bedroom. A tattered teddy bear from her childhood lay against the bed's pillow. She grasped it and nuzzled its head. On her old dresser sat a ceramic horse that she used to wish would magically come to life. Faded posters of Counting Crows, Bach, and Mozart hung on the walls. The room even still smelled of her old lemon shampoo. Why didn't Mom turn this room into an office or even downsize and sell the house?

Suzanna flattened herself over the top of the dresser and looked along its back. The chalk marks were still there. One dash drawn for each month—her countdown to moving out and independence. Silly, though. In the end, her freedom involved nothing more than living a few miles away and refusing financial handouts. Spending the night in this room painted a picture of how easily her fragile independence could slip away.

She peeked into her old closet and spied a small bookshelf. Something new? All right, Mom, finally using this room for something else. Maybe just the closet, but it was a start. She snooped through the books. Travel books. Not a very subtle hint. To her mother's endless chagrin, a high school trip to Rome was Suzanna's only experience globetrotting. For years, her mom had pestered her to go on a mother-and-daughter excursion to Europe, as though travel were the cure for everything. As much as she loved her mother, she didn't want to be stuck alone with her on another continent. So the journey never happened. That didn't stop her mom from continuing to push for it.

One of the books was about travel in New Jersey. She paged through to see if it mentioned the Jersey Devil. Not a word.

Suzanna propped herself up on the bed and flipped open her computer. Wouldn't hurt to learn a little more about the Jersey Devil's history. A simple search brought up loads of information. She read the first paragraph:

The story of the Jersey Devil began in the 1700s, a time rife with belief in witches, curses, and mystical creatures. It started the way many myths do, based on a suspicious person. The dubious person in question was named Mrs. Leeds, later labeled Mother Leeds. Her two-room, stone house sits on a hill in what is now Leeds Point, New Jersey.

Switching to Google Maps, Suzanna looked up Leeds Point. It was by the shore, an hour or so from Haddonfield. The article said the house sits—not sat—near Leeds Point. Interesting. Does that mean the house still exists? She read on:

Mother Leeds and her husband arrived as strangers, with twelve children and a thirteenth on the way. Allegedly, Mother Leeds was tired of having babies and cursed her last born to be a devil instead of human. After the child was delivered, it transformed into the Jersey Devil and flew up and out the chimney.

Only in New Jersey!

Chapter 19

Joan sat alone at her kitchen table long after her daughter went to bed. Ever since Suzanna moved out, the house felt empty—the same kind of emptiness that cramped her heart all those years ago when she'd returned from Europe. She never did get used to living alone. Always half-hoped Suzanna would move back. She loved the rare occasion when her daughter did stay over. The sound of her humming, cooking for two, the sense of family.

She put on her headphones and turned up the music. Concern for her daughter pinched at the corners of her eyes as she poured her last glass. Even at twenty-four, Suzanna didn't seem to understand the kind of danger she could be in. She wouldn't know real danger if it bit her on the nose.

Still, she had to hand it to the girl; she was resolute about forging her own way in the world. Even as a child, she'd never wanted help with school projects, and after the conservatory, she had struck out on her own, pursuing a musician's scrappy living.

Joan often wondered if Suzanna's independent streak came from never having a father. Over the years, she'd tried to make up for the missing dad, striving to be a "Super Mom," but usually coming up short. She did her best to be a good example. Maybe her own independence had been an influence.

If only she hadn't made that one slip. So stupid. Like a rite of passage, she'd saved the revelation for Suzanna's high school graduation night. But then she drank too much and lost the ability, or the will, to follow through. If not for that, Joan suspected Suzanna's search for her father wouldn't have even started.

Tonight had been a particular disappointment, though. She thought Suzanna was letting go of the whole father mystery, but the shock of the explosion must have changed things. A glimpse at mortality could dredge up all kinds of yearnings. Getting her hands on that old yearbook didn't help, either.

She put on another album and was surrounded by that aged voice—no, that eternal voice. Like so many nights in the past, Joan listened to Bellow and wrapped herself in the warm image of her daughter safely asleep upstairs. Hopefully, Suzanna had noticed the strategically placed shelf of travel books. She'd so love to revisit the sites from her own youth and share them with her daughter. Maybe someday, Suzanna would change her tune.

Joan closed her eyes, remembering the smell of warm baguettes as she'd strolled along Paris's Pont Neuf, trailing her hand over the centuries-old stone walls. She had been such a wayward girl, gallivanting all around Europe. The Roman Colosseum, Venice, London, the orange blossoms of Seville … that trip had been one thrill after another. Sleeping in hostels, making new friends who didn't even speak English, getting close without words, and moving on. The drugs of the eighties—cocaine and weed—had been cheap and plentiful. Now, she was just grateful she landed on her feet.

She let the song wash over her. Isaac Bellow was singing about burdens and mercy. One of his early works that she had heard first as a child. His music was simpler then, just him and his guitar. That was before fame bought him pricy production and recording techniques. But it was always his lyrics, then and now, that really touched her. Pure poetry. Melancholy and beautiful.

Sometimes, it seemed that he spoke directly to her.

Chapter 20

Sunday, May 12

Sunday morning, Detective O'Brien was the only one pulling office overtime, apart from the usual skeleton crew. At his desk in the squad room, he welcomed the relative quiet of the weekend. It helped him think.

The Archer surveillance report he'd received from Smelly Higgins was clear-cut. He hoped it was accurate, too. He'd half-expected the guy to desert his post again. When Higgins actually answered the phone, O'Brien released a pent-up sigh of relief. Smelly Higgins was a detective, but not a good one. And that nickname! Apparently, the guys gave it to him after he ate a particularly spicy bowl of chili.

Per Smelly, Saturday night had been routine, no movement. And yet, O'Brien lacked confidence that any of the three Haddonfield detectives—especially Higgins— could, or would, do solid work. He rubbed his temples. Small police forces like Haddonfield's needed everyone to pitch in, regardless of rank. Those three mollycoddled snowflakes acted like the sun shone out their collective backsides. Not one of them had ever put in an all-night stakeout.

The detective smoothed the left side of his mustache, gently raking in any stray hairs, while his thumb and index fingers pulled the whiskers from above his lip through to the curled tip. With the same motion, he smoothed the right side. He decided his mustache could use a trim. Jokes around the squad room multiplied when it grew too long.

O'Brien tapped the pack of cigarettes in his suit coat pocket. He'd really been trying to quit. Really trying. It didn't seem to matter, though; there they were in his pocket. He took the pack out and chucked it in the wastebasket.

Taking a deep, cathartic breath, he sucked in the pungent odor of the squad room. It stank like a locker room … like a dirty, boys' locker room. Compared to his New York district office, the Haddonfield Police Station was a hovel. Its swinging glass door opened to a cramped reception-dispatch room that could've come right out of small-town Mayberry. Dusty neighborhood maps coated the walls, along with an enormous, framed image of the Haddonfield Police insignia. In the corner hung an American flag that needed washing. Two paces from the door, a high counter separated the public from Marge, a stoic widow with steely, gray hair. Cool and efficient, she answered phones, did all the filing, and single-handedly kept the station running. Marge had always been O'Brien's favorite coworker, perhaps because he identified with her antisocial tendencies.

A door by Marge's desk led to the tunnel-like squad room crammed with rows of desks backing up to tall, grimy windows. O'Brien would have preferred an office, but like everyone else, including the captain, he had a desk by the windows. As far as resources were concerned, he found the station remarkable for what it lacked. It had no interview rooms, no holding cell, no secure evidence storage, no break room, and only two computers. Not even a phone on every desk.

Along with all the shortcomings, it irked O'Brien that not one woman worked on the Haddonfield Police Force. Not only did it offend his sense of professional staffing, but it gave the guys license to spew a continuous stream of misogynistic banter—banter he could do without. In New York, his partner had been a woman, and he missed her influences, both good and bad. Here in Haddonfield, he didn't even have a partner. Inclined to keep to himself anyway, O'Brien trudged along on his own. Who needed a partner to manage Haddonfield's minor crimes?

That's what he used to think. This new case's sheer number of suspects brought it in line with many of his New York investigations. Of course, this car bomb investigation might lead nowhere, but the hit man idea nagged at him. Ordinary citizens didn't just go around making bombs. The hit men he'd chased down in New York used car bombs and bullets as their weapons of choice. They weren't dummies, but ruthless and methodical. Like ghosts, they'd slip into town, kill, and get out fast. So why was a hit man in Haddonfield? Why Suzanna?

O'Brien scraped back his chair and strolled down the length of the squad room to the water cooler beside Marge's desk. He pulled out a paper cup and filled it. "I quit smoking."

Marge handed him a mass of files. "I'll believe it when I see it."

"Would you like to make a wager this time?"

"I refuse to take your money. Find the bomber yet?"

"Working on it."

The detective walked back to his desk, thinking about his suspect pool. Nothing he'd discovered so far pointed to a specific culprit. To get to the bottom of this case, he would have to put in the work to interview everyone and investigate all leads.

He loosened his tie, pulled a handful of blank index cards out of his drawer, and stacked them on his desk blotter. He flipped one over and, with a black Sharpie, wrote, *Mom—Joan*. Positioning it on the left side of his blotter, he contemplated Joan Archer. What was her real story? Without a doubt, Suzanna had been sold a bill of goods about her father.

He placed the next card, labeled *Father—?*, to the right of Joan's card. The question mark made his nose itch. Nothing about the father added up. If the mother didn't come clean, he'd have to do some major digging.

O'Brien wrote out two more cards, *Roommate—Chris* and *Boyfriend—Adam*. He arranged all the cards in a neat row across his desk. None of these people appeared capable of assembling and installing a car bomb, but as far as he knew, any one of them could've hired a hit man. Of this lot, the missing father was his prime suspect. The guy might be entangled in any number of criminal activities that somehow roped Suzanna in.

He labeled his next card, *HB owner—Harry*. Only Harry could possibly have the know-how to make and plant that bomb, but O'Brien's gut rejected the idea.

On his final card, he wrote, *Hoodie Guy*. His nose itched so much, it started to run. This hoodie guy was the worst kind of suspect. Did some weirdo actually gawk at Suzanna through a window, or was Harry trying to cast suspicion onto someone else?

He blew his nose. If he didn't start getting some answers, he'd have to take a decongestant.

Detective O'Brien swept up the index cards and tucked them in his breast pocket. He checked the time. Two o'clock. On Sunday nights, he religiously watched *60 Minutes* while he ate dinner. That gave him enough time to conduct one interview—the roommate. He'd tackle the others first thing tomorrow morning.

Reaching under his desk, he reclaimed the cigarette pack from the trash. There was no way he could quit in the middle of this case. On his way out, he nodded to Marge, and with her face fixed in its perpetual frown, she nodded back.

Chapter 21

After a quick shower, Chris suited up in his performance clothes—black shirt, black slacks, black everything. Surprised by how loosely his pants fit, he cinched them up with his belt. He donned clip-on sunglasses, snuck into Suzanna's room, and stood in front of her full-length mirror. He was ready. Now, for the long drive to his posh gig.

He was surprised to see Suzanna's guitar case leaning against her dresser. It only took a glance at her neatly made bed to know she hadn't come home last night. Must be at her mom's, or maybe she'd hooked up with some guy. Who knew? Wherever she had spent the night, she better get back soon and pick up her gear, or she'd be late for her brunch job. It was like he didn't know her anymore. Hard to believe that just six months ago, he'd wanted to get back with her.

Chris grabbed his guitar case and music and headed out to his old Mustang convertible. The trunk opened with a screech, and he swung his beat-up case inside with an experienced, fluid yank. With the back of his hand, he wiped the sweat from his upper lip and inspected the old case. Dammit. Why was Suzanna walking around with the best guitar case on the planet? He slammed the trunk closed. "She gets all the breaks."

Before getting in his car, he took a stealthy look over his shoulder at the patrol car parked across the street. Cops had been hanging around since Friday night. It got on his nerves. The police wouldn't look too kindly on some of his bad habits or associates.

Shading his eyes with his hand, he peered into the open patrol car's window. The cop was holding a phone in front of his face and yelling into it. If that guy was supposed to be monitoring Suzanna, he screwed up. Chris scuffed through the gravel lot and stood on the curb, where he could clearly hear the cop's blaring voice from the other side of the street.

"Nothin' happened all night, and nothin's happening now … Archer hasn't moved. Yeah, yeah … tonight? Aw, man, I'm exhausted. I'm not used to working hours like these. Listen, I'm a detective, I shouldn't be sitting out here … No, no, I'll do it."

Helping the police could have advantages. Chris crossed the street, put one hand on the patrol car's roof, and tipped his head in the window. "Hey, man, Suzanna's not here."

The cop turned off his phone. "She's not? Where is she?"

"Sorry, but hell if I know."

"Wait a minute. I sat here all night. I didn't see her go anywhere."

"Last night?" He shot the cop a quizzical look. "She never came home."

Expletives rang out from the patrol car as the cop sped away. Chris chuckled as he made his way back to the Mustang.

It was a two-hour trip down the freeway to the Bala Country Club. Chris gave himself plenty of extra time for the journey.

The way Suzanna had given him hell yesterday morning weighed on his mind. He could control his drinking just fine, thank you very much, and his opioid use, too. As far as he could tell, she didn't even know about the drugs, but he felt guilty about them anyway. Back when they were dating, she wouldn't have cared. She'd been so tolerant and accepting. But after rooming with her for six months, she'd become remarkably unforgiving and nothing less than irritating. Chris could hardly stand being around her anymore.

And then there was her stupid threat. Suzanna didn't have a clue how real blackmail operated. There had to be a clear risk. Did she actually think he gave a damn about his parents? He stuck out his tongue and blew a raspberry. Well … he did worry about them cutting off his allowance.

Chris eased on the brake at a traffic light and peered into the glowing bulb. Red meaning stop. Stop meaning no.

Like all the orders his fundamentalist mom and dad had bombarded him with as a child.

His mother had forced him to practice classical guitar for hours every day, against all his protests and tears. Like any ordinary kid, all he'd ever wanted to do was go out and play ball with his friends. But looking back on it now, he was reluctantly grateful for the rigorous training.

Most of his competition at the conservatory could get by on talent with minimal practice, but he was the kind of musician who had to sweat for every crumb of progress. Chris had to tamp down his jealousy whenever he thought about how much more talent Suzanna had. A lot more. While he'd put in years of strenuous drilling just to be accepted into the conservatory, she practically cakewalked in. He still had to practice more than she did. Maddening!

The car behind him beeped twice, snapping him out of his funk. He grimaced into the rearview mirror and stepped on the gas.

The club's private entrance snaked around ponds, fountains, and lush, emerald grounds. Chris felt at home amongst the meticulously groomed shrubs and ornate buildings. This setting suited his professional standard—high-class, elite, elegant. Everything about the place screamed wealth. He licked his lips and could almost taste the caviar.

He pulled into the parking lot and parked his old junker amid luxury sedans. If only his parents would buy him a new car. He'd hinted at it but got no response. Not wanting to push his luck, he let it go.

Adjusting his clip-ons, Chris scanned the grounds. His lungs filled with the scent of newly mowed grass. The whole world looked shimmery and golden. His chest swelled as he made a show of hoisting his guitar on his back. Strutting through the heavy, gilded doors, he oozed with confidence. The tuxedoed banquet manager rushed up, shook his hand, and ushered him to a padded chair on a small stage.

Chris tossed back his hair with a grand flip, imagining the gesture in slow motion, and sized up the room. Round tables covered with bone-white tablecloths sat on plush, red carpeting. Each table held a crystal vase at its center, brimming with calla lilies. Attendees mingled, holding drinks and chatting. A few celebrities drew his attention— a state senator, a major league baseball player, and a local news anchor.

The perfect gig ... not only lucrative but also an excellent networking opportunity. After his performance, he would mix with the notables and drum up more concerts. He tried to recall how he'd landed this gig but couldn't put his finger on it.

One by one, he unlatched the tarnished clasps on his guitar case. He opened the lid and reached down to pull out his guitar.

He gasped in horror. *How?* Shock and confusion rippled through his chest.

The case was empty.

Chris fanned his burning cheeks with his hand as he explained his situation to the manager.

Seeming to weigh his words before speaking, the manager said, "Too bad. I was looking forward to hearing you." He shook Chris's hand. "But no problem. We'll play a CD."

Chris sighed in relief but then noticed the guy was looking anywhere but into his eyes.

With a more businesslike tone, the manager said, "Tell your parents I said hello, and thank them for recommending you." He put a solid grasp on Chris's shoulder and turned him toward the door. "Maybe we'll try this again sometime."

The car seemed a million miles away as he plodded forward with his empty guitar case and no five hundred bucks. His stomach felt thick and heavy as a cement block. The hard reality sank in. The whole gig had been nothing more than a favor to his parents. The forgotten guitar wasn't his only failure; he was never wanted in the first place.

On autopilot, he drove home in a shadowy stupor. Would his concert career ever take off? Or, at twenty-five years old, was it already over?

Chapter 22

This time, the thump rocked the floor. Arty dropped his buttered toast and rushed into the living room. He stopped in his tracks when he saw his favorite, worn-out armchair—the one he always fell asleep in—pushed over on its side. That ratty chair had seen almost as many years as he had and weighed a long ton. A beam of morning sun glinted off something underneath. He pulled the chair upright and found the pile of glossy, Florida brochures he'd picked up last week in Center City.

What the heck was going on here? Studying the paranormal was one thing, but having it upend his home was a whole other can of worms. All of a sudden, the occasional shifting item or weird noise had turned into a daily barrage of perfume whiffs, falling books, misplaced photos, and now this. He noted the gooseflesh on his arms. Worst of all, the spook in his house seemed pissed off.

Arty wondered if he could get in touch with the guys from *Ghost Hunters*. This would make a fantastic episode. When they investigated a haunting, they went in with lots of cool gadgets—night vision goggles, full-spectrum camcorders, thermal meters, motion sensors, electronic voice recorders, and more. But then again, if this ghost was his mum, and she was upset, no sense letting the whole world watch her have a meltdown.

He gathered up the shiny, Florida leaflets. The last time he saw them, they'd been on the kitchen counter. Shaking his head, he returned to his breakfast and plopped the brochures on the table. From years of reading and watching shows like *Ghost Hunters*, there was one thing he knew for sure: ghosts remain in the human realm to take care of unfinished business. What could Mum's unfinished business be? And why is it heating up now?

Rebuttering his toast, Arty considered the possibilities. Is it because he's moving soon, and his mum doesn't want him to sell the house? Does she know he lost money? Or could it have something to do with the Jersey Devil? Lately, everything else did. Or maybe she didn't want him making this last hit. She never did approve of his pop's profession, and it wasn't a secret that she didn't want Arty to follow in his footsteps.

The Polaroid photo from 1948 lay on the table beside his toast. His mum's curly, dark hair fluttered in the breeze. A full-skirted swing dress made her waist look so slender that Arty was sure he could encircle it with his bare hands. As for him, he just looked like an awkward tyke. Plaid shirt buttoned wrong and hair uncombed, he slouched on the cement steps with a big grin on his face.

Back in those days, a Polaroid camera had passed for newfangled magic. His pop's camera had been his pride and joy, but it lit a fuse under the nastiest fight Arty had ever seen his parents have. His mum had wanted to know where it came from. They'd screamed at each other, and his pop stormed out. Arty figured his pop had nicked the camera from a cleanup job.

He wished he could remember that trip to Florida, but it was a total blank. He wondered if they actually went. What he did recall from that time was his mum getting cancer—the puking, sallow skin, and losing all that weight. And the yellow eyes. They stuck in his memory and still made him queasy. They were eerie, no white left. The yellow had eaten it all up. Every time he'd looked at her, his eyes watered. When she'd gone to the hospital for the last time, he was almost relieved.

Arty looked at the clock. Better step on it. Today's operation was gonna be a breeze, take no more than an hour. He had a special surprise all laid out for his target's trek into Philly. On the way out of Haddonfield, the secluded bridge over Cooper River would be the ideal place to nudge a car off the road. If the crash didn't do the trick, the engorged, rushing stream would.

At the door, he turned, cupped his hand around his mouth, and yelled, "Just going out for groceries, Mum." In case she was watching, he didn't want her to know what he was really up to. He shut the door behind him, and with a loud clank, the doorknob fell off and rolled to his feet. His mum never did have a great sense of humor.

By the time he got his toolbox and fixed the doorknob, it was too late to pull off his hit job. Referring to his notes,

Arty plotted a strategy for the next day. He savored that old rush of adrenaline prickling his chest as he devised the new plan. The perfect plan.

Chapter 23

Suzanna trotted to the bottom of Ristorante Buena's brick steps, her gig bag banging against her guitar case. Six minutes late. Not *that* bad. But Jonathan, the very proper maître d' and her boss, would not be pleased.

She could kick herself for sleeping—rather, oversleeping—at her mom's last night. What a mistake. She barely had enough time to stop at the apartment, throw on her gig clothes, and grab her guitar. Only an idiot would be late for work at Ristorante Buena, the most exclusive restaurant in Philly. They paid an upscale hourly wage, plus the tips were so generous, they covered most of her bills. She would never admit it to the owners, but she'd have played for the tips alone.

While Suzanna adjusted her gear, she gazed up at the entrance's crown of scroll pediments flaunting colonial–era charm. Smart marketing. Tourists spent big bucks on anything historic in Philly.

She bounded up the steps, almost knocking over a stocky man in a gray hoodie coming out the door. Over her shoulder, she glanced at him, but he'd already turned his back. "Sorry," she called out. The Ristorante required a suit and tie. This guy wasn't just underdressed; he looked like he was going to the gym. Jonathan had probably just thrown him out.

When she pulled open the thick, burgundy door, the delicious aroma of mushroom risotto drifted out. Wonderful. Risotto for lunch today. Every week, her free Sunday meal consisted of gourmet cuisine, quite a step up from HB's burgers and salads. But she had no complaints. On her days off, she had to eat modestly. Her mom accused her of surviving on peanut butter and jelly, tuna fish, and popcorn.

As she stepped into the vestibule, her feet sank into the cool-gray carpeting. The grand door swept shut behind her with a whisper, instantly muting the city's tumult.

Suzanna hurried past the empty podium where the maître d' greeted guests, grateful for Jonathan's absence, and slipped down the steps to the bar. That lower floor was a study in contrasts where history stood shoulder to shoulder with modern elegance. But in her opinion, the whole setup did the colonial features a disservice. The low ceiling's rustic, exposed beams butted up against recessed lighting, the original 1700's rough-hewn timber stairs touched down on golden, wall-to-wall carpeting, and the contemporary, crescent moon-shaped bar sloped gracefully in front of a stone, colonial, walk-in fireplace.

Hugging her gear close to her body, Suzanna threaded around clusters of high rollers waiting for tables. The bartender, in formal vest and bow tie, didn't even glance at her as she passed; she didn't know his name anyway. Out of the corner of her eye, she glimpsed him, offering a martini on a tray to a shapely woman in a white cocktail dress. The woman's fingers sparkled with gems. Suzanna much preferred HB's workaday bar, with Vinny serving pints in his black jeans and polo shirt, all the while wisecracking with the customers.

In record time, she reached the back coat closet and shoved her jacket into one of the employee slots. She hoisted her guitar, pulled her shoulders back, and prepared to meet the wrath of Jonathan. Only six minutes late, but Jonathan was about as flexible as a disco beat.

As she climbed the stairs to the lengthy main dining room, she savored the heady scent of fresh-cut flowers mingled with whiffs of buttery Hollandaise sauce. To Suzanna, the decor upstairs seemed more about setting a mood than reflecting any notion of history. Casements wrapped in full-length, burgundy curtains combined with modern chandeliers to block out all natural light and create a romantic glow. The only old-world charm in the room hung on the latte-colored walls, lithographs of Philadelphia's landmarks—Independence Hall, the Liberty Bell, the Betsy Ross House, the Art Museum, and, of course, the Rocky statue.

A waiter flew past her with a flaming dessert in his raised hand. Suzanna ducked and zigzagged around the tightly spaced tables rife with stylish guests dressed to the nines. Despite the high prices and posh setting, the Ristorante packed in as many customers as possible. It took finesse for Suzanna to cross the massive dining room while carrying all her gear.

While edging into her performance area, she searched the room for Jonathan. There he was, standing stiff as a spike beside the marble fireplace, reeking of pretension in his tuxedo. His eyes rose to meet hers with an intense glare. With a curl of his finger, he summoned her.

Suzanna tiptoed toward him like a guilty child. "I'm so sorry I'm a little late, but my car blew—"

His hand shot up, palm out. "No excuses. Just don't do it again." Such a jerk. Jonathan didn't care about anything except the Ristorante. He certainly didn't care about her car problems. The very idea of socializing with the help, the category she knew he dumped her in, would likely make his stomach turn.

From the first time she played at Ristorante Buena one year ago, Jonathan's concept of a performance area consisted of squeezing her between two guest tables. As far as she was concerned, it was the worst performing space she ever had. Of course, any comparison to the HB was unfair; her roomy spot there stretched in front of huge, glass windows looking onto the sidewalk. Outside the HB, everyone walking by could watch her playing, and inside, every customer had to pass her tip jar on the way out. But at this chic Ristorante, she was an afterthought. If Jonathan had his way, he'd make her sit and play beside the kitchen door or, worse, by the restrooms.

Suzanna made short work of her setup. She plugged in the power strip and hid it under her chair. Positioning her amp slightly in front to avoid feedback, she inserted a wedge underneath to make it point up for better projection. She unfolded her portable music stand, put her setlist of music pieces and binder on it, and clipped her mic to her guitar's sound hole.

While skimming her setlist, her eyes fell on the teeny etching of a guitar peeking up from the bottom of the page. The memory of her mom's excitement over giving her that ream of paper made her smile. Guitar presents might be dopey, but the gift givers, especially her mom, meant well.

Suzanna gradually introduced her sound to the room by gently plucking the strings. Her chords harmonized with hushed conversations, silverware clinking on china, ice jangling in crystal glasses, and popping corks. The thick drapes and carpeting softened the edges of her tone, making her guitar sound dark and warm.

Just as she finished her first song, State Senator Bancroft's imposing figure entered the dining room. Gray hair and a midriff bulge gave away his age, despite his vigor and clean-shaven, boyish features.

Strolling beside him was a much younger man who was positively South Philly but not handsome like Vinny. He had a long nose, that must've been broken at least once, and oily slicked-back hair. In a flash, Suzanna realized that this young man and Chris's event planner were one and the same. That's why he looked familiar last night; she'd seen him here at the Ristorante a week ago with Bancroft. She remembered because Jonathan had seated them directly beside her, so close that she could smell their aftershave. Why on earth would Chris's event planner be working with the senator? Could Bancroft be hiring Chris for an event? Why not her?

Jonathan seated the two men beside her, even closer than last week. Suzanna cringed when their tablecloth brushed against her leg. As he turned on his heels and bustled away, a little ball of fury toward the maître d' bloomed in her chest. She took several deep breaths to tamp it down. Trying to shrink from the awkward position—practically on top of the senator—she pulled her gear in as tightly as possible.

Bancroft flashed her his senatorial, ear-to-ear grin. "Hi, Suzanna, how's it strumming?"

The forced laugh she saved for stupid guitar jokes escaped her lips. Double-quick, she transitioned to her standard welcoming smile, but that smile was phonier than usual. Since hearing about the intern, her comfort level with Bancroft had taken a nosedive. Suzanna searched the senator's smiling face and shining eyes for some sign of impropriety.

"That's quite an impressive guitar case you have there." The senator pointed at the silver techno-case by her side.

The event planner glanced at the case and then at her setlist. He moved only his eyes, not his head. He looked at her that same way last night, like he had a stiff neck.

"She's brand new." Suzanna gave the case's handle a proud pat.

The senator nodded and turned back to his companion. They spoke in subdued tones. That's when it struck her. Wasn't it her mom's job to deal with event planners? Was Bancroft planning something her mom didn't know about? Suzanna's chest tightened, considering her mom's problems on top of her own. She tried to eavesdrop, but she couldn't hear a thing. Why were they speaking so softly?

Focusing back on her work, she placed a Baroque suite transcription on her music stand. Suzanna always played her most difficult pieces in the first set when her fingers were fresh. The only material she avoided altogether was concert repertoire because it called for the audience's full attention. She accepted that the goal of background music was the exact opposite.

Usually, diners paid little attention to her music, unconcerned with its quality and difficulty. But they did notice mistakes. When her hands were fatigued, generally around her third set, she could only pull off easy pieces without a hitch.

It was hard to turn off her musings, but she dove into the Baroque suite. A sour note slipped out, and she skillfully slurred into the right one. Suzanna sighed.

Mistakes on guitar were the most frustrating thing about playing the instrument. Battles with Piano Dan about how a piano key is either struck or not, a fifty-fifty chance, brought her little sympathy. On the guitar, a correctly played note can still result in any number of goofs that people interpret as mistakes—a buzz, a blur, bending the string, a squeak, a twang, a botched slur, or missing the string altogether. She found it difficult to shake an imaginary scene she'd conjured on her very first gig ... she would make a whopper mistake, and all the diners would freeze in mid-bite and stare at her. Some would drop their forks.

Suddenly, Bancroft pounded his fist on the table and exclaimed, "Devil's teeth!" Suzanna muffled a snort. Must be a heated discussion for him to use that nasty phrase.

By the time she started her third set, the crowd was loosening up, and the room resonated with an unusually spirited buzz. Probably all the complimentary glasses of champagne and mimosas. Suzanna flipped through her binders. Along with music organized by difficulty, she had collections that enhanced a room's energy. To accompany a subdued crowd—slow, new-agey waltzes. For a lively group like this—upbeat tarantellas. She switched binders and played through several aggressive Spanish works with robust strums.

Rippling the back of her fingernails over the strings, she ended her set with a surging Rasgueado flourish. A crisp, twenty-dollar bill poked out the top of her tip jar. Suzanna turned toward Bancroft, but the table was empty; it had already been bussed and reset.

While packing up her gear, a handsome woman wearing a stunning strand of pearls stood in front of her and cleared her throat.

Suzanna stopped packing and smiled.

The woman said, "Lovely. That was so relaxing!" Delicately, almost like she was embarrassed, she slid a folded bill into the tip jar.

Relaxing wasn't quite what Suzanna was going for with her Spanish pieces, but she smiled. Keep the customer happy.

The woman cupped her hand to her mouth and whispered, "I especially liked 'The Godfather Theme.'"

Suzanna nodded, thanked her, and waited until she left to chuckle. She'd never played "The Godfather Theme" in her life.

Checking her time, she only had a half hour to get to the other end of town for her first date with Adam. In the kitchen, she gobbled down her risotto. Then, she changed into jeans, gave a fist bump to the next shift musician (a harpist wheeling in her behemoth of an instrument), and sped across the city to the Kimmel Center, the home of the world-famous Philadelphia Orchestra.

Chapter 24

An usher showed Suzanna and Adam to what appeared to be the worst seats in Philly's Kimmel Center—the nosebleed section with a slightly obstructed view. Suzanna wasn't surprised. Kimmel tickets went for up to two hundred apiece. These lousy seats wouldn't break the bank, probably sixty bucks. Still, Adam must work a second job to be able to buy even the cheap seats. The gigging musicians she knew didn't have the money for concert tickets. Most wouldn't be able to afford a ticket to hear themselves play.

They eased into their seats just as the string section pulsed the initial soft chords, and the woodwinds took up the melody. Squinting in the dark at her program, Suzanna read that only the first half of the concert would be Beethoven. The second half contained two twentieth-century works by obscure composers. She wasn't a purist, but so much twentieth-century classical music had been experimental that it just didn't stand the test of time. As she slumped in her seat, it squeaked slightly.

Adam was frowning and holding his program so close to his face it almost touched his nose. Tilting his head to the side, he whispered in her ear, "Would you mind if we left at intermission?"

She whispered back, "I was thinking the same thing."

"Looks like total rubbish, doesn't it?"

"Total!" Her relationship barometer tipped toward optimism. Suzanna nestled into her velvety seat and enjoyed the Philadelphia Orchestra performing her favorite Beethoven symphony.

When the lights went up for intermission, they filed out to the atrium, the symphony's final chords still ringing in Suzanna's ears. They passed back through the majestic Kimmel doors and merged into the flow of pedestrians on the busy sidewalk.

"The spring weather feels good, doesn't it?" Adam's voice had a slight tremor.

It sounded to Suzanna like he couldn't think of anything to say. She took a sidelong glance at him strolling beside her. With his straggly, brown hair and slender build, he reminded her of anything but corporate America. She liked that about him.

Tipping her head back, she let the sun warm her face. Adam's arm shot out, stopping her inches from a mud puddle. What a gentleman! She dodged the wet patch, a reminder of yesterday's miserable storm, and imagined Adam in Elizabethan England throwing down his coat for her to step over.

Philadelphia street vendors lined the sidewalks, hawking their wares. Aromas from a variety of cuisines mingled in the mild breeze. Adam bought hot dogs and soft pretzels from a plump vendor wearing a long, white apron.

Suzanna and Adam laughed as the vendor popped the hot dogs over his shoulder into the rolls and loaded everything in a brown paper bag.

Food in hand, they set a leisurely course for the Academy of Music Opera House, a nearby historic landmark. The Academy's brownstone exterior incorporated a tier of marble steps that ran the length of the building. The perfect place to sit and eat. In time to their footsteps, Suzanna hummed the theme from the symphony's second movement.

At the opera house, she settled on the highest step and transformed the simple task of spreading mustard on her pretzel into a major operation. "I've been listening to Randy Newman," she said, "per your suggestion."

Adam squatted on the step below her, his dark eyes shining. "What do you think?"

"I like that his voice isn't …"

"Traditional?" he suggested.

"Yes. I find his voice compelling, like Isaac Bellow's. The fact that it isn't perfect somehow fits." Suzanna faked an offended tone. "I'm not sure about that 'Short People' song, though."

Adam laughed. "Yeah, satire's his thing."

Her mustard-spreading process complete, Suzanna peeked down at Adam. "So, where'd you get your degree?"

"Temple. Not quite as classy as your conservatory."

"Don't put Temple down. They have a fantastic music department! I would've gone there if I didn't get into the conservatory."

"But when you've played an instrument all your life, the Holy Grail is to go to a conservatory." Adam's lips curled into a brittle smile. "The competition was just too steep."

"Ah, the advantage of being a classical guitarist— there aren't a lot of us. Less competition."

Stuffed from hot dogs and a salt-luscious, Philly soft pretzel, Suzanna tilted back on her elbows. She figured Adam must only be a moderately talented cellist. If he was a superstar, it was true—he would've gone to the conservatory, and he wouldn't be playing in a dinky orchestra like Haddonfield. Not that it made any difference to her.

She tilted toward Adam and asked, "When did you start studying cello?"

A cloud fell across his face. "Around seven."

Suzanna knew the score. When someone starts playing that young, it's rarely their own choice.

"Did your folks force you to practice?"

"No more than normal. How old were you?"

"Fourteenish. Mom was supportive but didn't push. I was pretty self-motivated." She could still picture her mom bringing home a classical guitar. Someone in the office had been giving it away, and she took it on a whim. From the first moment Suzanna had picked up the instrument, it felt natural in her hands. The following week, after only one lesson, she could already play the classical guitar standard "Romanza." Her mom's open mouth and raised eyebrows said it all.

"How about your dad?"

Suzanna hung her head and forced out a heavy sigh. At some point in every new relationship, this question had to be answered. Might as well be now. Grudgingly, she trotted out her mom's story. At the end, she said, "So, I have no idea who he is."

Adam didn't say a word. He just stared at his hands.

Suzanna attempted to fill the dead air. "I know it's weird. I think about getting a DNA test—"

He spun around and looked up into her eyes. "Your car exploding yesterday? Could someone be after your missing dad instead of you? Like he's in some kind of trouble."

Suzanna's jaw tightened at the thought of her birth father being involved. Could he be a criminal someone's after? Or a numskull caught up with some bad actors? Or worse, did her mother have to run away from him? Those thoughts first crossed her mind the night Baby blew up, but she'd swept them away and buried them deep. Pulling her jacket tight around her waist, she said, "Don't think I haven't considered it. But if Mom doesn't know who he is, and he doesn't even know I was born—"

"You know, I'm worried about you. It's all so …"

"I just hope Detective O'Brien unravels the whole thing soon." That was an understatement. She shook off the conversation and forced a cheery tone. "Have any plans for tonight?"

"Orchestra rehearsal at seven. How about you?"

"Probably hang with Em at HB. Can't practice. My hands are spent after three hours of constant playing."

He spread his legs out over three steps and turned his face up to the sun. "Don't you take breaks?"

"Usually. Ten minutes every hour. But if people are tipping or about to leave, I keep playing."

"Even when your fingers hurt?"

"Tips stop during breaks. It's like people forget you were there."

Adam nodded but said, "Not worth it."

As they stood up, he stretched his arms behind his back. Suzanna brushed off her jeans and calculated his height. Around five-foot-sixish? If she wore heels, she'd be able to look directly into his eyes.

The breeze swept Adam's hair into his face, and it took him a second to control the stray strands. "Where are you parked? I'll walk you to your car."

No one had ever suggested walking her to her car before. He might be a little *too* gentlemanly. "I'm down Locust. I got OSP."

"OSP?"

"On street parking."

Adam laughed. A promising sign.

They strolled down tree-lined Locust Street, past high-end, colonial townhouses. Pink-edged, green buds poked out of the cherry tree branches.

Suzanna had a thousand questions for Adam but was worried about sounding nosy, so she kept to basics. "Where abouts do you live?"

"Only a half hour from Haddonfield, in Pipers Corner."

"That's out in the middle of nowhere!" She immediately regretted blurting out the words, but Adam didn't seem fazed by it.

"It's very affordable. I'm right in the thick of the Pine Barrens."

Suzanna agreed. Living out there in no-man's-land *must* be cheap, but this time, she held her tongue. She'd only visited the Pine Barrens a few times with her mom to tour Batsto Village, a restored, historic town deep in the forest. She remembered the desolate woods and earthy odors. Adam's gruff tone sounded a bit defensive. She studied his face and decided it was cynicism, something she'd have to keep an eye out for. "Hey, wait a minute … are you close to Indian Mills?"

"A couple minutes from my house."

"I found a shop online in Indian Mills, the Devil's Lair."

"I know that shop. It's a dive."

Suzanna filled him in on the Jersey Devil book the police took into evidence and her search for another. By the time she finished, they'd reached her car.

"I'm checking out the Devil's Lair tomorrow." Touching the roof of the Civic, she said, "This is me."

"Are you sure you wanna go there?" Adam's forehead bunched up. "It's sort of … rustic."

"It's the best place to find the book, don't you think?"

Adam caught hold of her arm. "What time are you going? I'm not working tomorrow. I'll meet you there, and you won't have to go in alone."

Suzanna turned and gently slipped her arm free. She reached for the car door, but Adam jumped in front and opened it for her. The gesture felt strange and formal. As she got in, she considered his offer. What made him think she needed protection? It was true the bomber, or whatever, was still out there. It would probably be prudent to have company. She would also get to know Adam better. She slid down the driver-side window, the only control she'd figured out on the Civic. "Okay, if you're not busy, I'll meet you there. How's two?"

Adam flattened his back against the car to let a van pass but then tilted his head in the window. "Why not bring your guitar, and afterward, we can play duets at my place."

A red flag went up. Was this an innocent proposal or some plot to get her into bed?

Adam's tone became eager. "I've got at least one piece written specifically for cello and classical guitar. I can probably dig up more."

That piqued her interest. "Really? Such an unusual combo. Who's the composer?"

"Friedrich Burgmüller."

Suzanna shut her mouth tight. How embarrassing. She'd never heard of Burgmüller. "Should I bring my amp?"

"No, the balance will be fine without."

"I'm not so sure about that."

"You'll see."

Adam nodded toward the hatch crammed with Suzanna's gear. "That looks like a thief's dream."

She groaned. "That's the only issue with this car … no trunk."

"I bet guitars are a popular target."

"For sure. Guitars attract a lot more thieves than, say, trombones."

"Easy to carry, too. Not like the hassle of dragging a bulky cello around."

"Don't complain. The girl who plays after me at the Ristorante is a harpist. Imagine wheeling that thing around all the time."

"She must hate flute players. I know I do." Adam laughed and walked back to the sidewalk.

Suzanna started the Civic. "In my next life, I want to come back as a piccolo player!"

Still humming symphony melodies, Suzanna hauled her guitar up to the HB's bar. She wondered why she never saw the cop who was following her. He must be good at his job to stay so well hidden.

"Yo, what's up?" Vinny asked. "You ain't playing tonight."

"Just chilling after my date."

"With Cello Boy?" Vinny arched one thick brow. "How'd it go?"

She gave him a thumbs-up. "His name is Adam."

Vinny put down the glass he was drying and searched her eyes. "You two an item now?"

"Too soon to tell." Suzanna maneuvered her guitar between the barstools. "Can you keep this behind the bar? The rental has no trunk."

"Sure, but why ya got your ax?"

"I totally forgot to drop it at home. I've been spaced out since Friday."

Vinny's bicep bulged as he straight-armed her guitar over the bar as though it weighed no more than a toothpick. His sculpted, muscular build was so different from Adam's slender frame. The majority of guys she'd dated looked like Adam; none of them were hunks like Vinny. Most were musicians. What did she expect?

"Want anything to drink?" Without looking, Vinny reached up and pulled down a wine glass from the hanging racks. "How about some cab to calm your nerves? I've got a half-finished bottle left over by one of the tables. Expensive, too."

"Sounds good." Suzanna swiveled her back to the bar and studied the room. The bare, wooden tables and paper napkins were poor relatives to the Ristorante's embroidered chairs and tablecloths. Em was serving a table near the windows. Suzanna caught her eye and waved.

Vinny swept the glass of cabernet onto the bar, tucking a napkin under it at precisely the same time. "How's your noggin'?"

"Better." Suzanna patted the back of her head. "The lump is almost gone."

A plate shattered, and all eyes turned toward Emily. "It wasn't my fault," she said to the room at large.

"What was it then?" asked Vinny with a chuckle. "A sudden burst of gravity?"

With a puckered mouth and steely eyes, Em smoothed her apron, tightened her ponytail, and went for the broom closet. After sweeping up the mess, she dragged herself up to the bar. Tired creases gathered around her eyes as she flopped down on a stool and stifled a yawn.

"Up late studying?" Suzanna asked.

"Yeah, plus a long day waitressing. My feet feel like two bitches on a bitch boat." She sat down, folded her arms on the bar, and buried her head in them. Vinny set a cup of coffee next to her.

"You off now?"

Emily's voice came muffled through her arms. "Yep. Just have to cash out."

Vinny pulled out his condiment tray and lined up lemons on his cutting board. He looked up at Suzanna and asked, "Where'd you go on your date, anyway?"

Lifting her head, Em butted in and said with a snobbish lilt, "They went to the Philadelphia Orchestra." She bent her wrist affectedly while sticking out her little finger, then plunged her head back into her arms. Emily could be a challenging best friend.

Vinny layered his lemon slices between compartments of cherries and olives. "Gonna go out with him again?"

"Tomorrow."

Em's head popped up. "Moving a bit fast, aren't you?"

"We're only playing duets."

Narrowing her eyes, Em asked, "And where will you be playing these duets?"

"At his place, but—"

Emily sat up and half-laughed, half-snorted. "Ah, the horizontal tango."

"Why does everyone think I'm going to sleep with him right away?"

Em tugged her ponytail loose and let her hair fall down her back. "Who else thinks you're gonna jump in the sack with him?"

"My mom. And she has no room to talk."

"Just be careful."

"I can take care of myself." Suzanna wondered if she sent out vibes of helplessness or something. "Stop with the overprotective thing."

Em pursed her lips. "It was your car that burned up, right?"

"I was trying to forget about that." Suzanna hung her head.

"Any word from the cops?" Vinny asked.

"Nothing so far." She poked a finger at his chest. "What do you think? Why would anyone want to hurt me?"

Vinny stroked his chin. "Could be they think you're somebody else. So they're not after you, but somebody you sorta look like, or somebody with the same piece-a-junk rust bucket as you."

Suzanna frowned. "Unlikely."

"How 'bout this. Somebody wants to keep you quiet. Got some juicy dirt on anybody?"

"Oh for God's sake, Vinny." Suzanna put down her glass with a clink. The only secret she knew was that one of the waitresses got pregnant last month. Hardly a reason to bomb someone's car.

A customer at the other end of the bar waved, and Vinny glided over.

Emily sat up and propped her cheek in her hand. She plucked a cherry from Vinny's tray, pulled off the stem, and popped it in her mouth. Then she leaned in toward Suzanna and whispered, "Maybe Chris owes money to somebody like the Mob, and they're coming after you for it."

"They wouldn't get any money out of me. If they want bucks, they should go after his parents."

"Maybe they're only trying to scare you. You weren't actually killed Friday night, right?"

"Detective O'Brien thinks it was a botched job— basically, they missed. He even put an officer on protective duty, and he's shadowing me. I think."

Vinny nipped back just as Em reached for another cherry. He gave her hand a mild slap. "Cut it out, Emmy."

Em shook her hand as though his slap really stung.

Suzanna lowered her voice. "What do you think, Vinny? Could the Mob have planted the bomb?"

"If that was the Mob's doing, you'd be dead right now. Those guys don't make mistakes." He tucked a celery stick in a Bloody Mary and handed it over to a waiter.

Em tipped her head at the booths across the room. "There's two over there," she whispered. "I know a made man when I see one. Cute, too."

Vinny threw his drying rag over his shoulder and pointedly looked in the other direction.

Occasionally, Suzanna had noticed them, too. Not like she was an expert or anything, but after years of playing background, she could tell. They showed up at the HB or Ristorante Buena sharply dressed, dripping with confidence, but at the same time, watching their backs. The staff would run around and wait on them like they were royalty.

Vinny reached back and pulled down a bottle of Jack Daniel's. Em nabbed another cherry and threw it in her mouth. He shook his head at her. "I saw that."

Children's laughter surged from a corner booth. Three kids were climbing on a booth's leather backing and scraping their muddy shoes all over the seats. The parents ignored them.

"Look at that." Vinny chucked his towel down on the bar and glared at the family. "I'm getting Harry." He rushed away just as one kid did a handstand on the booth's seat.

"How's Chris?" asked Em.

"No idea."

"You should check the cabinet over the fridge in your apartment."

Suzanna pictured herself scrambling up on the counter to reach it. "Are you kidding?"

"That's where I saw him stash his booze."

"If I find hidden bottles, it just puts another nail in his blackmail coffin."

"Blackmail, hmm … I still say extortion."

"Blackmail, extortion." Suzanna swayed her open palms up and down like she was weighing something. "They both sound like I'm doing something illegal. All I want is the rent money."

A deep, brassy voice rang out above and behind Suzanna's back. "What's that about extortion?"

Looking over her shoulder, she saw State Senator Bancroft.

"This must be my lucky day." Bancroft bellied up to the bar alongside her. "Are you playing here tonight?"

Suzanna shook her head and tried to smile, but she could only think of that poor intern. Bancroft looked like he wanted to ask her something. What could he want from her? She hoped it had nothing to do with her mom's job. He looked a little tipsy, too. So awkward.

Em leaned across Suzanna. "Hey, Senator Bancroft, you're a lawyer. What's the diff between blackmail and extortion?"

"Blackmail is a type of extortion." As he delivered a detailed definition of each term, Em stuffed her head back in her folded arms, and Suzanna's eyes glazed over. "Bottom line, blackmail involves threatening to divulge damaging information for money."

Suzanna wished Em hadn't asked.

"Why do you ladies want to know about this?"

"Just wondering …" Suzanna rubbed her eyes.

"By the by, where's Vinny? I came over here to order another bottle of wine, not give a lecture on the law."

"Vinny's chasing down the boss," Suzanna said. She couldn't help thinking that Bancroft had had enough wine. His eyes were literally drooping. The man needed a nap and a glass of water. A second later, Harry and Vinny edged in behind the bar.

Harry's face lit up. "State Senator Bancroft! So nice to see you." He extended his hand.

While they chatted, Suzanna paid attention but couldn't decide whether Harry really liked the senator or was pandering to an important customer. She wondered what Harry would make of the intern incident.

Carrying a new bottle, Bancroft strutted back to his table. Everyone he walked past turned and gazed at him. Watching his command of the room, Suzanna worried even more about her mom. Maybe Bancroft was planning something behind her mom's back. Something to do with his opponent? Her mom once complained that Wallace played dirty, but she refused to stoop to his level. Maybe Bancroft was doing the stooping instead.

Vinny pulled the Guinness tap, filling a pint glass while he used his elbow to point out the offending booth to his boss. When Harry glanced over to size them up, the family was already packing up to leave. "Let them be."

Vinny's jaw dropped. "You're not gonna say something?"

"Not when they're about to go. Anyway, what's a little mud on the booths. Customer relations are more important."

Vinny shook his head and walked away. Sometimes Vinny and Harry seemed like best buds; other times, it was pretty clear who was the boss and who wasn't. Right now, it was plain as day. Vinny disapproved of that family, but no one was asking him.

Harry turned to Suzanna. "Any news on the explosion?"

"No, but we've been discussing it and agree on one thing: the Mob's not involved."

"Well, *that's* good to hear!"

Suzanna recoiled. Harry's sarcasm hit her hard. It wasn't like him.

He smiled and patted her shoulder. "Sorry, just on edge." Lowering his voice, he said, "And tired of putting on the happy face for people I can't stand." He turned around and went back to his office.

Did he mean Bancroft? If Harry didn't like the senator, there must be a good reason.

Suzanna cocked her head at Vinny. "Forget the Mob. How does the Jersey Devil book fit into all this?"

Vinny's face went blank. "What book?"

"Didn't you notice? The explosion blew it in with me."

Vinny leaned over and, in an ominous half-whisper, said, "That's spooky stuff. Don't mess with the Jersey

Devil." He tapped his fingertip down on the bar. "Lots of people right here in Haddonfield seen it."

Mid-sip, Em choked and spluttered her coffee back into her cup.

Vinny's tone switched to a hushed bark. "He's half dragon, half kangaroo, and possessed by the devil."

In the same solemn tone, Suzanna said, "That's the stupidest thing I ever heard."

He shook his head. "It's real."

Surprised Vinny took the legend seriously, Suzanna looked at him with a baffled frown.

Em elbowed her. "The Jersey Devil's a specialty subject of one of my psych professors."

"Is he the resource you were talking about yesterday?"

She nodded. "He's a well-known expert. Been on the radio and everything."

Vinny's brows pulled together, crinkling all the skin on his forehead toward his nose, while his gelled hair stayed in place like a helmet. "What's the Jersey Devil got to do with your psychology stuff?"

Em grinned. "Only people needing therapy believe in it."

Vinny snorted.

"Come on, Em," Suzanna said. "What's the connection?"

Em tilted her head back and studied the ceiling. "I don't know. It's my prof's specialty, not mine. We should go talk to him. He might have a lead on the book."

"Aw, come on. Anyone could've bought that book. How can your prof help?"

"I bet the crazies into the Jersey Devil are a pretty small group." Em glanced sideways at Vinny. "You never know."

Vinny swiped a sponge across the bar and gently shoved Em's propped arm from under her head. As her chin bobbed, she shot him an icy glare.

Turning back to Suzanna, Em said, "His lectures are fantastic. You should see him in class. He's really cool and hilarious."

Suzanna swiveled to Em and gave her a dubious glance. "Wait a minute. Is there some other reason you want to meet with this prof?" She fixed her eyes on her friend. "Let's have it."

Emily raised her pinched thumb and index finger and opened them an inch. "I may have a little crush on him." Her voice turned to a whisper. "I think he likes me, too, though."

"He flirts with you at school? That's not ethical … probably illegal."

"It's not like that. You know, we joke around a lot. Anyway, I'm only guessing."

It was just like Emily to think the professor flirted with her while thirty other students watched. "Okay, let's find out more about the kangaroo devil and, at the same time, see if your prof has a crush on you. Better than sitting around worrying about a mystery bomber."

"I'll text him right now." Emily grabbed her purse from behind the bar and pulled out her cell phone. "If he's down with it, I'm off Friday. You okay to go?"

Suzanna nodded. "Have to be back in time for work, though."

From a table near the bar, a customer let out a huge belly laugh and blared, "Then he took them to the cleaners!" Together, Suzanna and Vinny turned toward the voice.

"We got a loud talker today," said Vinny. "What makes him think we're all dying to hear what he's got to say?"

"Yeah, loud talkers come through clear as a bell when I'm playing," Suzanna said. "We get them at Ristorante Buena, too. At least he's not on a cell phone."

"Can you hear softer conversations when you're playing, too?" Vinny asked.

"When tables are close to me, I hear everything. People forget I'm there. They think I can't play and listen at the same time."

"They think you can't walk and chew gum." Vinny smiled down at the glass he was drying.

Suzanna took a sip of wine. It was nice to chat with someone who shared the same concerns. Vinny was her comrade in arms.

Em jumped off her stool. "All set. He said he'd be happy to help."

"Great. Friday, right?"

"Right. Gotta go cash out." Em turned and went back to the office.

Suzanna drained her wine glass and hopped down.

"Going home already?" Vinny asked.

"Need to rest my head and my nerves."

Vinny hauled her guitar out from behind the bar.

She gave him a grateful smile, gripped the handle, and wrestled her case through the HB's front door.

When Suzanna got home, she walked into an intense interrogation. Detective O'Brien was questioning Chris— more like grilling him. Chris sat meekly on the sofa, looking up at the detective. O'Brien towered over him, scribbling on his notepad.

Suzanna took a seat at the kitchen island and eavesdropped. The brisk professionalism of the detective's questions impressed her. O'Brien certainly knew what he was doing. She surprised herself; she was warming up to him.

There were dark circles under Chris's eyes when he walked up to Suzanna after O'Brien ended the session. He tapped the side of her guitar case. "Want me to take this to your room?"

An unusual offer. She nodded. Just when she thought Chris was going down the drain, he makes a decent gesture.

O'Brien turned to Suzanna. "The driver who struck your car and set off the bomb came to the station and confessed." His eyes stayed locked on Chris scuffling down the hall with Suzanna's guitar. "He's from down in Elmer and thought he caused the whole thing. Said he had to get it off his chest. And wanted his bumper back."

Suzanna sprang up. "Did he plant the bomb?"

"He had nothing to do with it."

"So, no news that actually helps."

"Don't think that way. He was never high on my list, but now we can eliminate him."

Suzanna plopped back in her chair.

O'Brien sat next to her in the kitchen. "I struggle to understand how the two of you make ends meet. Harry can't be paying you all that much."

"True. Chris's folks help him out, and I get decent tips. That's where the money is."

O'Brien squinted at her. "Does everyone tip you?"

"There are prime tippers and never tippers—nothing in between. And, of course, you've got your verbal tippers, who are useless."

"That's some serious profiling."

"Prime tippers are senior couples, single women, LGBT couples, men, and drinkers." Suzanna propped her head in her hand. "Never tippers are young people, like under twenty-five, and married women."

"Interesting. What are verbal tips?"

"People compliment you on your playing but don't put any money in the tip jar."

O'Brien winced. "I may have done that once in a New York restaurant. I didn't have any cash on me."

Suzanna shook her head. Point against O'Brien.

He yanked one side of his mustache and stood to go. She hoped he was chewing over his future tipping strategy. He looked her in the eye, a rarity for the detective. "Contact me for any reason. Even the smallest thing."

A hasty nod was the best she could muster.

"Keep your hopes up. We'll figure this out. Detective Higgins has been assigned to watch you tonight and tomorrow."

"Oh, wait a sec." Suzanna took a round lapel pin from her pocket and placed it in the detective's palm. "Emily asked me to give you this."

O'Brien glanced at the pin. A drawing of a bushy mustache filled the center. Above it read, *I mustache you a question*. Below it read, *But I'll shave it for later*.

Suzanna walked him to the door and watched him stomp down the stairs.

Chapter 25

Chris angled Suzanna's guitar carefully against the wall in her room. He pressed the button by the case's handle and inspected the empty, rectangular compartment. Then he spent some time investigating all the other compartments. Sighing, he snapped all the flaps shut and crossed the hall to his room.

He lay on his bed, staring at the ceiling and grumbling as he waited to get the kitchen to himself. He heard the creak of the apartment door closing and the bolt latch. Suzanna's footsteps tapped along the hardwood floor to her room. The coast was clear. As he slogged out to the kitchen, he considered making some dinner. Chris hadn't eaten anything since breakfast, but the detective's third-degree had crushed his appetite. Instead, he pulled down his half-empty bottle of gin and made himself a martini. He plopped in two extra olives to make it count as dinner. Tonight, the glass's slender stem felt clunky and wrong in his hand.

While he sipped, he vaguely worried about how hard it was getting to go without a drink and even harder to stop once he started. He knew that after this martini, he wouldn't stop drinking until he passed out.

When he finished off the gin, a vivid craving, the taste and smell of H, took hold of his tongue and nostrils. The desire was stronger than ever, but Chris was broke, and his stash was empty.

It had been a week and a day since a stupid snafu put him in the position of owing his dealer, Micky, a bundle. A thousand dollars, to be exact. He had a plan in motion to bring in the dough, but he'd just hit a stumbling block. And then, he lost the five hundred bucks this afternoon, too. He was supposed to pay Micky tonight, but now he'd have to ask for more time.

Chris steeled himself and made the call. Micky was so pissed. It was tricky, but he managed to sweet-talk and negotiate a week's extension. Another week *should* be more than enough time to get the thousand. Better be. Coming up with convincing excuses was getting harder by the day.

He had first met Micky a few months back at a seedy bar called Randy's in Pennsauken, a few miles from Haddonfield. Chris remembered it was right around Christmas, and almost half a foot of snow was on the ground.

Sitting at the bar, he'd downed shots of Kentucky bourbon using the holiday money his folks had sent. No one knew him at Randy's. That's why he was there. One too many drinking binges had made him infamous in Haddonfield's more fashionable bars.

A mucky film of snowy sludge covered the wood floor, and cold air whipped around him whenever someone opened the door. Micky took the seat beside him. Through Chris's bourbon goggles, Micky looked thoroughly respectable. He'd have won the best-dressed contest if there was one.

They got to talking, and somewhere along the way, Micky offered him eight Oxycodone tablets for a hundred bucks. If Chris hadn't been feeling flush that night, he never would have bought them. He had no clue that he was getting a sizable discount.

By the end of January, he was one of Micky's regulars. Then he ran out of cash and couldn't buy his weekly bag of Oxy.

Micky suggested a solution. A big haul was coming in, and he needed help with distribution. One of his crew had gotten busted and was in jail. Plus, he wanted an assistant his buyers didn't know. Chris fit the bill. With the promise of twenty bucks for every gram he sold, Chris jumped at the chance. Micky entrusted him with a thousand dollars' worth of dope and told him where to sell it. The scheme sounded painless … at first. That night, to sanction the deal, Micky gave him his first shot of China white.

The next day, Chris drove to his first buyer's house in a rough part of Philly near Temple University. Towers of garbage lined the neighborhood's sidewalks. The sanitation department had clearly just given up. The foul odors of urine, gas fumes, and rot made a potent stink. He wiped his watering eyes and held his nose.

Even with the less-than-perfect surroundings, completing the sale was a breeze. Easy money. Chris left, confident the rest of the deals would be a cinch, too. But as he swaggered back to his car, the sharp sting of a kidney punch knocked him to his knees in the filthy street. There were three of them. A swift blow to the side of his mouth splayed him out facedown. They took his puffer jacket, his backpack, and even his sneakers. The entire thousand dollars' worth of drugs was in that backpack.

Practically crawling, Chris crossed the city block to his car. When he'd reached the front bumper, he fell against it and retched, spitting out the metallic taste of blood along with the bile. Then he sat on the curb and waited for waves of nausea to pass. When he finally got in his car, he glanced in the mirror and flinched at his swollen eye and bloodied lip. With his sleeve, he mopped away the blood and filth from his face.

Close to tears, he'd agonized over what Micky would say or, worse, do. Sweat beads popped out on his upper lip. The mugging had been painful, but Micky … he meant business. Chris had witnessed firsthand how he tore into buyers who owed him. And one night, over drinks, Micky casually admitted that he had whacked someone as though it was a badge of honor.

Seizing the steering wheel in a death grip, his stocking foot on the gas, Chris escaped back to New Jersey.

Relieved to find Suzanna out, he paced the apartment, rehearsing explanations for Micky. By the time he was ready and made the call, he was panting.

"They got everything."

"What do you want me to do? Stupid idiot, carrying your whole supply!"

"All right, but now what?" Chris tensed his arms, and pain ran through his ribs.

"You get me the money for all of it—whether you sold it or not."

Chris's eyes filled with tears. "How?"

"Not my problem. Just get me the dough by next Saturday."

"Saturday? But that only gives me one week!" An icy shiver slipped down Chris's back.

Micky let out a snide chuckle. "Okay. A week and a day, then. Next Sunday." His voice turned menacing. "That's the 12th I'm talking."

Chris was numb. "How can—"

"Let me lay this out for you. You bring me the money, and I won't have someone break all your fucking fingers." Micky hung up.

He couldn't remember now what story he'd given Suzanna about the bruises, but she bought it and left him alone. So many lies to keep track of. Already his lie to her about the event planner stuck in his dry throat.

Focus. With no concerts or big gigs lined up, Chris had to find a way to get Micky's money. An old and unwelcome money-grubbing strategy popped into his head: play background music. No. No way. He could never earn enough in time *that* way. Obviously, he needed more gin.

Anyway, if he ever did return to playing background jobs, he'd never be able to admit it to Suzanna. Besides, background gigs had horrible working hours, always when other people were out enjoying themselves—nights, weekends, and holidays. His meager social life would go to hell. And all the holiday songs he'd have to learn come fall. God, he hated Christmas music. And the stupid guitar jokes: if you keep picking that thing, it won't get better; don't fret, no strings attached …

As he tossed the empty gin bottle in the trash, he spotted Suzanna's gallon jug of cheap sangria on the kitchen counter. She'd bought the wine for some dinner party that never happened.

Chris sat at the island and drummed his fingers. His gaze returned to the gallon jug. Usually, he wouldn't touch such rotgut. He opened the fridge and closed it. He looked back at the jug. In the morning, he was gonna have a hangover from the gin. Why not make it epic?

At three in the morning, Chris sat bolt upright in bed, wide awake. Everything after his second martini was a haze. He still felt drunk and had a blazing headache. Propped against the wall by his bed, the wine jug stared at him. It didn't hold a drop. Did he drink all of it by himself? His aching head answered the question. Damn. Crappy wine, and so much of it. He tried to swallow, but his tongue was stuck to the roof of his mouth.

After several attempts, he stumbled out of bed and seized the jug. If he got rid of the evidence, Suzanna might not notice. Cradling the jug in his arms, he bumped back and forth between the hallway walls to the kitchen.

He sloppily yanked the front door open, and it banged against the wall. Frozen in place, he listened for any movement from Suzanna. Silence.

By moonlight, he lumbered down the wooden stairs to the recycle bin that sat on a cement slab. He lobbed the jug into the bin like he was shooting a basket. It missed by a mile. When it smashed into pieces on the cement, a light switched on inside the apartment. Across the street, a car door slammed. Chris twisted around. Standing beside a patrol car, a cop glared at him with his hands on his hips.

Chapter 26

Monday, May 13

Suzanna drove down King's Boulevard on her way to the Devil's Lair. She'd left early. If she beat Adam to the shop, she would have breathing room to explore on her own. She didn't cross paths with Chris before leaving. The thought of seeing or talking to him made the bump on her head hurt. Smashing that wine jug in the middle of the night was the final straw. Detective Higgins had helped her clean up the glass and drag Chris upstairs.

As she passed the tiered gazebo in the center of town, Suzanna slid the driver-side window down and let the breeze ruffle her hair. Children ran circles around the gazebo's edge, shrieking in high-pitched bursts.

Wincing, she slid the window back up and wondered if Adam wanted kids. She could ask but didn't want to jump the gun. Most of the guys she'd dated, especially musicians, had agreed that when you added up all the hours needed for daily practice, evening gigs, and self-marketing, there was no time left over to care for a child. Not enough to be a good parent anyway.

Suzanna cruised out of Haddonfield and over Route 30 into the rural farmland of South Jersey. Orchards of blossoming peach trees alternated with green fields of lettuce, scallions, and young corn. At the same time, cheek-by-jowl suburban cottages dwindled to a handful of weather-worn farmhouses. She could see for miles over the flat New Jersey landscape. At least, it seemed that way. Not a mountain, not even a hill in sight.

An ever-increasing number of pitch pines poked out of the fields signaling, or warning, that she was closing in on the Pine Barrens. An earthy odor of rotting wood and wet leaves made her sniffle. She rifled through her purse for a tissue.

The farmland abruptly transformed into a thick forest of soaring evergreens. Suzanna was thrown into a dark shade and silence, like she was driving into a tunnel. The pine needles coating the ground muted the woodland sounds. Only the harsh crunch of pinecones under the car's tires broke the stillness.

Potholes peppered the road's surface, challenging the Civic's shock absorbers. The ruts grew deeper and more ragged with each mile. Speed limit signs and mileage markers were either missing or trashed and illegible. Clearly, state tax dollars were not being spent on road maintenance in the Pine Barrens.

By the time Suzanna pulled up to the first major crossroad of the trip, the crisp tang of woody pine had invaded every inch of the car. The odor was refreshing but overpowering. A green, metal signpost stood on one side of the road—the first sign in decent condition she'd seen since entering the Pine Barrens. She strained her neck to read it.

Welcome to Indian Mills
Celebrated Ann Roberts, Indian Ann, last of the
Delawares in the state
resided here until her death in 1894. She has become a
legend in the Pines.

That sort of explained where the Indian part of the town's name came from, but was there a mill, too?

Ahead on the right, well back from the road, sat an ancient gas station with grubby, white stucco siding. Across the building's top, the words *Indian Mills Auto Repair* were barely visible in faded, red paint. On the other side, a boxy, brick, two-story building housed a mom-and-pop grocery store and the Indian Mills Pizzeria. A slim, wooden porch ran the building's length and held two sun-bleached Adirondack rockers. As the breeze rocked the unoccupied chairs, Suzanna imagined the ghosts of two young country girls sitting out, enjoying the spring weather. On the porch's far end, a dingy soda machine leaned against the brick siding, looking tired.

Downtown Indian Mills—the dictionary definition of Hicksville.

The Devil's Lair, per Google Maps, could be found two miles beyond the Indian Mills intersection. As she drove on past the grocery store and auto repair shop, thick forest surrounded her again. Not another building appeared until she came to the Devil's Lair itself.

Suzanna pulled into the dirt parking lot and surveyed the shop's sloping porch and rotting cedar shakes. In better times, the parking area would've been the shack's front yard, but it was hard to imagine a lawn ever existed. The only hint that she'd come to the right place was a crude three-by-four mounted on the roof with the words *Devil's Lair* burnt into the wood.

As she got out of the car, a pulsing energy vibrated across her shoulders, urging her heartbeat to get in sync. She stamped her feet, trying to force out the sensation. Unsuccessful, she concentrated on calming her breathing and walked toward the porch steps. Up close, the shack looked even shabbier.

Suzanna tested each ramshackle porch tread with her toe, skipping the rotten ones that had a slight give. On the top step, she froze as a mouse skittered across the sloping planks. Steeling herself, she crept up to the front door.

The warped door required a shoulder thump to even budge. She muscled the doorknob, and when it finally gave way, she toppled inside, almost falling over. Straightening up, she looked into the fierce snarl of a man-size bear rearing up on its hind legs. The dark-brown grizzly loomed over her, its claws gleaming and at the ready. She flinched and hopped back.

Looking closer, Suzanna saw light shimmering off the glass eyes. The faint scent of animal hide drifted out as she patted the velvety fur. It felt so real.

A voice boomed from the depths of the room. "Don't touch the bear."

Suzanna pivoted toward the voice. Behind a long, glass display case sat a man of indeterminate age with a straggly beard. He was reading a book and looked so content, that she wondered if someone else had called out the warning.

The merchandise mounted on the walls—guns and fishing gear—looked foreign and threatening. The floorboards creaked under her feet as she crossed the room. A rifle, obviously not for sale, was balanced against the wall. Where was all the Jersey Devil stuff?

With a final, creaky footstep, Suzanna reached the front of the case. Now she could see that the man's T-shirt featured one of the scarier drawings of the Jersey Devil. The glass case's top served as a counter. Inside, an extensive selection of Jersey Devil memorabilia stretched across a stark-white cloth—hats, books, T-shirts, figurines, jewelry, mugs, posters, and most notably, a bobblehead.

She cleared her throat and summoned her boldest assertive voice. "I'm interested in a specific book about the Jersey Devil. *The Jersey Devil: Phantom of the Pines*."

The man flipped his book over and spread it on the counter facedown. He looked up at her and frowned through his beard. "Why that one?"

Not up for sharing her story, Suzanna ignored the question. "Do you have it?"

"Out of stock." He snatched up his book and went back to reading.

"Will you order it again?"

He slapped his book closed and put it on a shelf behind him. That's when she realized he was sitting on a rolling desk chair. He pushed off with one foot and rolled to the opposite end of the glass case. Pointing at a different paperback, he said, "We got this one."

Suzanna edged along the display case and inspected *The Strange History of the Jersey Devil*. It looked interesting, but it wasn't what she came for. "No, thanks. Can I order the other one?"

With one push, he rolled back to the other end of the case. "Can't. The guy only comes once in a while with a box of them."

"So he's self-published?"

"Guess so. Makes 'em himself. I just sold the last one."

Suzanna perked up. "Have you got records of everyone who bought it?"

He snorted and shook his head. "Nah, don't keep lists like that."

"Do you remember who bought the last one?"

The man raked his fingers through his beard and looked at the ceiling. "I think … some tattooed, greasy-haired geek."

Considering this fellow's beard, shaved head, and, now that she looked, multiple tattoos, it seemed a strange criticism. "Know his name?"

"No idea." He handed her a yellow legal pad and pen. "Name and phone number. When the guy brings more in, I'll call."

While she wrote, Suzanna asked about the town's history. The man grudgingly explained that Indian Mills used to be the one and only Indian reservation in New Jersey. The Lenni Lenape tribe, aka the Delawares, worked out some deal with the state, built a sawmill, and tried to scrape by. With no success, they ended up migrating to Wisconsin.

"So there *is* a mill. And Indian Ann?" she asked.

"A few Lenape stayed. Ann was the last of them to die off."

Suzanna considered the fate of the Delawares in New Jersey but couldn't make the connection. "How does the Jersey Devil fit in?"

"Why ya wanna know about the Jersey Devil? He's pure evil."

"How do you know?"

The man's eyes grew dark. "I've seen him."

Her pulse surged. "Where?"

"Over by the old sawmill. Follow the trail back of here." He jerked his thumb over his shoulder. "Takes you right to Mill Pond."

He pulled his book down from the shelf, signaling the conversation's end. But Suzanna still had questions.

"Is the mill working?"

Without looking up from his book, he said, "Nah. Been empty for years, gone to rack and ruin."

"And the Jersey Devil?"

He sighed and dropped the book again. "The Devil likes that old mill, his favorite spot outside of Leeds."

The conviction in his voice was disorienting, like believing in the Jersey Devil's existence was the most natural thing on earth. It didn't make sense that so many people thought the monster was real, even Vinny. "Maybe I'll check out the mill and catch a glimpse of him."

"You'll find his claw marks on a big, old rock beside the log chute. But lady, go in daylight. Night's his feeding time."

"If I met the Jersey Devil at night, what would he do?" Suzanna asked.

The man locked eyes with her. His upper lip curled to show a row of rotting teeth. "Rip the flesh off your bones and eat it!"

At that moment, the warped door behind her scraped open. She let out a faint, anxious whimper and spun around, not knowing what to expect.

Adam bounded into the shop and shook his head at her. "I thought we were coming in together?"

Suzanna exhaled noisily and relaxed her shoulders. "I'm not helpless, you know." She appreciated his concern over the bombing, but he was babying her just like Harry did.

Adam pouted like a lost puppy. "You could've waited for me."

The man's nose was back in his book. As they turned to leave, she peeked at the name of his book. *Moby Dick.* Could it be that he equates the White Whale with the Jersey Devil? Interesting.

They left the shop without disturbing him. From the porch, Suzanna spied a blue Toyota, old but in decent shape, parked next to her rental. "Yours?"

"Not as nice as your new Civic."

"Jealous?"

Adam laughed. Suzanna liked the way he laughed. Genuine but not too loud. Without being obvious, she tried to look him over. His coffee-colored shirt brought out his black-brown eyes, and he'd made a questionably successful attempt at tidying his hair. He appeared to be growing a five-o'clock-shadow beard. Trendy. Adam was full of contradictions. His hair, clothes, and now this fashionable beard all clashed with his traditional manners.

"Did you see the sign about Indian Ann at the crossroads?" Adam supported her arm as they went down the porch steps. No one had ever held her arm before. Did she like it? She wasn't sure.

"I got the whole story from that guy in there." At the bottom of the stairs, she took her arm back.

"How about the sign in the back about the sawmill?" He led her behind the Devil's Lair to the start of a trail where another well-maintained green marker stood.

Sawmill

"Site of water-powered sawmill in operation for more than two centuries built on the site of original Indian sawmill. Operations ceased in early 1900s."

Suzanna imagined sawmill workers in baggy overalls and flat, wool caps using harpoons to float logs through the pond to the mill. Younger laborers, maybe children, would guide them up a chute to be sliced into wood slabs.

"How cool." Suzanna hopped onto the trail. "Let's go take a look."

"But we won't have time for duets." Adam shuffled his feet.

"It'll only take a minute. Come on, it's an adventure."

She took the lead, and Adam followed close behind. Their shoes sank into the spongy moss covering the path. An occasional pinecone flattened underfoot.

The trail's end opened to a wide, grassy field beside the pond. Across the field, along the edge of the water, sat the derelict sawmill.

"It looks a lot like an old barn, doesn't it?" Adam asked.

Suzanna sized up the mill's mostly intact stone foundation. It contrasted with the bleached and tattered wood of the two upper stories. "An old barn with a wheel attached." She pointed at the giant wheel sagging into the pond.

Adam crossed the field to a long chute jutting out from the mill's upper floor, while Suzanna held back to scrape mud off the soles of her sneakers. She put all her weight on one foot and braced her back against a tree. Something hard rolled under her foot and then snapped. In the soil by her feet, she discovered a handful of scattered, frail bones. Examining one, she could make out teeth marks. It had been chewed.

"Find something?" Adam called from the mill. He jogged back and examined the bone in her hand. "Interesting."

"A small critter?"

Adam sniffed the bone. "It must be old." He poked the other remains with his toe. "I think they're from a dog."

"Oh no!" The thought of it being a dog skeleton tugged at her heart. A slight shudder ran through her shoulders. She dropped the bone and turned away.

They walked together along the pond's bank to the mill. A gentle incline led up to a gaping entrance at the front where double doors should've been. Suzanna crouched by a huge rock and brushed her fingers over three long scrapes on its side. "The guy at the shop said these marks were made by the Jersey Devil."

"Local nonsense."

She held her tongue, unsure and frankly confused about the whole Jersey Devil story. Talking to Em's professor and getting an expert's opinion would help. She looked forward to it.

Adam turned and walked into the mill. Suzanna watched him disappear. Surprised by sudden goosebumps, she leaped up and hurried after him.

Suspended from the mill's inside walls, hung rotting gears and pulleys mixed with dirt and cobwebs. Suzanna tried to take one of the pulleys down, but it fell into pieces.

In the center, she came to a scary contraption resembling a guillotine but without a blade. Just looking at it triggered her frayed nerves. She anxiously searched over her shoulder for Adam. He was examining a long, worn table crammed with a pile of flat belts, cables, and ropes in varying states of decay. He held the back of his hand up to his nose. "It smells like something died in here."

Suzanna joined him at a broad window where a log chute poked through. Her nerves settled down as soon as she stood beside him. A good sign. "You know what? This would be a cool building to turn into a restaurant or dinner theater-type thing."

"I can totally see that." Adam's gaze scanned the room's perimeter. "But as proprietor, I would only allow the performance of classical music or Randy Newman."

She laughed with him. "Or Counting Crows."

"Who?"

"The indie rock band. They've been my favorite for years."

"Did they do 'Round Here?'"

Suzanna nodded with glowing eyes. "I think their longevity makes them unique. And they just recorded a new CD this year—one of their best!"

Adam held up his hands as if at gunpoint. "Okay, okay. Classical music, Randy Newman, and Counting Crows."

"Perfect. We can display all these mill relics behind glass and have booklets full of information on how it used to work."

"And a stage along this side." He swept his arm across one wall.

Suzanna let out a sigh. "It would cost a fortune."

"Good idea, though."

She wandered outside and down to the pond while Adam inspected the guillotine wannabe. Standing on the pond's edge, she was surprised by a school of carp. The fish glared up, puckering and unpuckering their mouths. Somebody around here must feed them. She held on to a tree branch and bent over the water to make faces back at them.

Pounding footfalls rushed toward her from behind. Out of nowhere, Adam's arm flashed in front of her. "You'll fall in!"

Suzanna jerked backward, pushing Adam sideways. One of his legs splashed into the pond, the murky water up to his knee. His arms shot out, trying to regain his equilibrium, but he lost the battle. She grabbed his elbow, keeping him from falling in altogether. As he clambered up onto the bank with her pulling him by the sleeve, a massive shadow flew over them, shading the entire pond. She threw her head back, but the sky was empty. Her throat tightened.

Adam sat in the tall grass, attempting to wring out his sock. "That musta been an eagle or big owl, something like that."

He put his sock and shoe back on and stood in front of Suzanna. A bit of red crept up his face. "Thanks. I meant to save you, not the other way around."

Suzanna wanted to tell him she wasn't a damsel in distress but figured it would only make him feel worse.

Adam turned toward the trail. "Let's get out of here." He shook out his pant leg and started back, his shoe squishing with every step. The sun, low in the sky, reminded her of the bearded man's warning. She jogged after him, and they set a brisk pace.

At the cars, Adam glanced at his watch. "Almost dinnertime. Can't play duets on an empty stomach. We could drive to Haddonfield, or I could try to cook—"

"Have you tried the Indian Mills pizza?"

"Perfect idea."

Suzanna followed Adam's Toyota to the pizzeria and waited for him on the porch. How odd. Pizza in the middle of nowhere.

Chapter 27

Adam pulled out from the pizzeria and waved for her to follow. In less than ten minutes of driving through deep woods, a *Welcome to Pipers Corner, NJ* sign appeared made of beat-up metal. The town amounted to nothing more than dense woodlands—no downtown, no traffic light, and not even a convenience store. Not that Indian Mills was a snappy hot spot, but on her way to the Devil's Lair, she'd driven right through Pipers Corner without even realizing it.

Adam turned sharply onto a single-lane, paved road that sliced into the forest. Suzanna peeked at the mint-condition street sign as she turned—*Owl's Way*. The street looked like someone had hacked it out with a machete, then hastily spread macadam before the wilderness could reclaim the land.

Owl's Way ended in a parking lot attached to four long rows of upscale, multistory townhouses. Brand-spanking new, tucked away in the heart of the Pine Barrens, they almost glittered.

As Suzanna unloaded her guitar, Adam took it out of her hand and carried it to one of the knotty pine front doors. How in the world could he tell which townhouse was his? They all looked the same.

He held the door while she crossed the threshold and passed a convoluted wall security panel. The entryway opened into a spacious area with cathedral ceilings, featuring long, skinny skylights. Muted recessed lighting filled the room, and oriental rugs spread across the hardwood floors. She assumed this space was the living room, but it was bigger than her kitchen and living room combined.

Everything was spotless. The furniture and decor were brand new and ultramodern. Suzanna's taste ran more traditional, but she appreciated the quality. She understood why he lived way out here. This townhouse would cost big bucks in Philly or even Haddonfield.

Adam stowed her guitar beside his cello under a bay window overlooking the parking lot. He shook his wet pant leg and pointed up a flight of stairs. "I need to change."

On her own in the lofty living room, she took a good look around. Not snooping. It was impossible to snoop. No personal effects were on display. There weren't even photos for her to examine.

Suzanna wandered to the back of the house and found the kitchen. It was pristine. Adam must never cook. She peeked in the refrigerator, only ketchup and milk. Footsteps echoed on the hardwood floor, and she shut the refrigerator door just in time.

"Do you like to cook?" Adam asked in a way she thought sounded hopeful.

"Not really. Most of the time, I eat at my gigs."

"I have trouble just boiling water." He nodded his head at a set of sliding glass doors. "Let's have our pizza on the back deck." He pulled out plates from the glossy cupboards.

Suzanna stepped out onto a roomy pine deck with a lovely woodland view. She sat at a round umbrella table and ran her hand over the top. Pricey.

The setting sun lit the swaying pine tops as Adam poured sparkling water. They shared the pizza and talked music. It was the most delicious pizza she ever ate.

As dusk settled in, she noticed the other decks were empty. "Does anyone else live in this development?"

"So far, only me and two couples. It's so new, the units haven't sold out yet."

Suzanna tried but couldn't make it add up. Everything · was too upscale. "Do you have a roommate?"

"No, I'm on my own. I only moved in a couple months ago."

Suzanna gave up on subtlety. "Well then, what's your day job? Even way out here in Pipers Corner, you're not living like this on a Haddonfield Symphony paycheck."

Adam laughed and shook his head. "My other gig is in Atlantic City playing in the Trump Casino backup orchestra."

"What a great gig!" She gave him an elbow nudge. "Now I get why you live in Pipers Corner—it's halfway between Haddonfield and Atlantic City. Smart. Do you like working at the casinos?"

"Yeah, but it's a huge compromise from a concert career."

"Everyone graduating from music school ends up making some compromises." Suzanna patted his shoulder empathetically, then pulled back her hand. This relationship had too much potential to jinx it by moving too fast. "We all leave college thinking we're gonna become famous concert soloists, but then, survival gets in the way."

He sat back with a wistful smile. "It's just impossible to make a living playing concerts if you're not Yo-Yo Ma."

"Or Segovia."

Adam folded his arms and smirked. "But at the casinos, I played backup for so many of the big stars— Barry Manilow, Tony Bennett, Tom Jones—the list goes on and on." He lowered his eyes, and his voice softened. "You must know how it is, Suzanna. You play so beautifully, and yet you're plucking out background music in restaurants."

"Sure, I know what you're saying. Get this. My conservatory class was lucky enough to perform all our senior recitals at Carnegie Hall. And I have to admit, I got a standing ovation."

"Looks impressive on your resume, I bet."

"Yeah, not that it gets me any background work." Suzanna took a sip of water. "That very night, I was back playing at the HB. I'll never forget one woman criticizing me for 'making some bloopers.' I wanted to shout to the rafters, 'But I just got a standing O at Carnegie Hall!'"

"Ouch! That's gotta hurt." Adam edged toward her, studying her face with those puppy dog eyes.

Sensing he was about to kiss her, Suzanna sat back in her chair. It felt too soon. "My roommate is idealistic about playing only concerts." She shook her head. "Half the time, he can't pay all his rent. And his ego …"

Adam sat back, too. "I know the type."

Suzanna put on a British accent. "What is the intrinsic value of being a musician, and what propels us to perform for little reward?" She sighed and, in her regular voice, said, "I mean, I do get it. There is something special about what we do. But that doesn't make us superior."

Adam got up and leaned against the deck railing, looking out at the forest. "No. It makes us lucky."

Suzanna joined him, rubbing her hands together to warm them. "Chris says it makes us exceptional, but then, he thinks he's better than everybody else."

"He doesn't have to make his own living, does he?"

"Not completely; his folks help."

Adam nodded. "Figures."

"He says background music is more than a compromise. It's a surrender."

"He's asking for a hard life."

"What do you think about tips? Chris thinks they're demeaning."

"At gigs, where they're approved, I'm all for it. But you have to be careful. Once, I played a job where parents let their children put tips in my jar. It was adorable, and the kids got such a kick out of it."

Suzanna listened to Adam's story about children with uncertainty. She'd decided so long ago she didn't want kids. Anxious to know his view, she considered bringing it up. Maybe this was the right time … or perhaps she would wait.

"Three little girls kept coming up to my tip jar and scrounging in their tiny purses. I thought it was so cute." He chuckled softly. "Later, their mother apologized and put like ten bucks in my jar. Turns out those naughty girls weren't putting money in my jar—they were taking it out." Adam bumped his shoulder against hers.

What did that bump mean? That he really liked kids or that he really liked her? Either way, the familiarity was pleasant. Quite chummy. It was the perfect moment to have the 'kids talk,' but she wimped out. Suzanna sat back down at the table, not sure why she was being a coward.

After clearing the plates and pizza box, Adam joined her. "You get requests at the HB, right? That should bring in tips."

"Right, hefty tips at that, but there's no guarantee. One time at the HB, a man requested a fairly obscure Renaissance piece. I just happened to know it, a fluke. As I played, the guy stood in front of me and watched every note I plucked."

"How much did he tip after all that?"

Suzanna held up her index finger. "One dollar."

"No!"

"He must think every guitarist just happens to know that piece. You don't get that kind of treatment at the casino, do you?"

Adam pursed his lips. "It's different. But the megastars we play backup for should at least talk to us. Only the nice ones do." He put his elbow on the table and his chin in his hand. "Any bigwigs come to Ristorante Buena?"

"Some famous Eagles football players come in, and sometimes local politicians." She raised her eyebrows and tilted her head. "And one time … Willem Dafoe!"

Suzanna laughed at herself, and Adam chimed in. It was great talking to someone besides Chris about music life. "Someday, I want to get a job in academia."

"Hope you liked going to school. You'll need a master's, maybe a PhD."

"I know. But I want to work in music *and* have a reliable income."

"Far as I know, a college gig is the only way to do that."

With the sun gone, the wind gusted cold across the deck, a reminder that it wasn't summer yet. Suzanna tugged her jacket around her neck.

Adam reached for her hand. "Come on. Let's get inside and make some music."

He led her to a pair of upholstered chairs near the bay window. She sat down and tapped her heels; she'd been looking forward to this. A lot could be learned about a person from playing music with them. And duets, in particular, generated a special connection between the players.

Peering up at the cathedral ceiling, Suzanna wondered about the acoustics. To hear the echo, she clapped her hands. "Wow, natural reverb."

Adam smiled, obviously proud of his house. She reached out and touched the glass end table beside her. It was stiff and cold like she imagined the rest of the furniture would feel. Maybe he had hired someone to furnish his place. The stark house didn't reflect any part of the guy she was getting to know. Adam opened his cello case, and the light scent of spruce and varnish filled the room.

Suzanna took a deep breath and savored the familiar odor. "I love that smell. My guitar is made of spruce, too."

"Don't you worry that your guitar will get chipped or smashed at the HB? All the waitresses and clumsy customers."

"I should. Good classical guitars can cost up to ten grand. My mom had to help me buy mine."

"Don't get me started on instrument prices." Adam took out his bow. "This bow alone was two grand."

Suzanna eyed the bow and shook her head. The cello must've cost a bunch more. His parents probably helped him, too, but she wasn't going to ask. She noticed he never talked about his family. Doubtless, there was a story there, but she'd wait for him to tell her in his own time. "I think about getting a cheap guitar for gigs, but I can't stand playing anything but this." She patted her guitar case.

Adam's voice took on an edge. "No such thing as a cheap cello."

"At the HB, I worry more about the noise. It's not like playing for a concert audience where everyone is quiet."

Adam perked up, and his words flew out. "Why don't you play in Atlantic City? The money's better, and I never see any classical guitarists."

"There's a reason for that." Suzanna's shoulders drooped, hating to stifle his enthusiasm. "The rooms in AC are ginormous, so even with amplification, I wouldn't be heard."

"Too bad."

"No big deal. I enjoy playing background in restaurants."

Adam tightened his bow and swished it through the air. He handled it so gracefully that she had to pry her eyes away. "Background gigs can double as practice time." He bent over and set up his endpin. "I hate to say it, but I doubt many people would notice if you only played scales."

Suzanna nodded. "I just don't want to turn out like this guy I ran into at a wedding reception a few years back." She shut her eyes, picturing it. "He was playing a keyboard near an hors d'oeuvre table. A crowd of people had filed by, loading their plates. He smiled at each person while pounding out 'Memories' from *Cats*."

"I've seen that, too."

"But I *knew* him. He was in my conservatory class. We had a long chat, and the whole time, he played 'Memories' over and over. He might as well have been a recording."

Adam nodded. Then, as if gently holding a baby, he rested the cello's neck against his shoulder. He flicked his hair back and pointed his bow, motioning for Suzanna to take out her guitar.

She bent down and unfastened her case's latches. As she pulled out her guitar, a molded flap opened underneath the case's handle. It revealed a small, rectangular nook that she hadn't seen before.

Adam stretched his arm past her and ran his fingers around the edges of the empty compartment. "Bet that's for a cell phone."

Suzanna bit her lower lip. His movement had looked incredibly sensual. He probably didn't mean it that way. Her libido was working overtime. Quickly removing her teeth from her lip, she chucked her phone inside the chamber and snapped it shut. "You're right. Perfect fit." Cradling her guitar, she settled into her chair and watched Adam tuning. With his instrument in his arms, he looked so confident … confident in a way she hadn't seen before. His fingers moved nimbly over the cello's neck.

"Nocturne for cello and guitar by Friedrich Burgmüller," he said, stretching around his cello to set the scores on two polished-brass music stands. "I think you'll like it."

"I'm still skeptical about this combo without amplifying my guitar. You'll have to be careful not to play over me."

"Let's give it a try and see." A slight smile came and went from Adam's lips. "I'll make sure not to overpower you."

Was there a double entendre in there, or was she still imagining things? Checking his face, she couldn't tell. Suzanna turned her attention to the music, noting the composer's dates at the top of the page. The piece had been composed in the late 1800s, specifically for cello and classical guitar. The pairing was as rare in that era as today. A rare pairing … maybe like Adam and her?

He set the tempo and they began, the guitar plucking graceful arpeggios while the cello bowed a slow, elegant melody. From the first phrase, Suzanna was astounded by its beauty. The volume of Adam's cello balanced perfectly with her guitar.

She gave herself over to the music, her pulse quickening to the beat. The strings' vibrations beneath her fingers melded with the low, throaty sound of Adam's down-bowing. Their bodies swayed with the entwining harmonies. Instinctively, they played off each other's phrases. The theme crescendoed, and their physical effort increased. Movements and emotions in sync, they merged with the music and each other. The intimacy raised Suzanna's artistry and her passion. It was an intimacy that only came from playing duets or making love.

As their instruments blended for the closing cadence, Suzanna closed her eyes as she played. Her final chord and Adam's last vibrato lingered in the air for what seemed like hours. She didn't open her eyes until Adam took her hand and kissed it. A slow shudder shimmied up her arm. He looked like he was going to do or say something else. She held her breath.

He gazed into her eyes. "You are so beautiful—"

Suzanna stifled a snicker and looked away. "Except for my nose."

Adam blinked and released her hand. "What's wrong with your nose?"

"Well, it's a little on the large side, don't you think?" This was so embarrassing. But she couldn't get away from it. She had a big nose. "Chris says I should get a nose job."

"What a jerk."

"It's not just him. Once at the HB, a little boy asked me if I was Jewish. He said his mother told him that people with big noses were Jewish." She lowered her gaze and shook her head. "Kids!"

"Don't blame the kids. Blame the parents."

"I guess. You really don't mind my nose?"

"Not at all. I love that your face is pretty *and* unique. Your nose is the crucial part."

Suzanna stared at him, unsure what to say or do. This could be a turning point—someone actually liked her nose. She thumbed a faint melody on her bass strings.

Adam turned in his seat and pulled more music from a back shelf. They played through several Baroque suites, though none held the magic of the Burgmüller. She stood up to stretch out her back but stopped mid-stretch. Time had flown by. It was pitch black outside.

"There are two more Burgmüllers we can try," Adam suggested.

Liking her nose was one thing, but Suzanna could see where this was going. She knew if they played another Burgmüller she'd be in his arms, and her mom was right. It was too soon for that. "Sorry, but I really have to go now." She crouched down and put her guitar in its case. "Thank you for a lovely time."

"Wait, before you go, I want to show you something. Grab your jacket." Adam took her hand and led her out onto the deck. Tiny, twinkling lights outlined the railing, doors, and windows. He stood her at the railing. "Close your eyes."

She didn't hesitate.

"Hold on." He clicked a switch. "Now, look up."

Suzanna gasped. Adam had turned off the sparkling lights, exposing a vast, black sky speckled with crystalline stars. Without light pollution, it was like she could see for a million miles.

The sight of the stars' icy mist, combined with the cool night air, made her shiver. He put his arm around her and kissed her forehead. His soft, scruffy beard nuzzled her brow.

They stood, staring up at the Milky Way in silence.

Adam spoke first. "Do you think you'll ever stop performing?"

"Why would I stop?"

"Some women do—"

"Are you talking about having children?" Suzanna looked at him with a pained frown. They were gonna have the 'kid talk' after all, and she didn't like the way it was starting. "Children were never part of my plan. You know, the musician thing, the career is too consuming. And if I'm ever going to go back to school …"

The corners of Adam's mouth drooped, and he focused on the ground. "Oh, right."

To break the tension, she gave him a gentle jab in the ribs. "Come on. I'm an only child. I was never exposed to children and never got the 'have-a-kid' memo." She turned her head back toward the sky. "Now Emmy, she wants a ton of kids. Of course, she helped raise four younger brothers."

"You're set on this?"

That scared her. Was this an imperative for him? "I've been set on this for a long time. How could I keep up practicing, work toward a college gig, and take care of a child? I can barely take care of myself." Suzanna chuckled but felt Adam stiffen beside her.

He withdrew his arm and turned to face her. "Don't you like children?"

"Sure. I just don't want any of my own." Trying to read his face, she fixated on his charcoal eyes. Until that moment, she'd considered those eyes intriguingly brooding. "How about you?"

Adam pinched his lips into a flat line and lifted his chin. "I was an only child, too, but I always wanted a big family. I don't understand why anyone wouldn't."

The statement stung. Of course. She'd have to be an idiot to think this traditional guy wouldn't want children. She hung her head and let the disappointment shower over her. "I should go." She turned and walked into the house.

Adam trailed after her. "Is something wrong?"

Suzanna looked up from snapping the clasps on her case. "Nothing's wrong. I just find kid talk upsetting. I have to go."

His voice turned gentle and low. "Are you upset because you have your—"

"What?" Was he about to say period? She glared at him wide-eyed while the color drained from her face. Old-fashioned was one thing, but sexist … What century was he from, anyway? She felt tears coming.

Adam's eyes widened like a frightened animal. "What did I do?"

Suzanna grabbed her guitar in its hefty, silver case and got out as fast as she could.

Chapter 28

Back on Owl's Way, not one streetlight shone along the entire stretch of macadam. The Civic's headlights barely cut through the gloom.

Suzanna wiped away tears that were making it even harder to see. Maybe if she'd grown up with younger siblings, she would've learned to be comfortable around children. But as it was, she had no desire, and the responsibility terrified her.

Turning onto the road toward Haddonfield, she expected visibility to improve, but the deserted highway's dim streetlamps were few and far between. She coughed away a tickle in her throat. The damp, musky scent of the night woodland was seeping into the car. She fished in her purse for a cough drop, but no luck.

Suzanna tried to stop thinking about Adam. She could've dealt with his medieval social moves, except for the kid thing. And prehistoric ideas about women? But she hated to just give up on him. They were compatible in every other way, and that Burgmüller! Could there be a way to change his backward ideas? Her mother always said that you can't change men; you've got to either take them as they are or leave. Sigh.

In daylight, the Pine Barrens had been a bit intimidating, but now, in the dead of night, with her emotions running high, the towering pines seemed to close in on her. The massive trees lining the roadsides were so crammed together, it was impossible to see beyond into the forest. A pair of glittering, yellow eyes blinked between the tree trunks, and her melancholy fused with worry.

Suzanna noticed a chilly mist rippling along the roadside, chalk white and floating in wispy waves. It climbed up into the forest, covering the knobby tree roots. She pictured the milky fog enveloping the car with her inside. Shaking her head, she forced away the vision.

Squinting through the windshield, she longed for more light. Instinctively, she reached around the steering wheel to turn on the high beams. Why hadn't she thought of that before? The high beams would make all the difference! But the location of the Civic's brights was anybody's guess. After running her fingers over the steering wheel controls, she took a guess and pulled the most prominent lever. The windshield wipers whisked across the glass with a piercing squeal. She flinched and banged her head on the headrest. A rush of adrenaline surged through her body. Feeling like an idiot, she flicked off the wipers.

Her search moved on to the armrest. Suzanna pressed one of the buttons. Both rear windows slid down. It took a while, but she managed to bring them back up. She tried another lever on the wheel, but the wipers slapped across the windshield again.

With a groan, she started randomly pressing buttons and pulling levers. The gas cap flapped open, the hazard lights flashed, the radio blared, and the sunroof sailed back and forth. After all that, she gave up and continued squinting through the regular beams' dim light.

Taking a glimpse in the rearview mirror, Suzanna noticed a car behind her. Not wanting to look stupid, she kept her hands off all controls and settled back against the seat. She checked the time prominently displayed on the dashboard, information she could never have hoped to gain from Baby. Only 10 p.m. So much had transpired with Adam that she was surprised it wasn't three in the morning.

Periodically, she peeked in the mirror, trying to figure out the trailing car's make. Could it be Adam coming after her to apologize? Or maybe she forgot something at his house.

Suzanna craned her neck and looked over her shoulder to be sure her guitar was there. She remembered putting it … The Civic swerved, and Suzanna found herself on the wrong side of the street. She whirled forward. Heart thudding, she guided the car into the proper lane.

Willing herself to calm down, she stole another look in the rearview. The car behind her had crept closer. She kept checking. Each time, it gained on her. Now she could see that it would dwarf Adam's little Toyota. Maybe it was a cop. Could she get pulled over for drifting into the other lane? She concentrated on her driving but kept one eye on the mirror.

Soon, Suzanna recognized the car's make and model. It was an enormous, coal-black Lincoln Continental. Not a cop. Not Adam. She knew the model well; it was the same kind Harry drove, except his was off-white. He used to have fits parking it in the tight spaces of Haddonfield until he created a spacious parking space behind the HB just for his car.

She tried to look inside the car at the driver, but the windows were a sheet of black. The night and shadows couldn't be enough to make the inside of that car completely invisible. Tinted windows? Aren't they illegal in New Jersey?

Suzanna slowed, expecting the Lincoln to pass her. But it didn't. Instead, it matched her speed and stayed dangerously close. She stomped on the gas pedal, and the Civic jolted forward. A brief peek in the mirror showed the sedan staying inches away from her back bumper.

Suddenly, almost playfully, the Lincoln tapped her bumper. She shot straight up in her seat. Who'd do that? Clumsily searching the dash for something—anything—to help, she pulled a lever. The wipers slammed across the windshield again. Not now!

Abandoning the Civic's controls, Suzanna drove on in a panic, her knuckles white. Her eyes darted up and down between the hulking car in her mirror and the road ahead. If only she had her cell, but it was stupidly locked away in her guitar case.

Her pursuer sped up and began to pass. She forced a sigh of relief through her clenched teeth as the Lincoln inched up on her left. But he didn't pass her. The black monstrosity slowed to her speed and cruised alongside.

Suzanna hammered her foot on the gas. "Come on, little car!" The Civic strained but made no headway. In a flash, the Lincoln made a razor-sharp turn and slammed headfirst into the side of the Civic. The little rental lunged sideways like a bumper car. Cowering behind the steering wheel, she watched, open-mouthed, as the Civic hurtled to the right shoulder of the road.

Reflexes kicking in, she heaved the wheel. But the car lurched, aiming for a speed limit sign. Sweaty hands slipping, she frantically spun the wheel back. The Civic rose up on two wheels, tires howling. Her scream joined the screeching tires as the car blasted across the street.

A gigantic pine sprang up in front of her. Suzanna stomped on the brakes. The car spun out in a wide arc, and a sea of pines flew by in slow motion.

The Civic bounded off the road, thorn bushes scraping the doors. It streaked down a wooded slope. Branches thrashed and cracked the windshield. Over tree roots and into gullies, the car sped wildly downward. The rough bark of a pitch pine was the last thing she saw.

Chapter 29

Tuesday, May 14

It smelled like a doctor's office. Antiseptic. In the glare of fluorescent light, Suzanna blinked her eyes. Her head was pounding. A blurry version of her mother's face materialized. She swallowed hard and winced at her burning throat.

Wait a minute ... car wreck ... attacker ... hospital! Her eyes snapped wide open. "Are my hands all right?"

Joan responded to Suzanna in the same brisk manner that she had asked the question. "Yes."

"Is my guitar all right?"

"Yes. Your new case did its job."

Every muscle in Suzanna's body relaxed.

Joan patted her hand. "I'm so glad you're finally awake." She let out a long, slow sigh.

Suzanna tried to sit up, but a sharp stab radiated through her shoulder, forcing her to collapse back onto the pillow.

"Easy now," Joan said in a hoarse whisper.

A stinging pinch made Suzanna look down at an IV running into a fat, bluish vein on the top of her hand. When she raised her head, a dull ache spread behind her eyebrows.

She reached up and ran her hand over a thick gauze bandage and a streak of caked blood.

"You're a little banged up, but you're fine."

A squat nurse breezed into the room with an official air. "You're awake. Excellent." Holding Suzanna's chart, she read dryly, "Slight concussion from trauma to skull … minor forehead laceration … bruise to right shoulder … no broken bones … no other injuries." She hung the chart on the bedrail and fixed her eyes on Suzanna. "You must have a very hard head, young lady. I'm told you received a bump a few days ago, too."

"Thank goodness for the rental car's airbags!" Joan pulled her cardigan tight around her. "If you'd been driving Baby, I think we would've lost you."

"How'd I get here?"

"A local man driving down that godforsaken road saw your taillights flashing and called 911." Joan sat on the edge of the bed. "Do you remember anything?"

"Hitting an enormous pine tree!"

The nurse edged along the bed, examining an array of beeping machines. "We can release you later today, but the police want to talk to you now. Do you feel up to it?"

"I guess so." Just what she needed—another blow to the head and another interrogation. And now it was definite. Someone was trying to hurt or kill her.

Detective O'Brien strode into the room and stood at the foot of the bed. "I'm hoping this was just an accident,

Suzanna." He glanced up at her. "Did you fall asleep at the wheel or something?"

"I'm fine, Detective. Thanks for asking." She paused for the sarcasm to sink in, but he only inched along the side of her bed, waiting for an answer. She sat up, supporting herself with her uninjured arm. "No, I did *not* fall asleep. I was forced off the road."

O'Brien's upper torso seemed to sag. "I was afraid of that. I need the whole story, every detail." He dragged a chair beside her bed, took out his notepad, and waited.

Suzanna recounted the entire episode, from when she drove out of Adam's parking lot to when she crashed into the tree. She even told him about her embarrassing attempts to find the Civic's high beams.

When she described the black Lincoln, O'Brien sat up and asked, "Did you see the license plate?"

"No, sorry."

"Too bad. We got the security footage from the jewelry store, but the angle showed the front of the HB rather than the side where the explosion occurred. However, a large sedan with Pennsy plates came down King's Boulevard and turned onto that street. Couldn't make out the plate numbers, though."

"Was it black?" Suzanna asked.

"Maybe. Couldn't be certain."

A sudden pressure seized Suzanna's head like a vice, and she slammed her eyes shut.

Joan cut in. "Can I help you now, Detective? Suzanna should rest." She reached out her hand and said, "I'm her mother, Joan. I've been meaning to talk to you."

Instead of shaking her hand, O'Brien placed a business card in her palm. Joan took a long look at the card and then his mustache. "Hold on. Are you supposed to be Poirot or something?"

"Right." His surly tone made it clear he was in no mood for ribbing. He moved to a table across the room from Suzanna's bed and motioned for Joan to join him. Suzanna half-listened and half-slept while they talked. They were discussing potential suspects when she fully woke and eavesdropped in earnest.

"Is there someone who might want to harm you, Joan?"

Joan shook her head. "I can't think of anyone."

"These attacks might not be directed solely at Suzanna. You or one of her friends might be in danger, too."

"Well, I guess, at my work ..." Joan's face clouded. "There's a chance—"

"What exactly is your job?"

"I'm in charge of Donald Bancroft's campaign for U.S. Representative."

While the detective jotted in his notepad, Suzanna was struck by an unsettling possibility. Could her problems be connected to her mom's politics? Just how dirty did the Wallace campaign staff play?

Joan shifted in her seat. "I suppose a political rival could target me, but …"

O'Brien tapped his pencil on the side of his head. "Interesting angle. How rough do these campaigns get?"

"Depends. Ours isn't that bad."

"If the investigation goes in that direction, I'll have to meet with your coworkers."

"Okay, but let me know if you need to speak with the senator. I'll want to brief him first."

"Will do." O'Brien lightly struck his pencil on the table. "Know anything about this new boyfriend?"

"Your guess is as good as mine. I haven't met him yet."

O'Brien glanced down at his pad and frowned. "What about Suzanna's father? She claims he's not in the picture."

Joan clicked her tongue and looked away. "Correct, he's not."

"Are you sure he's not trying to get at you through her? Like a domestic dispute?"

Joan flushed, and her voice took on an icy edge. "Not possible." She twisted her hair and pulled it behind her head. "He doesn't even know she exists."

Suzanna turned on her side, straining to catch every word. All the pain would be worthwhile if the investigation helped track down her father.

"Right," O'Brien said with dry irony. He stuffed his pad and pencil back in his pocket and leaned toward Joan. "I've been wondering if Suzanna's father is involved in some sort of criminal activity. Something that's indirectly affecting her. Maybe someone is trying to get at him by getting at her." He lowered his voice. "Can you put me in touch with him?"

Joan peeked over her shoulder at her daughter and then back at O'Brien. "No."

Spotting her mother's furtive glance, Suzanna was all ears.

The detective bent forward, resting his elbows on his knees. "You know, you can be fined or even jailed for withholding evidence."

Joan's eyes flashed at the detective but then hardened into a distant stare.

O'Brien stood, casting a long shadow across the floor. "I *will* find out who he is and where he is. But please, save me the grunt work."

Just hearing those words, Suzanna's heart beat faster. Now that she thought about it, she should've hired a detective years ago to locate her father. Maybe she could team up with O'Brien on the case.

O'Brien looked down at Joan. "Call me anytime. You've got my card."

Emily poked her blonde head into the room, startling everyone, and exclaimed, "Yippee-yo-ki-yay, Detective

O'Brien!" As she laughed heartily, she pivoted to Suzanna. "Hey, you're conscious. Look who I brought with me." Emily held the door and Adam walked in. Suzanna closed her eyes and tried not to panic. She vaguely remembered being mad at Adam. Even so, she didn't want him seeing her like this. She had a stupid bandage on her head, no makeup, and wasn't at all sure she looked decent in a hospital gown that felt three sizes too big. Only Em could've thought this was a good idea.

Adam ventured to the side of the bed. Suzanna glanced at her mom, concerned that Adam's first impression was coming off less than stellar.

He feebly murmured, "I can't believe this happened after you took off from my place. I'm so sorry … about everything."

Without giving Suzanna a chance to respond, O'Brien closed in and asked, "Are you Adam Damon living in Pipers Corner, New Jersey?"

Adam turned to the detective and nodded.

"I have some questions for you, son. Come outside with me."

Suzanna watched, speechless, as a stunned Adam left the room, tagging along after the detective.

Emily sat in the detective's vacated seat and talked to Joan in a half-whisper.

Suzanna strained her ears. Em's voice dropped in and out, but she got the gist.

"… your house … don't let Chris near …"

She clearly heard her mom's panicked question. "Why? What's going on?"

"… booze, and maybe … addictive … don't trust him."

Joan stood and squeezed Emily's shoulder. "Thanks."

Em bustled to Suzanna's side, her purse banging against the metal bed. "Since you're getting outta here, I'll scoot. Got a final to study for." Pressing Suzanna's hand, she said, "Feel better," and bounded out of the room.

Folding her arms, Joan sighed and walked to her daughter's bedside. "That detective of yours isn't very sociable."

"Well, I'd say he's not a people person. You have to get to know him."

"He's handsome enough. But that mustache …"

"Mom! Really?"

"Like you said, I'll just have to get to know him better."

"I think he's a great detective. That's all that matters."

Chapter 30

Detective O'Brien shifted from one butt cheek to the other, trying to get comfortable in a metal chair across the hall from Suzanna's hospital room. He'd always disliked the sounds and smells of hospitals—who wouldn't—but the chairs should be classified as torture.

He'd just finished questioning Adam Damon and felt as clueless as ever. All the guy's answers had been "I don't know," a blank stare, or both. Damon was either totally oblivious or stonewalling. O'Brien was sure of one thing—he didn't like the darkness of Adam's eyes.

The detective took out his cell phone and looked up the contact info on the local yokel who called in Suzanna's wreck. She'd asked O'Brien to get it for her so she could thank the guy. With full knowledge that he was procrastinating, he sent her a detailed text message.

He stroked one side of his mustache and pulled out a loose hair. He couldn't put it off any longer. It was time to get Smelly's account of last night. Higgins had been tasked with shadowing Archer all night. So, how could the accident have happened? He was almost afraid to ask, but with a dispirited sniffle, he dialed Higgins.

"Where are you, and where were you last night? Archer was attacked."

"Well, a howdy-do to you, too. I guess that's the way they talk to each other in New York City."

O'Brien waited.

"I was at her apartment all night. Nothing happened."

"But you were supposed to tail her."

"Well, I wasn't going to follow her into the Pine Barrens. I turned back and stayed at her apartment."

O'Brien's face flushed red as he kneaded his temple. "This was your second chance."

"Aw, man, we never do this tracking bullshit. Besides, at her apartment, everything was fine."

"That's it, Higgins, you're off the case." O'Brien hung up with a click, wishing he had a receiver to slam down. Now he'd have to write up a report on Smelly. He hated messing with anyone's career, but he couldn't help hoping there'd be a demotion in store for Higgins.

O'Brien eyed the officer standing guard outside Suzanna's room. His name was Jason, and he couldn't have been more than in his late twenties. Even so, in the time O'Brien had been with the Haddonfield Police, Jason had proved himself to be one of the most responsible cops in the department. He'd been one of the first on the scene at the HB bombing. He could think on his feet. And he was in fantastic physical condition. How was it that he was only a beat cop and Smelly was a detective?

"Hey, Jason. Want to work a case with me?"

"Is it okay with the captain?"

O'Brien cheerfully contemplated making the recommendation for Smelly to switch to Jason's beat. "I'll make sure it is."

"Then a big 'yes, sir'!"

Em bounded out of Suzanna's room and stopped in front of Jason. "Hi, again, remember me?"

Jason had been leaning against the wall but snapped to attention. "Yes, ma'am."

"Don't ma'am me. My name is Emily." She stuck out her hand, and he shook it. "Wow, that's some grip," she said while giving his bicep a gentle squeeze.

O'Brien looked up and wagged his head. Em was certainly a firecracker. He could see that Jason was a bit flustered. He would be, too, if the flirting came his way.

Out of the corner of his eye, O'Brien glimpsed a man of medium build wearing a gray sweatshirt, getting on the elevator. He sprang up and elbowed past Emily just in time to see a flash of yellow as the elevator doors slammed shut.

"Watch it!" Emily steadied herself against the wall.

Jason's eyes were on O'Brien, waiting for an order. O'Brien pointed at Suzanna's door. "Hang tight."

The detective ran to the nurse's station, skidding in his dress shoes. Puffing, he rammed into the counter. "Did any of you talk to a guy in a gray hoodie?"

A candy striper raised her hand.

"What did he say?"

"He asked about Suzanna Archer's condition. I told him she was fine, and he left."

O'Brien sprinted down the steps, two at a time. He hit the lobby with both feet, but all he saw was a blinding flurry of white coats. The open elevator was empty. He flew out the door and coasted to a stop on the sidewalk. The guy was gone.

Chapter 31

A middle-aged doctor whisked into Suzanna's hospital room, his gray comb-over flapping. He glanced at her chart and beamed. "Everything looks fantastic." Rubbing his hands together, he said, "Let me remove the bandage, and you'll be released!"

As the doctor unwrapped the tight gauze, the sharp pain in her head dulled. Each layer he unwound relieved more pressure. The final layer came off with a swoosh.

Suzanna explored her forehead and detected a sore gash with two stitches above one eyebrow. She scratched away the caked blood beneath it.

On his way out, the doctor turned to Joan and snickered. "My advice is, don't put her back in the game!" He threw his head back and burst out laughing. "You know, concussion?" He laughed even louder. It didn't faze him that no one else even cracked a smile. He waved as he left the room, still chuckling.

The nurse shoved several papers in front of Suzanna and pointed rapidly from one sheet to the next. "Sign here … here … here … and initial here." Handing a pamphlet and pill bottle to Joan, she said, "This gives instructions on treating concussions, and these are pain meds. Only give her one if she really needs it."

At her mother's house, Suzanna climbed into her old bed and gingerly laid her head on the pillow. Joan placed an oversized pair of sunglasses with dark-green lenses and rainbow frames on the bedstand. "The pamphlet says no TV, and you should wear sunglasses."

"I think I can manage that," Suzanna said, yawning. "What's written on the sides of those glasses?"

"Bancroft for U.S. Rep. They're all I've got."

Suzanna tried them on. They were the biggest and most colorful sunglass frames she'd ever seen. The campaign slogan was imprinted in shining silver across the wide length of both temples.

Joan handed her a pain pill and a glass of water. "What a relief that you don't have to work tonight. You can rest and not worry about losing a night's pay."

Suzanna smiled weakly and sat up. "I knew there had to be a benefit to the gig economy."

Joan shook her head and stuffed two more feather pillows behind her daughter.

Suzanna took the pill and settled back. "I'm off tomorrow, too, so I can nurse my wounds for another whole day. Then it's back to work."

Recognizing her mom's concerned frown, she said, "Come on. I'll be fine by Thursday."

It was the second night in a row Suzanna was sleeping in her old room, her old bed. She was floundering. And that hurt much worse than her bruises.

Chapter 32

Arty slouched into his chair and wrapped the heating pad around his creaking knee. Last night, when his Lincoln made contact, his bumper stuck for a split second. The release had jolted him forward, jamming his lousy knee into the gear shift. Now, the knee was screaming. Yesterday had been brutal from start to finish. Eight hours of following his target all over the lousy Pine Barrens! And it'd been cold as penguin shit.

Now, toasty and warm in his living room, he turned on the TV and settled in. The Florida brochures were beside his chair again. Arty couldn't remember if he'd moved them from the kitchen, but he didn't care one way or the other. He propped his feet up and thumbed through a shiny, Tampa flyer flaunting a white beach and cresting waves. Now, that's first rate.

Just as he entered full kick-back mode, the doorbell rang. "Christ! This better be important." He limped to the door with one hand on his knee.

He spied his geeky neighbor, Rick, out the window, sighed, and opened the door.

Rick peered out through greasy strands of hair. "Hey, man! I've been listening to police reports on my Ham radio. You know, hoping for some Jersey Devil buzz from the cops."

"I haven't told you about my visit to the birthplace."

Rick's eyes widened. "What? When?"

"Sunday. You should've seen it. As spooky as they come. Only a two-room shack but—"

"Did you see him?"

"Nah, but I swear I could feel him." Arty crossed his arms.

"Did you look in both rooms?"

"The door to the back room was shut tight. I didn't force it."

Rick nodded. "I think he was out causing trouble last night. I heard on my Ham—"

"While you were fooling with that crap, I was getting some shut-eye." Arty brushed some sleep from his eyes and yawned. One more symptom of old age to add to the list … being tired all the time. Irritating as hell.

"Jersey cops reported a car crash in the Pine Barrens."

"Wait." Arty stopped short. "Last night?"

Rick bounced on his toes. "A girl ran off the road and plowed down an embankment. Lots of police and ambulance activity. Lots of excitement."

"Did they say how it happened?"

"No, but I bet it was the Jersey Devil's work! We'll find out soon enough. They say the girl is all right."

With a smack, Arty bashed his hand into the doorjamb. Rick nearly jumped out of his skin. Arty's rage sizzled hot in his chest. He set his jaw and spoke through gritted teeth. "Are you sure the girl is okay?"

Rick tilted his head to the side and eyed Arty. "Yep, in the hospital but not critical. I'm thinking about paying her a visit. Ask some questions. Wanna come?"

Arty couldn't believe it. He'd screwed up again. How'd she survive in that little shitcan of a car? He'd seen the wreck with his own eyes. It was totaled!

"You okay, Arty?" Rick looked vacantly at him with his mouth open.

Arty lost it. "Why don't you go take a flying fuck at the moon!" He slammed the door in his neighbor's face.

Leaning his back against the inside of the door, Arty held his knee in both hands and grimaced in pain. His worst job ever. This damn target keeps coming back like a bad penny! And a dent in his bumper, for nothing.

This time, he didn't wait for the furious phone call from his client. He had to get this job done and remove himself from the situation before he got nabbed. Step One: Put the house on the market. Step Two: Find a place in Florida. Step Three: Put this job to bed and pocket his pay. Step Four: Get out of town, warp speed.

Arty called his shady, fly-by-night lawyer. "Morty, need your help. I'm leaving for good and want you to handle a few things. Can we meet tomorrow … right away?"

"Hi there, Arty! What did you say? Tomorrow you wanna meet?"

"Yeah, can't you hear me? The day after today."

"Is the heat on?"

"Philly's hotter than the last man's seat on a short toboggan! I'm not waiting to move to Florida."

"On the morrow then. Are we selling the house?"

"Yeah, that and I'll need a new identity."

Arty would manage all right in Florida with this last rotten job's pay. It would be tough, but he'd get by. Once the dough from the sale of the house came through, things would ease up.

With a surge of energy, he stood up, the ache in his knee fading. He had to get organized and lighten the ship so that moving out would be quick and painless. Taking an inventory of the house, he decided to pack only the absolute necessities. No furniture or knickknacks required. He started throwing clothes in a duffel bag.

A new attack plan was forming in his mind. It would mean smoking out his target, up close and personal. Completing this job wasn't just a matter of money anymore. Now, it was a matter of pride.

When Arty finished packing, he'd filled two large suitcases and his duffel bag. Is that really all he needed? He staged everything by the front door. Ready.

His energy boost fizzled, and he collapsed into his living room chair. That's when a dull thud came from upstairs. Dammit. First, the neighbor, now the ghost. Wouldn't anybody leave him alone? He climbed the stairs, and at the top, an icy chill prickled his arms.

Arty peeked into his bedroom. He still slept in the same room he had as a kid. But he knew the noise hadn't come from there. It came from farther down the hall, his pop's room. When his pop dropped dead of a heart attack twenty years after his mum died, Arty had packed all the old man's clothes and toiletries into cardboard boxes and piled them high in the room's closet. Out of sight, out of mind. Then he'd closed his pop's door and never opened it again. That was over forty years ago.

He cracked the door and stuck his head in. Some folks believe ghosts can't hurt you, and some think they can. Arty was on the fence and not about to take any chances. The smell hit him first. Even after all those years, the room still stank of his dad's cherry pipe tobacco. That sweet, woody stink could gag a maggot.

The closet door hung open. Hadn't he closed it all those years ago? He eased into the room, his teeth chattering in the sudden cold. Checking inside the closet, he saw that the stacked boxes of his pop's things had tumbled to the floor.

Arty set about sorting the mess and uncovered a rose-colored, cardboard carton he'd never seen before. It was taped shut. He pulled the tape and popped it open. The fragrance of his mum's perfume rushed into his nose and mouth—jasmine and rose. The box was crammed full of her clothes. His dad must've packed them away after she died. The scents of both dead parents mingling in the tight space made him woozy.

He sat on the closet floor and fumbled through his mum's clothes, not sure what he was looking for. Underneath the clothing, cocooned in a scarf, he discovered a shoebox—his mum's knickknacks. Link by link, he pulled up a gold necklace with a cameo pendant. His mum had worn it every day. Arty stroked the cameo with his thumb and lowered it back into the box with a gentle flump. Her silver-and-rhinestone barrettes were scattered over some Polaroids. The rubber band around the photos had all but melted and fused onto the glossy, white border of the one on top. It showed his mum in front of a diner, laughing, an ice cream cone in her hand. He set his mum's box on the floor. He'd give her odds and ends a closer inspection later. After restacking all of his pop's junk, Arty jammed the shoebox under his arm and closed up the room.

Back downstairs in his chair, he put the box on his lap and turned on the TV. It was time for the special anniversary show of *Ghost Hunters*. The once-a-year program was one of his favorite things. This year, it specialized in reluctant spirits and their reasons for staying in the earthly realm. He hoped to glean some insight into his mum's situation.

As the intro played, Arty dipped into the shoebox. The band around the photos snapped. Bits of elastic clung to the stack. The images were all of his mum before she got sick and of him as a baby. He flicked through and studied her face. He didn't remember her hair being so dark. And how did he forget that she'd been drop-dead gorgeous?

Ghost Hunters explored a number of reasons why spirits stay put and the ways they haunt. Ghosts looking for resolution were supposed to be big on electromagnetic interference. His mum hadn't done anything to his electrical system—no lights going off and on, no fuzzy TV. Arty dug back in the shoebox and brought out a silver pin shaped like a cat in a sitting position. It wasn't familiar to him like the cameo necklace. One item at a time, he emptied the shoebox. The last thing in the box was a folding hand fan with a faded Chinese design. When he picked it up, it crumbled in his hands.

Chapter 33

Wednesday, May 15

In a borrowed nightshirt, Suzanna shivered while rummaging in her mom's closet. She was searching for a housecoat or sweater, maybe some slippers. The only clothes she had were the shirt and jeans she wore in the crash, and they still stank of pine forest and burning rubber.

She pushed her sunglasses up on her head. A long cardigan, its shoulders stretched on a misshapen, metal hanger, looked cozy and woolly warm. She pulled it on and continued searching the closet. Not snooping, just curious.

Earlier that morning, she'd been roused by a gentle touch on the arm. Her mom couldn't miss another day of work and was going to the office. Still groggy from yesterday's pain pill, she barely grasped the directions for reheating the beef stew in the fridge.

When Suzanna heard her mom go out the front door, she dragged herself to the window and double-checked that Jason was still across the street in an unmarked SUV. He'd been assigned general protective duty and would shadow her from now on. She felt safer already. With a satisfied sigh, she drifted back to her bed. When she finally woke again, it was two in the afternoon.

Now, snug in her mom's sweater, Suzanna surveyed the fantastic accumulation of footwear lining the bottom of the closet—heels of varying heights, flats, sneakers, and boots. She had to chuckle. Her mom never met a pair of shoes she wouldn't buy. Unfortunately for Suzanna, not one pair of slippers made it into the mix.

Near the back, a black, lacy dress hung on a wooden hanger. Price tags still attached and a thick layer of dust covering the shoulders, it looked forlorn. Holding up the dress, she wondered why her mom had never worn it, then squeezed it back into place.

Stuffed behind all the other clothes, Suzanna discovered a zippered garment bag. When she peeled back the flaps, a cascade of dust spilled out. She sneezed and waved it away. Inside, she found a minidress made from scraps of old clothes and bits of ribbon. What was this, a Halloween costume? She zipped the bag shut with a twinge of guilt.

Out in her mom's bedroom, she looked at all the combs, brushes, and makeup scattered on the dresser and kicked-off shoes in the corner. The house was becoming solely her mom's space, whether she kept a room for her daughter or not. That was the way it should be. That's how Suzanna wanted it to be, but she still got a slight, wistful pang. Feeling like an intruder, she tiptoed out of the room.

In the kitchen, the smell of her mom's beef stew hung in the air. She took the Tupperware from the fridge and swung around to the table. Hot pain shot through her forehead; she'd moved too fast.

Suzanna sank into a kitchen chair and held her head in her hands, waiting for the aching to taper off. Her fingers hovered over the Band-Aid above her eye. Those stitches were supposed to dissolve in about a week and be absorbed into her body, which kind of creeped her out. She pulled her sunglasses down. They helped.

While the microwave whirred, she checked the clock. Detective O'Brien was stopping by at four with follow-up questions. Plenty of time to eat.

Relaxing at the kitchen table, Suzanna enjoyed the crisp vegetables and tender beef swimming in thick gravy. She considered her mom's peculiar dress, the torn bits of clothing sewn together with ribbons. Something about that dress seemed familiar. Had she seen it before? Perhaps when she was very young. She'd have to own up to snooping and ask.

After putting her dishes in the sink, she went to the tiny office off the living room and logged on to the oldest PC in existence. Its fat keys and huge monitor didn't bother her as long as it connected to the Internet.

Suzanna searched for a clue about any dress fashioned from old clothes and ribbons. None of the search results were remotely relevant. Then she tried *dresses made from cloth and ribbons* and *rags and ribbons*, but nothing. Torn, old clothes could be hand-me-downs. Or castoffs. Of course!

She typed in *castoffs and ribbon* and laughed out loud. A dozen references to Isaac Bellow. Now, she remembered. It was a phrase from her namesake song, "Suzanna Unfolded."

Suzanna dances beneath the bridges of Paris,
Wearing castoffs tied up with ribbons.
Is she a courtesan or a newspaper heiress,
She keeps it all well-hidden.
No matter how hard you try, you can't help but want her,
You can't help but want her tonight.

She sent a text to Em. "Call on your break. Something weird."

The phone rang immediately. Suzanna chuckled. "You're on break?"

"Sure, sort of. What's weird?"

Suzanna told her about the dress and the web search. She had to keep waiting for Em to stop laughing.

"Man, I love your mom," Em said. "Obsessed doesn't cover it. I bet she made the dress for Halloween, or maybe that's how they dressed when she was young … what year do you think?"

"I guess sometime in the eighties."

"Were miniskirts even a thing then?"

"Hate to break it to you, Em, but you didn't invent sexy. I'll get the scoop when she gets home." Admitting that she'd stumbled on the dress would be awkward, but there had to be a silly explanation, and she couldn't wait to hear it.

Em lowered her voice. "Now, tell me about how things went with Adam. *Before* you smacked into a tree, that is."

There was an insistent triple knock on the front door. "Can't. O'Brien is here." When she opened the door, O'Brien's mustache somehow looked bushier. Maybe it was the sunglasses.

"Just a few more questions," the detective said.

"Sure. Let's sit in the kitchen. Do you want some stew?"

"No, thanks, I'm good." Detective O'Brien followed her down the hall. "I wouldn't say no to a glass of water, though."

They sat at one end of the long kitchen table. Suzanna watched the detective drink the water and wondered how he kept his mustache dry. Turned out, he didn't.

"You still have a couple drops of water on your mustache." She pointed at the same spot on her face where the drops hung on his.

"I'm saving that for later." He stretched out his tongue to the corner of his mouth and ran it over the bristly hairs, lapping up the water droplets.

Suzanna cringed. Thank God it wasn't food.

He smoothed both sides of the mustache with his thumb and index finger, removing any stray droplets.

"Did you get your guitar back, and is it okay?" O'Brien asked, taking out his pad and pencil.

"Jason dropped it off. Not a scratch."

The detective wet the pencil's tip on his tongue. "When you figured someone was following you, why didn't you call 911?"

She took her sunglasses off and set them on the table so that they were staring at O'Brien. "My cell was in my guitar case. So stupid. I couldn't get to it."

"What part of the Lincoln slammed into your car?"

Suzanna thought back to the moment of the collision. When she breathed in to respond, her lungs prickled and her heart raced. For no reason, she surged with dread. Was this a panic attack?

O'Brien put his hand across the table a few inches from hers. "Are you all right?"

She slumped back and nodded. Her voice came out breathless. "Only the bumper, I think." Suzanna inhaled, long and slow. The fear disappeared as quickly as it had cropped up. She slid her sunglasses on top of her head and met the detective's eyes. "I did get some info yesterday that might help with the investigation."

"Info?"

"Before the accident, I went to the Devil's Lair shop and ordered a copy of that Jersey Devil book."

Detective O'Brien nearly spit out a sip of water. "I told you not to do that."

The corners of Suzanna's mouth drooped. "Sorry, but I think the owner can tell us who bought it."

"I'll look into it, but please, Suzanna, don't try anything like that again."

"Okay." She peeked up at the detective. "Maybe."

Detective O'Brien sighed heavily. He swiveled and glanced up as Suzanna's mom walked in.

Joan had stopped at Suzanna's apartment and brought back a bundle of clothes. She handed them to her daughter and sat down beside O'Brien. Suzanna held up the clothing, looked at the detective, and pointed a finger upstairs.

O'Brien nodded. "We're done."

Suzanna pulled down her sunglasses and went to her room. She never thought putting on a pair of stretch pants could feel so fantastic. Before slipping on her T-shirt, she crumpled it up and ran the soft cloth over her cheek. Feeling more human, she took her guitar out of its case and played for the first time since the accident. Her swollen shoulder felt stiff as she plucked the strings but didn't hurt. Tomorrow at the HB, she would play her easiest repertoire.

The murmur of voices floated up from the kitchen. She practiced Carcassi Etudes while waiting for the detective to leave. When she heard O'Brien's dress shoes click across the tiled foyer and the front door latch, she looked out her bedroom window to the street. O'Brien was leaning against the white SUV, chatting with Jason. It was strange to see Jason in plain clothes. Looking at the clock, she guessed her mom had been with the detective for almost two hours.

Returning to the kitchen, Suzanna watched her mom put a steaming bowl of stew on the table for herself and point at it. "Want some?"

"I ate before, but I'll keep you company."

They sat down in their usual spots. Suzanna crossed her arms on the table and rested her chin on them. "What were you guys talking about?"

"He gave me an update on the case. Nothing much, really. How are you feeling?"

Suzanna reviewed each injury and its improvement, leaving out any symptoms that might cause worry.

Joan shoved her dish to the side, folded her hands in front of her, and leaned toward her daughter. "Now, tell me about this Adam fellow. What's going on there?"

"I'm not sure. Everything seemed great and then …"

"Details."

Suzanna reported the finer points of the Kimmel date, the sawmill, the duets, and the having-children disagreement.

"Sorry, sweetheart. You two sound like a good match." Joan's voice turned plaintive. "Would one kid be so awful?"

"Don't start. I won't change my mind." Suzanna sighed, knowing her mom would love a grandchild. "Too big a commitment."

"I guess you're right. But it means that you'll have no family when I'm gone."

"I'll be fine."

Joan let out a quiet moan and took her bowl to the sink. "You're making an unusual life choice."

"I know I'm bucking the system, and some people—Adam, for one—don't like it."

Joan faced her daughter. "You have to accept the downside. The world's attitude toward motherhood isn't changing any time soon."

Suzanna pursed her lips. "I waited too long to bring it up with Adam."

Joan nodded with a sulky frown.

Wiped out by the day's activities, Suzanna yawned and dragged herself up to her room. That's when she realized she forgot to ask about the dress. It could wait till morning.

Chapter 34

"Relax. Like I said, I'll have it on Saturday." Chris patted the sweat forming at the small of his back through his polo and sulked at Micky. "You agreed to the extra week. All I'm asking for now is one hit to hold me over."

He figured he might as well get something out of Micky's "double-checking on the Saturday payment" visit. So, he asked for some Oxy. He knew he sounded desperate but didn't care.

Chris sat down at the kitchen island and, out of habit, pulled out his nail kit—a skinny, black, leather case the size of a cell phone holding an array of files and buffers.

"Stop whining." Micky glimpsed the case full of nail files and let out a short bark of laughter. "What the hell is that?"

"Nail kit. All classical guitarists have them."

"No shit?"

Chris didn't want to talk to Micky about anything, least of all his nail kit. But he needed to stay on Micky's good side. Whatever that meant. "Right-hand nails need to be filed special."

Micky smirked. "What about your left hand?"

Chris held out both hands, palms down, for him to see the difference. The left-hand nails were clipped down to the quick, and the right-hand nails were long and sloped sideways into a thirty-degree angle. When Chris noticed his fingers were trembling, he drew them back.

"Jesus, what a pack of fags," Micky said.

Chris ignored him. He took out a smoothing buffer and tried to steady his hands to work on his thumbnail. "To get the best tone, they must be shaped and smoothed."

Bending his wrist, Micky put on a lisp. "So what if you're playing a concert and a nail breaks?"

"Cancel." Chris scraped the file over his thumbnail. "Or try a fake nail, but that never works." Micky's anti-gay slurs rubbed Chris the wrong way, but he was in no position to complain. Micky probably held anti-attitudes about plenty of things.

"So how about that Oxy?" Chris asked.

"Fuck you and your stupid nails." Micky spat out his words.

"Just one hit."

Micky shrugged and pulled a rolled-up, plastic baggie tied with a rubber band out of his pocket. He chucked it at Chris, who tried to catch it but failed. It bounced off the island and landed on the floor.

"I'll be here Saturday night for the dough." Micky hitched up the front of Chris's shirt and drew him in, face-to-face. "And no more extensions." He let go, and Chris collapsed back in his chair. Micky walked to the door, but before he left, he turned and said, "By the way, I got the lowdown on your folks. If you don't come through, I'll be taking the situation to them."

Chris went back to buffing his nail while his stomach did backflips. Did Micky just threaten his parents? He wasn't sure, as sometimes Micky spoke in code. Was he saying he was gonna shake down his folks for the money or kill them? An awful tightness climbed up Chris's throat. He felt like he was on a cliff's edge, and one more problem would push him over.

He wondered, too, about the debt extension Micky had given him. And now he'd fronted him drugs. Was Micky setting him up, getting his claws into him deeper?

Chris examined his polished thumbnail, scrutinizing every angle. Perfect, even with shaky hands. The first phrase of Beethoven's Fifth rang out, his ringtone. He picked up.

Em's voice sounded harsh and strained. "Have you heard about Suzanna?"

"Now what?"

Em told him a somewhat agitated version of the accident in the Pine Barrens. "Didn't you notice she's been gone two days!"

"I thought it was quiet around here. When she coming back?"

"How should I know? But she'll be at her mom's tonight."

"You think she'll come back tomorrow?"

"*Whenever* she comes back, take good care of her."

"How? Like make her tea or something?"

"Just stay sober!"

Chris held back a snicker and clicked off the phone. So, no Suzanna tonight. Great time for a party. He called Piano Dan. "Can you buy the beer again? Cool, bring the gang."

Chapter 35

Thursday, May 16

Suzanna helped herself to the oatmeal on the stove and sat down at the kitchen table with her mom. Joan fiddled with her turquoise ring until it fell off. Suzanna noted that her mother had lost some weight since working on the Bancroft campaign.

Joan picked up the ring and fixed her eyes on the stone. "I know your head's throbbing, and you're scared to death about these attacks—"

"Do I hear a 'but' coming?"

"But I've got to tell you something. Something you won't like." Joan reached across the table and gently stroked her daughter's arm. Suzanna's gaze darted to her mother's eyes. Even through sunglasses, she could see trouble. She gently extracted her arm from her mother's touch and poured herself some orange juice.

"I've wanted to tell you this for many years. But these attacks … if anything ever happened to you …" Her voice broke. "I put it off long enough." She flopped back in her chair. "Take those sunglasses off for a minute. Prepare yourself." Joan pulled her hair back in a pony and jammed her ring back on her finger. "This will be upsetting."

As she removed the glasses, Suzanna's spine tensed. They locked eyes.

"I know who your father is. I wasn't promiscuous in my youth, not like I've said. In fact, he was one of very few."

A tidal wave of shock washed over Suzanna. "I knew it, I knew it, I knew it!" With each word—each one louder and higher in pitch—she rapped her fist on the table, rattling the spoon in her bowl of oatmeal. "Why tell me now?"

"Why now?" Joan rubbed her eyes. "I meant to tell you so many times. Like when you graduated from high school or got your apartment. There never seemed to be a right time." She held her palms up pleadingly. "I never had a good enough reason until now."

Joan pinched the bridge of her nose, and her crow's feet deepened. "Yesterday, Detective O'Brien forced the issue." Her face flushed as she turned her head away. "There's a chance, an extremely remote chance, your attacks have something to do with your father. The truth is, he's a celebrity."

Suzanna jammed forward into the table. "Get out!" She couldn't help asking, "Senator Bancroft?"

Joan rolled her eyes. "No, of course not the senator." She pulled her chair in and thrust her shoulders back. "Let me explain."

Suzanna sagged back in her chair. "Well, who—"

Reaching across the table, she pressed two fingers to her daughter's lips. "Just listen."

Joan folded her hands and focused on her ring. "When I'd tooled around Europe for those years before college, I was actually following Isaac Bellow's tour. Back then, his concerts were growing bigger. But occasionally, he still played small venues, sometimes just a pub or coffeehouse. When I wasn't going to his shows, I'd experimented with being an adult. One of those experiments happened in Paris after an intimate concert in a lovely café along the Seine." Joan's eyes drifted up to the ceiling as she remembered. "I was sitting at a table, sipping espresso. He'd come up to me and said, 'I see you.'"

"Who came up to you?"

"Isaac Bellow, of course. We'd connected. Deeply. He said he respected my freedom. My independence. Called me a courageous warrior." Joan feigned a matter-of-fact tone and said, at top speed, "One thing led to another, and I ended up in his bed."

Suzanna screwed up her face. "What?"

With a spell-like focus, Joan stared into her daughter's eyes. "When I'd returned to the States, I found out I was pregnant. Your father is Isaac Bellow."

Suzanna sprang to her feet, knocking over her orange juice. It leaked into a small puddle by her bowl. "But how do you know for sure?" She smacked both hands on the table and leaned in. "It still sounds like your experimenting was pretty intense, and any number of men—"

"I'm certain it's him." Joan gently pushed Suzanna back in her chair and wiped up the juice. "He was the only one in the six months leading up to my pregnancy. He's the only one it can be." She snatched an LP record jacket from the shelf beside the stereo and held it up. "Look at him."

Suzanna took the album cover and, although she'd seen it many times before, looked with new eyes. A black-and-white photo of Bellow's face filled the entire record jacket. As she inspected the haunted face, her mouth opened, but no sound came out. Isaac Bellow stared back at her, his nose the mirror image of her own.

She tried to do the math in her head. When she was born, her mom was twenty-two. Bellow's first album had come out during the early seventies' folk scene, and he'd kicked off his music career relatively late. "Mom, wasn't he kinda *old* for you?"

"Old? What's twenty years or so? Men in their forties and fifties can still be studs. Grow up."

Suzanna pictured a mature George Clooney and had to grudgingly agree.

"Should I go on?" Joan almost whispered.

"There's more?"

"I returned to the States, gave birth, and started college. But I was still obsessed with him." Joan folded her hands together and squeezed. "Paris clearly was a one-night stand, but I thought it extraordinary … he called me his Joan of Arc."

"Joan of Arc? So what?"

"In '94, when he'd settled in a Yoga ashram outside of Boulder, I just had to see him again." She blew out a long, strained sigh. "This is the weird part."

"How can this get any weirder?" Suzanna struggled to look her mom in the eye. Instead, she picked at the scab on her hand where the IV had been.

"A neighbor watched you. You were about eight then."

Suzanna slammed back in her chair. "I remember that! It was the first time in my life you left me for more than a day."

"I'd gone to the ashram way up in the mountains and wore nothing but castoffs and ribbons, exactly like in the song you're named for."

Suzanna's eyes grew wide. "I saw that dress!"

Overlooking the comment and evident snooping, Joan looked through Suzanna and into her past. "He was staying in a one-room cabin slightly apart from the main building. When he'd opened the door, he took one look at me and broke into a smile." Joan's voice became small and distant. "He reached out, stroked my breast so tenderly, and pulled me to him. We made love. Again, he called me his Joan of Arc."

Suzanna *really* didn't want to hear any specifics of her mom's sex life. "Joan of Arc was a soldier. What's that got to do—"

"He said I'd saved him that night. That's the last time I saw him."

Acid disillusionment rose in Suzanna's throat. The woman sitting across the table twirling her turquoise ring was a liar, a fraud, and a groupie to boot. The independent lifestyle that Suzanna had always admired and emulated was nothing but a series of bad choices. Suzanna fixed her eyes on a jagged scratch in the table and asked softly, "Did you tell him about me?"

"No, I didn't want to hang that on him. He has no idea you exist."

Suzanna thought about her mom's turn of phrase, "Hang that on him." That "that" was her! The insult felt like a sharp slap to the face; she stroked her cheek.

Hinging her elbows on the table, Joan tucked her chin in her hands. "It was like everything that night happened in slow motion." A tender smile played across her lips. "Slow … in fact, he wrote a song called 'Slowly' on his last recording." Coming out of her reverie, she turned back to her daughter.

Bitterness crept into Suzanna's voice. "Do you think that song was about you?"

"Well, of course not. That's just the way it was for me … and probably lots of others. Frankly, it was him." Tears glistened in Joan's eyes. "He said I was his Joan of Arc."

"Wait a minute!" Suzanna's stomach tightened as she made the connection. "Is Joan Archer your real name?"

Joan turned her face away. "My first name was always Joan, but I changed my last name after Europe. Used to be Smith, so no great loss." She pulled a tissue out of her pocket and dabbed at her eyes. "If your grandma and grandpa were alive, we'd still be arguing about that name change. Your legal surname is Archer, but it should be Bellow."

Suzanna touched her own cheek again and found it wet with tears. As a child, she'd created a mental image of her never-seen father—an everyman type wearing khakis and a golf shirt. The kind of dad her friends had. That impression had stuck. She tried to make Bellow fit into that box, but couldn't.

Funny, she always thought she'd be happy to learn who her father was, but instead, she felt hollow with loss. Loss of trust and solidarity with her mom. Loss of the hope that one day she'd meet and get close to her father. Suzanna could barely recognize her mom now. All the pieces didn't fit anymore. But it wasn't just that. She couldn't recognize herself, either.

"Were you afraid to tell me before?"

Joan's voice shook. "I was afraid you would go and bother him. I didn't want to put him in that position."

"You're kidding me! This is my father we're talking about. I had a right to know."

"For two shining moments, I was his Joan of Arc. That's all I want him to remember." With shoulders tense, she held her head high. "I'm not suggesting I handled the situation well."

Suzanna let out a sarcastic snort.

Joan stoically allowed a tear to fall. "I'm sorry, but now you know."

Suzanna glared at her. "I need time to digest this." She shoved her sunglasses back on and stood up, scraping her chair on the floor. She walked through the kitchen, trying to look dignified. She couldn't say why. In the hallway, she called out, "Take me back to my apartment," and stumbled up the stairs to gather her things.

They didn't speak during the ten-minute drive. Suzanna felt like she was in an altered reality. When they reached the apartment, Joan simply said, "I'm truly sorry."

Without so much as a word or a glance, Suzanna got out and slammed the car door.

The apartment smelled like Lysol. The hallway and kitchen were immaculate. Chris leaped out from the living room, holding a cleaning rag, and sweat dripped down his forehead from underneath a soaked sweatband. "You're back," he said between gasps for air. "Sorry about your crash."

Suzanna looked at his frown and heaving chest. It was hard to be sure through her sunglasses and still-teary eyes, but he seemed genuinely concerned. Resting his back against the wall, he pulled the sweatband off. "Emily said you'd be back today."

As she walked toward the living room, Chris sprang in her path. She peeked around him. The living room was a disaster of beer bottles, pizza boxes, and filled ashtrays. She rolled her eyes in exasperation, and sudden pain drilled through her skull. She mashed her fingertips into her eyebrows; the pressure helped. Her fingers drifted to her stitches. Closing her eyes, she said, "I need to lie down," and dragged her guitar down the hall.

Chris hurried behind. "Why don't you eat something first?" He tugged at her sleeve. "I can make you an omelet."

Suzanna brushed him off, opened her bedroom door, and found Piano Dan asleep in her bed. More like passed out. She kicked the bottom of the bed, and Dan bounced up, all arms and legs.

Suzanna pointed at the door. "Out!"

He lurched forward and slammed into the door face-first. Apparently, that woke him up. He staggered into the hall, and Chris hustled him out the front door.

Suzanna stripped the bed, lay on her back on the bare mattress, and stared at the ceiling. She didn't have the bandwidth to worry about Chris's mess, not while dealing with the news about her dad. The extent of her mom's selfishness gnawed at her, but she couldn't help feeling some empathy. It was her mom, after all. She shook out her tense hands.

The next time she spoke to her mom, she'd have a million questions.

Chapter 36

Joan's confession to her daughter had taken longer than she expected. It was already mid-morning. She let Suzanna leave the car without a word. Her heart told her to chase after her and try to fix things, but the prudent course was to give the girl time.

She played a mental video of how she'd thrown the father bombshell at Suzanna. It was the last way she had hoped to do it. She ran her fingers through her hair, raised her chin, and put the car in gear.

Over the years, Joan had fantasized about revealing her secret during their mother-daughter trip to Europe—if she could ever convince Suzanna to go. They'd follow the same footsteps she'd taken in 1986, and then she would confess at that little café along the Seine. Perfect. Lately, though, she'd considered not telling her at all ... just leaving her in the dark forever.

But when Detective O'Brien interviewed her yesterday, she realized she had no choice. He'd been clear. He was hell-bent on finding Suzanna's father. As they talked, he'd been firm and direct but, to her surprise, also sensitive. Her story came tumbling out. The last thing she'd imagined was telling this detective her secret before telling her daughter, but she did. O'Brien had listened to her without judgment. She felt safe with him. Suzanna was right. You had to get to know the man.

Deciding that she should stop feeling sorry for herself, Joan turned the car toward the office. Work always made the best antidote. She wondered if it was the same for O'Brien. He seemed so wrapped up in Suzanna's case, she guessed his job was all-consuming like hers. Even at the end of their interview, he'd tried to delve deeper, asking her why she'd lied to Suzanna for so long. No answer came to her. She had no excuse. He suggested that she might want to keep Bellow all to herself, not share him even with her daughter. She admired his insight. After all, hadn't she been doing just that all this time? On the way out the door, O'Brien had asked a final question. Did she have a significant other? She told him no. But what she didn't say was that she rarely dated. How could she? She'd never met a man who measured up to Bellow.

Joan stopped at a light, stretched her arms, and yawned. She had planned on confessing to Suzanna last night but lost her nerve. Instead, she'd spent a sleepless night going over what she would say. This morning, when the time came, she didn't use even one of her imagined speeches. In any case, getting that secret off her chest was like letting a heavy burden drift away.

Only two more blocks to the office. She flipped her hair back and considered making some changes in her life. Maybe something out of the ordinary, something big.

Finally, selling the house? Some beautiful condos were being built one town over. Would it bother Suzanna not to have a house to come home to?

When Joan pulled into the campaign parking lot, she was surprised to see Bancroft's car. He was supposed to be at a fundraiser. He missed a function last week, too. Just as well; she wanted to talk to him. Hopefully, she wouldn't find him asleep at his desk like yesterday. She'd tiptoed up and gently tapped his shoulder, but he was out cold. Holding in her disappointment, she'd left his office without saying a word. Not everyone held the same high standards of leadership that Joan did. She understood that. But what kind of a leader naps while their staff works overtime?

Putting on her managerial face, she walked briskly into the building.

On her desk sat an overflowing pile of Post-it notes, all with the "critical" box checked. She returned the first call, only to find she'd have to redo the following week's fundraising plan. Burying her concerns for Suzanna in the back of her mind, she got lost in the hectic uproar of phone calls, emails, and staff questions. She loved her work, but some days, it felt like she was giving birth to the election itself.

Her scheduling coordinator breezed in. "I need your help to firm up the rally's TV coverage."

"What can I do?" Joan's voice came out stressed.

"I need you on the conference call."

Surrendering, Joan finished the letter on her desk and spent the rest of the morning working on news coverage for the Trenton rally. Unlike most of Bancroft's speaking engagements, this rally would be streamed online. The interns were particularly excited. This was new and complex territory for Joan, but only the beginning. Over the next year, she intended to double their Web initiatives.

Glancing at her watch, Joan wasn't surprised to see it was already lunchtime. No doubt, today's lunch would be delivered Chinese. While waiting for her food, she scanned through yesterday's glossed-over emails. One was from Suzanna and read, "His music makes me smile, even the sad songs. Give it a listen. You need some music to make you smile." An MP_3 was attached with Randy Newman singing his song titled "Suzanne." The cheery email had been sent before Joan's confession. With a deep sigh, she wondered how her relationship with her daughter would change.

In the lunchroom, Joan ate with the interns and discussed volunteer strategies. Crammed around the oval table, they hung on her every word. Those fresh, young faces yearned for guidance. Remembering the fantastic coaching she'd been given during her trainee days, she took to heart the responsibility of paying it forward. She prioritized managing the interns, and their work had become crucial to the campaign. It would be rough going without Anne on board, but they'd just have to get by.

"When does the door-to-door canvasing start?" asked a pug-nosed girl with a full head of flaming red hair.

To Joan, the redhead looked so young, only a baby. She fought the urge to stroke the girl's hair and push an unruly strand behind her ear. "If I can get the project plan off my desk, we'll start tomorrow."

"How's your daughter doing?"

Every face turned toward Joan; she wasn't sure who asked the question. The story of Suzanna's attacks had blazed through the office. "She's fine, but they still haven't captured her attacker."

"Think it has something to do with her work?" asked a young man with a mouth full of braces.

"Don't know." Joan shook her head. "The police are on top of things."

Donald Bancroft swept into the lunchroom, sporting a handsome smile and radiating authority. All the interns stopped eating and sat up straight.

"How's everyone doing? Do we have the rally all organized?"

"We sure do!" said the redhead.

Joan set aside her takeout bowl and chopsticks, too. She enjoyed watching the enthusiasm of the troops. If only she could stop worrying about how Bancroft's assault on Anne might be affecting them. She assumed they were still talking about it among themselves but had no idea which way the wind was blowing. Joan worried about Bancroft losing their loyalty and respect. By association, could she lose their esteem as well?

Halfway down the hall to her office, Joan's finance director stopped her. "Could you help me review the accounts this afternoon? I think I found a problem."

Joan sighed and looked at her watch. "You bet. I wasn't planning to leave on time anyway."

Chapter 37

Suzanna reluctantly cleared space on her bedside table for Chris to plunk down another cup of tea. He was attempting to wait on her, but everything he did made her bristle.

"Thanks, really, I'm fine. Only a little headachy."

"Sure thing, Miss Hollywood," he said, mocking her sunglasses. "Must be nice to laze around in bed all day."

She paid no attention. "There's something you *could* do for me since I'm now carless. Give me a lift to the HB tonight?"

Chris saluted. "I'll be your chauffeur."

"Great. I'll grab a ride home with Em. Think insurance will offer me another rental?"

"Doubtful." Chris left her room, shutting her door behind him.

The first phrase of Beethoven's Fifth echoed from out in the hallway. Suzanna could hear Chris pick up and say, "On track." She pressed her ear against the wall, but the call had ended. The odd statement bugged her. Exactly what was "On track?"

Chris propped the HB door open with one foot, his eyes fixed on a patrol car parked across the street. Suzanna lugged her guitar through and followed his gaze.

"That's Detective Higgins," she said. "You remember him?"

"Why would I?"

"It's a total blank then?"

"Don't know what you're talking about. But doesn't it make you paranoid?" Chris jerked his head at the street. "Cops hanging around like that?"

"Are you kidding? It's awesome."

Suzanna saw Jason was out there, too, his white SUV parked in front of the HB. He wore wire-rimmed sunglasses and appeared to be reading a newspaper. Half-smiling, she imagined him as an international spy.

Chris removed his foot and let the door swing free. "Good night, Suzanna. Have a good gig." He turned and walked out.

How odd. Chris had never wished her well for a background gig before. Usually, he'd be all huffy and say something like, "Haven't you got better shoes?"

As she was finishing her setup, out of the corner of her eye, she saw someone outside the window—someone in a hooded sweatshirt. She ripped off her sunglasses and looked full-on. Nobody. Must be the glasses. She slid them back on and headed for the bar.

Vinny cracked a broad smile. "Cool shades!" His voice softened as she got closer. "Em told me what happened. I'm sure glad you're okay."

Suzanna climbed onto a barstool. "Aw, thanks, Vinny." She swiveled and surveyed the customers, hoping for some lavish tippers. The two days off last weekend put a strain on her already-stretched budget.

Vinny tossed his towel over his shoulder and leaned toward her. "Suzanna, I been thinking. Remember what we talked about the other night? Why somebody might be after you?"

Tilting her head, she peeked up at him. "Yeah?"

"I been wondering … maybe somebody thinks you overheard something. Something you shouldn't have." Vinny's eyebrows rose. "Know what I mean?"

"But I'd remember hearing something important."

"Maybe you didn't hear it. They just think you did."

Suzanna frowned at him.

"You said when people sit nearby, you catch every word."

Vinny leaned closer. "At Ristorante Buena, too?"

"Sure, but people ignore me like there's an invisible fourth wall."

"Fourth what?"

"Like actors. I can't look customers in the eye. It would break the fourth wall. They think I shouldn't see or hear them."

"Here at the bar, it's different. They don't ignore me." With his dark eyes shining, Vinny grinned and pointed up and down the bar. "They think I'm their psychologist."

He snickered and poured a glass of seltzer, Suzanna's traditional work beverage. She never drank alcohol while performing. The motor responses of little finger muscles were the first to go south when combined with a drink. With a swoop of his arm, Vinny slid the glass in front of her.

Suzanna took a nose-tickling sip. "Some people act like sitting near me is extra private. Once, I heard a woman, no more than two feet away from me, break the news to her husband that she had breast cancer."

Vinny nodded and rubbed his neck. "How about the Mob? What if a made man thinks you overheard something? Maybe at your fancy place?"

"But you said it couldn't be Mafia, that they wouldn't make a mistake. And now, we're talking two mistakes."

"I'm gonna ask my uncle Guido if he knows anything anyways. That okay with you?"

Suzanna lowered her voice. "Your uncle is in the Mob?"

Vinny bent over the bar. "You didn't hear that from me."

She dialed her voice down to a whisper. "Is Guido honestly his name? He may as well have 'mobster' tattooed across his forehead."

Vinny put his finger to his lips. "Shh." One side of his mouth curled up, and he said, "Yeah, he named my cousins Micky and Joey."

"Vinny, Micky, and Joey. Sounds like a sixties' doo-wop group. Did you guys sing on the street corner?"

"Nah, none of us can carry a tune. I'll let you know what he says."

Emily stomped up to the bar. "They can kiss my big, fat, white ass!"

Suzanna never understood how Em reined in her language on demand. Not one expletive dropped while she dealt with customers.

"That table stiffed me!"

"No kidding?" Vinny said. "No tip at all?"

"Not a fucking cent." Emily just stood there, panting in disbelief, then swung around toward Suzanna. "What's with the glasses? You a movie star or something?"

Suzanna pointed at her head. "For the concussion."

"Your face looks like a bowl of fruit loops."

"Campaign swag. Ask my mom if you want a pair. Actually, you don't even have to. You can get them free at every gas station from here to New York."

Suzanna headed back to her performance area and tuned up. On her music stand, she opened a binder of pieces from the 1800s—a little trite but charming and, most important, easy. She adjusted her amp to the room's volume, careful to make it loud enough to be heard but not louder than the general customer murmur. At the end of her set, she packed away her guitar and was about to go to the bar when a tiny woman using a cane tottered up to her. The woman held up a five-dollar bill and said, "I wanted to make sure you got this."

Hesitating, Suzanna tried to figure out what she meant.

The woman stuffed the bill into her tip jar. "I've asked waitresses to put money in your jar for me before, but I think they keep it."

Suzanna sighed, knowing some waitresses resented her. They thought that her tips cut into their own. Emily always said it wasn't true, but this woman was living proof. Suzanna smiled sadly as she walked to the bar.

Em sat with her back against the bar, her bent elbows resting on the rail. She was swinging her feet while monitoring her customers, evidently entirely recovered from the "no tip" incident. Suzanna climbed onto the stool next to her.

Em tilted toward her. "Feeling better?"

"My head only hurts when I shake it. The sunglasses help." She took them off and blinked until her eyes adjusted to the light.

"And how are you mentally?"

"Ah, now we're talking a whole different ball game."

Em examined Suzanna's puffy eyes. "Been crying?"

"Maybe." She slid the sunglasses back on.

"Still on for meeting the professor tomorrow?"

Suzanna's face went blank.

"You remember our plan to visit Professor Gardener … the Jersey Devil expert."

Suzanna stroked the Band-Aid, covering her stitches. "I completely forgot."

"We don't have to go. I'm getting cold feet anyway."

Suzanna swiveled to Emily and grasped her arm. "No, I really want to. Especially after the Devil's Lair."

"What was that like?" A customer enthusiastically waved. Em hopped down and bustled toward the table.

Suzanna called after her, "Tell you tomorrow."

"Noon?" Em asked over her shoulder.

"Noon."

Chapter 38

Friday, May 17

Emily pulled up to Suzanna's apartment in her old, engine-knocking Subaru coupe, her elbow hanging out the open window. Across the street, Jason shifted his white Ford SUV into gear.

Brandishing her own pair of Bancroft-swag, multicolored sunglasses, Em gave Suzanna a silly, lopsided grin. "I'm joining the club!"

Laughing, Suzanna slid into the passenger seat, and they took off for Philadelphia's Main Line, the notoriously wealthy group of suburbs in northwest Philly. The professor lived smack-dab in the middle.

Suzanna gave Emily a rundown of her Kimmel date with Adam and their trek to the Devil's Lair. She skimmed through the sawmill and rushed to the eating pizza at Adam's place. That sparked a deluge of questions from Em about the townhouse. Suzanna had to detail every room, right down to the empty refrigerator. Then she glossed over the steamy duets and went straight to their disagreement over children.

Emily shook her head. "Girl, you blasted things *way* out of proportion!"

"But he really wants kids, *plus* he's a little chauvinistic."

"Didn't your mom think you overreacted?"

"She says you can't change men, so if you don't like something—"

"Nobody's perfect. You should try to work it out."

Unusual advice from Em, but it made Suzanna wonder. Was she rejecting Adam too soon?

With some confusion and only a little arguing, they found Professor Gardener's street, Darby Road. Emily haltingly steered down the block while Suzanna checked the house numbers.

"There it is." Suzanna pointed at a massive corner property.

Em slammed on the brakes, whipped off her sunglasses, and scanned the estate with her mouth half open. A spectacular, three-story, Pennsylvania bluestone mansion loomed in front of them. On one side, a turret spiraled high above the slate roof. On the other, a single-story annex adorned with leaded-glass windows stretched into the side yard. The groomed landscaping looked naturally wild, like a flawless English garden. Juniper bushes edged the foundation, interspersed with pearl-white hydrangeas, their snowball blossoms bobbing in the breeze.

Em jabbed her finger at the windshield. "Look at that enormous pitch pine at the end of the driveway. Maybe that's his tip-o-the-hat to the Jersey Devil." She inched the Subaru up the circular, cobblestone drive and parked beside a flight of slate steps leading to the front entrance.

"Are you sure this is the right house?" Suzanna squinted at the elaborate entryway. Its chestnut door stood nine feet tall, flanked by shimmering, stained-glass side panels. "He didn't get all this on a university professor's salary."

"I heard he inherited old Philadelphia money, but this is more than I expected." Emily pulled a comb through her hair and applied lipstick in the rearview mirror.

The silver Tesla on the other side of the driveway was enough to impress Suzanna. "What's his first name?"

"Not sure. We just call him 'Professor' in class."

Typical Emily. She didn't even know her crush's full name. Suzanna nudged her. "Come on, let's go."

Leading the way, Suzanna climbed the steps. Behind her, Emily stubbed her toe on the first sharp edge of slate. She let out a yelp and snatched the hem of Suzanna's jacket, almost pulling her backward.

"Sorry. I didn't hurt your head, did I?" Emily asked in a whisper.

"No, but why are we whispering?"

"It's this place." Em took another big-eyed look at the grounds. "It's out of our league."

Standing in front of the imposing door, Emily rolled her shoulders back and straightened her blazer. As she rang the doorbell, she checked her breath.

A baritone voice blared out, "Who's there?"

They both jumped.

The intercom was neatly concealed under a wrought iron monogram. Em clicked the button. "It's Emily?"

Several padlocks unlatched, and a muscle-bound, thirtysomething man in sweats swung the door open. "Hi, I'm Jack." His baritone had transformed into a cheerful tenor. With sparkling blue eyes, dimples, and killer traps, he looked more like Chris Hemsworth than a psychology professor. His thinning, blond hair was cut super short, almost shaved. Suzanna shot Em a questioning glance.

"We're here to see the professor," Em said.

Not sure why, Suzanna was relieved that Jack wasn't the professor. But then, who was this fellow with the biceps bulging through his sweatshirt? A butler? The prof's son?

Jack held the door while Em and Suzanna wandered into the foyer. Sunlight streamed through the stained glass onto the oriental carpet's deep garnets and vermilions. Inside, the hushed house possessed a kind of reverence. It reminded Suzanna of a cathedral she'd visited in Rome, where the colored light silently played off ancient, wooden pews.

With a smile that wouldn't quit and dimples ablaze, Jack cast his arm toward a draped archway. "Right this way, ladies."

They tagged after him into a drawing room. Suzanna's entire apartment could've fit inside. She came to a standstill in front of the room's centerpiece—a magnificent staircase spiraling up to the second floor. Per Jack, the carved newel post and railings were made of antique chestnut. The same stunning woodwork trimmed the entire room.

Tracking Em's gaze upward, Suzanna looked past the elegant furnishings and wall hangings to an enormous chandelier. Its icicle-shaped crystals cast flecks of crimson across the ceiling.

Jack led the way to a side parlor through two lofty pocket doors. Professor Gardener sat in a wingback chair behind a grand oak desk. Built-in bookshelves lined the walls, and the furniture was upholstered with rich, brown leather. The room smelled of books and money.

"Hello, Emily. This must be Suzanna." He smiled and shook Suzanna's hand vigorously. "A pleasure."

Professor Gardener looked more like a professor to Suzanna than Jack, but not by much. In her mind, professors were doughy, white-haired pipe smokers. All her profs at the conservatory had been, at any rate. This professor was lanky and appeared to be in his forties. His long-lashed, blue eyes and straight nose were topped off with a neatly cropped beard. The only stereotypical "prof" thing about him was his loose-fitting tweed jacket with suede elbow pads. It was easy to see why Em was attracted to him. The money didn't hurt, either.

He gestured for them to sit in two club chairs across from his desk. Suzanna was surprised he didn't stand—not when they entered the room or when he shook her hand. She smiled inwardly at herself. Why should she expect that kind of old-fashioned etiquette from Professor Gardener yet think it peculiar coming from Adam? Perhaps she wasn't as modern as she thought.

When Emily sat, she crossed her legs smartly. In her cargo shorts, her long, tanned limbs took center stage. She was in full flirt mode.

Taking the other chair, Suzanna sank deep into the soft leather. The whole arrangement felt a little like sitting in a doctor's office.

The professor folded his arms on the desk. "Now, how can I help you two?"

Struggling to boil down her situation to a single, sensible statement, Suzanna hesitated. The professor shifted awkwardly in his leather wingback chair like it was a piece of clothing that didn't quite fit. She didn't know about him, but *she* wouldn't be comfortable living in this kind of luxury. Every time she turned around, she'd worry about breaking something.

Emily tipped her chin at Suzanna. "Go on."

Still unsure where to begin, Suzanna just said, "I'm looking for a specific book about the Jersey Devil."

Professor Gardener smiled at her, good-natured, little creases pinching the corners of his eyes. "What's the title?"

The book's name, now so familiar, rolled off her tongue—*The Jersey Devil: Phantom of the Pines*.

Twisting in his chair, the professor pulled a book from a bookshelf on the wall behind him. He held up a paperback, the multicolored cover gleaming. "Do you mean this one?"

"That's exactly it!" Suzanna shimmied forward and balanced on the edge of her seat. It was identical to the one she had found, except in pristine condition.

The professor placed the book on his desk and regarded Suzanna. He wore a troubled expression. "What's your interest in this publication?"

Emily broke in. "Why don't you listen to her story first?"

The professor nodded. The leather creaked as he settled back in his chair.

Flashing a shiny, pink-lipped smile, Emily shifted in her chair and swept her hair over one shoulder, letting a blonde waterfall spill down her arm. Keeping her eyes trained on the professor, she said to Suzanna, "Tell him about both attacks."

Suzanna's lips clamped together tightly at Emily's coquette pose. The only way Em could flirt more transparently would be to bat her eyelashes. She sighed internally at Em and launched into her story. As she sped through it, she emphasized finding the book and the mystery of her attacker's identity. Only a few short outbursts from Em interrupted her recap.

The professor drew a pair of reading glasses from his breast pocket, then positioned them low on his nose. He flipped through the first pages of the book. "This is self-published with a limited publication run."

"I noticed the author gets no credit. Isn't that unusual?" asked Suzanna.

The professor let out a heavy sigh. "Yes. Yes." He slapped the paperback down on his desk.

"Sorry," Suzanna said. The professor sounded like he was fed up with something. She hoped it wasn't her.

"I guess I'll confess," he said, his voice in complete surrender, his face somewhat sheepish. "I wrote this book."

Suzanna gasped.

Em choked back laughter. "No way."

A troubled crease crossed the professor's brow. "I can give the police a list of the stores where it's been sold. They're all in New Jersey. But it seems unlikely it would help them find your attacker."

"But why leave out your name? Don't you want credit?" Suzanna asked.

"It's not my typical kind of academic treatise. I aimed to educate the New Jersey public about the Jersey Devil's legend, that's all. I didn't want my name on the book because it's a bit embarrassing. My colleagues at the university wouldn't understand."

Suzanna turned to Em. "I guess we're two of the people the professor needs to educate. I thought it was weird that we didn't know more about the whole thing. I mean, we grew up here."

"That's not unusual," he said. "New Jerseyans all know *of* the Jersey Devil, but it's the rare one who knows anything *about* it."

"I've seen the hockey team play," Em offered.

"That's what I'm talking about." He bobbed his head. "The hockey team's the only scrap of the story most Jersey folks know."

He handed the book to Suzanna. "You can have this one."

"Thanks! Search over." She paged through, checking out the pictures. At home, she would read it cover to cover.

Jack strolled into the room. "Anyone want iced tea or lemonade?" A playful glint twinkled in his eyes. "I'm getting a head start on summertime quencher recipes."

The professor tossed a grin across the room at Jack. "I'll take an iced tea." He turned back to Em and Suzanna. "Jack here is turning into Martha Stewart."

While Em requested lemonade, Suzanna thought about the Martha Stewart comment. Something was going on here, and she didn't think Em would like it. "I'll take lemonade, too."

"Magnifique." Jack got busy setting up a small serving table. "I'm finally getting used to the juicer in this kitchen."

Suzanna directed her puzzled gaze at the professor. "Did you just move here?" The question slipped out before she considered how intrusive it was.

"Two years and counting," Jack said cheerfully.

The professor shot him a stern look.

Two years wasn't much time to settle into a Main Line mansion. Suzanna could only imagine the hassle of furnishing the place. And cleaning a house this size? She squashed down all her nosy questions and switched gears. "Professor, do you know a store called the Devil's Lair?"

"Of course." His face brightened. "I sell my books there. We've been there many times."

Beaming, Jack added, "Yeah, it's a freak show, but a hoot."

The professor pointed at the book in Suzanna's hands. "Did you look for my book at the Devil's Lair?" That sparked a lively discussion between Suzanna and the professor, comparing notes on the shop. Professor Gardener thought it a better resource than she did, but they agreed the owner was *quirky*.

Suzanna's conversation with Professor Gardener was like talking with a friend, not a snobby millionaire or stuffy college professor. He was down to earth. No wonder he looked uncomfortable in this mansion. He appeared just a little uncomfortable in his own skin, too.

Emily plucked the book from Suzanna's hand. "Let's see that." She scooted back in her chair and leafed through the pages.

Jack finished with the table and went to the professor's side. He lowered his voice and said, "I'm having trouble with the stove again." In undertones, the two chatted about the appliance problem.

Suzanna was pretty sure Jack and the professor were an item, or else she was a very bad judge of character. She reached over and tugged Em's sleeve. Their eyes met. Suzanna glanced from Jack to the professor and back again and arched her eyebrows. Then, she repeated the gesture.

Em frowned and whispered, "Huh?"

It was going right over Em's head. At best, she'd figure it out soon. At worst, this was going to get embarrassing.

The professor's gaze followed Jack leaving the room. Suzanna studied his eyes. They were brown like Adam's but not so dark. More of a chestnut color, as though reflecting the glow of the mansion's woodwork.

"I've been researching the Jersey Devil online," Suzanna said, "and I came across scads of drawings. Each one was supposed to be the Jersey Devil, but they were all different." She rubbed the back of her neck. "Like, drastically different."

The professor chuckled. "There's no consensus on the Jersey Devil's appearance, but everyone agrees on a few basic features." He ticked off a finger for each. "A serpent-like body, a face shaped like a horse, segmented bat wings, cloven feet, a forked tail, and he stands upright like a Tyrannosaurus." He pulled a stuffed binder from his desk drawer and passed it to Suzanna. She held it up so Em could see. While they flipped through various renderings of the Jersey Devil, he continued. "No photographs of the creature exist, only a variety of witness descriptions, anecdotal sightings, and these drawings."

Eyes glued to the pages, Em shoved a hand over her mouth and giggled. "So who were these witnesses? Wackos?"

The professor frowned. His lips disappeared behind his beard, and his voice took on a prickly edge. "All sorts of people wrote witness accounts." He fixed his eyes on Emily. "Commoners and people of stature, like police chiefs, mayors, even clergy."

Suzanna's back stiffened. Why did the professor sound so defensive? Could he actually believe the Jersey Devil exists?

In a calmer voice, turning to Suzanna, he said, "The most famous account came from Napoleon's brother Joseph, who spent the majority of his life in New Jersey."

"But no one still believes the thing is out there, do they?" Em asked.

"They do," Suzanna said. "The Devil's Lair guy said he saw it. And Vinny said people in Haddonfield did, too."

"Well, that's Vinny for you." Em leaned toward the professor. "He's just a friend."

The professor twisted back and searched his bookshelf. "I think I have a book specializing in Haddonfield's experience."

Suzanna took the opportunity and yanked Em's arm. She drew a finger across her throat and then mouthed the word *gay*.

Em's eyebrows scrunched together and she mouthed, "What?"

The professor turned and handed a hardcover book with a blue binding to Suzanna. "Want to borrow it?"

"Thanks." An aged, yellow-tinted photograph of King's Boulevard filled the cover.

Still paging through the binder, Em pointed at the goofy-looking sketch from the *Philadelphia Bulletin*. "How could someone believe that thing's real?"

The professor took a fat book with leather binding from the shelf. It looked like a bible or a fancy dictionary. "Belief in the supernatural is hardwired into the human brain. That's where most of our myths and conspiracy theories come from." He cracked the book open at a tattered bookmark. "There's also no consensus on the type of sound the Jersey Devil makes." He read, "Some witnesses claim the Devil's cry combines the scream of a human child with the snarl of a beast, some say it resembles a woman's shriek, and still others say it sounds like a bloodcurdling wail full of rage." He closed the book with a thump. "Imagine being the first humans to live in those deep, dark forests of pines. Woodlands like that are gloomy and eerie, almost primeval—especially at night."

Suzanna raised her hand. "I can attest to that!"

The professor's eyebrows arched up. "Chilling, isn't it?"

She nodded. His voice held such conviction. He must've gone through a disturbing night in the Pine Barrens, too.

"How'd this whole bizarro thing start, anyway?" Em asked. "Does anybody know?"

"The Jersey Devil's story began in 1750, a homegrown legend from the first settlers of the Pine Barrens."

"If I had to live in that creepy forest, I'd make up stories, too," said Suzanna.

"Especially if, like the locals, you had no education and lived in poverty. They still do."

Emily smiled. "Yeah, we call 'em Pineys."

The professor leaned back and cleared his throat. "Yes, I'm familiar with the term." He tilted his head and considered Emily over his glasses. His lips disappeared again.

Em didn't seem to catch the professor's disapproval, or she didn't want to. Opting to deflect, Suzanna asked, "But Professor, the whole Mrs. Leeds and her cursed child thing … is any of that real?" A mental image that she had created of Mother Leeds popped into her head—a bent and wrinkled, old woman in a ratty, winter coat wearing a babushka and carrying a gnarled walking stick.

"Oh yes, Mrs. Leeds existed, and descendants of the family are still in the area."

"Imagine. The Jersey Devil would be their relative," Emily said.

The professor nodded. "The origin story I come across the most has Mother Leeds moving to the Pine Barrens pregnant for the thirteenth time. Penniless and with a drunkard for a husband, she could barely feed her existing children. When she found herself pregnant again"—he tossed his hands in the air—"she threw up her hands and exclaimed, 'Let this one be a devil!'"

In a hushed tone, Em said, "Cursed her own child." She shook her head. "Then gave birth to a monster instead of a baby?"

"Sort of," the professor said. "When she went into labor, the local midwives came to her two-room, stone house. Her husband and other children waited in one room while she gave birth in the other. At first, the baby appeared normal, but then it multiplied in size and transformed. Talon-like claws ripped out of the tips of its fingers, sharp fangs shot from its gums, wings unfurled, horns sprouted, and its eyes glowed fiery red."

Em gaped at him. "Like *An American Werewolf in London*!"

"But the Jersey Devil doesn't change back and forth like a werewolf. Its transformation was permanent. More like Bigfoot or the Yeti."

"After he changed, did he just go off and live in the woods?" asked Emily.

Suzanna remembered this tidbit. "Yep, he flew up the chimney."

"Like a backward Santa Claus!" Em said.

"Not quite." The professor held up a finger, signaling for them to listen. "First, the Devil savagely attacked his mother, killing her. Then he tore the midwives, limb from limb. Next, he bashed in the door to the next room and mauled his father and siblings, leaving only a few alive to tell the tale. Then he flew up and out the chimney and has lived in the bowels of the Pine Barrens ever since."

"That version is a lot grislier than the one I read online," said Suzanna.

"Versions, with varying degrees of horror, have circulated for over two hundred years."

Emily bent forward and strategically propped her elbow on the corner of the desk. "Did it kill any other people?"

Suzanna couldn't see it, but she felt certain Em's lips were curved in a suggestive smile.

"As far as we know, it never killed a human again. But now, every strange thing seen or heard in the Pine Barrens gets blamed on the Jersey Devil."

Leaning in, Suzanna asked, "How about you, Professor? Do you be—"

"Here we go!" Jack squeezed through the pocket doors sideways, carrying an enormous tray filled with tall, slender glasses, two crystal carafes, and a foot-long, mother-of-pearl cocktail stirrer. He placed the tray on the serving table with a gentle clink.

"Well done," Emily said.

Jack nodded at her. "Did I hear you guys talking about the musty, old 1700s? Let me bring you back to the present." With a crisp whipping motion, he stirred the carafe of iced tea. When he was finished, he popped the slender stirrer up into the air. As it came down, he caught it by the tip and balanced it on the back of his hand. Quivering slightly, its iridescent handle gleamed in the sunlight. Emily laughed out loud at the flair trick, while Suzanna watched in wonder.

Next, Jack held a glass at waist height. With his other hand, he raised the iced tea carafe almost over his head and poured a graceful stream into the glass, not spilling a drop. He handed the iced tea to the professor. Suzanna suspected Vinny could do the identical tricks, even though she'd never seen him do any. Jack poured the lemonade in the same manner but ended with an extra flourish. Emily applauded like mad, and Jack took a bow.

The professor smiled at Emily. "Jack used to be a bartender. That's how we met."

"I've come a long way since South Philly!" Jack said. "And now that Gerry has inherited—"

"Jack, please. These are students."

That nailed it for Suzanna. They're a couple, all right. Maybe even married. Same-sex marriage had just become legal in New Jersey a few months ago. She wasn't sure about Pennsylvania. Regardless, it was obvious the professor didn't want to talk about it in front of them.

Jack left the room, saying, "I'll let you get back to the 1700s."

Suzanna turned to the professor. "That era, the 1700s, was a transitional time for European music. I wonder what kind of music the folks in the Pine Barrens made back then. Maybe they wrote songs about the Jersey Devil."

"Sounds like a perfect doctoral thesis."

Suzanna's gaze dropped to the floor. "I haven't even got a master's."

A sudden clickety-clack of scraping claws echoed from the other room. A small dog raced in and jumped playfully on Suzanna's legs. She pulled him up onto her lap and patted his head.

Emily squealed with delight. "Do you know what I'd name a little Jack Russell dog like that?" All eyes were on her. "*Little Jackie!*"

Suzanna stifled a groan. Em was still in flirt mode.

"He's a Basenji, not a Jack Russell." The professor took off his glasses and pinched the bridge of his nose. "Two very different breeds." He turned his attention to his pet, sitting calmly with Suzanna. "I've never seen Sigmund take to anyone so quickly. He's usually on the shy side with strangers."

Sigmund curled up his solid, little body and settled down on Suzanna's lap. His short fur glistened white and burnished brown. She ran her palm down his back; he was quite muscular for such a small dog. His slim head tapered through the muzzle like a fox's head and was topped off with erect, little ears. And at the other end, she couldn't help playing with the cutest curly tail she'd ever seen. As a child she never had a dog, but always liked them. This one was quickly stealing her heart. She stroked the thick wrinkles of skin and fur that covered Sigmund's forehead. They made him look like he was deep in thought or trying to puzzle out a mystery.

"Adorable," Emily said. "How long have you had him?"

The professor's forehead wrinkled in thought, not unlike his dog. "Close to a year."

Sigmund looked at each person in the room with his dark, almond-shaped eyes. All the while, his curly tail wagged with gusto. Emily reached over to pat the dog's head, but Sigmund took one look at her hand and let out an eerie, guttural wail that wobbled like a bad, slow vibrato. Emily froze. It was the strangest dog howl Suzanna had ever heard. Almost unearthly.

"That's about the only sound a Basenji can make," the professor said. "They can't bark."

Em tossed her head toward Sigmund. "Well, what was that racket?"

"The Basenji yodel. They have an abnormally shaped larynx. The breed's nickname is 'the barkless dog.'"

Sigmund settled down. Suzanna gently stroked his head until he nodded off. The professor's eyes were locked on his dog in her lap.

Em crossed her arms and leaned to one side, trying to put herself in the professor's line of sight. "Why do people still think they see the Jersey Devil nowadays? It all happened so long ago."

The professor blinked and looked at Em. "The sightings didn't just stop after the 1700s. Throughout the twentieth century, there were several major incidents. Like in 1904, all hell broke loose." His eyes shone. "Did you read about that, Suzanna?"

"Guess I didn't get that far."

"Here's where things get interesting." He twisted around and rifled through his bookshelf.

Suzanna cleared her throat, leaned over, and softly said, "Hey, Em. Stop the flirting. They're gay."

Em only frowned and asked, "What are you talking about?"

That was it. Suzanna gave up.

The professor turned back to them with another thick book. While he searched through the pages, he said, "Within one week in January 1904, the Jersey Devil was seen by thousands of people in New Jersey, Pennsylvania, and Delaware." He laid the book on his desk and flattened one page. "Fourteen different towns in New Jersey were terrorized, including your Haddonfield. The local papers were filled with it."

Jack rushed into the room. "Sorry for the Sigmund interruption. He got away from me."

With a wave of his arm, the professor pointed out Sigmund on Suzanna's lap.

A surprised smile flashed across Jack's face. "Well, look at that! Do you mind holding him?"

"No, he's fine," she said.

Jack cleared the empty glasses, and the professor turned the book on his desk to face Suzanna and Emily. It held a map of New Jersey and the surrounding states. "This shows the progress of the Devil over that week in 1904 from one sighting to the next."

Suzanna's eyes grew wider as she followed the lines crisscrossing the entire state of New Jersey and spilling over into Pennsylvania and Delaware. Emily traced the patterns around Haddonfield with her finger.

"It began with frantic reports of mysterious tracks in the snow and mangled dogs and chickens."

Suzanna couldn't help thinking the professor believed the scary story he was telling. His words resonated.

"Then, witness sightings poured in to police stations. And not just an individual here and there. Large groups of people claimed to have seen the Devil at the same time. A general panic erupted. All the schools closed. People padlocked their doors and stopped going out at night."

Suzanna felt a chill. "Smart. Night is his feeding time." She could still picture the huge shadow soaring over Mill Pond.

"Search parties were formed to find and kill the beast. Public fear went off the charts when bloodhounds refused to follow its trail. They say police fired at it as it flew overhead, but to no avail. All that week, people reported livestock slaughtered."

Em rubbed her arms. "Wow."

"There were two other major sightings in 1951 and 1960, but they didn't match the intensity of that week in 1904."

"So give it to us straight. Is the Jersey Devil real or not?" asked Em.

"I can't answer that," said the professor. "We've no hard evidence to prove it exists—no bones, no blood, no DNA. But we have hundreds of witness accounts over multiple generations." He sighed. "There's only speculation about why so many people could've seen the Jersey Devil if it *doesn't* exist."

"Maybe that Leeds family made it all up. They probably murdered each other," Em said.

The professor half-smiled but didn't meet Em's eyes. "There are plenty of theories about how the legend could have started. For instance, Mother Leeds's new neighbors in the Pine Barrens could've labeled her 'strange' for any number of reasons: She was from another country, had an accent, was a recluse, or simply that her child would be the unlucky thirteenth. And then, once suspicion was cast in her direction, the locals' imaginations could easily have run wild."

"Do you believe that?" Suzanna asked.

"It's possible. Also, the baby could've been born physically deformed, and that brought on the legend." The professor flipped his palms up. "No one knows."

"Well then, maybe the story's true," Em said with a trace of irony.

"There's one explanation I'm partial to," said the professor, "and it doesn't require belief in the supernatural—the psychological disorder called 'mass psychogenic illness.' The more common term is 'mass hysteria.'"

"You mean like mass hypnosis?" Suzanna asked. "Then all the sightings were just in people's heads?"

"How could so many people be hypnotized," Emily asked, "or mass hysteria-ized?"

"Collective delusion. False or exaggerated beliefs running rampant within small, enclosed settings like schools and convents."

"But the Jersey Devil was seen all over the Tri-State area. That's not enclosed," said Suzanna.

"It doesn't quite match the definition, but it's the most credible explanation."

Em scooched up and asked, "Have you ever seen him?"

Suzanna held her breath.

"No." The professor spoke softly. "But sometimes at the house in Leeds, I can almost feel a presence."

"You mean that two-room house still exists?" asked Suzanna. "I'd love to see it."

The professor opened a laptop on his desk, clicked on a website, and turned the computer to face them. The screen reflected a small, dilapidated, stone house on the peak of a sparsely wooded hill. All along the hillside, straggly pines jutted up, cloaked in fog and shadows.

"It's near the expressway toward Atlantic City." He scrolled through several photos taken from different angles.

"You've gone there?" asked Emily.

"Many times. I'm including these pictures of it in my forthcoming book on the occurrence of mass hysteria throughout Western history. I'm dedicating a full chapter to the Jersey Devil."

Emily's face lit up. "Let's all go and check it out." She eagerly looked back and forth between the professor and Suzanna. "How about tomorrow? I'm off again."

"I'm in!" Suzanna gave Em a thumbs-up.

Emily bounced in her chair. Apparently, she still had no idea that her romantic intentions were falling flat.

The professor pushed back from the desk. "In fact, I wanted to go last weekend. I still need shots of the fireplace to finish up the Devil's chapter of my book." He put his weight on one leg and shimmied his chair out from behind the desk. "But I tore my Achilles tendon."

Em sprang to her feet. Suzanna wriggled forward as far as she could without nudging Sigmund awake. A cast and walking boot encased his foot and leg up to his knee.

Em winced. "That looks painful."

"If I'm careful, I might be able to avoid surgery. Poor Jack's been pushing me around in a wheelchair."

Em sank back in her chair. "So that's why you canceled class last week."

Suzanna could've smacked her forehead. That's why he never stood up.

The professor nodded and took off on a tangent about his injury. Suzanna and Em learned more about the Achilles tendon than they ever wanted to know. At the end, he said, "Tomorrow night's going to be especially tricky. We're flying to Chicago for a baptism. I'm afraid Jack's got his work cut out for him. It'll be difficult but exciting." The professor's face lit up. "We're going to be godparents!"

Suzanna's head spun toward Em, who appeared to be lost in thought. Did she hear what the professor just said? It had to be clear now. She looked at Em with a sympathetic frown. "So just you and me tomorrow. Road trip." Suzanna turned to the professor. "Want us to take those pics for you?"

"Yes, fantastic!"

Em's lower lip stuck out in a full pout. "Sure, we'll go there and take pictures."

"Should we use our phones?" Suzanna asked.

Professor Gardener pulled a canvas carrying case from a low desk drawer. Inside was a sizable camera with a long, bulky lens attached. "Snaps from your phones are okay, but I'd prefer high-res photographs for my book. Do either of you have experience with DSLR cameras?"

As she stood up, Suzanna slipped sleeping Sigmund from her lap to the chair. "I had a course in school." She lifted the elaborate camera from his hand. "Do you have instructions for this?"

He slid a thin booklet across his desk.

Suzanna caught the pamphlet, wishing it was a little thicker. "Only the fireplace then?"

"Try to get close-up shots from the mantel down to the hearth. And just a heads-up—cell phone coverage up there is spotty."

Suzanna put the booklet and camera in the canvas case and set it by her chair. She crammed in beside Sigmund and scooted him back on her lap. He didn't stir from his slumber.

The professor smiled at Sigmund. "He's snug as a bug with you."

"It surprises me, too." She stroked the dog's head.

"Here's an idea. How about dog sitting for me this weekend? My regular dog sitter is away, and I haven't found another. I would drop him at the kennel, but I'd prefer someone took care of him here in the house."

Suzanna was taken aback. What an extraordinary request, out of nowhere. "I've never dog sat. What would I have to do?"

"Come by tomorrow evening and a few times on Sunday. Feed, water, and walk Sigmund, play with him a little. You could even stay overnight."

Before Suzanna could answer, Emily enthusiastically said, "I'll do it!" and scooped Sigmund up. The little dog frantically bellowed his frightful yodel. She dropped him back in Suzanna's arms and stepped away.

"Sorry, Emily," said the professor. "Looks like Sigmund is partial to Suzanna."

Emily plopped back in her chair.

Facing Suzanna, he said, "If you can work it around your schedule, I pay well. What do you think?"

Suzanna really didn't want to get into the pet sitting business. It was an odd offer from someone she hardly knew. Why did he trust her to enter his mansion while he was away and take care of his precious dog? Was this the impression she gave people? Harmless and obliging?

"Would you give me a key or something?"

"Yes, of course. And Jack will teach you how to use the alarm system."

Jack appeared out of nowhere and leaned against the edge of the pocket door. "I'm still figuring out that alarm myself. When we lived in Germantown, we didn't have such fancy—"

"Jack," the professor snapped, "come on."

Through gritted teeth, Jack said, "Sorry."

Suzanna pondered the offer. Spending time with Sigmund in this beautiful house would be nice. But the request was weird, her life was in chaos, and she had obligations. "Thanks for the offer, but I have to work Saturday and Sunday. No rest for musicians."

The professor smiled and shrugged. "No worries."

Suzanna put Sigmund down on the floor. "Bye, Siggy." He scampered away, his little claws clicking out a tremolo. "We'll stop by tomorrow on the way back from Mother Leeds's house and drop off the camera. What time are you leaving for the airport?"

Jack jumped in. "The flight's at seven thirty, so six at the latest."

"If I'm already gone when you get here," said the professor, "hold on to the camera and bring it back another time. Jack will show you out."

Back in the car, Emily hummed a little tune. "What do you think? Cute and loaded. Do I have a chance?"

"Better turn on your gay-dar."

"What?" Em turned so fast toward Suzanna that the seat belt jerked taut by its safety lock. "You think he's gay?"

"Who did you think Jack was?"

"His personal trainer?" Emily asked weakly. She flopped her arms on the steering wheel and sighed.

Suzanna just shook her head. Out of the corner of her eye, she spotted Jason pull up across the street.

Chapter 39

O'Brien dunked one of Marge's donuts in the cold cup of coffee he'd schlepped from home and tried to block out the raucous noise of the squad room. The donut wasn't on his low-fat diet, but he couldn't help it. The vagaries of Suzanna's case were luring him back into old, bad habits.

He was determined to make more progress this morning than he did yesterday. His entire Thursday had been spent chasing down the Jersey Devil link with no result. During the drive to Indian Mills, his gut warned him that he was on a wild-goose chase. His gut was right. The owner of the Devil's Lair wasn't much of a conversationalist, and his record-keeping was even worse. Dead end.

On the way back, the detective interviewed Adam Damon for the second time at his swanky townhouse. It was hard to get a read on him, even though he'd answered every question thoroughly and without hesitation. The guy's upscale lifestyle surprised O'Brien, so he pressed him on his financials. It turned out that Damon was not only pulling in a decent salary from the casino, but he'd inherited a bundle when his parents died in a car accident. Another dead end.

As he licked the chocolate frosting off his donut, he laid out the six suspect cards he made on Sunday: Joan,

Father, Chris, Adam, Harry, and Hoodie Guy. He had interviewed each of them at least once, except the father and hoodie guy. One significant lead had changed—now he could put a name to the father.

When Joan had explained her story, his initial, harsh impression of her mellowed. He'd seen up close what it was like to be starstruck. Not something to be laughed at. One of his major cases back in New York had dealt with the murder of a groupie. The victim's ex stabbed her eighteen times because she'd slept with an up-and-coming rock star.

So many tragedies resulted from stupid, youthful choices. At least Joan owned up to her mistakes. O'Brien admired that. She certainly was an attractive woman. And scary smart. She'd noticed how he held his cell almost up to his nose and to one side when he read messages. Typically, he didn't discuss his vision problem, but somehow with her, it just came out. She listened to him without interruption. Then she told him that the University of Pennsylvania was conducting a new macular degeneration treatment study, and she had a friend working in it. She offered to try to get him in the program. That friend called yesterday, and he'd already been admitted into the research study and scheduled for testing. If he could stop the progression or just slow it down, he'd be forever grateful to Joan.

O'Brien focused back on the index cards. Knowing the father's identity saved him a good chunk of work, but a trip to Boulder to question Isaac Bellow could still be in his future. Before he went down that road, he wanted to learn more about Joan's political ties. Politics was a dirty business, and she ran an entire campaign. It wouldn't hurt to interview her again. Would it?

"How's your case going?"

The detective's head jerked up. Marge was standing next to his desk. He cleared his throat and tried not to show that she'd startled him. "Dragging on too long. It's been a week since the first attack. Every day that goes by brings Suzanna closer to more danger."

She placed a cup of coffee down beside the index cards. "Keep the faith," she said as she sauntered back to her typing and filing.

Marge's coffee was terrible, but he wasn't about to tell her. In the men's room, he poured the bitter sludge down the drain, then headed outside for a smoke. On the way, he snatched Chris's file from his desk.

Cigarette hanging from the side of his mouth, O'Brien slumped against the building and paged through his notes. A patrolman walked by and said, "Wild Bill, just come off the lone prairie?"

The detective didn't even look up. He had to get more info on this roommate, Chris Boyd. Something wasn't right there. During questioning, the guy shook like a jellyfish. Possible drug user. He squashed out his cigarette butt and walked back to his desk, nodding at Marge as he passed.

He glanced at Harry's card. After the hospital chase, it was clear Harry didn't invent the hoodie guy. He'd seen the gray-and-yellow sweatshirt with his own eyes. And the idea of the bomb being racially motivated went out the window with Suzanna's crash. He tore up Harry's card. There was no way the upstanding pub owner was involved in any of this.

But what about that hoodie guy? Why was he checking on Suzanna's injuries? What could his motive possibly be for murder? Total mystery. Itchy. He blew his nose.

The whole case frustrated O'Brien's sense of order. His New York cases were clear-cut—turf wars, drug deals, Mob hits. This investigation had a mysterious twist, and he felt like he was running out of time.

Chapter 40

Emily angled her head out the car window and yelled, "Don't take all day!"

Suzanna slipped into the apartment. No Chris. Relieved, she checked her watch. Only fifteen minutes until starting time at the HB. They'd taken longer at the professor's than she thought.

She rushed into her bedroom, grabbed her gear, and gave the room a speedy once-over. One of her dresser drawers was pulled open, and her pain pills were missing from her bedside table. The first thing that came to mind was that Chris had searched her room for money. Good luck with that! She was broke. But why steal her pills? Unless … Suzanna had enough on her plate. If he was doing prescription drugs for fun, that wasn't her problem.

Back in the car, she slipped her sunglasses back on. She didn't tell Em about the open drawer or the pills. A part of her was starting to feel sorry for Chris.

With Em's help, Suzanna hauled her gear inside the HB and got busy with setup. Behind the bar, Vinny stood, shaking a cocktail and straining it into a snifter. He called out, "Emmy, ain't you off tonight?"

Em marched to the bar and plopped down. "Line 'em up, Vinny. I can't think of a better place to hang out and drown my sorrows on my night off."

Searching through her music, Suzanna selected scores easy to read through the green tint of her glasses. She rotated her shoulder, trying to ease the lingering stiffness. The HB was packed, and the crowd was livelier than usual. Must be the warming weather after the chilly rain of the last few days. Everybody seemed to have spring fever. She'd have to turn up her amp. Despite the festive din, her guitar sounded bright and clear. No carpeting or curtains to dull her tone like at the Ristorante.

As she played, Suzanna stole glances away from her music, taking note of anyone or anything that didn't seem quite right. She didn't have an inkling who to trust anymore. That bald guy sitting alone next to the bar gave her the creeps. His beady eyes squinting at the menu *had* to be the eyes of a hit man. She looked away. Just last week, she would've considered him harmless. She pinned her eyes to her music and kept them there.

A half-hour into her set, Suzanna came out of a daydream about Professor Gardener's house. Crap, she'd stopped listening. Her hands were just going through the motions, the phrases mechanical and bland. She decided to cut herself some slack. So many hopes and fears were crowding her brain. Fears about the attacker. Hopes about her new father. And though she hated to admit it, thoughts of kicking Chris out, too. Only thirty minutes to go until her break. She stretched her back and did her best to keep her mind on the music.

Chapter 41

The HB was crowded, but Arty lucked out and got a small table near the bar. He strained to read the menu. Such tiny print! Prescription reading glasses were probably next. It was one thing after another with this raft of shit called growing old. Throwing the damn menu down, he just ordered coffee but asked the waitress to make it an Irish one, hold the whipped cream. He deserved it. His house was on the market, and he got a sweet deal in Tampa. Steps one and two of his Florida plan—done!

Now, Arty only had to finish up this hit job. In order to create a new strategy, he needed to collect more data, which is why he'd reluctantly driven back to New Jersey.

The waitress came by with his coffee in a glass mug, accompanied by a crunchy Pirouline wafer. Thank you kindly, don't mind if I do. The coffee tasted smooth, almost as good as Starbucks. Better, he thought, as the heat of it spread through his chest. Arty sipped and observed his target while she played guitar. His best ideas always came from watching his targets in action. Surprisingly, he liked her music. It was very relaxing.

Chapter 42

When Suzanna's break time finally came, she joined Em at the end of the bar. Vinny strolled over. "So how'd you like Professor Gardener, Suzanna?" He jerked his thumb toward Emily. "I understand Emmy had a little disappointment." Emily raised her head from her second glass of wine and sneered at him.

Suzanna tilted her head and reflected. "I liked him and learned a lot. He has the most beautiful house *and* the cutest dog. He even asked me to do a side job for him—dog-sitting Saturday night and Sunday. He said I could stay there overnight!"

"You can't!" Vinny exclaimed. "You have to play here Saturday. We can't do without you two Saturdays in a row."

"Don't worry." Suzanna smiled at Vinny and lowered her voice, hoping he might do the same. She hadn't expected him to react so strongly. "I turned him down. I might've been able to squeeze it in, but it would've been crazy hectic. Music comes first."

Harry walked by and asked, "All three of you on a coffee break or something?"

"Chillax, Harry," Emily said without turning away from her glass. "I'm not even working tonight."

Suzanna elbowed Em. "So, road trip tomorrow, right? Jersey Devil house and photos for the prof."

"You still wanna go?"

"Don't you?"

"I guess." Emily emptied her glass and swiveled to face the customer tables. Leaning back on her elbows, she said, "I hate people who take up an entire table but only drink coffee. Look at that old guy. He's been sitting there forever." She swiveled back to the bar. "His waitress is losing a good tip, and he's taking up one of Harry's tables."

Vinny glanced at the guy. "Never seen him in here before. But Emmy, some people just want a hot cup of joe."

Chapter 43

Arty tracked his target's movements as she joined her coworkers at the bar. It was easy enough to listen in on their conversation. He didn't catch every word, but the bartender was facing him, and that Philly accent came through loud and clear.

The waitress topped off his mug. "Sure you don't want something to eat, mister?"

"What?" Arty twisted in her direction.

"Sure, you don't want something to eat?"

"How many times do I have to say no? Are you always this boneheaded or just making a special effort today?"

The waitress spun around and left so abruptly that a puff of air whipped back into his eyes.

He returned to his surveillance. The inside info coming his way was golden. From force of habit, he checked for his lucky chip. But even without it, he could feel his luck returning.

Gardener … the name sounded familiar. Arty took his balled-up Jersey Devil notes out of his breast pocket and was amazed to see Professor Gerald Gardener's name and address on his list of experts. Small world.

The waitress slapped the check folder on the table. He went on eavesdropping, hoping to rake in another lead. But nothing. He took a long swig. Enough. He got what he came for.

When he passed his target's tip jar on the way out, he dropped in a dollar bill. He was wise to the irony but did it anyway.

Chapter 44

Shortly after Suzanna saw the old coffee drinker shuffle out the HB's front door, a group of four couples packed up and left. She stared at them with a vague frown as they walked past her tip jar. No tip.

"What's up?" Em asked.

"That crew comes in every Friday. They used to give me a supersize tip."

"No more?"

"I ruined it a couple weeks ago … broke the wall. They were sitting right beside me while I was playing."

"I know those guys. They drink a lot of wine and always have a great time."

Suzanna nodded. "I overheard their conversation about the Colosseum. That was like my favorite thing on my Rome trip. Without thinking, I spat out, 'Oh Rome, I loved the Colosseum!'"

"Oops."

"I knew the moment the words left my mouth that I broke the wall to pieces."

"And they were clued in to your eavesdropping."

"That's not all. I'm sure they wondered how I could afford to go to Rome. I mean, I was just the help," Suzanna explained.

"They probably thought you were a poor, starving artist."

"Right, and that image went down the drain. I put myself on their level. Always a mistake. Haven't gotten a tip from them since."

Harry dashed out of his office and jammed his face against the window behind Suzanna's performance chair. His eyes narrowed as he searched up and down the sidewalk.

"What's up, boss?" Vinny asked.

Harry pulled Vinny aside. "Thought I saw something on the new security system. Not sure. Did you see a guy with glasses staring in the front window?"

"Nope."

Harry strolled back to his office, a puzzled frown clouding his face.

Chapter 45

On his drive home, Arty considered his new scheme. It called for some extra prep, but his final job would be a thing of beauty. By tomorrow night, it'd be off his plate, and he'd be on his way to Florida.

He climbed out of his trusty Lincoln and went inside his old Cape Cod to get some supper. His chair scraped across the kitchen linoleum as he scooched up to a steaming bowl of canned chicken noodle soup. He idly poked at the stuff in his mum's shoebox while he ate. Sitting on top, the Polaroid of him and his mum on the steps seemed to be bullying him. Sick of looking at it, he flipped it over and stuck it under the other photos.

A cold chill ripped through the room and up his spine. All the lights in the house flashed on and off three times. What the hell?

With the last flash, the lights stayed off.

"Dogshit!" Arty fumbled for the flashlight on the counter. A crescent of light bounced ahead of him as he groped down the basement stairs to check the fuse box. The walls of his musty cellar were made of cracked and crumbling stone and clay. More clay crumbled off every time he climbed the stairs. Small water puddles filled depressions in the uneven cement floor, producing a dank stink that hit him in the face every time he opened the cellar door. The basement served only as a crappy storage area. He'd never thought of making it anything more.

His foot plopped in a puddle, and water splashed up his pant leg. Arty almost lost his balance but steadied himself against the old heater. A cold breeze crept up his back. He couldn't move. He tried to take steps toward the fuse box but was frozen, superglued to the spot. Then, like the negative of a shadow, he saw a white mist sweep across the dark wall behind the heater.

"Mum, knock it off!"

All the lights blinked on. At that exact moment, he could move again. The sudden change in his equilibrium made him tip over and bash into the heater. Pain flashed through his bad knee as it whacked the floor. Son of a bitch! He clicked off the flashlight and limped up the steps.

Back in the kitchen, Arty rubbed his goosefleshy arms and thought he knew what his mum was up to. He rifled through the shoebox for his crucial find—two sets of unused train tickets, one in his mum's name and one in his. None for his pop. This was his evidence. Evidence of why he had no memory of that trip. It never happened.

Everything was fitting together like jigsaw puzzle pieces. The info from *Ghost Hunters* and the train tickets added up to a confused ghost—his mum—whose last wish was to take him to Florida. This was the reason she'd remained in the human realm. This was her unfinished business. But why the electrical shenanigans tonight? Did ghosts have mental breakdowns?

Arty checked out the front window to see if his neighbor's lights were still on. He could bounce his latest spook experience off of Rick, and besides, he'd been feeling kinda bad about yelling at him the other day. Best to patch things up before moving. After throwing a few Advil down his throat, he shuffled across the street.

Rick opened the door. "Hey, Arty. What's up?" Arty waited for pot smoke to pour out. But it didn't.

"I'm here to say adios. I'm moving. You'll see a For Sale sign in the yard in two shakes."

"Be sorry to see you go. I was thinking we could start a supernatural investigators' club." Rick grinned at him. "Then dig into that poltergeist in your house."

"A club? Your elevator doesn't go all the way to the top floor." Arty took a long look at his neighbor. Something was different. What was it? He narrowed his eyes. Then he saw it—Richard Wacker had washed his hair!

"By the way," Arty said, "my minor ghost activity has mushroomed into an all-out haunting. I'm positive it's my mum. She started the electrical haunting tonight."

"Man, your *mother*."

Arty detailed the evening's ghostly visit. He noticed Rick was unusually alert, like he was sober.

"*Ghost hunters* say they stay around until their business is finished," Rick said.

"As soon as I move to Florida, it will be taken care of."
Arty turned to go.

"Do you think she'll cross over when you leave?"

Arty stopped midturn. He'd never thought about that.
"Not sure … wait … yeah, I guess I do."

"You hear I got a job?" Rick smoothed his T-shirt.

"Really? Where at?" Arty couldn't imagine anyone
hiring this stoner.

"Batsto State Park. Giving lectures about the Jersey
Devil."

"Well, cut off my legs and call me Shorty! Congratu-
fucking-lations!"

Chapter 46

Saturday, May 18

From the passenger seat of Em's Subaru, Suzanna pulled her cap off, pushed her sunglasses back and read the directions. Leeds Point sat on the easternmost end of the Pine Barrens, about five miles from the ocean. Suzanna had dressed for the expedition to the Leeds' house—hiking boots, baseball cap, and long pants. Emily wore shorts and flip-flops. Suzanna took one look at Em's outfit, pinched her lips together, and crossed her fingers for minimal climbing.

"Hope we don't run into any Pineys," Em said with a smirk. She backed up the Subaru and headed south toward the part of the Pine Barrens that skirts the shore.

"Come on, Em. That word is insulting. I don't think Professor Gardener approved yesterday."

Emily countered with a floppy, dismissive wave. "I just can't stand the way they dress. Every time it's jeans, work boots, and flannel shirts. And they all act like they've been bonked over the head with a baseball bat."

"Don't say that in front of the professor. Maybe we'll have a Bruce sighting instead."

"He's the biggest Piney of them all!"

"You need a filter."

The light traffic on the flat roads made for a smooth ride, even in Em's old coupe. The air blew noisily through the open windows, whipping Suzanna's thick hair across her face. She glanced over at Emily, who personified the word "chill." Driving with one hand on the wheel and sipping a soda from the other, she gazed out from behind sunglasses with a faint smile on her lips.

They motored through South Jersey's fertile farmland. Vibrant-green fields of snow peas proved that New Jersey really *was* the Garden State. The lush crops shimmered an even deeper green through Suzanna's tinted lenses.

Propping her head back, Suzanna relaxed the tension in her neck that had been building up for days. This trip was a good idea, slipping away for a little while. She was bursting with the news of her brand-new father and peeked over at Em. Not now. Telling Em such an astounding story while she was driving would be suicidal. She could wait until they stopped … completely.

"I gave Detective O'Brien your button."

Em chuckled, a glint of mischief in her eye.

"I'm not sure he appreciates your humor," Suzanna said.

"So many mustache jokes, so little time."

"Cut him some slack. Maybe it makes him feel dashing, like James Bond." Suzanna pictured a tuxedoed O'Brien at a roulette table, drinking a martini.

Em snorted. "Spare me."

"I wonder if he's married."

"Bet you five bucks he's not."

Em pointed down the road at a diner, its retro, silver-and-white facade gleaming in the sun. "Wanna stop for brunch?"

"Sure!" Suzanna set her taste buds for good-old, Jersey diner comfort food.

Inside, at first glance, the bustling diner appeared cliché in every way: gum-chewing waitresses taking orders, short-order cooks clanging ready bells, and a small lunch crowd chatting amid the scraping of knives and forks. But then Suzanna's eyes fell on a disturbing mosaic depiction of the Jersey Devil. It filled the wall behind the counter from end to end. Dull, purple tiles formed the monster's long, serpentine body. Years of splattered grease gave the impression of slimy scales scattered along the forked tail. Snarling fangs, fashioned out of silvery-white tiles, glistened in the fluorescent lights. This version of the Jersey Devil must've come out of someone's nightmare.

As they waited to be seated, the customer chatter died down, little by little, until there was near silence. Only the coffee machine continued to sputter and hiss. That's when Suzanna noticed that most of the customers wore jeans and flannel shirts and had rifles propped by their sides. All faces turned toward Em and Suzanna. And they weren't smiling.

Em caught Suzanna's eye and backed away toward the exit. Before Suzanna could respond, a bone-skinny, white-haired waitress appeared, toting two oversize menus. Red lipstick more than outlined her grin of protruding false teeth.

"How you ladies doing?" Her voice was smiley, but her expression was sour. Then, like a drill sergeant, she barked, "Follow me."

Emily raised her eyebrows, gave Suzanna a big-eyed shrug, and obeyed. Suzanna trailed behind as they passed rows of empty tables butting up against full-length windows. The waitress tossed the menus down on a booth nestled far back in the corner. They plopped down on the cushioned seats featuring shiny, red, fake-plastic leather. It felt like everyone in the room had watched their every step.

Suzanna surveyed the greasy menu, relieved to see nothing but standard diner fare. The waitress whisked paper placemats onto the table, along with sloshing glasses of ice water. She pulled a pencil from behind her ear, took their order, and snatched the menus away without a word.

When the waitress was safely out of earshot, Suzanna whispered, "Unfriendliness influenced by the Jersey Devil, you think?"

"Or just a bunch of creepy Pineys." Em sipped her water.

Suzanna leaned in. "I have news."

Emily froze.

"I found out who my father is."

"Aha! The yearbook!" Em leaned over and folded her arms on the table. "So, he's the senator."

"Not the senator."

Emily's eyes shot up to meet Suzanna's.

Suzanna paused, letting Em suffer for a moment. "My father is Isaac Bellow."

Em started to hiccup uncontrollably. "Holy shit!" she blurted out between hiccups. She raised her index finger for Suzanna to hang on while she held her breath. When the spasms stopped, she said, "Your mom said so?"

Suzanna nodded and narrated an account of her mother's confession, emphasizing the mature restraint of her dignified exit from the room.

"Wait a minute." Em's eyes sparkled with suspicion. "Why should we believe her now?"

"It's the first thing that's ever made sense."

"But—"

"The timeline works. I was born in 1989, she was twenty-one when she had me, and Bellow would've been forty-three."

"He was an old fart!"

Suzanna did the subtraction in her head. "He's twenty-two years older than her."

A whiff of fried onions drifted toward them as the waitress returned carrying a tray so massive, she could barely hold it upright. As soon as Emily saw the straining waitress, she jumped up and helped serve. Plates piled high with omelets, home-fried potatoes, and toast slathered in butter clattered onto the table. The waitress turned on her heel and left with the tray.

"Don't people say 'thank you' around here?" Em knit her brow at the woman walking away. "She took off like her ass was on fire."

Suzanna closed her eyes and sniffed her fluffy omelet. "But the food smells great."

They dug in.

With her mouth full of potatoes, Emily asked, "Can't you order a DNA test or something?" She swallowed. "Will your mom ever see him again? Will *you* meet him?" She jabbed her fork at Suzanna. "Are you gonna be rich?"

"Stop!" Suzanna clanged her knife down on her plate. "I have all the same questions but no answers."

For the rest of the meal, they debated hypothetical scenarios that answered Em's questions. After pushing her plate aside, Suzanna said, "Listen, don't tell anyone about my dad. Detective O'Brien knows, but you're the only person I've told. Without a DNA test, I can't go public with it. That is *if* I go public with it at all."

Em pulled a fake zipper across her lips.

As they strolled back to the car, Emily said, "Strange place."

"But good food." Suzanna crossed to the passenger side.

A flash streaked by on the highway. Suzanna spun around to see the back end of a black Lincoln racing toward Philly.

"Emmy, look!"

Em's eyes followed Suzanna's pointing finger. "Miss girl, nothing's there."

"I saw it." Suzanna's voice croaked. "I heard it go by."

"What are you talking about?"

"The big, black Lincoln that forced me off the road."

Em gave Suzanna a sullen look across the top of the car. "PTSD is playing tricks on you."

"What PTSD? That was real. I felt the draft from it."

"Let's go."

"But—"

"You're still messed up from that accident."

"You think I'm hallucinating?"

"Possibly."

Suzanna stroked the fading stitches above her eyebrow as they drove away. That was no PTSD hallucination, but she wasn't going to fight about it. Then honestly, what were the chances that it had been the same Lincoln that forced her off the road? Not good. And was she really sure that it had been black? Maybe it was blue. She fought back a sob rising in her throat and stared out the window.

As they drove on, the green countryside disappeared, and the Pine Barrens took over. The deeper they traveled into the forest, the more things deteriorated. They passed ramshackle houses, some no more than shacks, with junk cars strewn across the grubby lawns. Tacky signs for local attractions popped up on both sides of the highway. Ancient and battered, they looked more like a warning than a welcome.

Em took off her sunglasses and tapped them on the steering wheel. She surveyed the trash accumulating along the sandy shoulders of the road. "Boy, you can tell when you're getting near the shore. It doesn't just get crappy. It gets *really* crappy."

The forest thickened. Shadows flickered on the loose soil, creating a strobe effect that made Suzanna's head ache. She squeezed her eyes shut. The rank stench of damp pines and rotting wood flooded her nose and mouth—the same smell as Monday night's crash. She shivered and said, "I think the Pine Barrens are every bit as creepy during the day as at night."

"But it's kind of pretty," Em said. "Check out those white flowers. What are they?"

Suzanna opened her eyes and recognized the clusters of tiny, white blossoms amid the carpet of pine needles. "Mountain laurel."

"God, you're such a Girl Scout."

"Only for a nanosecond. What do you know about the Girl Scouts, anyway?"

Em shrugged. "Nada."

They approached a deserted, overgrown crossroad with an old-style traffic light dangling from a thick, wire cable. The light swayed from side to side, creaking in the breeze. It was hard to tell, but the murky, red lens seemed to be lit up. Em hit the brakes.

Across the intersection stood a weathered, metal sign, bent and sloping as though it had been the victim of many fender benders. Emily squinted and read out loud, "Welcome to Leeds Point."

Peering at her directions, Suzanna said, "We're close. A secondary road should be coming up on the left."

Ignoring that the light might still be red, Emily drove on.

Suzanna pointed a few yards ahead. "There." A narrow dirt road snaked up a slight incline before being swallowed by the forest.

Emily turned in and stepped on the gas. An enormous cloud of sandy dust ballooned out behind the car. She jammed on the brakes, smiled at Suzanna, who was coughing, and said, "Oops." She pulled out again at a slow, almost dust-free crawl.

The dirt road soon ended, and the dense forest gave way to a vast field of wildflowers. They both bent forward and squinted through the windshield. There it was, across the wildflower field, atop a tiny, craggy hill—the birthplace of the Jersey Devil. The house looked miserable, dank, and decidedly vacant. At the hill's base, mist hovered around the pines and wound its way up the incline.

Emily whispered, "Spooky."

Suzanna pushed her sunglasses up on her head and took another look. The house had a dark, depraved aura. A massive shadow crawled out from under its eaves and stretched halfway down the hillside.

Keeping their eyes on the house, they crept out of the car. Their feet sank in the soggy, sandy soil. Long scrub grass tickled Emily's ankles and brushed against Suzanna's pants as a horde of cicadas blasted their strange, buzzing chorus. Suzanna glanced at Em, dislodging her flip-flop from the muck, and wondered where Jason might be. She hadn't seen his white SUV all morning.

They crossed the wildflower field to the base of the hill. Suzanna put her hands on her hips and surveyed the line where the flowers stopped and the forest returned. "Let's split up and search along the tree line for a way up." They paced in opposite directions, poking at the brush with their toes and trying not to flinch every time a raven's shriek cut through the cicadas' drone.

Suzanna halfheartedly kicked at a ragged opening in the undergrowth. A cloud of gnats buzzed into her face. Thrashing them away, she got on her knees and pulled back the weeds. A well-traveled footpath led up to the house. She waved Emily over.

Together they broke through the brush, pine needles scratching at their arms. Like a door slamming shut behind them, the vegetation swept back into place, and they were plunged into a murky half-light. The towering pine tops all but cut out the sun.

The path in front of them was tight; they'd have to walk single file. Suzanna shook the damp needles off her sleeves. "Let's go." She elbowed Em and took the lead. Underfoot, sand and loose rocks made her feet slip sideways with each step. Behind, she heard Em stumbling and grumbling as the plastic soles of her flip-flops snagged on stones and tree roots.

The path grew steeper, and the pines thinned. Up ahead, through the gloom, Suzanna could just make out the silhouette of a huge boulder blocking the trail. The closer she got, the bigger it looked. Em followed on her heels. When they reached the rock, they had to tilt their heads back to see the top of it.

"There shouldn't be boulders like this so near the ocean," Emily said. "Only sand and pebbles."

Suzanna ran her fingers over the boulder's rough surface. At least a fourth of it was sunk in the earth. "It's like a rock you'd see hiking up near Allentown. Like it was plucked out of the Pennsylvania mountains and just dumped here."

"If the point is to block the trail, they gotta do better." Em nodded toward the trampled path skirting around the boulder.

Suzanna poked at a column of notches along the stone's smooth side. "Check it out."

"It looks like someone took a sledgehammer to it."

"Steps?" Suzanna asked, putting her foot in the lowest notch. She climbed up with Emily scrambling behind.

At the top, she gazed down at a fantastic view of an emerald valley blanketed with pines. From this height, the forest looked lush and green, not scary at all. She tugged off her cap and shook out her hair.

"What are these?" Emily traced her finger around three long gashes carved into the highest point of the boulder. "Claw marks?"

Suzanna gasped. They were the same scrapes she'd seen on the rock beside the old sawmill. The ones the Devil's Lair guy said came from the Jersey Devil. Did the monster actually tear a chunk out of the Appalachian Mountains and drop it here? To block intruders?

A raven shrieked, and their heads whipped up to the sky. Nothing there.

"This place is messed up," Emily said. Without looking back, she scurried down the stone's steps and took the lead. "Come on, we're almost there."

Beyond the boulder, the pines dwindled to a scant few, letting the full blast of the sun beat down on them. They could see the house up ahead.

At the end of the path, Em stepped out onto a small, sandy plateau and paused. An unnatural stillness hung in the air. "Why is it so quiet up here?"

"The cicadas," Suzanna said. "They stopped."

On the other side of the plateau, the house's darkened windows glared at them. The stone walls looked disfigured, as though years of suffering had caused them to bend in on themselves.

As they shuffled forward over the clearing, the wind picked up so fiercely, its wail cut through the silence. Suzanna caught her cap as it whipped off. Em's shorts and jacket flapped madly against her body. It was like the house was driving them away, telling them to escape while they still could.

"Can't say much for the landscaping!" Suzanna called out over the wind.

Bare patches of dirt and scrub grass scarred the turf surrounding the house's foundation, mingling with a confused mixture of trash … beer cans, candy wrappers, broken bottles, used condoms, you name it.

Emily grabbed at a flapping, plastic grocery bag clinging to the branch of a dead oak tree. "It looks like every high schooler in a ten-mile radius has partied here."

"Smells like it, too." Suzanna held her nose against the odor of skunky mildew and stale beer.

They plodded through stringy weeds and sticker bushes until they stood face-to-face with the front of the house. Up close, they could see the rough, stone exterior gleaming with slimy condensation. Suzanna took small, careful steps up to the rotting, wooden door. It hung cockeyed on one hinge, and its bottom edges suggested some animal had gnawed the wood. When a string of tiny, black spiders crawled through a crack, she jumped back. "Ick!"

Emily nodded. "Double ick."

They continued to creep along the remaining length of the house, passing the crumbling, stone chimney thick with ivy and creeping vines. Suzanna tiptoed up to a side window, trying not to touch it. None of the windows had glass—only dried-up, worm-eaten wooden frames. Em propped her head on Suzanna's shoulder, and together they bent over and peered into the darkness.

As their eyes adjusted, a room no larger than a prison cell appeared. The dirt floor was filthy with mouse droppings and mold, and the interior walls were the same slimy stone as the exterior. Ages of smut and grit coated the inside of the front door. A giant, char-blackened fireplace full of ash and rotten logs ran the remaining length of the wall.

"So that's the famous fireplace the Jersey Devil flew up?" Emily murmured. "It smells like a five-pound sack of dead marmots in there."

Sooty cobwebs swept across the ceiling's wood rafters and cascaded down to the massive mantel like a dingy, lace wedding veil. The flagstone hearth covered at least a quarter of the floor, and the walk-in firebox would've been large enough to hold several of Mother Leeds's largest cooking kettles.

Suddenly, an explosive rush of air smacked the tops of their heads. The flapping of furious wings seemed to come at them from every direction. Suzanna searched the sky. Emily cowered and clenched Suzanna's jacket. High above, an enormous, nut-brown owl circled with wings fully spread.

"It's a great horned owl. Must be a female." Suzanna stared as the owl silently coasted into the forest and disappeared. "The females are bigger than the males."

"Okay, science nerd. Let's just take the pictures and go."

"I can't take the shots through this window. We'll have to go inside."

"I'm not going in there." Emily backed up and crossed her arms. "That fireplace gives me chills!"

"Wait here, then. This'll only take a minute." Suzanna approached the decrepit door but had no idea how to open it without pulling the whole thing off its disintegrating hinge.

Emily yelled, "Just squeeze through!"

Suzanna nodded. The door hung ajar just enough. Once inside the icy room, she breathed through her mouth to keep out the foul odor. This house gave her the creeps the same way Ellis Island did … it was like she could feel the ghosts.

Little black spiders crawled along a cobweb that trailed from one windowsill down to the dirt floor. Cringing, she looked away. An ancient, lopsided, wooden chair that was layered with grime sat beside the hearth. Other bits and pieces of broken furniture were strewn about. Directly across from the fireplace, a smaller, wood door led to the second room.

Apart from two windows, the room's only illumination came from shafts of sunshine filtering through jagged holes in the roof. Suzanna hadn't thought to attach the camera flash. The dim light would have to do. She hoisted the camera onto her shoulder, pulled the viewfinder to her eye, and started snapping.

When she finished with the mantel, she turned to the door leading to the back room where Mrs. Leeds supposedly gave birth. That meant she was standing in the room where everyone got torn to shreds. Allegedly.

Suzanna tilted the camera and aimed at the door of the back room. Through the lens, she saw a whirl of mist drifting out from underneath the door. She ripped the camera away from her face and glared at the door with her naked eyes. No mist. She wiped her sweating hands on her pants. Swallowing hard, she looked through the lens again. The mist reappeared. This time, it morphed into a wriggling, snake-like phantom and slid back under the door.

She pulled the camera down. "Aw, weird!"

"What's weird?" yelled Em from outside the front door.

"Something's in there!" Suzanna wrapped her fingers around the doorknob and tugged. A flurry of dust burst out as it gave way.

"Leave it alone, whatever it is!" Emily shouted.

It was like Suzanna had opened a door to a cave. There were no windows in the back room. Feeble rays of natural light illuminated the first few feet, but the remaining space was blinding blackness. In the limited light, she could just make out the edge of a thin, dirty mattress. God, do kids have sex in here?

Suzanna took one step inside. The odor came at her in a wave. Blood and rotting death. She clapped her hand over her mouth and nose and jumped backward out of the room. With the camera clenched to her breast like a life preserver, she landed on her butt. The door slammed shut.

Her pulse thumped in her ears, but she clearly heard high-pitched babbling, like a child's voice, from behind the closed door. She froze. The babbling merged with a moaning animal snarl. The snarl slowly built to a piercing howl. She darted out the front door, almost knocking it down. "Emmy! I think I'm having another hallu—"

Em was running toward the path, waving for Suzanna to follow. Then she disappeared down the trail.

Suzanna sensed a rasping intake of air at her back. The breath was expelled with a hiss that grazed her neck. Without looking back, she sprinted across the plateau and skidded down the path, rocks and sand spurting out from under the soles of her boots. She slackened her pace at the boulder and, with a shudder, snuck one last peek at the creepy house.

Chapter 47

Operation Finger Safety *had* to work out, and it had to work out tonight. There was no more time. There would be no more extensions.

From under his mattress, Chris pulled out his *Calvin and Hobbes* wall calendar—the nerve center for Operation Finger Safety. It used to hang over his bed to track his practice schedule. Now, it was folded open to the month of May and hidden where Suzanna had no business looking.

The timing for each step of the plan was neatly noted in the calendar's dated squares. He had scrawled a checkmark through every task as he accomplished it.

A fire-red circle filled the day of Saturday, May 4. Exactly two weeks ago. It marked the day he'd been robbed, beaten, and then threatened by Micky. That day, he had gone into a dazed tailspin and proceeded to snort, smoke, and drink anything he could find, wasting two entire days. The calendar squares for those two days remained blank.

Wednesday, May 8, was the day he sobered up and got to work searching the web for instant moneymaking ideas. Blackmail had been in the back of his mind thanks to Suzanna's stupid threat. So when he'd stumbled onto the article, "How to Blackmail Someone in Six Easy Steps," naturally, his interest was piqued. The steps were super clear, painless, and just like it said—easy.

Chris grabbed his wooden mortar and pestle from the bedside table. He'd bought the tool at a yard sale, attracted by its dark cedar color and smell. Sitting at his small desk, he crushed Suzanna's pain pills into a fine powder. The motion of pestle against mortar was sensual—mash, swirl … mash, swirl—almost erotic. As he worked, he reviewed each dated step of Operation Finger Safety from Wednesday, May 8, through today, Saturday, May 18. He reveled in his ingenious methods for accomplishing the steps.

Step 1. Find a target and get to know them. Completed Wednesday, May 8.

Micky had often bragged about his high-level clients: local celebrities and the wealthy. Chris hadn't paid much attention until the name of someone he'd actually met came up. He nearly choked on his beer when he heard that State Senator Bancroft was one of Micky's customers.

So, step one was simple. Chris did some poking around online and found plenty on the senator's education, career as a lawyer, and entrance into politics. He'd learned that Bancroft was the Democratic Party's current darling, even rumored to be presidential material. Examining pictures of him on the campaign trail, Chris noted that the senator was popular with the ladies. Bancroft's arm always seemed to be around some young beauty while smiling with those bright-white teeth. In the photos with his wife and daughter, though, he just stood grandly beside them with a raised chin and puffed-out chest, reeking of power.

By the end of the day, Chris knew the senator inside out. That evening, he even did a little recon work and snapped pictures from his car window of the Bancroft family in their front yard.

Step 2. Decide amount and method of payment. Completed Thursday, May 9.

Chris only needed a thousand to keep his fingers safe, but why shouldn't he make a profit, too? With a few grand more, he could hire a manager and get on a concert circuit. Maybe even buy a new guitar. Twenty grand would set him up nicely. Why not? If he was really going to do this, go big or go home. And as for the method of payment … cash only.

Step 3. Write the Blackmail Letter. Completed Thursday, May 9.

He'd crafted a perfect letter, properly typed. No identifying handwriting. Chris knew there was a reason he hadn't trashed that old Corona Selectric his mom had given him. The letter contained the blackmail amount and where to put it on Sunday, May 12. The threat? That he would tell the press about the senator's drug use and infidelity if he didn't pay up, and a warning to not contact the police.

Chris included "infidelity" as a guess. He'd assumed, from all the pictures, that there had to be something there.

The fun part was the "where." He'd told Bancroft to put the money in the compartment under the handle of Suzanna's case while she played at Ristorante Buena. It felt like such a coup, arranging it so Suzanna would unknowingly deliver the money. That cubby was just the right size for an envelope of cash.

He copied the exact words of the letter on the back page of his calendar for reference. Looking at it now, Chris saw he'd been cutting things close between the time he would get Bancroft's cash and the time he had to pay Micky. Same day. Blackmail growing pains.

Step 4. Ensure the letter will be opened. Completed Thursday, May 9.

Chris bought a self-sealing, non-bendable, Priority Mail envelope at the post office and three mailing stickers: *Open Immediately*, *Time Sensitive*, *Private and Confidential*. He plastered the stickers on the envelope and sealed the letter inside.

Step 5. Deliver but keep off the radar. Completed Thursday, May 9.

The chances of the letter getting directly to Bancroft were better at his office than at his home. Chris attached a label with the senator's office address printed in red and dropped it in a public mailbox. He worried about not having a way to check that Bancroft received it. He was pretty sure it would get there within a day, but … Without a solution, he just rolled with it. Neither snow nor rain nor heat nor gloom, right?

Step 6. If target doesn't comply, follow up. Completed Monday, May 13.

Sunday night, Letter #1's payoff date, Chris had checked Suzanna's guitar case while she was talking to that detective. No cash. The fact that step six existed assured him that his situation was routine.

The next day, he sent a follow-up letter along with family photos. This time, he told Bancroft to put the money in Suzanna's case while she played at the HB. But when he wrote it, he'd been seriously high. Off his game. Chris had upped the payoff amount to fifty grand. That might've been a mistake. But with that kind of dough, he could rent out halls for his own concerts and have the cream of the crop in management. Twenty grand sounded like chicken feed in comparison.

Chris wondered if Bancroft blew off paying on Sunday because he needed more time to get the cash. His follow-up blackmail letter gave a gentler deadline of Saturday, May

18—today—a whole week. It had included all the previous warnings, along with a further threat to his wife and daughter's safety. He inserted the photos he'd taken of Bancroft's family.

That final payout was due tonight. If Letter #2 hit its mark, he would have the money in a matter of hours. Nothing to do now but wait. He decided to make a list of the concert halls he'd like to rent out. That would give him something to look forward to, and visualization was a powerful tool for success; Piano Dan was always telling him that. Then again, Piano Dan was held captive in front of a computer screen for a paycheck. Maybe he'd visualized the wrong keyboard. All the same, Chris snatched up a pen and the stack of paper he'd *borrowed* from Suzanna. Holding one of the sheets up to the light, he scrutinized it. He'd never noticed that little guitar at the bottom before. Goddammit, that was just like her. Such a commercial sellout!

Chapter 48

Following their harrowing visit to the Jersey Devil house, Suzanna and Em drove to Professor Gardener's neighborhood to return the camera. The cottony clouds were starting to mirror the oranges and reds of the setting sun, except it was only late afternoon. Too early for the sun to go down. Suzanna took her sunglasses off and examined the sky. Splotchy orange tinged the clouds.

Emily turned onto Darby Road and slammed on the brakes. Smoke and chaos were everywhere. The professor's house was ablaze. A police blockade of sawhorses and yellow tape sealed off the front of the estate. Fire trucks and ambulances streamed down the street, their sirens wailing. A fleet of firefighters scurried around the house, their yellow slickers flickering in the flashing lights. Everyone was shouting.

A white SUV sped past Em's Subaru and came to a screeching halt at the blockade. Jason bounded out and joined the battle.

Em pulled over to the curb. They leaped out and raced toward the house. Ash was floating through the air like snowflakes. At the blockade, Jason's arm shot out and stopped them cold.

"Hi, again!" Em shouted over the mayhem and gave Jason a zesty smile.

Was Em flirting at a time like this? Of course, she was. Her default setting was flirt.

Suzanna called out through cupped hands, "Is the professor all right?"

Jason nodded. "Everyone's out."

The flames were attacking the center of the house. That gorgeous door and stairwell! The antique woodwork would be impossible to replace. Through the smoke, Suzanna glimpsed movement in an annex window. She tore off her sunglasses and saw Sigmund, clear as day, jumping up and down. Water was pouring from the ceiling, and his little body was soaking wet. His neck was stretched high and his mouth open wide, but with all the yelling and sirens, no one heard his pitiful yodel.

"The dog's in there!" Suzanna strained against Jason's arm.

"Stand back and let the firefighters do their job," Jason yelled as sweat dripped off his chin.

"But they aren't doing anything for Sigmund!"

Four Philadelphia Police SUVs rocketed down the road. A flurry of uniformed officers exploded from the cars, adding to the confusion.

Taking Emily by the elbow, Suzanna led her to the end of the driveway under the immense pitch pine. She shouted in Em's ear, "Can you distract Jason? I'm going to get that dog out."

Emily pulled a tissue from her purse and shoved it in Suzanna's hand. "Hold this over your mouth and nose. And put your sunglasses back on. They'll keep the smoke out of your eyes."

Emily sauntered up to Jason. "One of those fire guys pinched my butt!"

"What?" A puzzled frown passed over Jason's face.

"It's harassment. I mean, just because major shit is going down doesn't mean you can go around pinching people's asses."

"Which guy?"

"I think it was that tall one by the truck."

"Emily, this isn't the time."

"What? When *is* the time to pull the plug on butt pinching?"

"We'll see about that later."

"I think you should go check now. And why aren't you in uniform? How do these guys know you are police?"

As Em continued to serve up a baffling mess of complaints to Jason, Suzanna slipped through the blockade and dashed to the back of the annex. Black smoke was pouring out of the mansion's rear windows. She crept along the building, trying not to take in the acrid, smoky air.

Eyes itching and watering, she went to the first annex window. She rubbed her eyes with her knuckles, but it only made the itching worse. Through the leaded window, she could just make out Sigmund bounding up and down on the other side of the room. His poor yodel sounded frantic.

Suzanna scanned the window but saw no clear way to open it. Lacking a better idea, she turned away, shielding her face with her hands, and kicked at the glass with all her might. The pane broke in half, and the heavy shards fell into the basement. Only the window frame remained.

Billowing columns of smoke swirled from the new breach. "Sigmund!" With his little snout snuffling and his curled tail trying hard to stick up straight, he cast his head from side to side looking for her. When their eyes met, Sigmund galloped across the room and leaped through the window into her arms. She clutched him to her chest and burst into a coughing fit. Sigmund wagged his tail like crazy and licked her face.

When she stopped hacking, she heard a wheezing cough inside the house. Then a sneeze. "Siggy, someone's in there." She opened her mouth to yell for help but started coughing again. Who could still be in the house? If she didn't get help, they might die.

A beefy hand latched onto her shoulder, jerking her away from the window. She desperately held on to the soggy, wriggling dog. The burly firefighter's grip tightened as she struggled to get free. He yanked her to the front of the house.

"Someone's in there," Suzanna screamed at the guy holding her. "Why isn't anybody doing anything?"

"I have my orders. No one gets near the house, it's not safe. Let the firemen do their job, lady!"

She wrapped her arms tighter around Sigmund. "But they're not doing their job!"

From the mansion across the street, a woman in a cocktail dress and spike heels rushed toward them carrying a full martini glass. The gin and vermouth sloshed from side to side in the glass, but she didn't lose a drop. For a second, Suzanna thought the woman was bringing the firefighter a drink. But instead, the woman yelled in the guy's face with a screeching soprano. "What are you doing about all the other houses? Just because this guy lets his go up in flames—"

The firefighter gritted his teeth and growled, "We're doing everything possible to contain the fire."

Suzanna tried to take advantage of the distraction and pull away. Sigmund nipped at the firefighter's sleeve, but the guy held firm.

"It's a blessing his parents died in that accident and don't have to see this," the woman said. "This was never supposed to be his, and now look at it!" With watery eyes, she turned toward Suzanna as though she was her confidante. "You know they disowned him when he came out of the closet but died before changing their wills."

Men in khakis and polo shirts, alongside women in designer jeans, swarmed out of nearby estates and stomped in their direction. It looked like an angry golf outing. The firefighter faced the gathering horde. Sigmund flailed in Suzanna's arms and bit their captor's hand. Finally, the grasp on her shoulder eased. Dropping Sigmund, she squirmed out of her jacket and raced for the barricade. The firefighter was left holding Suzanna's jacket in his outstretched hand.

"Good one, Siggy!" she yelled as she ran, the little dog trotting along at her heels.

Chapter 49

Arty crouched in the bushes behind Professor Gardener's house. This guy had quite a mansion, even for the snazzy Main Line, but it burned like any other house.

That morning, he'd gone back to the Jersey Devil birth house. He couldn't get that back room out of his mind. But when he had attempted to open its door, it stuck fast. It reminded him of the used bookstore's sticky door. He'd tried again and again but never got it open. So, he gave up, left the house and the room behind, and hightailed it back to Philly to finish his job.

It was early afternoon by the time Arty stationed his car catty-corner to Gardener's estate. He parked beside a neighbor's weeping willow tree, giving him partial coverage. These Rockefellers with their damn spick-and-span yards. While he waited, he entertained himself by spying into the neighbors' houses with his binoculars. Eventually, a muscular, young man emerged from Gardener's house carrying an armful of suitcases to the driveway. When the car doors opened like wings, he realized he was staring at a Tesla. It looked like it came off the set of some sci-fi movie. Crazy-ass rich people.

As Mr. Muscles loaded the suitcases, an old sedan pulled into the drive. Arty snickered—the change of auto was his doing. His target musta borrowed this old junker; it was almost as bad as her crappy Maverick.

Mr. Muscles and Arty's target talked beside the Tesla and then disappeared inside the house. As time wore on and they didn't come out, Arty worried that the muscle guy might not leave with Gardener. He didn't want to deal with Arnold Schwarzenegger. But just then, the guy reappeared, steering Gardener in a wheelchair. The two made a huge production out of getting Gardener and the wheelchair into the Tesla. They finally settled in and sped away. What a relief. His target was alone in the house. Time to get down to business.

Arty took his trusty bottle of chloroform out of the glove compartment, wrapped it in a handkerchief, and put it in his pocket. He lifted his knapsack from the passenger seat, being careful not to jostle the can of gasoline inside.

A job in broad daylight was always a gamble. He reached in his pocket for his lucky chip and ground his teeth, remembering again that he'd thrown it in the ocean. He shook it off. He didn't need that stinking chip.

Picking the annex lock was a cinch, and disengaging the alarm, only a little trickier. Arty slid into a long stretch of room. The floor was covered with thick, beige, wall-to-wall carpeting. That carpet was hard to miss because the room was completely empty. No furniture, no pictures on the walls, no nothing. He soft-shoed it along the side wall and up a flight of steps to a closed door. With his ear against the door, he could hear his target moving through the house.

This was the delicate part of the operation. Arty softly unlatched the door, held it ajar, and waited until she walked by. Without a sound, he crept up behind her, reached his arm around, and crammed his chloroformed handkerchief over her mouth. Then, dragging her by the ankles, only stopping once to sit and gulp in some air, he pulled her into a closet. He kept her facedown, not wanting to look at her for his mum's sake. Funny, though. She seemed taller and heavier than he'd expected. She was still out for the count when he shoved her against the closet's back wall.

To lock her in, Arty sealed off the door using the fork trick he'd learned from his pop. Very handy for doors without locks … like, for instance, a closet door. He'd prepared the fork by breaking off the handle and bending the tines. He placed the hooked tines into the strike plate, closed the door, and slid the fork's handle through the base of the tines. If she tried to open the door, it would hit the fork handle and press the tines farther into the strike plate. Locked. Classic.

Arty doused the place with gasoline and lit the fire, then slipped out the back and snuck up an embankment to a thicket of leafy bushes.

And now, Arty sat amid those bushes, watching his masterpiece unfold. He leaned back on his elbows and chewed a beef jerky. The plan had gone without a hitch, and he felt pretty smug about it. But when he casually glanced down at the barricade in front of the house, he sprang to his feet and refocused his binoculars. *What the fuck?* That jacket, that hair, and those damn sunglasses. He looked without the binoculars and then with them again. He knew right away he'd screwed up. She wasn't locked in a closet but running down the street toward the burning house!

Goddammit! He felt like the one-legged man at an ass-kicking contest. No sense putting it off. He called his client from his cell. He had to yell to be heard. "I missed again. She's here at the scene."

"Of course, she's there. What do you mean?"

"She *just* got here. My timing musta' been off."

"Not again! Grab her. Go someplace private—out of the way." His client's voice was tremulous. "Someplace where you can get it done. And use a gun for Christ's sake!"

Arty wriggled through the bushes. Firefighters were erecting more barriers at both ends of the block, and a news van had pulled up, spewing cameramen and reporters. He edged down the side of the main house, staying out of sight. Squatting in the shrubbery, he waited for a team of firefighters to jog by. When they bulldozed past him, they came so close that their long, yellow coats flapped against his legs.

A swell of smoke whooshed out as the last runners passed and smacked Arty in the face. He lost his balance and fell flat on his ass. "Goddamn douchebagglers!" His burning eyes teared up as he took in a lungful of black fumes. Behind the bushes, he braced his back against the house and coughed until he almost puked. The whole time, a fine mist from the fire hoses soaked through his clothes. Crackerjack working conditions!

He sidled down to the driveway, staying by the hedges, and tried to take stock of the blockade. Everything was blurry and fuzzy, like static on a TV. People were running in every direction. Rubbernecking neighbors were straining and shouting over the sawhorses. Trying to stop the burning, he swiped away tears, but his eyes filled up even more. Then, he spotted his target again. Blurry-eyed or not, he couldn't miss those big-ass, rainbow sunglasses.

Chapter 50

Suzanna skidded into the barricade and pounced on the first firefighter she found. "There's still someone in there!" Her urgency and anguished cry must have been convincing because he turned on his heel and sprinted to the house.

She twirled in a circle, searching the barricaded area for Emily, but her friend wasn't there. The Subaru was still parked along the curb a block down the street. Where the hell was she?

Glancing back at the burning house, Suzanna watched as the firefighter she'd swooped on disappeared inside. She hoped he'd get that coughing person out in time.

Again, she looked around for Emily. She returned to the pitch pine tree and looked around the bottom branches. Not having any luck, she hunted through the straggling neighbors, sawhorses, and police tape. Em had vanished.

Something was shimmering by the leg of a sawhorse. Em's sunglasses! A few feet away, Sigmund was sniffing and clawing at Em's purse. It lay on its side, twisted and deserted.

Suzanna looked back at the Subaru and saw a stocky man bear-hugging something beside the passenger door. "What the hell—hey!" It was Em. She was thrashing and kicking. One flip-flop flew through the air and bounced off the Subaru's hood. The man forced a cloth over her mouth.

She couldn't believe her eyes. Suzanna blinked away tears, whether from the smoke or the shock, she wasn't sure. She tried to run, but her feet seemed to be frozen in place. All she could do was stare with her mouth agape as the man half-walked, half-dragged Em to a car across the street.

Sigmund jumped up on her legs, startling her into action. She bent down and scooped him up. By the time she looked back, Em's hands were tied behind her back, and the guy was putting a black hood over her head.

"Police!" Suzanna shrieked. No one responded. Firefighters, police, and reporters were all fixated on the fire. She made a panicky grab for her cell phone from her jacket pocket, but her jacket and the phone were still back with the shoulder-clamping firefighter.

Suzanna ran toward the cars, carrying the wriggling dog and Em's purse banging against her knees. Sweat dribbled down her forehead. As she ran, she saw the man shove Emily into the car trunk. It was the trunk of a big, black Lincoln.

When the man climbed into his car and powered up the engine, she tucked in her chin and all-out sprinted. But before she could get there, the Lincoln, with Em in the trunk, had eased out onto Darby Road.

She dashed to the Subaru. With sweaty fingers, Suzanna pulled Em's car door open and tossed Sigmund in the back. She dove behind the wheel, upended Em's purse on the passenger seat, and rifled through the junk for the car keys. No keys. Her eyes zeroed in on the ignition. There they were. Unbelievable. Em had dragged a purse with her but left the keys in the ignition.

As Suzanna started the Subaru, she glimpsed the Lincoln halfway down Darby Road. She grasped at a lever, hoping for the gearshift, but the windshield wipers swished across the glass. "No!" she wailed, "not again!" Closing her eyes, she could picture Em using the gearshift between the front seats. She jammed the Subaru into drive and tore after the Lincoln.

The black sedan cruised, almost floated, to the barrier at the end of the block. Suzanna lagged well behind, her hands shaking on the wheel. The Lincoln had to stop for a crowd of bystanders clogging the blockade. The group sauntered slowly out of the way, giving Suzanna precious seconds to catch up.

She glanced in the rearview mirror. Through the burnt and shattered front door, EMTs carried a stretcher. That must be the person she heard coughing. The dog sitter, maybe? With sudden realization, she cried out, "That's supposed to be me!"

The Lincoln cleared the barrier. No time to worry about the person who should've been her. Staying on the black car's tail, Suzanna settled on a plan—dial 911 from Em's cell, then keep following the Lincoln until the cops showed up. Reaching over to the passenger seat, she fished through hair ties, lipstick, coins, and cough drops before finally clutching the phone. One glance told her it was out of power. Completely dead. And no way to charge it in the old Subaru.

Suzanna smacked her hands on the steering wheel and frantically weighed her options. Should she keep going after the Lincoln or go back for help? Jason was still at the fire; she could get back to him in minutes. But then, how would they know where to find Em? It was anybody's guess where the man was taking her. Suzanna's only choice was to keep trailing the Lincoln.

But what could she do when they stopped driving? With no phone and no Jason, her only weapon was surprise. When the guy got out of the car, she'd have to sneak up and take him out. Somehow. Most importantly, she couldn't let him know she was on his tail. She stayed as far behind as she could without losing him.

Sigmund vaulted into the front passenger seat right on top of Em's junk. He perched on his haunches, looking forward through the windshield. Ears erect, he peered down the road as though searching for something. She reached over and patted his head. "Gonna help me, Siggy? Be quiet. We can't give ourselves away." Not making a sound, Sigmund sat and stared straight ahead, his muzzle taut like a hunter in pursuit.

Missing her jacket, Suzanna shivered. She resented having to leave it back with the firefighter and the martini lady. That lady said the professor had been disowned. He wasn't meant to inherit. Could he have had a hand in his parents' accident? The neighbor certainly was suspicious.

Exactly what kind of accident had it been? If his parents had died in a car accident, he could've tampered with the brakes, or he could've thrown them overboard in a boating accident. Or maybe he threw them off a cliff. That would be hard to do to two people at once. And having met the professor, Suzanna didn't believe he could do any of those things. But the fact that he'd expressly asked her—a stranger—to dog sit in his house on the very day it went up in flames was way too freaky.

A streak of lemon yellow hurtled across Suzanna's path. She slammed on the brakes. Sigmund slid off the passenger seat and lay on the floor, making a pitiful, guttural moan.

"Sorry, Siggy!"

A bumblebee-colored Mini Cooper drove away unconcerned, as though it hadn't just cut her off. Sigmund hopped back up on the seat, and his warm, brown eyes became hard and dark. She knew an incriminating look when she saw one. His eyes said, *Stop wondering about the professor. Focus.*

Ahead, the Lincoln turned off Route 70 in the same direction she and Em had gone that morning. Suzanna almost lost sight of them. "You're right, Siggy. I need to keep my eyes on the road." She stroked his back, and he rested his head on her arm.

They drew closer to the shore and dusk set in, filling the sky with streaks of deep purple and scarlet. Fearfully, she watched the thickening pitch pine forest rise up on all sides. This route was all too familiar. The traffic thinned, and she relaxed her aching jaw muscles. She'd been clenching her teeth for miles. Transferring her stress to her hands, Suzanna squeezed the wheel tighter. Sigmund wagged his tail. He seemed to enjoy the chase.

"Siggy, it can't be. It just can't be," she said as she tailed the Lincoln through the deserted intersection with the *Welcome to Leeds Point* sign. Even though everything pointed to it, she still gasped when the Lincoln turned onto the dusty dirt road leading to the Jersey Devil's birthplace.

Suzanna parked Em's car on the shoulder of the main highway. There was no way she could drive up that road and stay incognito. The Subaru's knocking engine alone would give her away, but driving, even slowly, would kick up a mountain of dust.

She opened the window, a crack for Sigmund. "You'll be fine," she said with a forced, reassuring tone. "Don't pee in Emily's car." The wrinkles on Sigmund's forehead deepened into a frown that said, *What kind of a dog do you think I am?*

She gently nudged the Subaru's door shut and crouched beside it. When the Lincoln's rear lights disappeared, she rubbed her cold arms and jogged up the dirt road after them.

Dusk was turning to night in the pine forest, and Suzanna started to second-guess herself. Even with surprise as her weapon, how could she overpower this guy? She was no hero. Worst case, she'd end up like Em—tied up with a hood over her head. And what if the guy was purposely luring her to the Jersey Devil house? But why in the world would he do that?

Suzanna's eyes began to tear up; this was all her fault. All the dreadful events of the past week centered around her, even though she couldn't explain any of it. If it weren't for her, Em would be safe, the professor's house would be intact, and Baby would still exist. She had to make things right. Somehow.

At the wildflower field, she stopped jogging. She could almost taste the spicy-sweet scent of the mountain laurel. By the remaining snippet of red-purple sunset, she could make out the guy dragging Em along the path to the house. A flashlight tied to his belt swayed and bounced, its harsh, white beam streaking back and forth across the pines like a deranged searchlight.

Chapter 51

Arty hauled his target up the path.

At the boulder, he took a breather and propped her against the huge rock. His mum wouldn't approve of his kidnapping this girl and dragging her up a hill. Arty's mum wouldn't approve of any of his methods. Maybe she'd jinxed him, and that's why his other plans failed. But why wait until he was older than dirt to pester him? If she just wanted him to retire to Florida, he was happy to oblige. Tonight, after he got out of town, she'd be batting a thousand in resolving her unfinished ghost business.

The cloth hood swayed as his target came to. In a flash, she dove into battle like a wild animal. Arty tried to control her thrashing, but she was strong. From under the hood, she spat out, "Let me go, you pig-fucker!" She kicked in every direction. One shot caught Arty's bad knee.

"Dogshit!" Arty stamped his foot. "Stop or I'll cut off those guitar-plucking fingers."

His prisoner froze. "I don't ha—" Tilting her head back, she groaned. "Am I supposed to be Suzanna?"

Arty pulled the hood off. "What the—" This girl didn't look anything like his target. In fact, she was the complete physical opposite. Stand them next to each other, they'd be Mutt and Jeff.

"Hey, you're that coffee guy!" She glowered at him.

"Shut your trap." Arty poured more chloroform on his handkerchief, wrestled it over her face, and she sank to the ground. He pulled a roll of duct tape out of his knapsack and slapped a strip across her mouth. "Tough luck, honey. You just became target number two."

Chapter 52

Suzanna fought her way up the darkened path, only slowing after she passed the boulder. Squinting through the shadows, she found a branch the size of a baseball bat and tested its strength by slamming it against a tree trunk. With a crack, the branch shattered into a pile of kindling.

At the end of the path, she stumbled on a shorter, firmer branch. To inspect it, she dangled it between two fingers in front of her face. Gagging, she threw it down. It wasn't a stick. It was a bone. A bone the size of a human femur. What kind of animal has a bone like that? Trying to rub away the dirt and disgust, she wiped her hands on the back of her pants.

The next step she took, her foot struck a half-buried rock. Suzanna pulled it out of the sandy soil. Small but hefty, the stone fit perfectly in her hand. It would have to do as her weapon. She could bash the guy on the head with it or throw it at him. But then, she was never known for her throwing arm. Best just to conk him with it. She'd have to get up close.

At the plateau, she braced for the wind of that afternoon but found it completely calm. She tiptoed around to the side of the house and crept up to the same window she'd looked through just a few hours earlier.

Emily was sitting in the center of the stuffy room, bound to the lopsided chair with bulky rope. The black hood was hiked up to her nose, held there by the strip of duct tape over her mouth. Suzanna couldn't help but note that Em's nose wasn't big enough to hold up that hood on its own. A little gush of guilt caught at her throat. What an idiot. Jealous of Em's nose at a time like this.

On the mantel, a flashlight balancing on its tail cap glowed upward. It threw a stark-white streak on the ceiling's wood beams and cast a ghostly gloom over the rest of the room. A man ranting into a cell phone kept shaking it and holding it up in different directions.

Suzanna gulped. In his other hand, he held a gun. And now she recognized him. The old coffee guy. At the HB, she'd been sitting only a few feet away from him!

"I got more bad news," Coffee Guy yelled into the phone.

The reply was muffled.

"I got confused at the fire. I snagged the wrong target. Speak up, it's a shitty connection."

Suzanna turned and pressed her back against the clammy house, gradually sliding into a sitting position on the ground. She could surprise Coffee Guy by running into the room and screaming. But then he would probably just shoot her. She could sneak up behind him and knock him out, as long as he didn't hear her coming.

She pushed her ear against the slimy stones. The voice on the other end of the phone came through clearer.

"You have someone else?" the voice bellowed. "What's wrong with you? Fix it."

"What do you want me to do? Jump up and down and spit wooden nickels?" Coffee Guy shoved off the wall and paced. "I could take out this one here, then go get the other one."

Crystal clear, Suzanna heard the voice roar, "Devil's teeth! This is my whole life!" She jumped up and glared through the window.

Only State Senator Bancroft said Devil's teeth.

A soft prickling tickled her wrist. One of those tiny, black spiders was creeping up her arm. Suzanna squirmed and swiped it away. The gravel shifted under her feet. She tottered and plunged downward. As she fell, she grabbed the window frame. Her fingernails dug into the rotting sill and scraped along its entire length. The scratching noise it made echoed in the night. She landed flat on her back.

"What the hell was that?" Coffee Guy's raspy voice trembled.

Suzanna waited, glued to the ground. Sensing a raw tenderness in her fingertips, she quietly arched her hand at the wrist to check the damage. Her precious plucking nails were cracked and broken.

Coffee Guy didn't say another word. The silence was worse than his ranting. She gripped her stone and rolled it around in her palm like a stress ball. An unearthly whine rose from the distance as she inched back up to the window. It seemed to come closer as it crescendoed into a wailing howl.

Coffee Guy cried out, "Fuck me, the Jersey Devil!"

Em mumbled through the tape, "You give stupid a bad name."

Suzanna was relieved to see Em conscious, but geez, did she have to insult a man with a gun?

"Put a cork in it!" Coffee Guy's eyes darted around the room.

Emily chewed half the tape away and said, "You can't find your ass with both hands."

Arty turned toward Em, raising the gun. "And you're nothing but a scum-sucking pus bag." He took aim.

No time to run up behind the guy. Suzanna threw the stone as hard as she could. It flew past Coffee Guy's head and hurtled toward the door to the back room.

The stone crashed into the door, the handle popped free, and the door yawned open.

Another eerie howl reverberated through the forest.

Coffee Guy stood rigid, every muscle locked in place. A funnel of mist swirled out of the back room and flew to the fireplace. It whipped by so fast that Suzanna wasn't sure what she'd seen, or if she'd seen anything at all. At the hearth, the mist churned up cinders, dirt, and cobwebs, blasting it all at Coffee Guy.

Coffee Guy swung around toward the noise. With soot flying in his face, he unloaded his whole clip in all directions. As the shots rang out, Suzanna ducked under the window.

"Fuck!" Em shouted.

"He's here!" Coffee Guy gulped in a lungful of ashes and fled, wheezing, out the door.

When Suzanna sprang up to the window, she thought she was really hallucinating. There it was, and there it wasn't, the misty funnel disappearing up the chimney.

Turning to Em, she asked, "You o—" She gaped at the stream of blood running down the chair leg.

Chapter 53

Joan was putting in another Saturday, and for that matter, another late night, at campaign headquarters when she heard a tantrum burst out of Bancroft's office. As she jogged down the hall, she overheard the senator talking to someone—a male voice she didn't recognize. Instead of going in, she backed up against the wall behind the half-open door and listened.

"I should've just called the cops," Bancroft said, his voice thin and weak. Joan had never heard him sound so wretched. "I used to have a couple of those guys in my pocket."

"Are you out of your mind?" The other man spewed the words out through his teeth. Joan pictured a human-size weasel hissing at Bancroft. "You would've been arrested, and this clusterfuck would be all over the headlines."

"I'd rather die."

"That's your big thing, isn't it? 'I can't be exposed,'" Weasel Man said in a whiny, childish voice. He chuckled. "Getting caught with your limp dick hanging out's more like it."

"Charming," Bancroft said and choked out a dry cough.

Metallic clanking punctuated their conversation. Somebody was jangling coins or keys; Joan couldn't tell which.

"Even if you go to the cops," Weasel Man said, "and they let you off, do you think they'd keep their mouths shut?"

Footsteps inside the room stomped toward the door where Joan was hiding. She pressed flat against the wall.

"Nobody can find out." Bancroft's tone wavered. "Nobody."

Weasel Man puffed out an exasperated sigh. "So finish getting rid of her."

"Don't forget, we're in this together, whether you like it or not," Bancroft said. "She heard us both."

"That's why I'm helping you handle things. Just cut out the problem and complete our deal."

Hands slammed on wood. "You threaten me with that photo and call it help?"

"How many fixers do you know? Oh, you don't?" Sarcasm saturated Weasel Man's words.

Joan weighed what type of photograph would be so threatening. Sex? Crime? Did it affect the campaign? Did it affect her?

"Between our deals and the threats …" Bancroft groaned as though he had a stomachache. "Front me a little more?"

"No way. Pay up."

"Just a little extra for holding your stuff?"

"Doesn't count. It's part of the deal."

"Come on, I'm broke."

"Heard that before."

Weasel Man must know the senator pretty well. Were they talking about some dirty political deal? The guy's taunting laugh was more sinister than anything she'd heard from any political rival. Even Wallace.

Weasel Man clicked his tongue in disdain. "You always find the dough somewhere. There's gotta be someone left you didn't steal from."

A drawer rolled open. There was a crinkle and a thud. Something must have been dropped on the desk. The sound was muffled and floppy, like jeans in an LL Bean mailing bag.

"There. That's my end of the deal," Bancroft said. "Now deal with Wallace."

"Got a pickup to make, then I'll do your setup. Don't worry, the guy won't know what hit him."

"Then it'll all be over." Bancroft let out a noisy sigh.

"Except for the cleanup."

Joan thought she heard her boss sob. Unbelievable. This man, whom she respected and supported, was talking about major corruption.

"And then there's the baby," Bancroft said.

"Can't help with lady problems."

Bancroft sniffed, and his voice took a sharp, bitter turn. "At least help me with this Arty guy you so *generously* recommended. He's crap!"

"Hey, he's my dad's guy. My dad doesn't mess around."

"But he keeps screwing up." Bancroft started yelling. "I need him to get it done."

"Not my suitcase."

"Should be. You're in this up to your eyeballs."

The jangling stopped with a jarring clank. The man spoke in a quiet, ominous voice. "Your little shitstorm is the least of *my* worries."

"Little shitstorm?" Paper slapped on the floor. "Devil's teeth! This is everything to me!"

That was enough. Joan barged into the room just in time to see Bancroft smash his fist down on a stack of campaign flyers. He was sitting behind his desk, his suit a disheveled mess. Several days of stubble masked his boyish features and accented dark circles under his eyes.

Weasel Man stood next to the desk. His stylish clothes clashed with his crooked nose and slicked-back hair. A key ring with ten or twelve dangling keys hung from his hand. He kept throwing them in the air and catching them. The gesture made it look like he would smash the keys into the senator's face at any second. In his other hand, he clutched a book-size parcel wrapped in brown paper.

"What's all the shouting about?" Joan's eyes locked on to Bancroft's. His stare burned with a desperation she'd never seen before.

Weasel Man ran his fingers over his greasy hair, then threw his keys up, catching them with a forehand grasp. All the while, his gaze bounced from Joan to Bancroft, finally stopping on the senator. "I'll come back later."

"No. Micky, wait—" Bancroft turned toward Joan. "Go away … please!"

She put her hands on her hips. "Not until I know what's going on."

"None of your business."

"None of my business?" Joan stalked past Micky and jammed her index finger down on Bancroft's desk. "I need to know everything going on in this office."

"You two enjoy." Micky's tone was all snark. "I'm taking off."

"Show some respect," Bancroft growled at Micky. "Dammit, I'm a state senator. I have the power to pull you down."

"You mean you used to." Affecting a singsong lilt, Micky said, "Don't forget the pic. Your closeup's in living color." His snarky tone returned. "You can't lift a finger against me." Micky singled out a tiny key on his key ring and waved it in front of Bancroft's nose. All the other keys swung and clanked underneath. "This little guy opens a safe deposit box holding a copy of that photo. It's in an envelope addressed to the *Philadelphia Daily News*. Ready to go at a moment's notice."

Joan found Micky's haughty posture appalling. The photo must be horribly damning.

Micky glanced at her without moving his head, just his eyes.

Bancroft withered in his chair. He mumbled to Micky, "Wait a minute in the hall."

Micky backed out of the office, the package tucked tight under his arm. His tacky aftershave made Joan sniffle as he passed by. From the hall, they could still hear him rattling his keys.

Joan sat down across from Bancroft's desk and jerked her head toward the door. "Who the hell is he?"

"Nobody you need to know. You have to go away."

"No. The accounts aren't adding up. What kind of trouble are we in?"

Bancroft bashed his elbows on the desk and covered his face in his hands. "Everything's in trouble," he said through his fingers. He looked up at her, his eyes tragic, then straightened his back and pulled open the top drawer of his desk. Joan followed his movement. Her defiant comeback caught in her throat when she spied the handle of a pistol.

Chapter 54

Suzanna ripped the hood off Em's head and used it to put pressure on the bullet wound. Bright-red blood was pouring out the back of Em's thigh. With her free hand, she removed the last of the tape from Em's mouth. Emily exhaled a lungful and started coughing. "The Jersey Devil's here?"

Suzanna yanked off the ropes. "Maybe. Does it hurt?"

"Yes, goddammit, he shot me in the ass!"

Red and blue flecks of light flickered across the ceiling beams. Detective O'Brien dashed into the room and tripped over a broken chair, sending both him and his flashlight flying. "What the hell happened here? Where's the shooter?" He tore out his phone from where he lay splayed on the grimy floor and called for an ambulance. As he hauled himself up, he was puffing hard. "Sorry … I took so long … to get up here." He bent down beside Suzanna and focused his flashlight on Em's leg. "I lost sight of you halfway up the road. Couldn't find this trail."

O'Brien checked Em's injury and took over applying pressure. "It's not bad. You'll live."

"He kidnapped me instead of Suzanna," Em said. "That guy must be blind!" Wincing, she adjusted the way she was sitting. "Shit!"

"Try to relax. The ambulance will be here any minute," the detective said.

Suzanna stood and gave Em's shoulder a gentle squeeze. Looking down at O'Brien, she asked, "How did you know where to find us?"

"Jason called me from the Philly fire. He saw the direction you were heading. I took over tailing you. He came after."

"Hey, Detective O'Brien." Em grimaced and blinked hard. "Where's that ambulance?" She forced a fake smile. "I'd love to stay and talk, but I really mustache."

O'Brien opened his mouth to respond but thought better of it.

Jason ran in and rushed over to Emily and the detective. "The guy got away into the woods, boss. We need a search team that knows the area."

Three paramedics hurried in hauling a stretcher and got to work on Emily. As they carried her down the path, she yelped obscenities with each bumpy step. Jason followed close behind.

Suzanna and Detective O'Brien climbed down after them. Noticing that the detective needed a break, she eased up at the boulder. O'Brien put his hands on his knees and gulped in air. When he stood up again, she said, "It was State Senator Bancroft. I heard him on the phone with the hit guy."

O'Brien whistled low. "Your roommate's been my primary suspect. Not sure how the senator fits in."

"He's responsible for the whole thing. But I don't get why."

O'Brien pulled out his cell and ordered all night shift officers still in Haddonfield to find and hold Bancroft. He hung up, shaking his head. "Senator Bancroft has a lot of powerful friends. We're gonna have problems making a charge stick."

Chapter 55

When a sudden siren blared, Joan and Bancroft looked at each other wide-eyed. As the siren got closer and louder, Joan understood. The cops were coming for Bancroft. But who—

"I'm outta here!" Micky's shout echoed from the hallway. His footsteps thudded as he ran down the stairs.

Bancroft pulled the pistol out of his drawer and pointed it at his temple. He tearfully focused on his desk.

Joan's nerves were jangled, but with a stern voice, she said, "Why are you doing this, Don?"

Bancroft flinched, but the gun stayed where it was.

"Please, talk to me." She took a gentler tone. "And put that thing down."

"I didn't want anyone to know, not even you."

Joan looked Bancroft up and down. Whatever he didn't want anyone to know had taken a toll. "What do you mean?"

"I've ruined everything—my marriage, my status, the election, everything." The hand pointing the pistol at his head went limp and dropped to the desk. The gun bounced out of his grasp and rolled over, where it rested menacingly on the desktop. "Every possible way out led to exposing the most shameful ..."

Joan put on her manager's voice. "Start from the beginning and start making sense."

"Last year, when I broke my ankle, I got prescriptions for Oxycodone. Lots of them. I got addicted to the stuff, and now … heroin."

"Hold on." Joan swept her hair back. "My God, we have meetings every day. Why didn't I …?" Now that she thought about it, she had spotted little things—his shaky hands, his sleepiness, appointments missed, and the intern incident. But addiction? *Heroin?*

"Why didn't you come to me?" she asked. "We could've worked something out. Still could."

"I didn't want you to find out. I don't want anyone to."

"Lots of people have addiction problems. We could even make this part of your campaign." Joan's political brain kicked in. "As a recovered addict, you could help other addicts and their families and make the opioid crisis a priority."

"Don't be ridiculous. My career would go down the tubes. Just think about the circus the Republicans would make of it."

"Why heroin? Why didn't you stick with the Oxycodone?"

"I can still get prescriptions, but my insurance stopped coverage. And the cost of buying out-of-pocket is outrageous. I had to go to the street. H is cheaper … and better." He cast down his eyes. The gun still lay on his desk. "Now I have a dealer bleeding me dry."

"Is that who Micky is?" Joan nodded toward the stairs. "Your dealer?"

A fat, telling tear ran down Bancroft's cheek.

"What about your Democrat friends or your law cronies? Couldn't any of them help you?"

"I'm a politician with sights on the presidency. Or I was. Why put my weakness on display? So my opponents can lap up the scandal? I don't trust *any* of my so-called friends to keep their mouths shut. They'd give me up in a minute. Especially to the press. Those reporters would have a field day."

Joan's patience was wearing thin, but the gun on Bancroft's desk made her keep trying. Even if he didn't blow his own brains out, he could turn the gun on her. "We can work this out."

"It's not only the drugs. I'm getting squeezed for money from every direction. My habit costs two hundred a day now and … I can't stop."

"Wait, you can't afford two hundred bucks a day?"

"Not along with my mortgage, my daughter's school tuition, my wife's shopping habit, which, by the way, is out of control. I already secretly drained my daughter's college fund and refinanced the house. Yesterday, my wife found out. She's leaving me."

Joan slid back in her chair and stared into space. She'd always considered Don wealthy and powerful enough to get out of any jam.

"And I owe my dealer. He's been jacking up the interest fees." Bancroft crossed his arms. "So I siphoned money out of the campaign."

Joan's mouth hung open. He'd said the words so matter-of-factly.

Bancroft sat back and studied the ceiling. "And then there's Anne."

"Anne? The intern?"

"She's pregnant."

Joan's head was spinning. "That innocent girl? She's only eighteen!"

"Not so innocent." Bancroft scowled at her. "She puts on a good act. Anyway, who are *you* to talk?"

Joan was getting the picture. Bancroft's ego and power had driven him to all this, and who knew what else. Then she remembered the assault. "You shoved Anne into a wall knowing she was pregnant?" Her old friend had changed; this powerful man was turning into a fiend.

"She's got this video and says she'll send it to the press if I don't leave my wife."

"What video?" Was there no end to this?

"She set up her phone to film while we were"—Bancroft tilted his head—"y'know."

Joan cried out, "You let her make a sex video? What's wrong with you?"

Bancroft picked up the pistol again and cradled it in his hands. He could've been holding a kitten. "I was stoned out of my mind. Now she says she'll go public."

Using her strictest mom voice, Joan said, "Put that down."

Bancroft sagged back into his chair and held the gun in his lap. "And now this blackmail."

"Blackmail?" Joan's eyes blazed. "What are you talking about? Anne?"

"Worse. Micky was under some heat and needed a place to store a shipment of cocaine for a week. I put it in my safe." He whispered, "In exchange, he was gonna plant some coke on Wallace and call the cops anonymously."

Joan wanted out of this bad dream. She kneaded her temples and thought about her own legal standing and how she might be pulled into this web by association.

"We hammered out the whole deal at Ristorante Buena one Sunday." Bancroft focused on the gun in his lap. "But your daughter was sitting right beside our table."

Joan's head shot up. "Suzanna?"

Bancroft wiped his forehead with shaky fingers. "I didn't realize she'd eavesdropped on us until she started threatening me."

"What?" Joan's heart pounded. "Suzanna would nev—"

"No!" Bancroft poked his finger at Joan. "Your daughter has been blackmailing me for a week, and I have proof!"

Joan tried to take deep breaths while Bancroft rummaged through his desk drawer. He pulled out two envelopes and pushed one across the desk. "That's the first one. I got it last Friday."

Joan picked it up between thumb and forefinger as if it held a contagious disease. The typed letter slid out easily. Once she started reading it, she couldn't pry her eyes off. "Twenty thousand dollars? And why in Suzanna's case?"

"Now, look." He pointed at the little guitar at the bottom of the page.

"Suzanna's stationery!" In a softer tone, she said, "I gave it to her myself."

"Right. It's on her music stand every Sunday. See where the letter came from?" He flipped the envelope over.

Joan studied the Haddonfield postmark. "Someone's framing her."

"Oh, no. You said it yourself in the lunchroom. Suzanna overhears all kinds of conversations."

"Yes, but—"

"I heard it straight from her mouth." Veins bulged on Bancroft's neck. His voice sounded strangled. "She was talking with her friends at the HB about blackmailing me, like it was nothing."

A red flush crept up Joan's cheeks. Now she got it. "Suzanna meant Chris, not you."

"Who's Chris?"

"Her roommate. You met him at the kickoff meeting at my house." No question, Chris was mixed up in this. He had access to Suzanna's paper and her guitar case.

"I don't know anything about any Chris!" Bancroft flicked the other envelope across the desk. "This came on Tuesday." Joan ripped it open, and two photographs fell out. She shuddered as she recognized Bancroft's wife's distinctive blonde bun and his daughter's shining smile. And she knew that McMansion in the background, too.

Joan read the letter and wondered how anyone, especially Don, could imagine her daughter writing it; it sounded like a fifth grader wrote it. She glared icily into his eyes while waving the letter in the air. "Listen to me. This is not from my daughter. Someone else is doing this."

"Oh, no. Micky checked everything out." Bancroft bristled with self-righteousness. "He verified that Suzanna eavesdrops on us."

Bringing her daughter into this crossed a line. Joan was so furious, she was having trouble breathing. Bancroft's shoulders drooped, and he looked miserably down at his hands. His tone changed to a whiny surrender. "He forced me. It was his idea. I had to do it."

"What? Make sense!"

"Micky has this phone pic of me sitting with two Philly drug dealers and … I'm there shooting up." His chin sank to his chest. He set the gun on his desk, resting his hand on top. "Micky threatened to give the photo to the tabloids if I didn't do it. I had to."

Joan's eyes shrank to slits. "Had to do what?"

Bancroft's whole body shook; the gun trembled in time on his desk. "Hire a professional. Suzanna was gonna ruin everything."

Joan sprang to her feet and yelled, "Are you crazy?"

"But the guy he recommended botches every—"

"It's you." Joan planted her palms on the desk and leaned forward, face-to-face, close enough to smell his stale-sweet Trident breath. "You're behind all these attacks on Suzanna!"

Bancroft pointed the gun at his temple again.

Two police officers charged through Bancroft's doorway and came to a sudden stop.

"What's going on here?" asked one cop.

The senator tearfully focused on his desk, still pointing the gun at his head.

The two cops edged over toward Bancroft and gently worked the gun out of his hand. Joan let out a huge sigh.

A third officer pushed Micky through the door in handcuffs. The cop's jolt made Micky's keys clatter to the ground.

"Looks like a kilo of coke, Sarge." The cop held up the parcel that Micky had been carrying.

Joan snatched up her phone and called the HB. Suzanna hadn't shown up for work. In a panic, she called Suzanna's cell. It went to voicemail. She turned toward Bancroft as he was being handcuffed. "Why didn't you tell me? My daughter. I thought we were friends!"

"You would've warned her, wouldn't you? Or gone in on the blackmail with her."

With an enraged glare, Joan backed out of the room. When she reached the door, in a contemptuous voice meant for Bancroft to hear, she told the police, "As far as I'm concerned, he can go ahead and put that bullet in his head."

Chapter 56

At the end of the path, Suzanna and O'Brien came out into the wildflower field amid a whirlwind of activity. The ambulance had ignored the end of the dirt road and bulldozed through the field to the base of the hill. Atlantic County Police cruisers zoomed up the dirt road, sirens blaring. Cops surged out of the patrol cars like clowns out of a Volkswagen, too many for Suzanna to count. They spread out in a line and burst into the forest, sniffer dogs at their heels.

"Jason," O'Brien said, "ride to the hospital with Emily. Smelly can drive the van back."

"Yes, sir." Jason hopped into the back of the ambulance beside Emily and yanked the doors closed.

As O'Brien watched them pull away, he tilted his head toward Suzanna. "I'll take you home, and we'll pick up Em's car later."

"No, I'll drive Emmy's car back."

Concern flashed across O'Brien's face, but he didn't protest.

"I've got to take care of Sigmund."

O'Brien's forehead scrunched up. "Who?"

Sigmund burst out from the brush at the path's entrance as though he knew they were talking about him. Delighted and panting, he jumped up on Suzanna's legs.

"Siggy, where did you come from?" She picked him up and hugged him like a teddy bear.

"Is that what all the howling was? A dog?"

"Sigmund must've gotten out of the car. What you heard was his yodel. It scared the crap out of the hit guy."

"Scared me, too." The detective smirked and shook his head. "It was eerie. From the path, it sounded like it was echoing through the entire forest."

They trudged through the wildflowers. Suzanna carried Sigmund, snuggled in her arms.

O'Brien took a pack of cigarettes from his shirt pocket and lit one up.

"You smoke?"

Sigmund sneezed.

The detective took a long drag on the cigarette, scowled at it, and flicked it away. "Nope."

"Right." Suzanna shrugged and let it go. "Do you know if Professor Gardener is okay … and that beautiful house?" She put Sigmund on the ground as they started down the dirt road toward the Subaru. He walked alongside them, wagging his tail.

"Gardener's fine. He was out of the state the whole time. But his house … that'll need work. Seems like he can afford it."

"Do you know how his parents died? Like, was it suspicious?"

"What? You think he had something to do with his parents' death?" O'Brien chuckled. "Cold."

"One of the neighbors said it."

"It wasn't suspicious at all. Their private jet crashed in a storm near Bermuda. They had a vacation home there. I guess Gardener inherited that place, too."

"I figured it was something like that." What a relief. She'd been right about the professor.

"It's a lot like your friend Adam. You know about that?"

Suzanna shook her head. "He never talked about his family."

"His parents died in a car accident a few years back, and he inherited a bundle. Did you really think he could afford that swanky townhouse just by playing cello?"

"It would be nice if some musicians supported themselves by playing music," Suzanna said wistfully.

Midway down the dirt road, O'Brien slowed to catch his breath. "I don't understand why the professor keeps teaching and Adam keeps playing cello. They've plenty of money."

It was no mystery to Suzanna. "There are some things you just have to do, whether you get paid or not. For me, being a musician isn't a job. It's part of who I am."

O'Brien nodded. "Sometimes that's how I feel about solving cases."

When they reached the main road, Sigmund trotted up to Em's car. The door that Suzanna had shut was wide open.

"You're one clever doggy." While lifting him into the back seat, she found three long scratch marks on the outside of the car door. Must have come from Siggy getting out. Em won't be happy about that. Then she noticed Detective O'Brien's car parked right behind Em's, and a smile tugged at her lips. He'd been with her the whole time.

O'Brien took a few steps toward his car but paused and pivoted back. "If the senator is our man ... *your mom*!"

He whipped out his cell and called Joan. "You all right? ... She's safe, she's fine ... Calm down." He handed the phone to Suzanna.

Chapter 57

One Week Later

After Suzanna finished her Friday night gig at the HB and locked her guitar in its case, Vinny came over from the bar and said in a soft voice, almost a whisper, "My uncle Guido says the problem has been my loose-cannon cousin, Micky. He was selling to the state senator."

"Wait a minute. Does he have hair like yours and a stiff neck? I mean, does he look around with just his eyes?"

Vinny replied with a crooked smile and a tight nod.

"Your cousin's in a lot of trouble. Detective O'Brien told me he was in custody."

"My uncle has his lawyers on the case, but Micky will do time, for sure. I'm just glad you're okay."

"Thanks for worrying about me." Suzanna hugged Vinny and asked, "Does O'Brien know he's your cousin?"

Vinny sniffed loudly and nodded. "Gave me the third degree about it." He picked up her guitar. "I'll put this behind the bar."

Em and Jason were sitting at the end of the bar near the front door. In only one week, they'd become quite the couple. Em sat fidgeting on a donut-shaped cushion designed to keep pressure off the gunshot wound. She grimaced with each shift of her butt.

Suzanna took a seat next to her. "How's your bum doing?"

"Just fine, dammit." Em was recovering, but not as fast as she wanted. "Is Chris still with his folks?"

"They finagled him into rehab. All their fancy lawyers are working on getting him off the blackmail charge."

"I should've seen that he was on the hard stuff."

"I knew something was up, too, but I thought the main thing was the booze."

Emily curled her finger for Suzanna to lean toward her and pulled Jason in by the arm. She lowered her voice. "Tonight will be my most devilish mustache joke ever."

Suzanna groaned at the impish glint in Em's eye.

"What's it this time, Emmy?" Jason snickered and shook his head.

Suzanna wondered if Jason knew what he was getting himself into. Em could be a handful.

"You'll see." Em threw back her head and cracked up. "It's fucking great."

"Ah, Emmy, try to hold back the language. Like we talked," Jason said.

"Okay, it's unfucking great." She stuck her tongue out at him.

Suzanna burst out laughing, not at all sure the relationship would survive.

Joan breezed through the door in her heels and business suit.

Smiling at her mom, Suzanna said, "I didn't know you were coming tonight." She and her mom had worked all week to patch things up. There had been some crying, some laughing, and some progress.

Joan was scanning the room. "Larry called and said he had an announcement about the case."

With a puzzled frown, Suzanna asked, "Who's Larry?"

"Larry O'Brien, of course." Joan tsked and kept looking for him.

"I thought his first name was Detective," Em said through a giggle. "Nice button."

Red and blue stripes ran across the top and bottom of an election pin covering most of Joan's lapel. It read, *Vote Joan Archer—Mayor 2017*. She mimed polishing it and said, "I thought this would be the perfect time to kick off my campaign."

"Mayor?" Em asked. "I would've guessed you'd run for the senator's old spot."

"Gotta start in the minor leagues." Joan handed out buttons to every person at the bar.

Detective O'Brien and Harry paraded out of the office, the detective holding a file folder high in the air. At the end of the bar, O'Brien stood as though it were a lectern and slapped the folder down.

Suzanna had never seen the detective so excited or happy. Her mom might have had a little something to do with that. Joan walked over and stood with the detective, and he gave her hand a squeeze. Suzanna had noticed things heating up between those two all week. She saw some surprised glances from her friends, though.

"The drug dealer, Micky Amoriella," said O'Brien, "rolled on State Senator Bancroft for the purchase of illegal substances and attempted murder. He had in his possession an incriminating photo of the senator injecting intravenous drugs in the company of known major drug dealers."

"What about the hit man?" Vinny asked, setting down a pint of Guinness in front of O'Brien and a glass of red wine by Joan.

"We lost him in the forest. But we nailed down his name and address in Philly. Only problem … when we got to the house, all we found was a pile of ashes. The fire chief said it had been an electrical fire. Nothing left." O'Brien pulled one side of his mustache with a frustrated yank. "None of the databases had a whiff of him. His trail just stopped cold."

Vinny's eyes hardened, and he said with a solemn lilt, "I bet the Jersey Devil got him. He probably never made it out of the woods."

Suzanna rubbed the scar above her eyebrow. Seemed like a suitable punishment to her.

"Most likely, he's out of state by now," O'Brien said, "but that doesn't mean we're giving up. We'll keep tracking until we find him."

Harry dashed out from behind the bar, threw open the front door, and ran outside. He returned, holding a guy in a gray hoodie by the scruff of the neck. The guy was middle-aged with a pasty, froggish face, wearing thick glasses.

"Okay, fella. Exactly who are you?"

With a shaky, high-pitched voice, the guy said, "My name is Ben. Benjamin Johnstone. I—"

"What the hell are you doing following Suzanna around?"

Head bent and eyes on the floor, Ben looked pitiful. "I'm ... I'm shy with women."

Harry's lips flickered with irritation. "Come on now. Why'd you show up at the hospital?"

Ben gave Suzanna a wistful look, sighed, and said, "I'm sorry. It's just ... I love your playing so much and ..." His eyes returned to the floor. "I was worried about you. That's why I went to the hospital."

O'Brien jumped up and pulled out his phone.

"Oh, for fuck's sake!" Emily practically spat the words out. "I can't believe my ears."

Suzanna's mouth hung open. "You've been stalking me. We talked the night of the explosion. And didn't I see you at Ristorante Buena?"

"Yeah, they wouldn't let me in."

Joan had her hand over her mouth. Suzanna looked at her and did a palms-up shoulder shrug. She didn't know whether to laugh or cry.

O'Brien put his phone away and nodded at Jason. "Hold him outside. Smelly's coming to pick him up."

"My pleasure," Jason said and hustled Ben toward the door.

"Wait. What's it say on that hoodie?" asked Harry.

Jason stretched the front of Ben's hoodie until the gold letters took shape—*American Dental Conference 2013*.

Harry's brows arched up in surprise. The wrinkles on his forehead nearly knocked off the glasses sitting on top of his head. "You're a dentist?"

Ben nodded.

Harry shook his bald head.

Suzanna got up and hugged Harry's broad shoulders. "Thanks for watching out for me."

As Jason dragged Ben out the door, Adam hurried in and sat beside Suzanna. "What's going on?"

"They found Suzanna's hoodie stalker," Em said.

Adam put his arm around Suzanna. "Are you okay?"

Suzanna liked his hair and his cello playing, but this overprotective stuff … Tonight was the first time they'd met up since the Devil's Lair, but they'd been talking on the phone. Their conversations had been honest and heartfelt. His interest in having kids stemmed from wanting to create a new family. Now that his parents were dead, he had no living relatives. Suzanna understood but didn't budge on her convictions. He swore he'd rethink his position. So, who knew where the relationship would go?

Thinking it best to keep things casual for now, she twisted out from under his arm.

At the other end of the bar, Vinny grinned slyly at Detective O'Brien. "Come on, Detective. Sit back down. When you finish that Guinness, I got some good Irish whiskey for you."

"Why, what's going on?" O'Brien's voice strained with suspicion.

Vinny took a bottle down from behind the bar and set it by the detective along with a shot glass. "You're gonna need it."

The detective probed Vinny's eyes but found himself in a staring contest. O'Brien lost. He hoisted his pint, took a gulp, and peered down the bar at Emily.

Em spotted him looking her way and shouted, "Looking for your mustache, Detective? It's right under your nose." She mugged at him and resettled on her donut.

O'Brien called back, "I guess you got to the *bottom* of things then, Em."

Em stiffened and glared at him. The detective's smug smile and her mom's valiant effort not to laugh sent Suzanna into stitches.

Eyes twinkling behind the taps, Vinny joined in as he poured a pint. "Yeah, Em, did the doctor give you *ass-pirin* for that gunshot?"

Em groaned. She looked through the door and nodded. "Let's see if you can top this one."

"I think you'll be bringing up the *rear*." O'Brien was on a roll.

A sudden, chilly breeze flowed through the HB's front door, drawing everyone's attention. Four men dressed in matching suits bustled in. They squeezed into Suzanna's performance area, side by side, each displaying a massive handlebar mustache. One of them took out a pitch pipe and blew a tone. The HB fell silent.

In perfect barbershop harmony, the four men belted out "If You've Only Got a Mustache" by Stephen Foster.

Oh! All of you poor single men,
Don't ever give up in despair.
For there's always a chance while there's life,
To capture the hearts of the fair.
No matter what may be your age,
You always may cut a fine dash.
You will suit all the girls to a hair.
If you've only got a mustache,
A mustache, a mustache,
If you've only got a mustache.

The next day, Suzanna flew to Boulder, Colorado on a red-eye. Her toes twitched inside her shoes the whole way. She tried listening to music on her headphones but couldn't focus. This visit was her life goal. One of them, anyway. She didn't want to offend or be misjudged.

Standing rigid in front of the chalet door, she hesitated. Her appointment time had come, but still, she lingered. This was more frightening than any of her exploits at the Jersey Devil house. When she finally did knock, the door opened, and she gazed at the ruddy face of a beautiful woman wearing an embroidered, Indian tunic.

The woman was welcoming but restrained. She guided Suzanna to a small room filled with Hindu pictures and statues. An enormous oak desk covered more than half of one wall. Directly across the room sat an ornate, antique loveseat. An electronic keyboard and recording equipment littered the back wall. Suzanna deemed it a very comfortable room. She wasn't sure, though, about the deep scent of patchouli tickling her nose. Her eyes locked on the curlicues of smoke rising from a burning stick of incense.

He had his back to her. Bent over, sitting at the desk, he was writing, or maybe sketching, in a notebook. His unoccupied hand rested atop an intricately carved walking stick. Slowly, he laid down his pen with a definitive, gentle thud and swiveled to face her. Smiling, he extended an open arm toward the loveseat, gesturing for her to sit. "What can I do for you?"

Chapter 58

Arty's fingers sifted through the sand beside his lounge chair on a beach near Tampa. Face basking in the sun, eyes closed, and sunglasses on, he chatted with Rick on a disposable, prepaid cell phone.

"Listen, my name's Roger now. Drop the Arty already."

"So you can't give me an address or phone number or anything?" Rick sounded flustered.

"Nope, I call you. Nobody calls me."

"You took off so fast—"

"Off like a prom dress."

"Did you hear that Senator Bancroft is in a bunch of trouble? He dropped out of the race for Rep."

"That dickhead. I wouldn't piss down his throat if his heart was on fire." Arty had actually read all about the senator's problems. Staying on top of things was part of being on the lam.

"Did you know they're rebuilding on your lot?" Rick asked.

"Uh-huh. I got the insurance *and* sold the property. Pretty sweet." Arty turned onto his back. He was gonna get his chalk-white legs tanned if it took all day. The insurance money he got from his house burning down padded out his retirement budget nicely. Ironic, right? Now, he was living his dream, tiki drinks and all.

"They say it was an electrical fire," Rick said.

"Mum's final act."

"Did your mom's ghost follow you?"

"Nah." Arty could still picture the columns of smoke coming out his front door and the bedroom windows. That fire snapped like it was happy and free, just like his mum. And now, he was sure. His mum was the reason he'd been drawn to Florida all these years. "I'm where she wanted me to be. Her business is finished."

"Didn't you say you had a cousin down there? Thinking about looking him up?"

Arty already had the address and phone number of his cousin. "Gotta wait a year or two until the heat dies down."

As he clicked off the call, the ocean breeze fanned his face. Breathing deeply, he took in the briny sea air and let it out a little at a time. He sat up and checked the color of his legs. After all, he didn't want them to burn.

The shade from a trio of palm trees a little ways off looked mighty inviting. Arty grabbed his lounge chair and shuffled through the sand into the shade. Before sitting down again, he took off his sunglasses and peered out over the white beach to the shimmering waves. The sky beyond looked like a million bucks. It was nothing less than fucking paradise. "Thanks, Mum."

Coda

The DNA test came back a match in the last week of July. Isaac Bellow had readily agreed to Suzanna's request and even seemed happy to do it. And not like she didn't believe her mother's story or anything, but still, it was mind-blowing to see it on paper. That same week, she turned twenty-five years old. Two milestones.

When Bancroft's trial began in June, it created a media frenzy. Suzanna spent hours at the courthouse. By the time it was all over, 2014 was well underway. Bancroft went to jail, a white-collar prison. Micky went to the state penitentiary. Chris was lucky; his expensive lawyers got him probation and rehab. The police never did find the hit man. Suzanna resigned herself to that mystery.

In the summer of 2014, the case finally closed. Suzanna was more than ready to move on. And she did. But then November came. Freezing rain and gloom set the stage. On the ninth, her mother, in tears, woke her. Joan couldn't say the words, so she just flipped on the radio. It was all over the news—Isaac Bellow had died. A cruel, quick cancer. Only a little over a year had gone by since her Boulder visit. If only she could've met with him once more. Her mother, unsurprisingly, dissolved into a basket case. They drank many bottles of red together.

On the last day of November, Suzanna received a letter inviting her to a special memorial service and reception in Boulder for Isaac Bellow. The event, almost a month after his burial, was invitation only.

The service was brief. Only Bellow's legitimate son spoke. Afterward, ushers herded everyone into a large reception hall. They directed Suzanna toward two round tables. She sat in the only empty chair and scanned the circle of faces. It was a shock, but she should have known. They all looked like her, especially their noses.

It didn't take long to figure out. These two tables held her half-siblings—her family.

Even though Suzanna only met with her father once, that single conversation led to significant changes in her life. During that visit, he gave her three pieces of advice. She was in the process of tackling all three.

He asked why she didn't write her own music. So now, she was composing classical guitar music. Why hadn't she tried it before?

He told her to expand her horizons and handed her a check that would more than cover her master's tuition. In September, she entered a master's program in composition.

He encouraged her to remove negativity from her life. So when Chris asked to room with her again after rehab— tone deaf much?—she declined and moved back to her mom's. Just until she graduates.

At the end of her Boulder visit, Suzanna stood to leave but paused and asked her father if he liked the music of Counting Crows. He said, "Not bad. Lyrics almost make it." Then she asked about Randy Newman. His face slowly broke into a smile. "He's a genius!"

ACKNOWLEDGMENTS

Thank you to my beta readers for suffering through the first drafts—Bonnie, Don, Nicole, Joan, Glen, Beth, Joanne, Howard, Marcia, Kerry and Diane. Your comments were invaluable.

Many thanks to Lieutenant Stuart Holloway of the Haddonfield Police Department for sharing his knowledge of local crime scene procedure.

Special thanks to my band of editors for dragging me through the process— Kelly Oliver-Barrett, Margo LaPierre, Eve Seymour, Mary Torjussen, and Joyce Mochrie. I've learned so much from each of you.

And a tip of the hat to the state of New Jersey, silly monsters and all.

ABOUT THE AUTHOR

Kathleen Mayes is a classical guitarist and a proud New Jersey resident. She taught classical guitar and music history at the university level for over thirty years while playing background music and concerts throughout Philadelphia and Southern New Jersey. She has recorded four CDs, published with Guitar Chamber Music Press, and performed at Carnegie Hall.

Now retired from teaching and the concert stage, she is dedicating her time to writing and having a lot of fun doing it.

Made in the USA
Columbia, SC
12 January 2025

51670935R00233